Leonard Bliss

and the

Accountant

of the

Apocalypse

by

Dominic Ossiah

Hope

you

enjoy it!

Ray

Cover design and artwork by Scribbleleaf

www.scribbleleaf.com

For Helen and for Norway

ONE

MARBLE, MAGDELENA DECIDED AS she stormed across fifteen miles of arid scrubland, wearing her second-most favoured suit and a fashionably impractical pair of high-heeled shoes.

Marble, limestone, granite and *slate*: collectively, the four words she hated most in all creation.

Stone tablets. She pushed a startled elephant out of her way. *In this day and age.*

A dazzle of young zebra stepped quickly aside; a wildebeest standing in her path received a less-than-gentle nudge, and his eight thousand companions, seeing that today was not the day to trifle with the CEO of Purgatory, stampeded out of her way. The wildebeest left a mile-wide path to Magdelena's office, a shaded tract of sparse flatland that lay at the centre of a spent volcano. Upon this relatively small patch of the basin stood a painter's easel, an executive chair upholstered in the finest Italian leather and a large, ornately carved desk hewn from the trunk of a prehistoric mahogany tree. There were no doors, walls or windows; instead, the boundaries of her 'think space' were marked by framed certificates in Divinity, Law & Business Administration that hung on copper nails driven into thin air.

Magdelena Cane took her seat and began typing another email dispatch to the three branches of the Afterlife. The communiqué explained, once again, why stone tablets were no longer considered a practical medium for communication. Her nostrils flared; her fingers rattled across the glass keyboard, addressing the email to the billions employed by Purgatory, Heaven and Hell.

Six hundred years ago, during a banquet to celebrate her promotion, Magdelena had made a fire-and-brimstone speech in which she'd promised to drag the Afterlife, gnashing and wailing, into what the human race would one day call the 20th century. Fighting words, she thought, glumly received and begrudgingly applauded by Leonard Bliss, Hell's Chief of Operations. But then, glumly and begrudgingly was how Leonard received everything.

Mr Gee, on the other hand, had clapped stoically during her speech. Wistfully, even.

Mr Gee, the CEO of Heaven and Chairman of the Afterlife: wise, omniscient and annoyingly difficult to read, even for a people person such as herself.

She remembered it was much later, after the festivities had begun to subside, that Leonard – drunk as men often were – had lurched lecherously towards her – as men often did.

'Two hundred years,' he'd said. 'Two hundred years and you will wish with all your heart that you were but a simple painter again.'

Magdelena reached down and stroked a lioness that had wrapped itself around her feet. As well as being a curmudgeonly individual, Leonard had always fancied himself as something of a doomsayer.

But it was Mr Gee who had applauded and smiled and who would have known, in his annoyingly omniscient way, that six centuries later she'd be at her desk, beset by anger and wondering if it would take a greater deity than herself to bring change to the Afterlife.

Yes, there was a reason the CEO of All That Is had looked stoically wistful that day. Magdelena looked to the painting set upon the easel: a half-finished picture of herself and Alfred Warr, making love beneath the shadow of the volcano. She'd realised long ago that the Afterlife was the embodiment of still life and as such there was little reason to capture it in oil, especially since she and Alfred were no more . . .

She steeled herself against a wave of self-pity and returned to the task at hand. Her keystrokes became key stabs, and the lioness, sensing that all was not as it should be with the Head of Purgatory, padded away to rejoin the pride still feasting on the remains of a zebra. Magdelena watched the lions for a few moments and then looked over what she'd typed so far.

Reason 1, the email read, *cutting and pasting text from stone tablets takes days of painstaking work and an inordinate amount of masonry glue.*

She read it three or four times until she was laughing uncontrollably, then stopped when she heard her own laughter mocking her from across the landscape. Magdelena shuddered and held her finger down on the backspace key. She hissed, 'Get a hold of yourself, woman,' and then typed again:

If we've learned anything from the incident with the thirty-nine commandments, the line read, *it is that stone tablets represent a serious health and safety concern when transported by the elderly.*

She sat back, chewing thoughtfully on the end of her pen. 'Wonderful,' she said. 'Now I sound ageist.'

The lions turned from their feast and looked to the sky. They sniffed restlessly at the air, and almost by reflex, Magdelena wheeled herself back from her desk.

A column of marble tablets fell from above and, with a thunderclap of biblical significance, embedded itself into the dry earth, scattering the pride in all directions.

The column stood in a plume of dust, glowing patiently with a strange inner light and throwing bolts of lightning into the sky. Magdelena waited for her heart to slow down before rising from her chair, smoothing down her skirt and brushing the fine white dust from her blouse. She stepped around her desk and stood in front of the tower of polished stone, running her fingertips over its surface.

It certainly didn't feel like a regular memo.

Then the phone on her desk rang. The red one. The one that hadn't made a sound in almost five years.

'Mr Gee?'

'Magdelena,' Mr Gee replied with not so much a voice as a memory, as though she'd heard his words spoken a lifetime before and was only now reliving them. 'And how is my Head of Purgatory this fine morning?'

Magdelena shielded her eyes and looked to the sun. The sun that never rose and never set. The mornings never came and never left, and whatever passed for weather in the Afterlife was always fine. 'I am well, sir, and how are you?'

'Fair to middling, fair to middling. Still haven't finished the painting I see.'

'I've been very busy,' she said, and instinctively looked behind her.

'Too busy to finish what would be your finest work?'

'Is there something I can do for you, sir?'

'Yes, yes, of course, if you can find the time. I've just sent a little something for your perusal.'

'So I see.' She eyed the tablets disdainfully. *Cumbersome and dangerous if delivered carelessly:* precisely what she'd been saying for the past two hundred years. 'What is it, exactly?'

'A testament.'

'Pardon me?'

'A new testament. Well, a *newer* testament. Just the first few chapters. Look it over when you have a moment.'

Magdelena suddenly felt quite sick. 'Has . . . something happened, sir?'

Mr Gee said nothing for a moment – long enough for Magdelena to draw breath and, someplace else, for an entirely new species to evolve.

'Not yet,' he said, wistfully. 'Soon, but not yet.'

'Another flood?' She took the first tablet from the column. It was written in English, not Hebrew, and every character was etched in gold.

'Just read it for me. Let me know what you think.'

'The Book of Leonard? You're writing a testament for Leonard Bliss?' She scanned the first paragraph, arching an eyebrow when she collided with the words *fucked comely.*

'It's a working title,' Mr Gee said. 'Always open to suggestions if you have something better.'

Well, yes I do as a matter of fact, she thought. *The Book of Magdelena*. She read on until her eyes fastened on Alfred's name. 'Shouldn't we leave this to Marketing?' she said with as much aloofness as she could inhumanly muster.

'The Catholics will be quite busy for the next few years. Best we handle this ourselves.'

'I'm a little short of time at the moment, sir,' Magdelena said, reading quickly, trying to measure Alfred's involvement in The End Of Days.

'Ah! The Hitler hearing.'

'He'll be here soon, and I really think I should be at the harbour to —'

'Yes, yes, of course. Do not concern yourself for now, but as soon as you have a moment. What's his argument this time?'

'Sorry?' Magdelena had counted only four, perhaps five occurrences of Alfred's name, which she thought was a good sign – a hopeful one at the very least.

'*Unteroffizier* Hitler,' Mr Gee said. 'What's his defence?'

She placed the tablet gently on the desk and picked up the case notes, rustling them near the phone's mouthpiece; a switch to paper would at least be a start. 'He submits that he was sent to Hell on the evidence given by his own conscience.'

'As is everyone.'

'He argues that since history judges him insane then his conscience cannot be considered a reliable witness.'

'That's desperate, even for him.'

'It is, sir.' She glanced at the tablet and saw that Alfred's name appeared again at the rightmost edge of the stone, surrounded on three sides by sadness, suffering and a slow, painful death.

'Magdelena.'

'Sir?'

'He must not win.'

'Who?' She bit at her lip and thought, *Please, not Alfred; he has suffered enough.*

'Hitler! He's not to win this appeal. Do you understand?'

'Perfectly, sir.'

'If I have to grant him entry to the Kingdom of Heaven, then I will have to admit Bundy, and Stalin, and West, and Shipman.'

'Yes, sir.'

'And I won't have Shipman here.'

'No, sir.'

'The man is unspeakably dull.'

'Yes, sir.'

Mr Gee sighed, and Magdelena thought she could hear ten thousand archangels sighing with him. 'I suggest you argue there is no official record of this alleged insanity and so no grounds for a retrial.'

'That was my plan, sir.'

'Yes, I know.'

'Then why did you mention it?' She snapped at him without thinking and immediately wished she could take it back. As an unspoken rule, Mr Gee tended to allow his staff two passes at verbal insubordination per century. This was her seventh.

But if I were you, she thought, *then I could take it back. I could do anything. I would know all things and I would act wisely upon them. I would not sit on my eternal throne and do nothing while . . . You're not listening, are you? Please, don't listen inside my head. I know you promised that you would never do such a thing, but if you are listening then please know that I didn't mean it. And if you are inside my head and you are seeking to punish mankind again then could you please not involve Alfred?*

'Magdelena!'

She shrieked into the handset.

'Are you all right?'

'Fine, sir, yes, I'm absolutely fine.'

'Good,' he said, warily. 'I'll leave you to get on.'

The line clicked softly and Magdelena allowed the air leave her lungs. Why mankind craved for him to answer its prayers was beyond her. She gathered her papers and pushed them into a glass attaché case, along with her mobile phone and a hairbrush. The desk intercom buzzed while she was thinking feverishly about hats.

'Rachel.'

'Ma'am, *Unteroffizier* Hitler has arrived at the harbour.'

'Thank you. I'll be down in a few minutes.'

'And Leonard Bliss is with him, Ma'am.'

She sucked at her front teeth. 'Leonard? Here? Are you sure?'

'I've just received a call from the harbour master. Mr Bliss wasn't expected?'

'No,' Magdelena said. 'No, he wasn't.' She decided against the hat. Leonard always laughed at hats, regardless of the occasion – or the hat.

'Best not to keep him waiting.'

'If he's come unheralded then I'll keep him waiting for as long as I wish.'

'Of course, Ma'am.'

She pinched the bridge of her nose and shook her head. 'No, I'm sorry. Seem to be a little out of sorts today.'

'You've just spoken to Mr Gee.'

'Yes.'

'Then I understand.'

Magdelena said, 'Oh, it's more than that.' She took a deep breath to explain then thought better of it; where Alfred Warr was concerned, explanations often took the better part of an eternity. 'Call the harbour,' she said, 'and tell them I'll be there in ten whatever-passes-for minutes around here.'

'Ma'am?'

'Just call them.'

'Yes, Ma'am.'

Another click as the intercom switched off. Like herself, a tiny echo in the wilderness. Across the plains, beyond the lions, and the zebra, the giraffes and the elephants; a single baobab cut into the horizon, a family of baboons playing near its exposed roots. Magdelena wished dearly that she could join them. She cast her gaze to the west; it was seven miles to the valley that led to the Quay of Purgatory, a distance she could cover in about a minute and a half, or faster if she carried her Pradas.

The Book Of Leonard

Chapter 1:1

AND SO IT WAS.

On the very same day his superiors crawled into feather beds, drank champagne and fucked comely French women thirty miles from the enemy line; young Ronald Weakes, surviving lance-corporal of the once proud and stalwart First Battalion, the Fighting Somersets, dragged his shattered body through the entrails of his brothers and the stinking, blood-washed mire of the Somme.

The half-man sobbed, spat teeth from his mouth, wiped mucus and blood from his nose.

Moments before, Captain Harris had blown the whistle. Ronnie could still hear it: a white tone inside his head that dulled the sound of the bombs, though not the voices.

German voices.

The half-boy's remaining hand fell upon Harris. The captain's lower jaw and throat, gone. The captain's skin, blistered and black. The captain's eyes, weeping blood, spun wildly in his head.

'Sir,' the half-man said. 'Sir, it's me. Weakes.'

The captain's eyes rolled to the sky, his arm burst from the mud and floundered until Ronnie took his hand.

'I'm here, sir. It's all right. I'm here.'

Moments before, they'd been a fighting unit, eager and afraid. Moments before, a mortar shell had careened low across the grey sky. They'd followed its path, legs rooted in the mud and their eyes trained on the shining black star that fell from the heavens. And Ronnie remembered swallowing bile as the mortar shell struck Private 'Lucky' Dice.

Moments before, Ronnie found himself lying in the mud, unable to hear his own screaming; his foot, his calf, his hand shorn neatly away. He wanted to cry, but his father had said weeping was a thing for women and queers. His father, the Cornish farmer who'd never raised arms in his life.

Shells struck close by, and the captain made a wet clicking sound from the remains of his neck. Blood foamed where his throat used to be and his eyes spun more frantically than before.

'I'm here, Captain. I'm right here.' Voices and shapes of the enemy. Harsh tongues and cold hands robbing the dead of their wedding rings and rifles.

'I'll be back, sir.'

The captain squeezed his hand, held it in a grip of cold iron.

'I promise, I'll be back. I need to find a gun. I'll come back.'

The grip tightened, pushing the bones of Ronnie's hand together. A numbness came upon the half-man; it drained the last of the warmth from his body while the blood ceased to flow from his splintered leg. The strafes of enemy fire showered them in mud, and in spite of his father's words, Ronald Weakes began to cry.

He pulled Harris across his chest and held him tightly.

'Tell you what, sir. Best we just wait here.'

The cold was grey and without end. It seemed to emanate from him, spreading out like the morning frost, pushing back the day to moments before.

'Captain . . .' Ronnie wiped his eyes and looked again. Men in retreat, walking backwards, along the path they'd taken to overrun the Somersets.

All but one.

A man, an old man, indistinct then solidifying, emerged from the mist. He stood over them, weeping blood as though his very soul was run through. Though he wept crimson tears so freely, he left not a stain upon his white suit, his white leather shoes.

'I cannot,' the old man said. 'I cannot do this anymore.'

'We surrender,' Ronnie said, and thirty dead men turned their backs on him. 'My friend, he needs help.'

'No,' the old man said, 'no, he does not,' and then sank to his knees and took the officer's ruined face in his hands. 'He is not here.' He called to the heavens: 'Dear Lord, I have lost him. I have lost them all.'

And again, Ronnie begged for his help. 'Sir, I don't know you, but if you have a Christian soul then you must save us.'

'No. It is pointless. So eternally pointless.' The old man turned to Ronnie, his eyes hardened. 'You. This is all you.' He took Ronnie by the lapels of his greatcoat and shook him with more strength than should have been possible, and Ronnie wished dearly that he could have felt it: the violent pull and push against the soft earth, the old man's heated breath upon his face. Instead, he found himself floating further away, prised from his own flesh. Strands of his own being, stretched and drawn. Fingers, toes, skin and memories. And then a burst of cold more primeval than anything he'd felt before, and when Ronnie opened his eyes he found he was gazing at the old man shaking his vacant form.

'No. It's not supposed to be like this.'

And to his horror, his words, his final words, were spoken by his body, expiring in the mud before his eyes.

It wasn't right. There was supposed to be a light, a glorious white light. And winged princesses in beautiful robes. And music, Ronnie thought. Where is the music?

'You, sir,' Ronnie said. 'Sir? Are you an angel, sir? If you are then could you take me to my friends?'

The old man clutched Ronnie's earthly shell close to his breast. 'I can do nothing for you now.'

Ronnie shivered, though not from the cold.

He looked to his friends: empty casks, devoid of light.

'If you are an angel, sir, then please, take me to my friends.'

'He is not an angel.'

And when Ronnie turned he saw the voice belonged to a giant of a man, as wide as he was tall, with skin as black as the night.

'Where are they, Alfred?' the Nubian said. 'Where are the souls of the Somersets?'

The old man did not reply, but stayed kneeling in the mud with his eyes pressed shut.

The Nubian made a sound like thunder from inside his throat, then spoke to Ronnie. 'You should not be here, Ronald Weakes. Your time is past.'

'But my friends. What of my friends? They should be here, now, with me. Where's the captain? Where's Sergeant Ffolkes?'

Dice and Holmes and Smith and Smith and Rowles and Baker: dead and lost, gone. They should be here,' Ronnie said, 'with me.'

The Nubian pressed a fingertip to Ronnie's forehead. 'Godspeed, Ronald Weakes,' he said, and Ronnie rose from the earth. 'No! I'm not ready!'

'No one is.'

The sky opened, two halves that stretched beyond sight. And from the rift shone the light, a luminescent stream carrying a boat, an iron gondola piloted by a creature whose glass skeleton moved and flexed beneath its transparent flesh.

And though Death had not extinguished his love for his comrades, Ronnie looked upon the light and thought, Yes, this is how it should be.

TWO

A DUST STORM TRAVELLED the seven miles of dry land that led to the Crystal Harbours of Purgatory. From their grazing lands near the edge of the crater, wildebeest and zebra paused from chewing the sparse yellow grass to gaze at the zephyr with passive curiosity. A storm was not an unusual sight inside the crater, though a tall, pale woman dressed in a business suit running at its head was a thing seldom seen.

Magdelena overtook a cheetah chasing down a Thomson's Gazelle. Her path divided a herd of ten thousand bison. She leapt over a family of twenty elephants and landed a mile later, cracking the parched land under her feet. The air thundered in her ears, stirring the maelstrom inside her head: thoughts of Alfred Warr, a prideful concern for her standing in the eyes of Mr Gee. The crater around her blurred into lines of white and green. She emerged from the valley and sprinted the length of a glass corridor rolled inside a perfect sky.

For when humankind dreamed of an afterlife they dreamed of God and Satan and skies without end. Over the course of several millennia this notion of Heaven and Hell, and Magdelena's small fiefdom between, had changed as humanity embraced science and reason: Mr Gee had lost his white beard and lightning; Gabriel Archer, the Head of Inhuman Resources, had lost his wings and his halo; Leonard Bliss no longer possessed horns, cloven hooves and a pointed tail – and had been very happy about it, as Magdelena recalled.

And best of all, no one was required to spend eternity wearing a billowy white smock.

The skies, however . . . the skies never changed.

In spite of humanity's crippled imagination, Magdelena missed her time outside with them. Mortals were aflame and lived at the speed of light, with little spared for self-reproach because they knew their time was short. There had been one mortal in particular, a married motivational speaker whom she'd worked for, and made the very human mistake of sleeping with, many years ago. His most favoured expression, she remembered, was that 'Self-pity achieves nothing.' A phrase he'd find an excuse to use whenever he had an audience. Still, despite his arrogance, one of the faults that came part and parchment of being human, Magdelena had loved the excitement, the *not knowing* of being with him; not knowing when she would see him again; not knowing if the affair would lay waste to everything around them; not knowing if he would gaze at her one morning and say he'd grown tired of her. She would lie next to him, waiting for him to awaken, her heart pounding with the thrill of possibility, the anticipation of unbearable pain. It was within their power to carve the heart from an immortal, and yet when they dreamed of an afterlife, they only saw sky. Lots and lots of sky.

Magdelena looked upward and realised she desperately missed opaque ceilings.

Not enough of them imagined the Afterlife as a ski resort, or a ladies club that served free cocktails during a happy hour that lasted ten thousand years. It occurred to her then that perhaps she'd spent far too long outside in the company of humanity. Yes, they were toxic and sinful, vibrant and alive; and now, with her time on Earth long since ended, Magdelena felt she was drowning in the timeless waters of the Ever After.

The glass corridor came to an end and the Head of Purgatory leaned back, anchoring her heels and gliding to a stop a few metres from where her personal assistant floated, holding her coat.

'You're going to be late,' Rachel said.

Magdelena slipped her stilettos on to her feet. She couldn't tell if the wraith was simply making an observation or chastising her: the creature's transparent skin made it impossible to see anything that could be translated as an expression. The subtle shifting of her bones, the beating of her heart, the pulsing of her intestinal tract, the movement of fluid under gossamer. Magdelena often found herself wondering if Rachel was beautiful.

'Are you even listening to me, Ma'am?'

'It's Magdelena,' she said, pulling on her coat. 'How many times do I have to tell you?'

'Very good, Ma'am.' The wraith turned a full-length mirror and Magdelena found herself facing the same reflection that had greeted her for two thousand years: a tall, slim, middle-aged woman with pale white skin and angular cheekbones; a roman nose; a strong, square chin and young, piercing green eyes etched with the wisdom of ages; and her hair, shining with the iridescent black of a raven, save for the moon-white streak flowing from her left temple to the end of the chequered braid that fell to her waist – an extraordinary blend of colour which Gabriel Archer, the Head of Inhuman Resources, had once drunkenly described as 'skunk'.

No, Magdelena had no use for a mirror. And it wasn't because she believed vanity a sin; it wasn't, not in her eyes. She found there was little point in staring at herself when, for better or worse, her employer and humanity's lack of imagination kept her perpetually unchanging.

A wooden box, decorated with carvings depicting tales from the Book of Genesis, descended from on high. The box rang an internal bell and announced that it was on the first floor: Purgatory. The doors opened and Magdelena heard herself sigh. Not him, she thought. Not today.

'Magdelena!' The angel in the lift beamed, all too broadly. He tilted his head slightly, ensuring that his hair caught the light in such a way so as to resemble a golden waterfall cascading from his crown.

'Gabriel,' Magdelena said tightly. He was wearing cricket gear – in pastel pink. Even the shoes. His sweater was draped casually around his shoulders with the arms tied across his chest, a style that made Magdelena think that he, like herself, had spent far too long on Earth – the English county of Surrey to be precise. 'What brings you down among us lesser immortals?' She reached past him and pressed the button for the harbour.

'Hah! Humour,' Gabriel said. 'Love it. Love it.' He made a gentle swing with the bat, ending with a stretch forward, a bent front knee and a loud click from under his tongue. Magdelena grimaced and wondered where in all creation one would travel to find a pink cricket bat.

'The big kahuna asked me to come down,' Gabriel said. 'Keep an eye on the Hitler hearing. Thought you could do with some moral support.'

'From you.'

'From me.' He smiled and dropped his head the other way, causing the elevator lights to reflect little stars that danced across his enamels. 'He says you seem a little distracted. Out of sorts, maybe.'

'Well when you get back to Heaven you can thank him for his concern and tell him the Hitler situation is under control.'

'Maybe – and these aren't my words – maybe running Purgatory is a little too much for you. I mean that and the whole,' he made quote marks in the air, 'modernisation of the Afterlife thing. At your age you should really think about—'

'Gabriel, I really wouldn't finish that thought – not in a confined space.'

The lift doors opened out on to Purgatory's harbour, an airborne pier of glass that stretched miles out of sight and was lined with soaring arches that bowed inward above the clouds. Countless wraiths stood behind computer terminals mounted on transparent columns, checking in thousands of bewildered arrivals as they stepped from the iron gondolas. Beyond the quayside, thousands more gondolas oared lazily through white clouds suspended in the stagnant blue sky.

'More glass, more sky, more fucking clouds.' Magdelena stormed from the elevator with Gabriel almost running to keep pace. Here at least, her plans for change had gained a traction of sorts: the giant plasma screens floated above the docks, displaying arrival and departure times, along with news reports and cartoons to entertain those taken before their time. A curious expression, Magdelena had always thought; no one was ever taken before their time.

Indeed, Purgatory was the busiest harbour mankind could imagine, with waiting times that ranged from a few minutes to several months. In any case, the arrivals needed distractions, and to that end Magdelena had recently commissioned the building of a shopping/cinema complex, a health club and a karaoke bar. Even Mr Gee had shown interest in her upgrade plans, going so far as to suggest she build a police station close to the leisure and shopping complex. And when she'd asked why, he'd simply replied, 'Well, you never know...'

But of course he did know; he did, in fact, know everything, so Magdelena had had the station built and staffed straight away.

She looked across the thoroughfare to see the harbour master rolling towards them, leaning right and left to avoid the other wraiths who were guiding the astonished dead to their place of judgement. He leaned back, bringing the glass Segway to a halt, then floated from its platform and saluted.

'A pleasure to see you again, Miss Cane,' he said. His vocal cords vibrated with excitement as he kissed her hand and pointedly ignored Gabriel Archer. 'He will be so pleased that a member of the senior management is here to greet him.'

Gabriel coughed loudly and stepped forward, closing the triangle. 'Two members of the senior management team, no less.'

'Such a great man. Such a great, great man,' the harbour master continued, ignoring the archangel completely. 'Humanitarian, visionary, loved and adored by millions...'

Magdelena raised an eyebrow and pointed it at Gabriel.

'...and a superlative orator, I'm sure you agree.'

'Well, yes,' said Magdelena, 'I agree with that, but—'

'You know, I believe his ideas and teachings will one day lead humankind to a new age of tolerance and enlightenment.'

'Excuse me?' said Gabriel.

The wraith was enraptured; his lungs hadn't drawn breath since he'd begun to speak. Magdelena placed a hand on his shoulder and told him to calm himself.

'I'm sorry, Miss Cane,' the wraith said. 'I haven't been this excited since . . . Well, no, I can't remember being this excited.'

'What are you talking about? He practically lives here.' She looked over his shoulder to where an excited crowd of wraiths and 'newly-deads', as the Archangel Gabriel liked to call them, had gathered in a frenzy of cheering and handshaking.

'Yes, in a spiritual sense, I suppose he lives in all of us,' the harbour master said, nodding earnestly. 'He certainly lives in me.'

Gabriel turned his attention to the crowd by peering through the harbour master's head.

'But now you're here, Miss Cane, perhaps you'd like to have a word,' the wraith said, treating the archangel to his most derisory look. 'He arrived early, so he's somewhat disorientated and very confused. Perhaps if you could explain his situation to him?'

'This is his eighth hearing in fifty years,' Magdelena said. 'I can't imagine him being confused at all.'

The harbour master made a worthy performance of being taken aback. 'You're talking about *Unteroffizier* Hitler.'

'Yes,' said Magdelena, and narrowed her eyes. A scuffle had broken out near the centre of the crowd. 'Who are you talking about?'

The wraith looked nervously over his shoulder, as though waiting for someone to hand him the magical clipboard that would shield him from a rapidly looming clerical error. 'Gregory XVII,' he said, his larynx vibrating in his throat.

'The Pope?' Gabriel said. 'The Pope is here? Now? He's not expected for another two days.'

The harbour master turned his head to look at the swelling crowd. There was shouting, and fists were being thrown. 'Apparently he took a sudden turn for the worse.'

The wraiths at the check-in stations looked nervously at one another. Some, urged by their colleagues, abandoned their posts and moved in for a closer look.

'And where is he now?' Magdelena asked, trying to maintain her composure as a bottle sailed across her line of sight.

The wraith closed his eyes, pointlessly, and raised a finger, waving it in the direction of the disturbance.

'Wonderful, just wonderful.' Magdelena kicked off her high heels and set off at a sprint. Gabriel ran past her, waving his cricket bat to separate the secondary gathering of transparent onlookers blocking their path. The harbour alarm sounded and a moment later a contingent of wraiths armed with stun batons sprang from the police station, riding pursuit Segways with sirens wailing.

The archangel shouted and pointed his bat at a gondola reversing erratically from the dock. Magdelena spared it a glance, and felt the ichor slow in her veins when she caught sight of its weeping occupant. 'Leonard!' she shouted. 'What do you think you're doing?' He couldn't hear her, and she knew it would make little difference if he could; Leonard listened to no one save Mr Gee. The gondola crashed into another vessel before straightening on its course and sailing into the distance at the speed of light. 'Someone get after him!' Magdelena shouted. 'He doesn't have a licence!'

But in accordance with the civil disturbance procedures, which she herself had instigated, the gondola pilots had left their vehicles to deal with the situation on the ground; there was no one to give chase.

The security detachment dismounted and began pushing everyone aside to allow Magdelena and Gabriel through to the centre of the crowd.

The harbour master, wheezing loudly and with his internal organs looking as though they might rupture at any moment, gasped to a stop a metre behind where Magdelena and Gabriel stood frozen in horror. He followed the line of their gaze, yelped, and began ordering more of the security wraiths into the affray.

Magdelena watched, white as a cloud, recalling the column of marble slabs next to her desk, and wondered, with a sense of cold foreboding, if one of the tablets mentioned her being fired . . .

I need to do something, she thought. 'Gabriel,' she said, 'get in there and do something!'

But Gabriel simply stared as the wraiths tried to separate a snarling Pope Gregory XVII from the bloodied, cowering form of *Unteroffizier* Hitler. The archangel swallowed, turned to Magdelena and whispered, 'Oh . . . fuck.'

THREE

ALTHOUGH HE DID NOT realise it, Elias Bjørstad had been at war with himself since the moment he was born. It was a battle that defined him as a man and as a priest and had taken him on a journey of frustration that began when, as a boy barely into his teens, he'd left the convent on the outskirts of Trondheim where he had been raised since the war.

Elias had travelled the world in search of himself and of God. He'd met a great many people and mastered many languages before entering the Sorbonne as a hungry, thin, travelling preacher. He left, some nine years later, as a doctor of Theology & Linguistics and a fully ordained priest of the Roman Catholic church. His time at the Sorbonne should have strengthened his love of God, but in the end it proved little more than a decade-long respite from doubt. The wanderlust returned and his search for the truth carried him to the most inhospitable places on Earth; the grim missionary armed with only a battered bible and his frayed convictions, plagued by inner voices that haunted him at every turn.

And then there were the dreams; dreams of alcohol, violence and lust.

His search became more desperate and his sermons a fiery melange of embittered Catholicism laced with Creationist platitudes. He hoped for a sign, a signal of the Almighty's displeasure, anything that would prove he was there, listening. Elias wanted his burning bush, or at least to be struck down for his disobedience. In the end there was only silence, and it was the silence that drove him to the North and South Poles; and to journey, alone and on foot, deep into the Amazon basin, until finally, half-mad, he joined an expedition to scale K2.

Whether it was the lack of oxygen or the malaise he'd laboured under for so many years, Elias would never know, but as they huddled in tents waiting for a break in the snowstorm, he burst from their shelter and, with the rest of expedition in pursuit, ran on to a ledge that reached out above the clouds.

'I hate you!' he cried. 'You took my mother and my father, and like a fool I serve you. You look on while children starve and the world burns. Well, Almighty God, I give you this one chance.'

His friends shouted to him as he stepped on to the rim with his toes hanging over the precipice. 'Your last chance,' he whispered. 'Your last chance to prove that you love me.'

Elias closed his eyes and fell into space. As his feet left the ice he felt his harness snap tight against his chest. The fall arrested, and almost as quickly he found himself in motion again, this time in reverse, falling upward. He landed heavily on the ice and rolled on to his back, trying to focus the voluminous shape standing over him in the haze of the snow.

'Bishop Bjørstad,' his saviour said, and Elias realised he'd been rescued by a priest . . . of sorts. The individual was tall, at least six and a half feet, with a torso that sloped out from his waist into a wide, muscular frame. His skin gave Elias the impression that the man had spent most of his life hidden from the light of the sun. His eyes, a cold and bright blue, were set beneath hooded lids. Even his vestments were something of an enigma; the regular apparel of a priest, though curiously inverted: white shoes, crisply pressed trousers and a clerical shirt beneath a white woollen overcoat. Save for the black leather gloves and the black cleric's collar, he would have faded into the mountain. Elias couldn't imagine such a man providing succour for the needy. In fact, Elias thought uncharitably, the man would probably be more inclined to rob the needy at knifepoint. Still, he was a priest. Elias struggled to his feet and extended a trembling hand. The priest looked at Elias's hand as though unsure if it was a gesture of friendship or an invitation to unarmed combat. He chose to ignore it and spoke again: 'Bishop Bjørstad.'

'My son?'

'Your presence is required at the Vatican.'

Elias nodded and adjusted his goggles. Excommunication: a fitting punishment after attempting to take his own life. God indeed watches over me, he thought, and was filled with more regret than he ever dreamed possible.

There was a helicopter waiting on the plateau. It too, like the priest who accompanied him, was painted white. On its doors it carried the seal of Gregory XVII: the supreme pontiff.

† † †

The helicopter delivered the bishop and the priest to a small airfield five miles from Lhasa, where they boarded a Vatican flight bound for Rome. The helicopter pilot disappeared into the cockpit, and moments later they were airborne. As soon as the seatbelt lights were extinguished, the white priest took a Bible from his seat pocket and proceeded to read from the first page, his brow furrowed with the intensity of his devotion. Watching him, Elias felt almost envious.

As well as the priest, there were two nuns in attendance who politely served wine and a meal of vegetable broth, lamb stroganoff and baked Alaska, all of which Elias devoured ravenously. The priest, sitting in the armchair across from him, ate nothing and did not respond when Elias offered him a warm bread roll. The nuns cleared the table without saying a word, and Elias wondered if he might be allowed to sit in the cockpit for a while. He'd flown a number of aircraft, but never a Lear, and would have loved dearly to give it his best try. When he moved to rise from his seat, the priest glanced over his Bible and presented him a look that spoke of how unwise such an action would be.

'I will need to get up at some point, my son,' Elias said. 'I'm afraid these days I'm ruled as much by the vagaries of my bladder as the word of God.'

The priest placed the Bible face down on his lap and laid his hands across it so it wouldn't hear. 'If I may say so, Your Excellency,' he said with an extraordinarily potent sneer, 'it is my honest and heartfelt belief that you are a poor excuse for a bishop and know little concerning the word of God.' He turned over his Bible and continued to read, tracing a gloved finger over each word as he quietly recited it.

Elias forced a smile and settled back into his armchair. The white priest's words scored him deeply, though he was determined not to show it. Besides, it was a long flight to Rome and he was grateful for anything that resembled a conversation, even if his travelling companion chose to throw insults from his seat for the duration of the journey.

'Your vestment is not one I am familiar with,' Elias began, still smarting. 'Would I be correct to assume that you are one of the fabled Apostles of the Inquisition?'

The priest turned a page and said nothing, the response Elias would have expected if this man was who he thought he was. 'Then if that is the case, may I also assume that if I had chosen not to accompany you I would have been excommunicated on the spot?'

The priest spared him a sour eye.

'And my companions; you would have killed them too. You would dispatch innocents in the name of the Church.' As he spoke he knew he was being foolish. The apostles were nought but a myth, a story told to young initiates caught masturbating after lights out; tales of assassin priests whispered in the night to discourage incidents of unseemly self-abuse.

Indeed, Elias himself had first heard of these 'enforcers of the Lord' when, as a young orphan of Trondheim, growing painfully into adolescence, he'd been chanced upon by Sister Constance while he lay in the convent grain store with his breeches about his knees and his Staff of Woeful Pursuits gripped firmly in his trembling hand.

'If you persist in this satanic practice, Elias,' she'd cried, vibrating a righteous finger high above her head, 'if you continue with this foul and baseless activity then his Holiness will have little choice but to dispatch his Agents of the Inquisition. And they will come to you, Elias Bjørstad; they will come to you in the black of the night and they will drive a nail through your Sceptre of Unholy Pleasures, as the cursed Romans drove nails through the palms and feet of our Lord Jesus Christ! Is that what you want, Elias? Do you wish a long and rusty spike driven through your Cudgel of Sin?'

When used to such cruel effect, her words had hammered the fear of the Almighty into Elias, so much so that a full three hours passed before she found him lying in the wood store, pleasuring himself yet again.

'Damn the evil tainting your soul, Elias Bjørstad,' she'd hissed. 'If you cannot cleanse your mind of impure thoughts then it falls to me to exorcise you, myself.' Then the aged nun had hitched her habit to her waist and slapped his Spear of Ignorance before impaling herself upon it. She'd felt dry and hot and, as Elias remembered, surprisingly robust for an octogenarian. She'd heaved and gasped, hoisted and crushed herself down on to him again and again.

'Can you feel me, Elias?' the cadaverous old witch had screamed. 'Can you feel me crushing the Trickster from your unholy loins?' Her motions became more frantic, pushing down so hard that Elias felt the old wooden planks begin to give way beneath his hips. 'Can you feel me throttling the putrefying vileness from your—' She'd grunted and slumped forward, smashing her head against his. He thought he'd heard her utter the word 'cock', though at the time could not believe this to be true; Sister Constance would never allow such a blasphemy to escape her toothless and shrivelled mouth – the same mouth she'd used to stir life back into his Rod of Deceit so his exorcism could continue.

The ordeal had lasted a painful and terrifying hour, and left him with scratches gouged deep into his chest, a fear of women that stayed with him until he entered the Sorbonne, and a pelvic misalignment that plagued him to this very day.

Elias swallowed and realised his eyes were watering. He looked across to the white priest, who returned the same look attached to a thin and humourless smile. Elias leaned across the table and said, 'This is about the condoms, isn't it?'

The priest returned to his Bible.

After nine hours of silence, the jet landed at Rome International Airport. Elias felt he should voice his concern when the pilot climbed behind the controls of another Vatican helicopter and began to prep for take-off.

'Should he not rest?'

'Do not concern yourself, Your Excellency,' the priest replied. 'Now please, take your seat.'

It was a mercifully short flight. Elias gazed down at the streets choked with evening traffic. How long had it been since he'd seen this proud and ancient monument? He'd always thought it fitting that the One True Church had found its home in the ashes of another great empire.

They circled the city for almost half an hour, indicating an unusually high level of air traffic around the Vatican. The white priest said it was caused by a 'swarm of journalists plaguing the city like locust', but didn't elaborate further. When they finally touched down at the Vatican City heliport, they were greeted by the plague the apostle had spoken of. The white priest drew a black overcoat over his raiment and bundled Elias from the helicopter as the journalists swept in around them. They thrust cameras and microphones at them in such numbers that Elias could not see which way to turn. They asked how he had found K2; if his misdeeds had finally brought him to the attention of the Vatican; what he planned to do after his excommunication; was there truth to the rumour that Pope Gregory had taken ill?

Elias followed the path the apostle cut through the crowd. 'His Holiness is unwell?'

The apostle didn't reply. He simply said, 'This way, Your Eminence,' and pushed the journalists aside, sending them sprawling as though they'd been run down by cars.

A Mercedes was waiting at the heliport entrance, its rear door held open by a sharp-featured little man in a black suit. Elias turned to thank the apostle and spoke to empty space. One hundred metres away, the helicopter was already lifting off, the steady chop of its rotors churning the air and ruffling the trim of his coat. He watched it until it had disappeared into the dark sky and wondered what further devices the apostle was set to embark upon this night. Yes, he thought, an apostle; he'd been snatched from eternal damnation by an apostle of the Inquisition. He thought sourly of Sister Constance and his hip creaked in agreement.

Another journey: a slow and respectful crawl along one of the many roads that serrated the Vatican Gardens. Another journey and another silent pilot. They passed numerous chapels and churches that stood in the shadow of the Basilica. Elias gazed at the vast grey dome and thought, This – this is the pivot, the focal point, the centre of all we believe. The Basilica poured light into him and he found his faith partially renewed, for the moment at least.

The car kept to the roads north of St Peters, skirting the city walls until it came to a stop outside the Apostolic Palace. The driver jumped out, hurried around and opened the passenger door. 'They're expecting you, Your Excellency.'

Elias climbed out of the car and creaked his way upright. The Papal Residence, he thought, staring with reverence and apprehension at the vast fascia of red stone. *Then I am to be excommunicated by Gregory himself.*

His legs moved as lead columns, so that he was almost exhausted when he entered the residence. A nun led him through a maze of corridors that eventually opened out into a grand hall, decorated without humility or reservation. The walls, leafed in gold, folded into arches which became part of the ceiling some fifty feet above, framing the life's work of some of the greatest artisans the world would ever see: effigies of angels and demons and strange transparent creatures that flew somewhere in between. His climbing boots echoed on the polished marble floor, and the deities looked down, disapprovingly.

Elias walked as quickly as his legs would allow, forcing the nun to run in order to keep pace. He wanted this to be over with.

The hall ended at a pair of immense oak doors and an old wooden chair parked incongruously several metres away. The nun took a moment to catch her breath, gestured for him to take a seat, then walked over to the doors, knocking once then opening one slightly so she could slip inside.

What a joke I am, Elias thought. What a sad and pathetic joke. He looked down at his feet; his boots had seen better days; they were caked in the red dust that had travelled with him from Tibet. A trail of it began at the archway to the great hall, then crossed a hundred feet of the polished floor, and ended just in front of his seat. He smiled warmly at a nun who shuffled past him carrying a laptop and a screwdriver. She replied with a curt scowl and steered an arc around him as though sin was something contagious.

He leaned back, resting his head against a fresco then sprung to his feet when he realised what he had done. He examined the painting; there was stain. God, a stain, from his hood, still damp with perspiration.

'It is a reproduction,' a voice behind him said.

He spun round and instinctively spread his arms to cover the scene of his crime, then gave himself away by saying how sorry he was. For many things, it seemed.

The nun smiled stiffly and bowed with just a slight movement of her head. 'They're ready for you now.'

† † †

In comparison to the great hall, the room behind the oak door was spartan. It was a quarter of the size, though the marble floor seemed to have seeped through from the corridor. The walls were a sombre vermillion, the ceiling, white. There were still more mounted frescos, less colourful but no less glorious. They depicted scenes of hell – sinners dragged wailing and screaming to the fiery pits of Perdition – leaving Elias with no doubt that in this room terrible things happened to the Church's wayward clergy. The chamber was inadequately lit by hundreds of candles, and in its centre, in front of a small and equally inadequate chair, stood a large crescent table of ancient cedar wood where twelve men laboured at portable computers.

And there was a thirteenth who seemed as seasoned as the others though not as old.

Each of them worked industriously by the light of screens that cast images of the world across their lined faces. Occasionally one of them would lean across to a colleague to clarify some point or share some small ecclesiastical joke. And as they worked, a group of nuns moved among them, pouring drinks and replacing empty plates with fresh rounds of sandwiches and cakes. Elias felt his stomach churn. He recognised them, most of them. Near the centre of the half-circle, next to a raised throne of cedar and gold, sat Carlos Giordano, Cardinal Secretary of State; to his immediate right, Leone Rossi, the Cardinal Camerlengo. Elias was numbly surprised to see the position of *Il Sositituto*, head of the Section for General Affairs, still held by Cardinal Möller. *The man must be near a hundred years of age.*

And Ignacio Martinez, the Secretary for Relations of States. Elias had seen him lecture once during his early years at the Sorbonne. He'd always thought of Cardinal Martinez as a liberal thinker; seeing the old man here, at his excommunication, made Elias feel he'd been somehow betrayed. The rest he barely knew, or knew vaguely from Vatican briefings which he, shamefully, skimmed through on the rare occasions they managed to reach him. The cardinals represented the upper echelons of the Roman Curia and were the highest authority in the Catholic Church. Only the supreme pontiff himself was missing.

Elias felt his knees suddenly weaken. The room began to spin, then came to a sudden halt when someone tapped a pen on the table. He blinked rapidly to clear his vision. Cardinal Rossi scowled at him and pointed his pen at the small wooden chair in the cradle of the semi-circle.

'Bishop Bjørstad.'

He looked up as he sat, trying to determine which of the cardinals had spoken. A loud cough drew his eyes to the far end of the table, where the younger clergy had risen from his chair. He was dressed in the vestment of a monsignor, a senior priest, which he wore more comfortably than Elias wore his own skin. His complexion was a strange affair: a patchwork of sun-darkened flesh next to uneven tracts of ghostly white. It was as if his skin was trying to tan but was finding it frightfully hard to remember how. He was of average height and perhaps a little thick about the midriff; his hair, a sandy-grey blond in colour, was combed back to reveal an intelligent forehead above a straight and narrow nose. He had a pronounced chin and slender, effeminate hands that Elias doubted had ever seen anything in the way of physical labour. The monsignor stepped forward with his eyes down, flipping between sheets on a clipboard.

'I am he,' Elias said. 'And who might you be, young man?'

The man raised an eyebrow as if to say, *How could you not know?* 'I am Salvatore Vecchi, private secretary to the Vicar of Christ.'

Though hungry and seized by fear for his future, Elias, nevertheless, found himself tensing his lips to suppress a smile. Was this not the sign he had asked for? Was this not the Lord's displeasure manifested as the twelve cardinals gathered in judgement? He would be punished for a career tainted by blasphemy, and for attempting to take his own life. 'And may I enquire as to the whereabouts of the Servant of the Servant of God?'

A vein in Vecchi's neck pulsed and undulated like a charmed asp. 'He is . . . indisposed,' he said brittlely. One of the cardinals – in the flickering light Elias could not see which one – coughed. 'We have been charged with speaking on his behalf.' Vecchi removed a page from his clipboard and placed it face down on the table. He took a deep breath, and for a moment, Elias thought he would burst into song. 'Tell me, Bishop Bjørstad, are you familiar with the Church's stance on contraception?'

And so it begins.

'Is it a point of Roman Catholic doctrine that you find somehow vague' – he fixed Elias with a look of unfettered disgust – 'or open to your own interpretation?'

Elias cleared his throat before he spoke, and still his voice sounded, to his own ears, as though he was being throttled. 'I am familiar with the Church's views on contraception, yes.'

Vecchi nodded vigorously, unseating a forelock that had been pressed neatly to his scalp. 'Good! Good, so you do understand. Excellent.'

'Have a care, Monsignor Vecchi,' Cardinal Giordano said without looking away from his screen. 'You will afford Bishop Bjørstad his due respect.' Elias felt his heart lift; an ally, perhaps, one to whom he could plead his case for clemency. Giordano peered at Elias over the rims of his tiny gold spectacles. 'While he is still a bishop.'

Vecchi smiled tightly. 'Of course, I beg the Curia's forgiveness.' He turned to Elias. 'And yours, Bishop Bjørstad. Now if you would be so good as to answer the question.'

'Yes,' Elias said. 'I am fully aware of the Church's position.'

The cardinals sat back and listened intently.

'Then perhaps you would care to explain how diverting church resources to fund condom drives in Cape Town, Nairobi and Dar es Salaam is in keeping with Roman Catholic doctrine.'

Elias fell silent, his eyes fixed fearfully on Vecchi who, once again, was examining his wretched clipboard.

'Eighty thousand euros,' the monsignor read. 'Almost a quarter of a million prophylactics distributed, for free.' He flipped the page. 'And in the name of the Roman Catholic Church.'

Murmurs rose from the seated cardinals. Some shook their heads; others wiped tears from their eyes.

'I sought to save lives.' Elias said. He suddenly felt very cold.

'And whose life did you seek to save when you misappropriated funds to pay for an abortion?'

The air inside the chamber grew slow and viscous. The cardinals gasped out loud and a nun dropped a carafe of wine and crossed herself frenziedly before running from the chamber in tears. One of the Curia – a smooth-skinned Ethiopian with an explosion of grey, wiry hair and whose name Elias could not remember – started from his seat and glared at him. He pointed a trembling finger and opened his mouth as if to speak. His eyes burned and his whole body shook with the effort of maintaining a semblance of self-control. His finger homed in on Vecchi and he said, 'I will not be a party to this . . . travesty.' And with that, he followed the nun from the chamber.

Vecchi himself could barely hide his satisfaction. He raised his hand and appealed for calm. Three of the cardinals were embroiled in a heated discussion; four more bowed their heads in prayer. Another cardinal threw down his skullcap and stormed from the chamber. And in the midst of all this, Giordano simply leaned against the arm of his throne resting his index finger against his temple, his eyes fixed on Elias. He neither smiled nor frowned, appeared neither outraged nor compassionate. Elias stared back, hoping that Giordano would read his plea for mercy in his eyes. How could I have been so wrong? he thought. With or without his faith, he had saved so many. Surely that was all that mattered? With or without his faith, he did not want to leave the church. The church was his home. 'The woman came to me from Darfour,' he shouted above the roar of disapproval. 'A victim of a most foul and vicious rape which left her with the curse of HIV and with child.' He wrung his hands until his knuckles cracked. 'She begged me to help her and I could not turn her away. I could not see her suffer, her child suffer, cursed to a life of—'

'And you are quite the satirist it would seem.' Vecchi said loudly. He held a newspaper above his head. Elias craned his neck and tried to read it. 'From the *Guardian* newspaper, dated January 6th 1993,' Vecchi said, helpfully. 'You wrote a letter under the embarrassingly banal pseudonym of CardinalX.'

'You called yourself a cardinal,' a voice from the table cried. 'For shame!'

'Quite.' Vecchi opened the newspaper and swept it in a wide arc for the cardinals to see. 'And on this date they chose to publish a letter in which you extolled your views on celibacy within the Roman Catholic clergy.' He cleared his throat when he plainly had no need. 'And I quote: ". . . *I cannot deny my calling any more than I can deny myself air. Yes, I feel truly blessed that I have been chosen to serve God and that he, in his infinite wisdom, has granted me a long and fulfilling life in which to witness the miracle of his handiwork. And yet I often feel alone, adrift, because my faith denies me the warmth and intimacy of female companionship.'"*

A hush fell across the chamber; Vecchi took a moment to bathe in it before dropping the newspaper at Elias's feet.

'So,' he said. A single word with the keen edge of a headsman's axe. 'You crave female companionship, Bishop Bjørstad.'

Yes, Elias thought, dear God, yes. A chorus of voices inside his head chimed their agreement. He pleaded with them: *Not now, I beg of you – not now.* 'It was a satirical piece,' he cried, wretchedly. 'My intention was to encourage a debate on the issue of celibacy within—'

Rossi slammed his fist against the table. 'There is no debate, Bishop Bjørstad! There is only the will of the See!'

And though it would not have seemed possible, the next two hours grew worse. Every misdeed and crossed word, every slight and transgression was dragged from history and theatrically dissected by Monsignor Vecchi under the unforgiving gaze of the Curia. In that time, Elias was offered neither food nor water. His chest grew tight, his vision tunnelled, and soon Vecchi sounded as though he was calling out to him from the fog. Elias's head fell forward and he whispered, 'Enough. Excommunicate me if you must, but please, enough.'

Strange and terrifying images snarled and clawed their way from the depths of his mind. Images of him beating one woman and forcing himself on another. Images of him drinking from barrels and fighting in taverns. Images of him torturing and killing Nazi soldiers. Memories of Sister Constance calling him Satan's little whore and running her tongue around the inside of his mouth.

'Did you hear what I said, Bishop Bjørstad?'

Elias raised his head and shielded his eyes. Vecchi was smiling, or at least contorting his face into what he believed to be a smile. The monsignor straightened and ordered a nun to fetch a pitcher of water. Elias's nightmares vanished to make room for the world in its entirety to tumble through his head. It is the lack of food and water, Elias thought. 'Did you speak of his Holiness, Monsignor Vecchi?' he croaked. His throat hurt.

'Indeed, I did,' Vecchi replied and poured him a glass of water. 'Following a short illness, Pope Gregory XVII passed away but a few hours ago.'

Vecchi's words left only the faintest imprint on him. Elias knew that on hearing such news he should feel the world shrivel to nothing. Have I become so disjoined, he thought, so far removed from my faith? The voices in his head said that he had. He gazed across the table and realised that only four cardinals remained. Giordano still rested to one side with his finger pressed against his temple. Vecchi looked to the Cardinal Secretary of State, who nodded solemnly.

'What is going on here?' Elias asked.

Vecchi cleared his throat, again, without needing to. 'Bishop Bjørstad,' he said, 'what would you say if I . . . We . . . were to offer you the position of Bishop of Rome?'

The world tumbled again. Elias tried to stand then thought better of it. Every movement of the clock sounded suddenly like a drum, and he was sure his heartbeat had slowed to keep pace. 'I'm sorry, what was that?'

Vecchi sighed impatiently. 'We would like to offer you the position of Bishop of Rome.'

'The Pope.'

'Yes.' Vecchi glanced at the Curia. They shrugged and nodded. He turned back to Elias and made another heartfelt attempt at a smile. 'Well, what do you think?'

'I think,' Elias growled, devouring a cut of rage as it was handed to him by each of the voices in his head, 'that if you wish to excommunicate me then you should do so without this cruel charade.' The voices roared their approval, and he thought he could hear swords clashing against wooden shields.

'It is no charade, Bjørstad,' Rossi said. 'Do you accept?'

'You are asking me if I wish to be the next Pope?' He placed the empty glass down, holding on to it as though it may somehow fall from the floor. His world stopped spinning and contented itself by folding inside out. 'But . . . I am just a bishop.'

'Technically, yes.' Vecchi said.

'You expect me to believe that you – any of you – would even consider elevating a disgraced bishop to head of the Holy Church?'

Giordano leaned forward and clasped his hands in front of him. 'And do you believe we would dispatch an apostle to retrieve you, just to excommunicate you?'

'And yet that is what you would have me think!' Elias said. 'You torture me and then ask me to lead you.' He wished dearly that he could find the strength to laugh.

'It was merely a test, Elias.' Rossi said, and Elias jumped in his seat, surprised to hear his name spoken after so many years. 'An interview ... of sorts.'

'Test me? There was no need. I can tell you that I am not the man you are looking for.' His mind stumbled and limped to keep up. Why? Why a such a lowly servant of the church? Why not one of the Curia?

'The Church has reached a crossroads,' Vecchi said, making Elias believe he'd voiced his thoughts aloud. 'Our flock is dwindling, seduced by lesser religions and the filth-ridden medium of the internet.'

Martinez snorted. 'Pornography is bad enough, but Buddhism, if you can believe that.' The others nodded sombrely.

'Under the most blessed and exalted leadership of Gregory XVII, the Church has enjoyed a return to the piety that was once the hallmark of our faith: traditional teachings, the restoration of Latin in many of our schools, greater influence in politics and the media.' Vecchi took a sheet of paper from his clipboard and thrust it under Elias's nose. 'He also brought about a dramatic reduction in church attendance figures worldwide.'

Elias could only make out a cacophony of words, graphs and numbers.

'As a result, the Peter's Pence contributions were down almost fifteen percent in ninety-three, twenty-two per cent in ninety-four, and this year they have fallen an unsustainable thirty per cent.'

'If this continues,' Martinez said, 'the Vatican faces bankruptcy.'

'The Church, bankrupt? That is not possible.'

'Even men of God cannot argue with the numbers, Bishop Bjørstad,' Möller said feebly, then slumped back in his seat, the effort having spent him.

Giordano rose from his chair. His height, a shade below five feet, took Elias by surprise. 'Desperate times call for extraordinary measures,' he said. 'The Church must at least give the impression of moving forward while staying fast with tradition and its core values. Wouldn't you agree, Bishop Bjørstad?'

Elias nodded, unsure whether he agreed or not.

'And that is where you come in.'

'I don't understand.'

Vecchi clasped his hands behind his back and leaned forward, far too closely for Elias's liking. His breath was cold and smelled of nothing, not even air, The monsignor gave the impression of a man who could slip through history without leaving so much as a ripple.

'Imagine, if you will, the reaction around the world if the Conclave chose an unknown wandering bishop to lead the Roman Catholic Church into the new millennium.'

'The Conclave will never agree to such—'

'The Conclave is a ceremonial gathering,' Vecchi said.

'More akin to a wake,' Rossi added.

'The decision as to who will serve as our next Pope is decided by those wise enough to serve the Curia.'

The four remaining cardinals nodded and murmured in agreement, while Elias wondered where the other eight had gone. He remembered one of them, the Ethiopian, had described the gathering as a travesty. Perhaps, he thought, perhaps this idea is not as widely accepted as the monsignor believes.

'You have led a long and interesting life, Bishop Bjørstad.' Vecchi flipped a page on his clipboard, and Elias wondered how so much incriminating information could be collected in so few pages. 'Norwegian by birth, orphaned during the war, raised by nuns. That would make you fifty-five, fifty-six?'

Elias nodded weakly and said he was fifty-five years old.

'And in excellent condition, if I may say so. No doubt due to the mountaineering, skiing, flying, hiking, fencing, boxing, karate . . . One wonders how you found time to minister your flock.'

'The Lord provides,' Elias said flatly. A plate of sandwiches travelled by, escorted by a young novice. She stopped to offer him one.

'I am sure,' Vecchi said with a smile that made no attempt to reach his eyes.

Elias took the entire plate and began cramming the small triangles into his mouth, two at a time.

'You see, Bishop Bjørstad, you are precisely the kind of man we are looking for,' Rossi said. 'Young – for a pontiff, dynamic, the kind of man that today's liberal Catholic can really get behind.'

The voices in Elias's head chorused: *Tell them!*

'And you're Norwegian,' rasped Cardinal Möller. 'People like Norwegians.' His tone, such as it was, suggested he did not understand why. 'Almost as much as they like Canadians.'

'Then why not choose a Canadian?' Elias asked with his mouth full and his voices screaming: *Tell them!*

Vecchi looked at him apologetically and tugged at his ear. 'Norway has a flourishing Roman Catholic community,' he said, 'which we are keen to nurture and support. What better way to demonstrate our commitment to them than by elevating one of their countrymen to supreme leader of the Church?'

'And as Norway is the world's second richest country, the benefits to the Church would be reciprocal.'

Vecchi stared at him, then quickly installed a slightly more pained version of his earlier smile. 'If that were our main concern, Bishop Bjørstad, then why settle for second best?'

Elias swallowed the mulch of his last sandwich and said, 'Perhaps you do not believe our followers are ready to accept an Arabic Pope.' The voices berated him, accusing him of base falsehood. He tried his utmost to ignore them, as he'd tried to for most of his life.

Vecchi's false smile broadened. 'Astute,' he said, 'very astute.' He walked back to the crescent and took his place behind it, fingertips resting lightly on the wooden surface, yet still suggesting he was trying to push the table down through the floor. 'We understand that this is much to ask of you, Bishop Bjørstad. Indeed, the position of supreme pontiff is much to ask of any man, but we wish you to consider it, carefully.'

The oak doors opened and two nuns in blinding white stood waiting.

'We have prepared quarters for you in—'

'There is something else,' Elias blurted before he could stop himself, 'something you should know.'

The Curia, collectively, clenched its buttocks.

'I have long suffered from—'

Tell them!

'I have suffered . . . I cannot accept. I am not sure, you see. I am not sure . . .'

'Sure?' Giordano said hotly. 'Sure about what?'

'I am not sure I believe in God. I am sorry. I cannot do this.'

The voices in his head cheered or rattled their shields or shot pistols high into the dome of his skull. The cardinals wilted, and Elias felt the weight of creation lifted from his back.

'Thank the Lord,' Vecchi said, fanning himself with his clipboard. 'Thank the Lord.'

Cardinal Möller made loud rasping sounds as he fought for air. Giordano reached beneath the table and produced an oxygen mask, placing it with practised ease over the old Cardinal's nose and mouth.

'I do not understand,' Elias said, staring at Möller and thinking, *One hundred years at the very least.*

'We thought,' said Rossi, glancing from cardinal to cardinal, 'we thought you were going to say . . . something else.'

'Something worse than being an atheist?'

Möller pulled the oxygen mask away from his face. 'We thought you were about to tell us that you're a homosexual.'

Rossi crossed himself, several times in succession. 'You're not a homosexual, are you?'

'He is not a homosexual,' Vecchi said, his fingers blurring as he rattled through the sheets on his clipboard. 'We would know if he were a homosexual.'

'I am not a homosexual,' Elias said, 'but I do not believe in God.' He sighed loudly. 'Or at least, I do not believe that I believe.'

'That should not represent a problem.' Vecchi looked to the remains of the Curia for approval. The ancient men glanced at each other before obediently nodding their agreement. Satisfied, Vecchi smiled. 'Though of course we would have to insist that you keep any such doubts to yourself.'

'I do not think you are listening to me,' Elias said, his head down and his hands clasped behind it. 'You cannot ask me to be God's representative on Earth when I cannot be sure he even exists!'

'You think you are the only one who doubts?' Martinez said. 'We all doubt from time to time. We are in the business of doubt. We are a religious faith, not a scientific certainty. If the existence of God was a known absolute then why would people need us?'

Elias was aghast. 'How can you say such a thing?'

'I say it because it is the nature of faith.' The cardinal wrestled his wine glass from a nun who had foolishly attempted to remove it. 'We seek the right man to lead us, Bishop Bjørstad, and it would be unwise of us to reject a suitable applicant merely because of his religious beliefs – or lack thereof. We seek a man who is just, honest with himself and others, capable and—'

'Norwegian,' Möller added, somewhat bitterly.

'In some countries,' said Cardinal Rossi, sagely, 'it would be illegal to withhold such an offer from you purely on the basis of your religious leanings.'

'Then perhaps one day we *can* look forward to a Muslim pontiff.'

The chamber fell silent for a moment before Giordano said, 'I do hope that you are not going to keep saying that.'

Vecchi coughed loudly into his fist. 'I think enough has been discussed for today,' he said. 'Bishop Bjørstad, make yourself at home here while you consider our offer.'

The white nuns stepped into the room and stood either side of Elias.

'Sister Hope and Sister Piety are both at your disposal. We will meet again in the morning.'

Elias rose unsteadily to his feet. He thanked the cardinals, shaking them coldly by the hand, except for Cardinal Möller who held his oxygen mask with one hand and waved vaguely in his direction with the other.

'Until tomorrow then, Bishop . . . Elias.' Giordano smiled pleasantly, as though they'd spent the evening exchanging recipes.

'Yes,' Elias said. 'Until tomorrow.'

† † †

'He is completely unsuitable, Vecchi,' Giordano said, slamming his laptop shut. 'What were you thinking?'

Vecchi gathered his papers and walked to the door beyond the crescent-shaped table.

'I have to agree, monsignor,' Rossi chimed in. 'He responds well under pressure, I grant you, but the man has no faith and no direction. Yet you think he should be the next Bishop of Rome.'

'Yes, he lacks faith,' Vecchi said, 'and that is precisely why we need him.'

'Explain yourself,' croaked Möller, while two nuns helped him into his wheelchair.

'We agree that Gregory, though a fine man, was a little too headstrong, and often did not act in the best interests of the Church.' Vecchi held the door open and bowed to each cardinal as they filed through. 'Bishop Bjørstad wishes to do the right thing, but he has no faith. In such a man, all that is required is a firm, guiding hand—'

'To show them what 'the right thing' is.' Rossi smiled, showing a mouthful of curiously pointed teeth.

'For the good of the Church,' added Martinez before disappearing into the dark passage beyond the door.

'Indeed,' Vecchi said. 'For the good of the Church.'

The nuns wheeled Möller through. He eyed Vecchi with suspicion, shook his head then vanished into the darkness.

Only Giordano remained; he stopped and hooked a finger at Vecchi who obediently stooped down so the cardinal could whisper into his ear. 'You have done well,' he said.

'I live to serve,' Vecchi responded, automatically.

'I am sure you do,' the tiny cardinal said. 'After all, when the time comes for you to lead the Church, I'm sure you would prefer if there was still a Church worth leading.'

Vecchi felt the muscle in his right cheek twitch. He forced his lips into a smile and bowed deeply. 'As I have said, Your Eminence, I seek only to serve.'

'Yes,' Giordano said ruefully as he entered the passageway, 'of course you do.'

The Book Of Leonard

Leonard 1:2

And so it was.

On the day that the much-beloved Pope Gregory XVII took his final breath, the Israeli government – believing that on such a day an incursion into the occupied territories would go unseen by the eyes of the world – plotted to remove PLO General Sufyan Amr-Mahmoud from his family home and headquarters, west of the disputed territories.

As the world mourned the passing of the supreme pontiff, five men – descendants of slaves, children of the chosen – crossed the border and stole their way through the dark streets of Rafah.

Their commandments had been very clear: Amr-Mahmoud was to be taken alive. Sergeant Jaron Rabin and his men, veterans of twelve such quests, devised another plan; one borne of necessity and a desire to avenge the persecution of their forefathers: they would simply slit the general's throat and return home.

But as their feet lit on Gaza's soil, Sergeant Jaron Rabin knew they would never again see the light of day.

'Are you with us, Jaron?' Lev spoke to him, and Jaron knew the last few moments had passed without the faintest echo left in his memory.

'Do not concern yourself with me,' he replied. 'Keep your eyes upon the rooftops.'

Robed as PLO patrolmen, the five moved as one and though they travelled with the stealth of serpents, to Jaron, every footfall in the sand was thunder in his ears, every step heralded by hell's demons.

Lev hissed his name again.

'You make enough noise to wake the dead!' Yoni said.

Noam cried, 'Down!' and by reflex alone they fell into a crouching circle with rifles raised. Then came the tracer fire, turning the cold night into the brightest of days.

Eshkol was the first taken by angels, his head almost severed by a sniper's weapon.

'Back!' Jaron cried. 'Fall back!'

And to each man, the twenty minutes that followed became twenty years, a running battle with an unseen enemy through the ramshackle streets and alleyways of Rafah. Rags were pulled across the empty window panes, stones and rocks cast from rooftops. Jaron's men were shooting wildly, into buildings that may have been barracks, or may have been homes, or hospitals or orphanages, or places of worship And then his conscience, silenced through years of conditioning and back-breaking training, spoke to him:

This is not right.

'Where are we going?' Ziv-El said.

Lev was struck below his chest He fell silently to the earth, and Jaron raised him to his feet. 'We must take shelter,' Jaron cried. 'We must plan our escape.'

They are before you, the voice in his head said. *Your enemy is at your front and behind. Redeem your sins and life everlasting shall be yours.*

His men followed him to a hut of mud and stone. They slew the two old women who cowered inside. They overturned meagre furnishings to form the semblance of a barricade. They waited in the silence.

'The shooting has stopped,' Lev said. With each breath the sound of shattered bone rattled inside his chest. Yoni crawled across the room and told him to take off his armour.

'We are beneath the guns of our enemy,' Lev said. 'I will do no such thing.'

'Let him examine you,' Jaron said. 'You are no good to us bleeding to death from the inside.'

'You have broken ribs,' Yoni said.

Lev sent him away and set about assembling the rifle from his backpack, a weapon as tall as himself and half again. 'Why do they not fire?'

'There is no need,' Jaron said, 'for we have nowhere else to run.'

'So what are we to do?' Lev said.

'We have to try to make it to the extraction point,' Ziv-El said.

'There will be no extraction,' Jaron said. 'If our lords and masters were to attempt to rescue us, then they would have to admit to the world that we were here.' They would be captured and tortured. They would be blinded with scalding knives, disembowelled and dismembered. Their flesh desecrated before the true God.

Lev, with his eye to the scope – the one Jaron knew he would lose, along with his other eye, then his gut, then his hands, then his feet – said, 'I see six.'

'And I hear a voice,' Jaron said 'I hear it like a light in my head. It has spoken to me since we arrived in Rafah.'

Yoni, who saw God in all things, said 'Does it tell you that you are about to die, and deservedly so?'

'Mine does say such things,' said Lev. 'But this I have always known.'

'What can it mean?' Ziv-El said.

'It means we are about die,' Lev said, 'and deservedly so.'

'We should escape to Egypt,' Yoni said. 'Lev said there are only six.'

'I said I could *see* six.'

'And if there are only six then we should come out shooting, divide ourselves and take our chances with the Egyptians.'

'We will find no mercy with the captors of our forebears,' Jaron said. 'And your plan tells the last moments of *Butch Cassidy and the Sundance Kid*. If memory serves, their story did not end well.'

And Yoni said, 'Jaron, it is better to die on our feet than like two old women, cowering in a mud hut.'

'Someone comes!' Lev cried, and the others took their places to defend their position.

'I cannot see, Ziv-El said. 'Is it one of them?'

Jaron said, 'He comes to offer us surrender.'

'End him, Lev,' Yoni cried. 'Show him what it means to be *Sayeret Mat'Kal.*'

Jaron cried 'No!' as Lev squeezed the trigger.

And as one did voice of their consciences laugh in echoes around them.

'He still comes,' Lev said.

You cannot stop him, Jaron's voice said. *For he is the devil. He is Lucifer. He is evil incarnate. He knows no beginning and for him there is no end. He is the end of the faith, the jailer of conscience. He is Leonard Bliss.*

Lev fired again. 'Still, he comes,' he said.

And Ziv-El, driven mad, struck his own head against the wall. 'The voice!' he cried. 'I can stand it no longer.'

'I can see him clearly now,' Lev said. 'He has been hurt.'

'Shot?'

'No. He looks . . . He looks as if he has been in combat with God himself. He bleeds from his nose and from his mouth. His eyes are blackened.'

The others took to the window and saw the wretched figure stumbling towards them, screaming at the injustice of creation.

And the Palestinians did follow in his wake.

'Leave me,' the madman cried. 'For I will have none of you! Do not follow me for I will lead you no more. Your consciences are free; may they take you where they will!'

Lev said, 'I do not understand that of which he speaks.'

'He speaks of temptation,' Jaron said. 'He will lead them no more into temptation.'

'You speak as though he is the devil, Jaron.' Ziv-El said.

'And what do you say he is?' Jaron said. 'Listen to what the voices tell us. He is the devil, here on earth.'

Heaven awaits you all, the voices said. *For it is no longer a question of faith. Heaven awaits your one act of redemption.*

'I shall go,' Lev said, and abandoned his post. 'I shall go and surrender. I shall pay for my crimes this night and enter God's kingdom with my conscience clear.'

'I too shall go,' Yoni said. 'I will seek the forgiveness of our enemy.'

'Then you are both mad,' Jaron cried. 'And I will not permit this.'

'Come with us,' Ziv-El said. 'We shall meet our God together.'

'You will not go, Ziv-El,' Jaron cried, a firearm in each hand, 'or by His Grace I will end you both.'

Go with them, the voice said, *Go with them and be with God.*

FOUR

Magdelena pressed her fingers to the bridge of her nose and took three deep, cleansing breaths. *And to think the day had started so well.* She rested her laptop on the crook of her arm and began making notes on everything she could see: the position of each witness and wraith; the damage to the gondolas; the pattern of the blood next to her shoes; the pattern of light reflected in the windows; the number of clouds overhead; every thought in the mind of the newly deceased; everything from where she stood, to the harbour's vanishing point a thousand leagues in the distance.

Gabriel Archer appeared at her shoulder, still carrying his cricket bat. 'Well, the wraiths lost track of the gondola,' he said, 'somewhere over the Middle East.'

'Earth?' said Magdelena, feeling as though she were being struck repeatedly between the eyes. 'He went outside – to Earth?'

The archangel nodded. 'They think he put down somewhere near Rafah.'

'But he hates it outside.'

'And he's never been overly keen on the heat.'

'So why leave? And to go to the desert of all places.'

'You know, this proves what I've always said: Leonard is clearly missing a screw or two.' The archangel examined the grain of his bat, running a finger along its edge. He made a tutting sound then stripped away a small pink splinter. 'Perhaps three.'

He'll be back, Magdelena thought. It's nothing to be concerned about. He'll come back. He always comes back. She turned her thoughts to the Führer and asked how he fared.

'Bruised, shamed. Threatening to lodge an official complaint.'

'Wonderful,' Magdelena said. 'Just wonderful. Try to talk him out of it, will you?'

'Me? Why me?'

'Because talking is what you do best, Gabriel.'

Gabriel opened his mouth to speak but, on this most rare of occasions, found he had nothing to say. He looked at her sideways, unsure if he'd been complimented, or insulted, or both. 'Now look here, Magdelena. You may think, as others do I'm sure, that I don't have any real authority, but as Head of Inhuman Resources, I think you'll find that my seniority is at least—'

'Gabriel, I just want you to talk to him. Tell him we'll schedule another hearing for the end of the week.'

'Fine, fine,' he said, 'but we're going to have a serious chat, you and I.' Then he stormed off to placate a man with the blood of six million staining his copybook.

Magdelena shook her head and turned to face the tall, elderly gentleman standing patiently with his hands clasped behind his back, his pigeon chest thrust out and the crescent of his chin pointing to the sky. His white hair sprang from under a lavishly decorated mitre, dented and perched precariously on his head.

Aside from all that, she thought, every inch the leader of men. 'Your Holiness, I'm so sorry to keep you waiting. Magdelena Cane, Chief Of Operations.'

Pope Gregory XVII shook her hand without conviction. Much like holding an octopus, she thought.

And his knuckles were still bleeding.

He looked over her shoulder and sniffed, loudly. 'So,' he said, 'this is the Afterlife, is it?'

'Part of it, yes.'

'I see,' he said, but Magdelena could tell he did not.

'I'm sure this is all something of a shock to you.'

'Not really, no. It's not at all what I was expecting, and yet I find myself unsurprised.'

She smiled gently through a raging migraine. 'A familiar strangeness.'

'Yes, I suppose you could call it that. Though I hadn't expected quite so many people to arrive at once.'

'When operating at full strength we can process one hundred deceased per minute,' she announced proudly then wondered if perhaps he really needed to know that.

Gregory sighed and removed his mitre, clutching it between his ribcage and elbow so he could scratch his head. 'I thought I had more time.'

'Everyone does,' said Magdelena. 'Perhaps I can get someone to look at your hand.'

The deceased pontiff looked at his knuckles as though seeing them for the first time. 'I used to be quite the pugilist when I was a young man.'

'Evidently.' Magdelena wondered why the holiest of men found it the hardest to adjust, to believe. In six hundred years, not a single pontiff has stepped on to the quayside and said, *Hah! I knew it!*

'Medical attention won't be necessary, Miss Cane. I'm unlikely to die from bruised knuckles. Thinking about it, I'm unlikely to die of anything.' His jaw trembled, his smile unable to support its own weight. 'The harbour master tells me that I am to remain here for the time being.'

'I'm afraid so,' Magdelena said. She touched his arm lightly, then drew her hand away when he flinched. 'This incident has caused us something of an administrative problem which, I'm afraid, will delay your departure to Heaven.'

'So, you're keeping me here.'

'Temporarily, yes. We have a hotel just across the—'

'You're keeping me, the Bishop of Rome—'

'*Former* Bishop of Rome.'

'You're keeping me here – in Purgatory.'

'Just until this unpleasantness has been resolved.'

He laughed suddenly, making her jump.

'A supreme pontiff, held in Purgatory. I daresay this doesn't happen too often.'

'More often than you'd think. And you have not been sentenced to anything, merely detained for the duration of our investigation.'

'What is there to investigate?' he said, reaching inside his mitre. 'I saw Lucifer and I reacted accordingly.' A soft tap with his fist and the dent popped out. 'I can't think of anyone in creation who would benefit more from a solid right hook.'

She made an additional note. Gregory leaned forward and tried to read it.

'There is much you do not understand, Your Holiness,' she snapped the notebook shut, causing him to jump back, 'about what we do here. There is much you don't understand about Leonard Bliss.'

'I knew who he was the moment I laid eyes on him,' Gregory said, wedging the mitre firmly back on his head.

'Not many recognise him.'

'Well "many" should look harder. When people see him then they should remember him. Remember the times he walked in their shadow, whispered in their ear, tempted them, lured them to do unspeakable things.' His face flushed and he cast a searing eye in Hitler's direction. 'And standing next to the most evil man in history, no less. An opportunity no pontiff worth his salt would let pass by.'

The Führer himself was incensed, shouting at Gabriel as though addressing his followers at Nuremberg, while a medical wraith weaved skilfully in and between his thrashing arms to tend his facial injuries. Magdelena heard Gabriel telling Hitler to calm down.

'Why didn't you hit him first?' she heard herself ask before biting her tongue.

Gregory looked surprised, amused even. 'You're the second person to ask me that,' he said. He pointed to a young man in his early twenties wearing an ancient uniform of the British armed forces. Though young in appearance, his hollow cheeks and weary grey eyes lent him the aspect of an aged veteran. He stood politely to attention while two patrol wraiths administered a firm and thorough reprimand for attempting to light a cigarette in a public place.

'Ah,' Magdelena said. 'Would you excuse me for a moment?'

'Take your time,' the former Pope replied. 'Apparently, I'm not going anywhere.'

She smiled apologetically then hurried off to where the soldier was demanding the return of his lighter.

'Good morning, Ronald.' She looked to the sky. 'At least I think it's morning.'

Corporal Ronald Weakes, late of the proud and stalwart Fighting Somersets, spun round, whipped off his cap and clutched it tightly to his chest. 'Miss Cane,' he croaked. 'Didn't expect to see you here. Not in person at any road.'

She whispered to the wraiths who nodded and melted away, literally, into the crowd.

'I read something about you today.'

Ronnie turned the colour of a lightly pickled beetroot and wrung his cap in his hands.

'Still waiting?' she said, promising herself that she would do nothing further to encourage him.

'They'd do the same for me, Miss Cane.'

'Yes, of course they would. I'm sorry.' He's just a boy, she told herself, alone and vulnerable and not for sport.

'That's quite all right, Miss Cane. I expect you'd have to be a soldier to understand.' He put on his cap and smiled with the blend of shyness and sympathy she'd always find endearing. 'They were my mates. Even the captain. I know he was posh and everything, but I swear to you Miss Cane, he loved each and every one of us the same. Follow him to the gates of hell if I could. You'd understand if you'd ever known a man like that.'

Magdelena said that she had known a man like that, a long time ago. 'Ronnie, you know you've been here for an awfully long time.'

'They'll be here, Miss Cane.'

'That's not what I meant. I meant to say we've known each other for a while now, so I think it wouldn't be inappropriate for you to call me Magdelena.'

'If it's all the same to you, Miss Cane, I'd rather just call you Miss Cane, you being a lady an' all.'

'Have you read the Bible, Ronnie?'

'Not really one for reading, Miss Cane.'

'Well, popular opinion has it that I'm not much of a lady.'

'If someone ever says that to your face, Miss Cane, be sure to tell 'em to come have a chat with old Ronnie.' He jerked his thumb at his chest and Magdelena had to set her teeth against her lower lip to stop herself from smiling. *Old Ronnie*, she thought. So sweet.

'Ronnie, listen. If your friends arrive—'

'When they arrive.'

'When your friends arrive, I will personally come and tell you myself.'

'I'm not leaving, Miss Cane. Not until they—'

'You belong in Heaven, Ronnie.'

'I belong with my mates.'

This same conversation, day after day, decade after decade. No matter what she said, offered or threatened, Ronald Weakes refused to accept the plain simple truth that, on this occasion, the Afterlife had fucked up.

No, not the Afterlife, she thought, and felt herself swallow. *Alfred.* It was Alfred's mistake, and now this young soldier's friends were lost in the nothingness between Purgatory and Earth, and it was far beyond her power to retrieve them.

'Don't be sad, Miss Cane.' He picked up his rucksack and moved past her to the edge of the quay. 'They'll be here. You'll see.'

Magdelena dabbed her eyes with the heel of her hand. 'Yes, I do hope so.'

'Y'know what's really funny?' He laid an old blanket on the quayside and sat down with his legs crossed, facing away from her. 'This place, the Afterlife. You told me once, a long time ago, it was an infestation.'

'I think I may have said it was a manifestation.'

'Yeah, that was it. A manifestation of human faith.'

'Yes.' She turned her head to one side when Ronnie took the sign from his rucksack. It was made from cardboard with *The Fighting Somersets* scribbled dyslexically on both sides.

'At least,' she said, barely able to breath, 'let me get you a proper sign.'

He thought about it for a moment. 'I could do with a pole, if you have one.'

'A pole?'

'Or a long stick, or something. Anything I can hang it on.' He tapped the sign with a grey fingernail. 'Then I can hold it up, see, while I'm down here.' He gave a few experimental blows on an old tin whistle and Magdelena fought the urge to snatch it from him.

'You want me to fix this,' she said. 'But I can't, Ronnie. There's nothing I can do.'

'You could ask Mr Gee.'

Magdelena felt the tendons of her throat tightening. 'I have tried . . .'

'You could try again. You could keep trying. He'll listen to you, Miss Cane. I know he will.'

'Ronnie, after all this time, you still have no idea how the Afterlife works.'

He played three notes and stopped part way through the fourth. 'Y'see, that's what's funny. This place is a man-i-f-estation of faith?'

'Yes.'

'So why is it the good folk who run it don't seem to have any?'

And for the briefest of moments – and she knew she would hate herself for thinking so – Magdelena decided that perhaps she wasn't quite as fond of Ronald Weakes as she once thought.

He played something ancient and sombre that she couldn't quite place. When she thought she had the name of the notes within her grasp, Ronnie added a sharp twist and snatched it away from her. Still, she waited patiently for him to finish before saying goodbye.

'Miss Cane,' he said crisply, and then returned to his tin whistle.

Magdelena turned and walked away, making a mental note to find him a pole or a stand or something. She looked to the left and to the right on her way back to the elevator, satisfying herself the crisis was over and that Purgatory was once again running with clinical efficiency. Still, Ronald's words made her skin itch, as though he'd held his lighter close to her flesh. She, Mr Gee, Gabriel, Leonard – all of them: all living embodiments of faith; the idea that they possessed none of their own was ridiculous. She stepped into the elevator and decided that if Ronald Weakes loved his flute so much then he could use it to whistle for his sign post, and again she felt terrible for thinking such a thing.

A pink cricket bat slid between the doors, preventing them from closing.

'That bloody man,' Gabriel said, squeezing his sizeable frame between the doors. 'Now he wants entry to Heaven without a new trial. Says being slapped about by a supreme pontiff would prejudice his case.' He leaned against a mahogany wall and looked across at her as though he was trying to see behind her eyes. 'Weakes is just playing on your compassion, Magdelena.'

'Face of an angel, ears of a bat,' Magdelena said, more sourly than she'd intended. The archangel answered her with an expression of suppressed pain and anger, veneered with an almost stoic calm, much like the one he'd worn during the painting of *The Annunciation*, Magdelena recalled, when he'd arrived late at the apprentice da Vinci's studio, having trapped his thumb in a taverna door.

'You'll end as Alfred did,' Gabriel said, 'unless you learn to be a little less . . . human.'

'Alfred cared,' Magdelena said. 'Why do people look down on him for that?'

'Because he is . . . Was . . . a Horseman and he failed in his duty. That's what caring got him. But you're right, Mags.'

Mags? she thought. *So help me . . .*

'Let's just forgive him shall we? I mean as long as he screwed up in a "caring" way, does it matter?'

Magdelena tightened her fists until she felt her nails piercing the skin of her palms. 'You know, Gabriel, you have a lot of front for someone working in personnel.'

'I am the Head of Inhuman Resources!'

'Then why didn't you see Alfred was suffering? That is your job after all!'

Gabriel, red in the face, clamped his mouth shut, keeping that which should never be said locked away behind his teeth.

'What?' Magdelena said, her eyes thinning to volcanic fissures. 'What were you going to say?'

'Nothing. Nothing you need to hear.'

'Oh, just grow up and tell me.'

'Perfection is expected of us, Mags; You, me, Alfred, Thomas, even Mr Gee doing his "moving in mysterious ways" thing – we're all part of it.'

'Part of what, you stupid and annoying little fop?'

'Religion, whore. It's all religion. It's how things work. It's the way things are.'

And for a moment, the angel and the penitent stared into each other's eyes with a hatred that would have left lesser manifestations of the collective human psyche cowering in fear. Neither gave nor pressed an inch until Gabriel coughed and said, 'I think you'll find this is your floor,' and then, as she stormed from the elevator, he added, 'You should think about attending one of our anger management classes.'

It was a throwaway remark which, nevertheless, earned him the Afterlife's second black eye in ten thousand years.

† † †

She found a second column of marble waiting for her on returning to her office. The dust had not yet settled from its arrival and the pride of lions was nowhere to be seen, though the half-eaten remains of a Grant's Gazelle lay festering a few metres away. Without the lions feasting near her feet, even a day such as this felt incomplete, as though part of it had yet to slide into place. She touched the first tablet, and the red phone on her desk rang.

'Magdelena,' Mr Gee said, somewhat sternly. 'Glad I caught you.'

How could you not 'catch' me? she thought. You know where I am every second of every day. You know where everyone, everywhere is, at any *when*. 'And how are you, sir?'

'Oh, you know. So-so. So-so. And you?'

'Well, to tell the truth sir, I'm—'

'Splendid! Now, first off, about that nasty business with Gabriel in the elevator.'

'You know about that?'

They both fell silent, and Magdelena thought she heard him raise an eyebrow. It occurred to her that being omniscient must be something of a chore.

'Anyway,' Mr Gee continued, 'just wanted to say I understand that he can be a little bit . . . forthright sometimes – and so can you – but you must understand that I cannot tolerate my senior management team brawling with one another, especially during office hours.'

Which run from the start of time until the end of days. And as fights went it had been fairly one-sided: Gabriel had collapsed like a sack of spoilt apples as soon as she'd landed the first blow. 'He called me a whore, sir.'

'A significant proportion of the human race calls you a whore, Magdelena,' he said, sagely. 'Are you going to assault them all in elevators, too?'

'No sir, but—'

'And didn't you call him a "stupid and annoying little fop"?'

Heaven is such a boys' club, she thought. But the argument was lost, so she wisely chose the path of silence.

'With Leonard gone, humankind will face the darkest of times, Magdelena. He must be found and returned to the underworld without delay. Someone must go after him.'

A lump coalesced in Magdelena's throat. 'Sir,' she gasped, 'if we leave him for a few days then I'm sure, after he's made an utter fool of himself, he'll fall out of some bar and come home.'

Again, the silence.

'Magdelena,' Mr Gee said, 'you do remember the "all-seeing, all-knowing" thing, don't you?'

'Yes, sir, I do, but—'

'So if I say we need to send someone after him, then we can safely assume that I'm right, yes?'

'Yes, sir. Of course sir. Forgive me.' The lump, unsurprisingly, grew larger. *No. Not him.* 'Sir,' she said hurriedly, 'if I may suggest a few operatives with proven field experience then I'm sure we can—'

'I'm going to send Alfred.'

No!

'Sir, I don't believe Alfred would be a good choice. He's still not himself, and I honestly don't think he'd cope with a field assignment. Thomas Mort would be a much more suitable—'

'I am sending Alfred.'

'If you must send a Horseman then send Daphne Unger,' Magdelena said, almost pleading. 'She's easily as capable as Thomas, and her work in the Sudan has been—'

'The choice has been made, Magdelena,' Mr Gee said with the great and terrible finality of a planet-wide flood. He darkened her skies and punctuated his words with lightning so intense she could see her bones through her skin. Thunder rolled across the land, bringing darkness in its wake.

Magdelena squeezed her eyes shut and turned her face away from the wind and driving rain. She held on to the edge of her desk and increased her mass by several tonnes, sinking her high-heels into the ground under her feet.

'Sir,' she yelled into the phone, her voice almost lost to the howling winds, 'this really is unnecessary.'

'In this afterlife, I alone decide what is and is not necessary.' His voice echoed from the handset and cleaved the air around her. Magdelena could hear the animals stampeding for the higher mountains; tens of thousands of wildebeest, antelope and zebra, shaking the earth beneath their hooves.

'You have become restless, Magdelena,' he said. 'You pace the Afterlife like a caged beast, looking to change that which is not yours to change, looking to rule that which is not yours to rule. You must learn patience, Magdelena Cane. You must learn humility.'

And then, in the space of a heartbeat, all was silent. Magdelena opened one eye and then the other. The skies reappeared, the clouds rolled back, and the animals stopped and looked at each other with an air of surprised relief. She straightened herself and removed her fingers from the indentations they'd made in her desk.

'Which is why,' Mr Gee said, his voice now coming from the handset alone, 'I have assigned you as Alfred's handler during this operation.'

'Sir, I really must protest—'

The skies grew ominously dark and Magdelena felt a tentative smattering of rainfall against her skin. She quickly raised a contrite hand and the sun shone again.

'You are worried for him,' Mr Gee said, 'I understand. But have you considered that perhaps moping around the Afterlife with no direction or purpose is not the best thing for him? Perhaps what would be best for him is the chance to make amends.'

She closed her eyes, took a deep breath and stepped across a line that had been scored in the earth since the crucifixion. 'I understand too, sir, but it occurs to me that these operations often lead to an intervention into the affairs of men, which, in turn, leads to one us having to make some sort of . . . sacrifice.' She half-expected the will of Mr Gee to rend her in two, and though the clouds adopted a more sombre hue, there was no more lightning, no fire and she wasn't swallowed by the earth. But the millions of animals that inhabited her office fell silent, sat, scratched and looked to the sky.

And when Mr Gee spoke, his voice was calm in the way that an eye of a storm is calm. It was calm in a way that said to Magdelena: *this will never be forgotten.* His words were flat and measured and in the time he took to say them, some place else, a vast civilisation rose then crumbled to dust.

'No one, you least of all, should speak so of my son.'

'I'm sorry, sir. I just want to do what is best for Alfred.'

'Alfred's fate is in his own hands. It is not for you to decide what is best for him. Do you understand?'

'Yes, sir.'

'You will brief him and then send him on his way. Do you still understand?'

'Yes sir.'

'It is time for our Horseman to get back on his horse.' Mr Gee made a strange wheezing sound in his nose that Magdelena assumed to be some sort of celestial chuckle. 'Anything you wish to add, Magdelena?'

'No, sir.'

'Splendid,' he rumbled. 'My will be done.' The phone clicked and was silent, and Magdelena realised she hadn't drawn breath in over a minute. She leaned against the carved wood, holding on to a table lamp, more for comfort than support, and thumbed the intercom.

'Rachel,' she said, her voice rising and falling between syllables.

'Yes, Miss Cane.'

'Could I trouble you—'

'For a towel and a change of clothes. Right away, Miss Cane.'

'And when you have moment . . .' she cleared her throat and delicately finger-tipped the tears away from her eyes, taking great care not to smear her make-up any further. 'When you have a moment could you find Alfred Warr's personnel file?'

'Yes Ma'am.'

Magdelena took her thumb from the intercom and turned to gaze at the half-finished painting. The colours had run. Fifty years ago she thought it would be her finest work, born, as it was, from love and desire. Now, only herself and Alfred, their bodies melted into one another, shone out from the canvas. Perhaps, she thought, it was time to put it away.

FIVE

BISHOP JULIEN DUPONT ARRIVED at his cottage on the outskirts of Montpelier, dropped his luggage on the hallway floor and walked through to his study without so much as a word of greeting to his startled housekeeper. He locked the door, poured himself a generous measure of whisky, switched on his ageing computer and began typing an email message to the Vatican, Rome.

In it, he thanked the Holy See for selecting him to attend the Joint Faiths Symposium held in Tel Aviv. He said he'd found the conference beneficial and enlightening. Judaism and Catholicism had branched so far from one another, he said, and yet the roots of their denominations remained firmly intertwined.

And then, with his conscience screaming expletives in his ears, Julien Dupont went on to explain that attending the symposium had also opened his eyes to one inescapable truth: he was not, quite frankly, a particularly good bishop. He then confessed to a bewildering catalogue of sins including murder, car theft, extortion, lying with women of questionable virtue, lying with men of a competing faith, embezzlement, the long and systematic abuse of minors in his charge, fraud, gambling, the trafficking of illegal narcotics, money laundering, substance abuse and shoplifting. He explained that while he had carried these crimes against God in his heart for the past thirty years, he could bear them no longer. He finished his email with a postscript stating that he would confess all to his flock before stepping down as their diocesan bishop and spending the rest of his days in solitary incarceration where he would seek God's forgiveness for the appalling way he had conducted himself throughout his adult life.

The Vatican's office of public relations responded within four minutes, sending an email headed: *'re: confessions of sins to flock'*.

They explained that, while they understood his need for redemption, it was a time of great upheaval for the Church; over the past several days, forty-eight Catholic officials who had attended the same symposium had made similar confessions. They said that, given his seniority and relatively high profile, a declaration of such magnitude would cause irrevocable damage to the Holy See. They asked if he had considered simply stepping down and spending the rest of his days in *silent* contemplation at a monastery somewhere; they could arrange for him to be accepted at a *silent* order just outside Rouen. They said *silence* had often proved a near-miraculous cure for a troubled soul.

Exasperated, Dupont replied that his conscience was now playing loud music inside his head. His conscience had an iPod and astonishingly poor taste. His conscience was threatening to play its back catalogue of Icelandic rap music on continuous loop for the rest of his life if he did not publicly declare his crimes against God. Dupont explained that he was a desperate man.

The Vatican Public Relations Office replied within two minutes. They told him to go to his church and await the arrival of a Vatican emissary who would provide counsel and comfort in his time of desperation. They instructed him to speak to no one. The Bishop of Rome's private secretary had taken a personal interest in his case; help was close to hand.

Dupont pounded his fists against his head and poured the remainder of the whisky down his throat. He typed a brief *Thank you, god bless you all* to the Vatican and slumped forward in his chair.

An emissary, he thought, and a hideous, rhythmic scratching noise assaulted his ears from within, followed by a blast of Slavic lyric he barely recognised as a grave and insidious slur against someone's mother.

How can a mere emissary help me now?

† † †

And so, two nights later, a silver Jaguar rolled quietly into the town of Montpelier, where it was much admired without really being seen by the hundreds of drunken tourists who stumbled from one apres-ski party to the next.

'You see Father, that is the beauty of the XJ series,' Raphael said. He brushed a strand of imaginary lint from the walnut dashboard. 'It is the epitome of ostentatious discretion.'

Father Luke smiled and wondered if such a thing were possible. His acolyte said the same of every vehicle they travelled in. Even the Vatican Learjets, and there was certainly nothing ostentatiously discrete about the apostolic flight. Raphael often spoke of the apostles themselves in the same contrary fashion; they clothed themselves in a garish inversion of the priest's uniform and yet were still able to walk the world without casting so much as a shadow.

'The target.' Raphael reached back over his shoulder to hand Father Luke a sealed dossier.

It carried weight, so Luke guessed that the target must be quite old. Unusual, he thought. It was often the younger, more idealistic priests that proved the most troublesome. He took his combat knife from the folds of his overcoat and sliced through the seal of Saint Fiacre, thinking that he perhaps should have read the documents on the flight. It would have saved time, but Father Luke disliked studying the subject of an excommunication in advance, though he was not sure why.

It is because you do not wish to humanise them.

'Did you speak, Raphael?'

'Father?'

It occurred to Luke that, unless his acolyte had suddenly found himself blessed with telepathy, he would have been unable to provide an answer to an unspoken question.

And yet the voice had been so clear.

Raphael frowned and slipped the car into a lower gear. 'Are you all right, Father?' A huddle of skiers tripped and cascaded into a heap, forcing the acolyte to swerve sharply.

'I am fine.' Luke said. 'Yes, yes, I am fine.' Fatigue, he decided, it is as simple as that. The Seminary had kept the apostles busy of late: numerous excommunications carried out; many damaging confessions silenced. Yes, fatigue; Luke promised himself a respite when he returned to Rome. Perhaps a few hours on the sniper range would help him regain his centre. He prayed for strength and fortitude, before returning to the open dossier. He studied Dupont's early life, noting both minor ailments and long-term medical conditions. There was a detailed section on the bishop's heart; it seemed the man had been afflicted with acute angina since his late forties.

Bless the seminary, Luke thought. They'd left a clear sign for the road he should take. Poison, then. A draught slipped into the bishop's evening drink would simulate a cardiac arrest. Then Luke remembered that Father John had poisoned a vocally homosexual priest in the south-west of England, and Father Bartholomew had used the infarction method on a bishop who had misappropriated church funds to support a gambling habit. He leaned back and tapped his front teeth with his knife. And hadn't Father Simon dispatched a Mexican priest in a similar fashion? Too many deaths of a similar nature would ignite the imaginations of conspiracy theorists.

Not poison then. While he often found cause to praise the efficiency and dedication of his brothers, Father Luke often had reason to curse their lack of creativity.

He put the folder down on his lap and questioned Raphael again: 'You did not accuse me of being afraid of humanising the Church's enemies?'

'I did no such thing, Father,' Raphael replied.

'So this is not one of your tiresome little jokes.'

Raphael slowed the car so he could turn in his seat to face him. 'No acolyte would dream of speaking to his apostle in such a manner.' He turned away. 'And my jokes are not tiresome.'

Raphael's sense of humour was considered by many within the order to be inconsonant with his role as an acolyte. But as far as Luke was concerned, the acolyte's jocular nature reinforced an almost overpowering sense of duty, unequalled by any of the previous acolytes he'd served with, and in his fifteen years as an Apostle of the Inquisition, Father Luke had served with many.

The last, barely a year ago, lost during an operation to excommunicate a priest living under the protection of a high-ranking mafia don. As the sun rose on that terrible day, blood ran freely into the gutters of Little Italy and twenty men lay dead: the don and his men; the priest – and Luke had long suspected their relationship was not in keeping with the priest's holy orders – and an apostle: Father Peter, killed by a stray shot to the throat. Luke's own acolyte, a tall, thin and dour man known as Able, had been critically wounded. His injuries, though not life-threatening, would have made their escape impossible.

So, Luke had prayed for him and then shot his acolyte through the head. Able had expected no mercy and had asked for none.

He had not even closed his eyes.

Luke felt himself swallow and turned his thoughts inward.

Perhaps unfairly, he had survived to a golden age for an apostle; many graduates of the seminary did not see out their thirties, while in a few days he would celebrate – if it was right and proper to call it that – his thirty-ninth year on God's Earth. Still, he was not immortal; his thick black hair was showing strands of grey; and though he subjected himself to a training regime worthy of any Olympian, Luke, nevertheless, had begun to feel the touch of time upon his flesh, if not his spirit. On the rare occasions he found himself looking in a mirror, he could see the embers of faith fading from his grey eyes. And the shallow lines on his face told as much about his life as the scars on his body. His thoughts now often turned to retirement, spending his remaining time training future generations of apostles and acolytes.

And you, Raphael, Luke thought, life for you must not be so very different. One of the few who had survived the apostolic training and yet, by the will of God, deemed unsuitable to take Holy Orders.

Commonly, it was found on the day of his final assessment that the initiate lacked the stomach for the kill.

Still, Raphael was everything a good acolyte should be: an exemplary driver and pilot; an accomplished medic; a disposal man; a decoy; something of a counsellor; something of a friend.

And he would be an apostle like you Father Luke, the voice said, *if he did not lack that faint black line drawn down the centre of his heart: the separation between a man of God and a murderer.*

Luke snapped upright. 'You must have heard that!'

'Heard what, Father?'

'A voice,' Luke cried. 'I heard a voice, as clear as your own.' He twisted in his seat and began smashing at the headrest speaker with his fist. 'It must be coming from the radio!'

'The radio is switched off.' Raphael tapped a switch on the steering wheel, filling the car with voices from a Swiss news channel that seemed less real to Luke than the one haunting him. 'You see, Father? There is nothing wrong with the radio.'

Luke slumped back in his seat, looking wildly about the car's interior. 'Something is not right, Raphael.'

'It is the strain of your calling, Father.' Raphael said, his tone as slick and colourless as crude oil. 'Once we have completed this operation, I shall request a break in our rotation. I think God would agree we have both earned it.'

'Yes, yes, of course,' Luke said. 'Respite, yes. We have earned it.'

He heard the sound of rustling paper, and then the voice said, *Tell me, Father, what do you remember of the fifth commandment?*

Luke started so violently from his seat that he hit his head against the car's ceiling. 'Raphael!'

Raphael slammed his foot down on the brake and brought the car sliding to a halt. 'Father, I hear nothing! What ails you?'

'A voice! I heard a voice. As clear as day! It spoke of the fifth commandment. You must have heard it!'

Raphael looked at him, a wary expression scored across his world-worn face. 'I swear to you, I did not hear any voices, Father.' He continued staring, searching Luke's eyes for any sign of fatigue or madness or worse – conscience. 'You said you heard the fifth commandment.'

'Yes, what of it?'

'Thou shalt not kill.'

'I am aware of what it says.'

Raphael turned to the front and put the car into gear. 'I've heard it said that some of the apostles are experiencing . . . doubts.'

'And you thinking that perhaps I am experiencing them too.'

'Ours is an arduous and thankless calling,' Raphael said. He turned the wheel and pulled away, pointing the car at a hill east of the town centre. 'To harbour the occasional . . . misgiving is to be expected.'

The enquiry seemed innocuous enough, though there was something in the way it was stated: an unfamiliar lilt to Raphael's voice that Luke could only describe as interrogatory. 'Raphael,' he said, 'has the Bishop instructed you to spy on me?'

Raphael looked into the mirror and smiled. 'I am always to spy on you, Father Luke. You know this.'

'What I mean is, do I still have the Cardinal's trust?'

'That I cannot say, Father, but I can remind you of this: you are priest of the Inquisition and, above all other considerations, your faith in your calling must be pure and absolute.'

'I have no doubts, Raphael,' Luke said firmly. 'I understand that we do the Church's holy work.'

'God's holy work, Father.'

'Of course, yes, God's holy work.'

At the top of the hill the road opened out into a cobbled boulevard outlined by a collection of mismatched buildings; most appeared to be ski lodges and alpine equipment stores, though ahead of them lay a tall and baroque tower of dark stone and stained-glass windows: the Church of the Repentant Son. Raphael found a space adjacent to the church and guided the car into it, while Luke checked the breach of his pistol and slammed a magazine into the stock.

'I thought that poison would suffice,' Raphael said, looking down at Luke's shaking hands.

'Something is not right in all of this,' Luke said.

'It is just a ski resort, Father.'

Luke stared out into the night, looking for his tormentor in the snow and in the shadows. 'Nevertheless, I would sooner we were away from this place.' Poison would take too far long, he decided, and he felt too unsure of himself for anything that would involve extended periods of stealth. No, a simple bullet to the head would suffice, then take the body back to Rome via Geneva; the apostolic flight was equipped with cold storage facilities for just such an emergency.

Clean, efficient, clinical: you are raising murder to an art form. I applaud you, Father Luke.

Luke swallowed, took a deep breath and opened the car door, stepping out on to the crisp grey snow. 'Wait here,' he told Raphael.

'Where would I go, Father?'

Luke set off, treading the deep snow across the stone boulevard towards the church. The pistol felt heavy in his hand, much heavier than it should.

And still you go, the voice sang.

'I am not listening to you, whoever you are,' Luke said through clenched teeth. The sound of paper rustled in the air around him. Ghosts, he reminded himself. You are jumping at ghosts.

The church was a thin, gothic affair, nestled conspicuously between a ski lodge and a boot store. A number of other buildings, another lodge and more cafes than necessary completed the circle of divergent architecture that stood at the top of the hill. Snow tracks criss-crossed the circle then funnelled into deep channels running down into the town square. Luke took a silencer from his pocket and threaded it on to the pistol. He made a final check of the rooftops before making his way to the church steps, leaving barely a mark in the snow. He was only a few steps from the oak doors when he heard a sigh that sounded, for all world, as though someone were whispering from behind his eardrum.

The fifth commandment, Father Luke; thou shalt not kill.

Luke wheeled round, his eyes scanning the white-capped edifices and snow-laden trees.

The night stared passively back.

He slipped the safety catch from the Baretta and trod the stairs backwards, watching for any sign of movement or the telltale star of metal reflected by the moonlight. He walked until his back met the church door then, without turning away from the boulevard, he reached down and felt for the latch, a large and heavy ring of ancient bronze which he turned slowly until it came silently to a stop. With a final glance across the rooftops, Luke slipped inside.

And he found himself home. He closed his eyes and inhaled the scent of burning incense. He felt the touch of Christ's penance soaking through his skin. Yes, he was home. He opened his eyes and thanked the maker that his training had kept him instinctively close to the shadows, though given the narrow windows and depleted candles either side of the altar – the church's only source of light, Luke decided it would have been far more difficult to stay clear of the darkness.

The interior of the church was small and shared the same gothic stonework as the outer walls. Oddly, the ledges and alcoves were more pronounced and extravagantly decorated with demons and gargoyles, giving Luke the impression that the church had somehow been turned inside out. He peered intently into the shadows. Though he was accustomed to working in the dark, it was a few moments before he was sure that the man he spied kneeling at the altar was, in fact, Dupont. He pressed his finger lightly against the trigger and took a silent step towards him.

Are you really going to kill this man? A man of God?

'He is not a man of God; he is an enemy of the Church.' Luke wondered if perhaps he were under the influence of some hallucinogenic, administered by Raphael as a test of his character, his resolve. 'I do God's holy work,' he reminded himself. Each step was as though he were walking across burning coals. 'I do God's holy work,' he said, again and again. Was he not one of the Apostles of the Inquisition? Had his order not secretly enforced the will of the See for more than five centuries? Was his sacred duty not blessed by the distant hand of the Bishop of Rome?

Thou shalt not kill, Father Luke, and yet here you are. The voice reverberated and Father Luke was unable tell if it was within in his head or without. It shook the steep walls and bowed the ornate ceiling. The frescos looked down upon him, and as he walked slowly beneath them, their heads seemed to turn away. The air moved around him in bursts: intense cold; then a warmth, a burst of heat from the heart of a furnace; then again, a cold so intense it clawed at the inside of his throat as he inhaled.

This church, Father Luke thought, *it breathes.*

Sweat ran from his brow and the weight of his own limbs began to pull him down towards the floor. Luke stopped to catch his breath, finding himself between two glass cases, each containing a sculpture of the Blessed Mother. He touched the glass and found his strength renewed. Luke inhaled deeply and drew himself up to his full height before calling out.

'Bishop Dupont.'

The praying figure turned his head slightly and replied, 'I am he. You are the specialist sent from the Vatican?'

'I am, Your Grace.'

The bishop slapped the side of his head with his hand. 'Then you are here to relieve me of my torment?'

'I am, Your Grace.' Luke raised his side arm and took aim, and as he did so, the voice in his head cried, *Look out, Father Luke!*

Luke whirled round, lashing out with his free hand, upsetting the statue case nearest him. He spun again on his heels and grasped the sides of the case, taking the weight across his back.

'I do not have all day, Father,' Dupont called from the altar and then slapped the side of his head, again.

'I will be with you in just a moment, Your Grace,' Luke gasped. The gun cut into the glass, making a painful scratching sound as he fought to set the cabinet upright.

Forgive me, the voice said, *but I did not appear to be getting through to you.*

Luke swallowed, positioned his legs either side of the case and rocked back and forth on his heels. 'What is it that you want of me?' He tensed his fingers against the glass and pushed with all his might.

Your immortal soul, Father Luke – I wish to save it.

'I am a priest of the Inquisition; I have no soul.' He leaned back, using his own body weight to push the cabinet back on to its plinth.

Every sentient creature has a soul, Father Luke, the voice said. Luke dusted down his jacket then continued walking the aisle towards the alter.

Does your heart not sing beneath the majesty of a perfect sunset? Are you not filled with joy at the coming of spring? Do you not feel God's blessing at the sound of children's laughter?

Luke said, 'No,' without breaking his stride.

Excuse me?

'I said no, as in no, I do not like the sunset and no, I do not care for the coming of spring and I actually find the sight and sound of children tedious and annoying. Now, if you'll pardon me, I have my duty to attend to.'

If I could just trouble you to wait here for just a moment . . .

And in that instant, Father Luke lost all feeling below his waist: his legs froze and his feet cemented themselves to the stone floor. 'What manner of evil is this?' He pulled frantically at his left leg, and then his right. 'You will release me, demon! You will release me this instant!'

Bishop Dupont laughed and hit himself on the side of the head with an ancient copy of the Old Testament, while from somewhere between his own ears, Luke heard the sound of pages being turned.

Sorry to keep you.

'Does your conscience trouble you, my son?' Dupont chuckled to himself and then smashed his head against the flagstones.

'My conscience?'

'Yes, mine has been giving me much trouble of late.' He half-turned, and in the light of the altar Luke could see the bishop's face was bruised and misshapen. 'Do you like Icelandic rap music, my son?'

Luke tried again to free his legs, aware that he could now hear a strange yet familiar rattling inside his head.

'I hear it all the time now, you know.' Dupont made a whimpering sound, as though he wanted to cry but his tears had run dry. 'There is one particular song: *Seal-clubbing at Sunset* by *the Red Herrings*; it is twenty-five-and-a-half minutes long.' He dropped his head to the altar and pounded it repeatedly against the stones then turned to stare at Luke. 'I see now that you are not the 'specialist' the Vatican promised me. You are an apostle of the Inquisition if I am not very much mistaken.'

The rattling in Luke's head grew more intense. 'Is . . . is that a computer?'

The voice in his head responded: *I'm sorry?*

'You have a computer . . . inside my head!'

Yes, isn't it marvellous? Makes everything so much easier, don't you find?

Luke was unfamiliar with the workings of the human conscience, if indeed that's what it was, but he had somehow expected it to be much less . . . efficient.

Won't keep you much longer.

'God protect me!'

Now, according to my records, you and your friend, Salvatore, slipped away from the orphanage in July of 1969. You found yourselves beyond the city gates watching the sunset from the walls of Castel Sant'Angelo.

'We were just children,' Luke whispered.

And you commented at the time, and I quote, "It is the most beautiful thing I have ever seen." It's right here in black and white. So Father Luke, you have a soul, and with a soul comes conscience.

'You cannot be my conscience! Who are you?'

Well, of course I am your conscience. The keyboard burst into life yet again with a furious roar of typing carried out at unimaginable speed. Father Luke dropped the pistol and fell to his knees with his fists pressed against his ears. *You're just hearing me a little more clearly now, which of course is down to Leonard. He has ceased his labours, you see. He has unchained the human conscience.*

Luke heard footsteps, though the sounds in his head made it impossible to ascertain where they were coming from. From the edge of his vision he saw a hand reach down and take the pistol from the floor.

'Raphael?' Luke craned his neck to see it was Bishop Dupont who held the gun.

'I understand what you are going through, my son,' he said. 'So I ask you to receive my confession and forgive me.'

'Forgive you? For what?' The pistol's maw seemed to grow until Luke believed he was staring down the bore of a cannon.

Dupont pressed the barrel beneath his own chin. 'For my selfishness.' The explosion shattered the bishop's jaw and blew a crimson pulp and fragments of bone from the top of his skull. He crashed to the floor, narrowly missing Father Luke.

And while Luke stared at Dupont's remains, something long buried inside him fractured its sarcophagus and tore its way free. In his mind's eye, Luke saw a man, a filthy, foul-smelling drunk of a man holding a gun and standing over the corpse of a young woman lying in a pool of her own blood. Luke began to scream.

Not something you see very often, his conscience said. *Hollow-point rounds, I take it.*

'You must stop this,' Luke cried. 'The noise, the memory; you must stop it.'

Only you can do that, Father Luke.

The apostle felt the life returning to his limbs. 'Then tell me what I must do.'

You must repent, Father. You must confess your sins.

'What you ask is impossible,' Luke said. He fought his way to his feet. 'Ours is a most sacrosanct order. I could no more betray it than I could betray the Holy Father himself.'

His conscience sighed and turned its rattling into a thunderous crescendo. Luke tried to close himself off from it, even as he stumbled back to the church doors. Raphael . . . Raphael would help him. His memory rolled forward: he saw the drunk place the muzzle of the gun between his lips and pull the trigger. Again, Luke screamed until his lungs hurt and his throat was raw. He pushed against the doors and fell from the church into the snow. A powerful wind drew the white from around his feet into cyclones that cut into his skin. He carried on, stumbling an uneven path across the boulevard to where the Jaguar was waiting. Luke dropped to his knees and called to Raphael. Raphael turned his head, slowly. He had been crying. Throughout his life in the service of the Church, Luke had never seen an acolyte weep.

'Raphael!' he called out again, over the roar of the wind and the metallic chattering inside his skull. 'Raphael!'

The acolyte spoke, his words lost to the elements, and then he shook his head and held up his hand. Luke fought on, on his knees. He shielded his eyes against the snowstorm. He could not read Raphael's lips. He looked to the acolyte's hand and saw that his fingers were curled tightly around a small metallic object; it was the size and shape of a penlight and featureless, save for a single flashing red light. He placed the metal cylinder on the seat next to him, closed his eyes then clasped his hands in prayer.

Father Luke's conscience said, *Oh my . . .* and the chattering in his head stopped; Luke jumped up, turned and ran. He stumbled over a loose paving stone, rolled and was back on his feet, sprinting for the protection of the church. He made it to the steps and then suddenly lost his hearing. The air around him burnt away and a wave of heat washed over him, setting the oak doors alight.

The Book Of Leonard

Book I: Chapter IV

AND SO IT WAS.

That on the 6th of June 1940, on the night the remnants of the allied forces sailed in defeat from Scandinavian waters, the legions of the Third Reich surged outward from the towns of Bergen, Oslo and Narvik to begin the rape of Norway. The centurions of the *Fallschirmjäger* swarmed into the hills that cradled the burning towns, and slaughtered the Norwegian resistance fighters with bullets and knives. And while the ground forces were about their murderous business, the *Fliegerkorps* laid waste to forest settlements from the skies.

And it was on this day that Thomas Mort and Alfred Warr disembarked from the warship *Scharnhorst* and set foot on the mortal plane for the first time in twenty years.

Thomas Mort looked upon the lines of troops and machines of war before him and said, 'Leonard has outdone himself.'

And Alfred Warr looked to the night sky, listened for the low drone of the German flight heading out to sea. He ran his finger under his collar and asked, 'Why am I here?'

At the dockside they were met by two German officers: a man and a woman who regarded Alfred with reverence and awe, for he wore the livery of an SS general. But the female officer did stare at Thomas and tried understand why this black man, this subhuman, this . . . *ape* did stand before her wearing the tailored suit, wide-brimmed hat and lapel pin of a Gestapo interrogator. Though her companion remained motionless, rendered mute by the sight of a Nubian Gestapo officer, she herself was not. But in the moment before she could cry for help, archaic machinery bolted to the underside of her psyche – between her emaciated conscience and the pit where her childhood nightmares lived – did hiss and churn and thunder into life.

The device, pre-dating science and installed in every human, served one simple task: to protect its host from madness should it ever encounter the byproducts of its belief system. The machine shrouded the Horsemen in the mists of reason, and the officers became satisfied that all was well. Thomas Mort smiled and then spoke, in an immaculate and over-precise German:

'You have a car for us.'

As the officers led them through the sea of uniforms, Alfred did say again: 'Why am I here?'

'You are here because Mr Gee wills it,' Thomas answered.

A rifle discharged not twenty paces from where Alfred stood. The gunshot, and the admonishment of the soldier by his commander, distressed the Horseman greatly. 'I should not be here,' he did say while he fought for breath. 'Magdelena has declared me unfit for work.'

Thomas did look upon him with pity and shame. 'Alfred, do you intend to spend the rest of eternity hiding under her skirts?'

'Do you call me a coward?' Alfred demanded.

Thomas raised a hand and gripped his little finger in preparation of a litany of evidence. But instead, he sighed and said, 'No one is asking you to work, Alfred. Just observe.' He saluted the two officers and asked for the keys to the staff car: a Mercedes, newly painted and freshly bullet-proofed.

'This is against protocol, Herr General,' the male officer said, his face drained of colour. He stared fearfully at Thomas, railing against what his own eyes were telling him. 'Lieutenant Drechsler here will drive you to wherever you wish to go.'

The woman nodded fitfully and wished dearly to go nowhere with either of them.

Seeing while trying not see, Alfred thought. A common enough reaction when mortals found themselves face to face with field operatives of the Afterlife. Though when he stood among mortal men, Alfred felt this veil was all too thin.

'Our destination is classified,' Thomas said. 'Hand me the keys.'

The captain hesitated, so Thomas added a heartfelt 'Dummkhopf!', and in his next breath the car keys were in his hand.

Lieutenant Drechsler, with much relief, opened the car door for the Horsemen. Alfred saluted weakly before climbing inside. Thomas started the car and raised an index finger to the air. The engine roared into life and the Horseman of Death smiled. 'Listen to that,' he said. 'German engineering; who can fault it?'

† † †

They left the harbour and took the northern road from Trondheim. Thomas drove like a man who knew he could not be killed, and Alfred clung fearfully to his seat as though he were someone who could. On their journey they saw people dragged into the streets, kicked, beaten, their homes set alight. Alfred began to weep, while Thomas cheerfully recounted events that were yet to come.

'Believe it or not,' he said, grinding his way through the gearbox, 'this will all come out in the wash.'

A woman screamed somewhere to their left; Alfred flinched and turned his head forth and back, trying to see where the sound had come from.

'Their experience will shape a nation of fairness, wealth and tolerance,' Thomas continued. 'A land to be envied by the rest of the world.'

The car lurched to the right, rebounding from a parked tank and then back on to the road leading to the mountains.

'And how do you know this?'

'Mr Gee allows me to see what will come to pass, to aid me in doing what needs to be done.'

Alfred could not remember ever being offered such foresight and was unsure if he desired it; he had difficulty enough coping with the present. If Mr Gee were to open his eyes to what was to come then he knew that such knowledge would drive him to madness. But Alfred Warr was all too human, and so when he found himself in the midst of an invasion being driven – poorly – by an immortal who could see the future then he had no choice but to ask: 'And what do you see for me?'

The Horseman of Death coughed in reply, and asked, 'How is dear Magdelena these days?'

'You know better than I.'

'She misses you, you know,' Thomas said. 'Misses how you were before the . . . you know.'

'Is that why we're here, Thomas? Is that what we're doing? Exposing me to my fears in an effort to cure me of this . . . What did she call it?'

'Post-traumatic Stress.'

Alfred slumped back in his seat, as would a petulant child on a long and tiresome journey. 'We're not seeing each other anymore, if you must know.'

'She tells it somewhat differently.'

'Well, she would, would she not?'

They drove on in silence until the track became a series of jagged rocks and loose boulders that forced Thomas to stop the car. He climbed out and looked up into the forest, to a group of small huts and timber dwellings nestled in a copse high in the hills.

'We walk from here.'

'If we must.' Alfred got out of the car and pressed his fists into the small of his back until his ancient bones cracked. 'What else did she say?'

'She said that your hatred of yourself smothered your love for her.'

'Are you sleeping with her?'

'No.'

'Are you?'

'If you ask me again Alfred, I shall have little recourse but to beat you soundly about the head and shoulders.' Thomas started walking, picking his way over the loose stones, sending small rocks tumbling downhill. 'Now come,' he said, 'we have very little time.'

The walk became a climb: arduous, painful on the ankles, strenuous on the knees. Alfred felt hot in his uniform. He was tired, weary, and he should not have been. Thomas, on the other hand, did look as though he'd risen from a hundred year slumber: vibrant and refreshed.

'I am sorry,' Alfred said. 'What I said about you and Magdelena...'

'Think nothing of it,' Thomas replied. 'You were lucky to have her.' He looked back and grinned.

Alfred lost his footing and slid down the hillside until his fingers gained purchase on an outcropping of rocks.

'Are you all right?'

'I am fine.' He brushed down his uniform, smearing blood and earth from his palms. 'But why did we not simply arrive at our destination? Why all this tiresome driving, walking and climbing?'

'I wanted to experience the mountain air,' Thomas said. 'The air in Heaven,' he said, 'tastes of nothing.'

'It is mankind's failing.' Alfred stood alongside him and took deep breaths of the cold Norwegian air. 'They lack imagination in many things.'

'And yet look at the wonder they've wrought in Magdelena,' Thomas said. 'Such a fascinating woman: statuesque, slim of waist, firm calves, beautiful eyes and her hair... Oh, Alfred, her hair!'

'Gabriel said her hair puts him in mind of a skunk.' Alfred wondered how intimate a man and woman need be for him to comment with such authority on the robustness of her calves.

'Gabriel says too much,' Thomas looked to his pocket watch, 'especially when he is drunk. It is almost time. We must hurry.'

And so on they travelled until they reached the cluster of huts where, with but a simple act of will, they faded from the sight of man.

'Now try to remain unseen.' Thomas walked past a group of men and women who were busy cleaning rifles in the near darkness. Others gathered logs, and still more fashioned them into barricades near the clearing that served as the entrance to the camp. They spoke in whispers, as though the trees themselves were listening, and they moved quickly but with a resigned determination Alfred had seen through a thousand wars in a hundred lands. These people, these brave brave people, were about to die. He hurried after Thomas who waited near a pile of munitions.

'Here.' The Horseman of Death pointed to a hut nestled in a horseshoe of young pine trees, and from where the most terrifying screams could be heard. The Norwegians stopped what they were doing and looked to the hut. Some shook their heads; others made the sign of the cross.

It was a cry Alfred knew well; it was a cry of battle. It was a call to war. And when he looked back he saw, to his horror, that Thomas was standing next to the hut. 'What are you doing?' he whispered, as though someone might hear him.

Thomas waved, smiled, took a deep breath and seeped through the dwelling's southerly wall.

Another scream did cut the air, and Alfred thought, *They have seen him. His concentration has failed him and they have seen him.* He tried to imagine the horror a mortal would suffer upon seeing a man of Thomas's stature suddenly come into being.

Thomas's head appeared through wall. 'Come on,' he urged, 'or you are going to miss it.'

Another scream, louder even that the first. 'If it is all the same to you,' Alfred said, 'I will wait for you back at the dock.'

'There is nothing to fear. Trust me.' Thomas smiled in a way that spoke of many things – many unknowable things – but trust was not among them. Again, against his better judgement – and it occurred to Alfred that he'd judged poorly for much of his long existence – he walked reluctantly to where Thomas stood with half his body inside the wooden dwelling.

'Ready?' said Thomas.

'No.'

'Excellent!' He grasped Alfred firmly by his wrists and pulled him inside.

Alfred passed through the wall with great difficulty, as intangibility was not a skill he possessed a particular talent for. He shrieked beyond the range of human hearing and landed awkwardly on his knees.

'How dare you!' he cried and raised his head to find himself between the thighs of a young woman on the cusp of expulsion. The woman looked down and her eyes locked on to his, or so it seemed. She was beautiful, even with her skin filmed in sweat and her abdomen stretched and contorted. Those eyes, Alfred thought. Clear and green, set below a deep, almost masculine brow. *So very much like my Magdelena.*

'Not yet, Marta. Not yet!' The midwife, a tall woman in her mid-twenties, as thin as a Nile reed and scrubbed almost as white, stepped inside Alfred's ethereal form. She rolled up her sleeves and hid her fear behind a smile. But she spoke with a confident authority that calmed Alfred as much as it eased the woman giving birth. She told Marta to breathe deeply and close her eyes, then she pushed both hands inside her. Marta howled, and Alfred wished dearly that he could remember how to faint.

'The child has not turned.' The midwife sank her arms to her elbows, and Alfred swayed most precipitously. 'And the cord is wrapped about its throat.'

Bile churned in Alfred's stomach. He turned an enraged stare upon Thomas and demanded that he do something.

'There is nothing that needs to be done,' Thomas said.

'The child will die! Is that what you want?'

'If that is its destiny then I will do my duty.' He looked at his pocket watch then turned his attention to the door. 'Any moment now,' he said, 'we shall have a guest.'

'A guest? Now? What are you talking—'

And it was then that a ghost of immense size and surprising solidity stumbled through the cabin door without taking leave to open it. He was at least as large as Death, with a moustache as black as coal and a latticework of scars covering his dark, weathered skin. His head was shaved and his nose was so crooked it appeared to be trying to point to his misshapen right ear. He appeared exhausted with the effort of staying anchored to the Earth which, Alfred knew, was an act of extraordinary will. His eyes, wild with rage, fixed on them.

'German scum,' he roared, 'in my home.' He did launch himself at Thomas Mort, who rapped him firmly on the nose with his fist. The ghost stumbled back through the table upon which Marta was giving birth.

The midwife fought to free the child from Marta's womb, and Alfred could see fear in her eyes; fear that the battle was all but lost.

Thomas stood over the ghost, who had decided, wisely, not to get up. 'Olaf Bjørstad?'

'Who the fuck wants to know?'

Thomas presented his ID card. 'Thomas Mort: Horseman of the Apocalypse,' he said crisply and tucked the card back into his pocket before Olaf had sufficiently gathered his senses to read it. 'Now are you—'

Marta cried out in agony and the midwife yelled at her to push.

'Push! Yes!' Alfred cried with every fibre of his being. 'Push, Marta!'

But Thomas Mort was about the business of death, and did not permit himself more than a moment's distraction. Returning to Olaf, he said, 'Now, are you aware that you are, in fact, dead?'

'Of course I am aware,' Olaf said, rising evenly to his feet as though he had merely stumbled upon the rug. 'I was there when it happened. Now you will excuse me; I wish to be with my wife.'

But before he could move towards her, Thomas placed a firm hand upon his shoulder. 'There is nothing more you can do for her.'

'Do not make me—'

'There is nothing you can do.' The grip tightened until the bones in Olaf's shoulder creaked.

The Norwegian growled and shook himself free. He entreated Alfred to a glare of unbridled malice then ran his hand across his scalp. In despair, he asked, 'Can you help her?'

'It is out of my hands.'

'Then why are you here?' He looked again at Alfred, a look blacker than before, if such a thing were possible. 'And who is your little friend?'

Thomas apologised for his poor manners. 'Alfred, it is my great honour to introduce you to Olaf Bjørstad: thief, gambler, bare-knuckle fighter, rapist, serial polygamist and, until twenty-two minutes ago, hero of the Trondheim Resistance.'

Bjørstad nodded approvingly, and made but a single correction: 'Hero of the *Norwegian* Resistance.' He drew himself higher until his head reached the ceiling, then pounded his fist against his cannon of a chest. 'I have butchered Nazis from Trondheim to Narvik.'

'And this,' Thomas continued, 'is Alfred Warr, former Horseman of the Apocalypse and now a casual observer.'

Though he'd found his ten millennia existence suddenly reduced to that of 'casual observer', Alfred managed to gather the shards of his dignity and extend a polite hand to the deceased Norwegian.

'You expect to shake my hand,' he said, 'while you kneel between the thighs of my wife?'

'There's nothing to fear.' Alfred jumped quickly to his feet. 'We are less than whispers to her.'

'That is hardly the point.'

And it was an opportune moment for Marta to scream. She did so, loudly and shrilly, like a shining pin pressed against Alfred's eardrum.

'He comes!' cried the midwife. 'Now push Marta! Push with all your might!'

And Marta Bjørstad did push, with every ounce of strength in her body and with the eyes of the unseen fixed upon her own, and every voice, whether it could be heard or not, crying out for her not to retreat, not to give way. And she did not; not until the midwife stood back with the child in her arms and declared, 'It's a boy! Marta, you have a son!'

'A boy,' Alfred whispered and he beamed joyously, swaying back and forth on his heels and toes. His smile faded and he crashed silently to the floor. Without consciousness and the power of will to anchor him to the earth, Alfred began to sink through the wooden floor as though it were marshland. The two ethereals watched him slide from sight.

'Will he be all right?' Olaf asked.

'Once he awakens,' Thomas replied. He turned his head at the sound of gunfire nearby. 'It is almost time.'

Marta heard it too, though she paid it little mind, her attention focused on the silence of her son. 'Why does he not cry?'

The midwife held the child by its feet and smacked it soundly. She tried again, then once more.

'Why does he not cry?' Marta asked again.

'He does not breathe.' The midwife laid the child between its mother's ankles and continued to strike the boy upon his back.

And Marta herself did hold back an anguish that would have consumed a goddess. 'You must do something,' she said.

'Yes.' Olaf turned an enraged stare on Thomas. 'Do something.'

'There is nothing I can do,' Thomas replied, examining his watch. There was shouting coming from outside the hut. The sound of gunfire drew closer.

The midwife raised the child's right eyelid with her thumb. 'Dear God in Heaven.'

'What?' Marta struggled to sit upright, the bench slick with the blood of her birthing. 'What is wrong?'

'His eyes.' The midwife covered her mouth. 'God in Heaven.'

Olaf walked through the table and looked for himself. The boy lay silently with his two eyes open; two shining black orbs that did stare blindly from an abyss.

Olaf stumbled back. 'What is this? What is wrong with him?'

'He is a vessel,' Thomas said. 'An amphora for a tainted spirit. He is a vessel for you, Olaf.'

'I do not understand.'

The ground shook with the force of an explosion, then came the stutter of gunfire within the camp boundary, and then the screams of the falling.

'You are an evil man, Olaf Bjørstad,' Thomas said. 'An evil man, like your father, your father's father and his father before him. An evil man doomed to be reborn as his own son and his son's son, until he finds redemption.'

'Help him!' Olaf pleaded.

'Men of debauchery and violence who beget men of debauchery and violence.'

Olaf fell to his knees and clasped his hands, shaking them at Death's Horseman. 'Please, I beg of you.'

'You must leave,' Marta said to the midwife. 'They're almost upon us. You must go now.'

The midwife struck the child again. 'If I go now then he will surely perish, Marta.'

'But you can save him,' Thomas said. He reached down and pressed his index finger against the flesh between Olaf's eyes.

And Olaf wept openly, something he had not done his entire adult life. 'I will do whatever you ask of me.'

As you always do, Thomas thought. He asked Olaf what he was willing to sacrifice to save his son.

'If you are asking if I will accept an eternity in hell then yes, gladly.' He looked to the midwife and saw tears of despair in her eyes. She counted softly to herself, struck the child again, counted softly to herself, struck the child again . . .

'Anything,' Olaf said. 'Just save the boy.'

Thomas sighed. Each time he came for this man – this evil man; each time the father became the son, he found himself in awe of this glimmer of nobility in an otherwise blighted soul. 'Nothing so dramatic,' he said, 'though perhaps equally unpleasant. You will be tested, Olaf; tested by your ancestors. They will spite you and belittle you. And if you fail Olaf, if you succumb to their temptations then Hell will be yours for all eternity. Do you understand what I have said to you?'

'I will endure,' Olaf said. 'Save my son.'

The sound of gunfire began to die away; it was almost over and there was still much that needed to be done. German voices filled the air from outside the hut, and Thomas felt the moments slipping away. Rare, he thought, for someone used to having all the time in creation.

† † †

A day and a night after the paratroopers left the encampment, Alfred Warr clawed his way free of the earth not one league from where his descent had begun. His thoughts were scattered, his lungs full of soil and he was barely able to keep himself anchored to the mortal plane. He closed his mind to the call of the Afterlife and ran, stumbling, back to the camp. He climbed the barricade and scrambled over the shell casings and corpses that littered the ground. The camp itself smouldered in the cold morning mist, every dwelling destroyed, every man and woman left to the crows.

He found Marta, sprawled naked on the ground, still with the pistol in her hand that had made the hole below her chin. He searched the surrounding hills for another day and another night, but did not find any sign of the child or the midwife. He returned to the camp, weeping and raving, half-mad with grief, and spent another night and another day burying the dead. Marta was last, and he interred her facing the moon, pressing the earth flat with the palms of his hands. Then he lay across her grave and wept for another day and another night, another week and another month, another autumn and another spring.

And so Alfred Warr remained there, alone and weeping, unseen by man, until Thomas Mort came for him, on the day the Reich surrendered Norway.

SIX

As soon as Magdelena had finished reading the last stone tablet, the telephone – the red one with no buttons or dial – annoyingly and predictably rang again.

She picked it up and said as briskly as she could: 'Mr Gee.'

'Magdelena!' he replied, smothering her austerity with a surfeit of enthusiasm. 'And how are you today?'

'I'm very well, sir. How are you?'

'Oh you know, mustn't complain.' He clicked his tongue twice before adding, 'Good days and bad days.'

'Is there something I can help you with, sir?'

'Well no, not really . . . Actually, yes. I was wondering if you'd perhaps had a chance to read the manuscript I'd sent you.'

You *know* I have, she thought. That's why you called. 'I finished the last page just this moment, sir.'

'Splendid! Splendid. And what are your first thoughts? Come on, honestly, off the top of your head.'

Magdelena wondered if clearing her throat would prove too obvious a delaying ploy. It would, she decided, but did so anyway.

'Oh dear, throat clearing,' Mr Gee said, 'not a good sign.'

'It's not that I didn't like it, sir,' she said hurriedly. 'I think I was just a little surprised by the tone. It's a lot more earthy than I expected. Gritty even.'

This seemed to please him. 'But that's precisely what I'm aiming for!'

'It is?'

'Of course it is! The events that are to come will affect all on Earth: those that are and those that are yet to be. The Newer Testament must engage everyone, no matter what they are or to whom they pray. No more of this "behold" and "unto you" nonsense. Yes, earthy; I like that. What else?'

Damn, she thought and cleared her throat again. 'Well, it could do with tightening up in places, obviously.'

'Obviously.'

'But if I may just make one small criticism . . .'

'Go on.'

'It was just this phrase on the very first tablet, sir.'

'Yes? Which one?'

'Fucked comely, sir.'

'Excuse me?'

She took the first tablet from the column and read aloud: *"On the very same day his superiors crawled into feather beds, drank expensive champagne and fucked comely French women thirty miles from the enemy line . . ."*

'You don't like it.' He sounded crestfallen.

'Just the phrase "fucked comely", sir.'

'A little too gritty, perhaps?'

'No sir, just too . . . odd. It puts me in mind of someone's name, sir.'

'A name.'

'Yes, sir.'

Mr Gee paused to consider this, then asked, 'Do you actually *know* someone called Fucked Comely?'

'No, of course not, sir. It's just that when I read it I thought . . .' Magdelena realised she wasn't sure what she thought. 'It just made me think of an adventure story from the turn of the century.'

'I'm not sure I—'

'*Who will save me?*' she proclaimed, affecting an overly dramatic swoon. '*For here am I, a pretty, defenceless maiden tied to a railway line by my wicked and grotesque Uncle Judas. He seeks to steal both my virtue and inheritance. And is that the 16:50 from Edinburgh approaching on time and at great speed? Surely, I am undone! But wait, is that the horn of an Oldsmobile I hear? Am I to be saved by my one true paramour? Why, yes! Here he comes: the roguishly handsome Sir Harry Devlin, accompanied as ever by his faithful manservant, Fucked Comely.*'

In the silence that followed, two people, someplace else, met, fell in love and built a small cottage on the edge of a great nation, where they spent their lives entwined, growing old and broken until the dust they became was carried out to sea.

'I think,' Mr Gee said finally, 'that you've taken the words somewhat out of context.'

'Nevertheless, sir, that's what I see when I read it.'

'I rather liked the phrase.'

'Well I am sorry about that.'

'Fucked shapely!' he ventured. 'Fucked shapely French women thirty miles from—'

'I think this is one those times, sir,' Magdelena said, 'when less is so very much more.'

Again, he paused, this time to consider every moment of two alternate futures: examining the infinite paths the universe could take, all hinging on whether he carved two words into the fabric of eternity, or not.

'Better without, then.'

'Much better,' Magdelena said and quickly pressed her advantage. 'And there's the part about Alfred, sir.'

'Yes, that business in Trondheim. Hardly his finest hour.'

'Exactly. He is highly-strung, emotionally, copes poorly in a crisis and, if I'm not mistaken, has a tendency towards agoraphobia. I think his best field days are behind him. In short, sir, he is completely unsuitable for this operation, and with that in mind, I've put together a shortlist of—'

'Magdelena, we have been through this,' he said, and there was a sadness to his voice that frightened her. 'What is, is.'

'Sir, if you would just take a look at—'

'Following the business with Hitler and the incoming Pope, not to mention your assault on Gabriel, I have to warn you that you're walking on very deep water, young lady.'

Young lady. Magdelena tried to open her mouth to protest but found she could not.

'Your insubordination, your lack of respect for your colleagues: these are traits most unbecoming in the general manager of Purgatory, wouldn't you agree?'

Hell below, she thought. What is this? She ran trembling hands over the metal contraption encasing the lower portion of her face. Flakes of rust came free beneath her fingernails. And it smelled, rancid with sweat and despair.

'Just nod,' Mr Gee said passively.

Magdelena held the phone at arms length and stared at it, trying to melt it with her eyes. *Nod?* Her other hand tried to find a catch or a hinge, but only found a padlock swinging just behind her left ear. She made an odd growling sound, something akin to stifled rage, brought the phone within a few inches of her nose and nodded.

'Good. Now I understand how you feel, really I do. But this is how it must be, Magdelena.'

But you can change things, she thought.

And some things must not be changed, he said, speaking inside her head. The padlock made a loud click and Magdelena found herself free again. She massaged her chin, moved her jaw from side to side. 'Then I will tell him.'

'As it must be.'

She wondered when creation had become so intransigent. Or perhaps it had always been so and she'd failed to see it. 'When must he leave?'

'Immediately.'

'And when will he return?'

Mr Gee exhaled and quietly hung up the phone.

Magdelena trembled. She stared at the phone, tightening her grip until the handset cracked in half. 'Don't you ignore me,' she screamed into the mouthpiece. 'I'm not one of your pet humans!' The phone had already been restored when she slammed it down onto its cradle.

The pride of lions sat upright and stared at her, then turned their attention to the flatlands beyond the river. They arched their necks, sniffing the air, drawing Magdelena's gaze towards the sun. She shielded her eyes, scanning the horizon until she saw the dust cloud approaching from the west. Her eyes grew wider. *It's him.*

The cloud grew nearer. She quickly tightened her braid and clipped a small silver flower just above her left ear. She wondered if she had time to change into a shorter skirt. She had attractive knees; Alfred had always said so. She stopped, rolled her eyes, cut sharply into her own train of thought, chiding herself for being so foolish; it was only Alfred and Alfred was her past. She sat down behind her desk and arranged a number of folders in front of her laptop. She chewed nervously at her fingernail then skewed two of the folders and scattered pages from the one uppermost across her desk; not so slapdash as to appear untidy and, at the same time, not so tidy so as to appear she had little to do. She nodded to herself, leaned forward with her hands clasped in front of her and waited for the cloud to arrive.

Deep breaths, Magdelena, she told herself. She looked down at her reflection in the dark wood and remembered that they had once made love on this very same desk. Almost one hundred years ago they had lain naked together under this very same sun, surrounded by the very same lions. She'd asked him why, unlike the other Horsemen, he'd never set foot on Earth; never witnessed mankind's endless folly for himself. Why he chose to balance the Book of Souls from the Afterlife, instead of harvesting the dead from the field of battle, as Thomas did.

'There is no need,' Alfred had said. He'd traced a fingernail across the areolae of her right breast and studied her face intently as she shivered. 'It is Thomas's duty to collect the souls of the fallen. I merely make sure that the correct entries are made in the Book. Since there are no true victors in war, I seek to maintain a balance between losses on both sides.'

She'd smiled and nuzzled the grey hairs on his chest, twisting the longer ones around her little finger. 'So, you're not so much a Horseman,' she had said, 'as a bookkeeper.' Then she had leaned closer to him and whispered into his ear: 'You are my Accountant of the Apocalypse.'

It was a joke, Alfred, she thought, just a fucking joke; though now she could admit that her timing had left much to be desired.

'Magdelena?'

She sat upright with a start. 'Alfred,' she said breathlessly.

He had changed since the last time she'd seen him; he was much less than he was. His hair was still long and white, and his imperial beard was all but lost in an untidy layer of grey stubble. His face was scored with deep lines, and his eyes, though still an inhumanly bright blue, looked tired and saddled. Impossibly, Alfred Warr looked much older than his ten thousand years. He stood before her, his hat held tightly with both hands, trying to find somewhere to fix his eyes.

'Mr Gee said you wished to see me.'

Magdelena suddenly felt the need to crawl out of her own skin and hide beneath her desk, to leave the empty shell of herself to dispatch him to the last place in creation he wanted to go. 'Take a seat, Alfred,' she said evenly, thinking that if she were a wraith then he could see inside her; see her heart pounding craters into her chest wall. 'It has been a long time.'

Alfred shuffled over to a rock and sat down, facing her with his hat on his lap and his toes pointing inward. He looks so small, she thought, so fragile. Part of her wondered what she'd ever seen in him, but the other part, the significant part, wanted nothing more than to cover him in mother-of-pearl.

'Where is the painting?'

Magdelena, in spite of herself, found her eyes drawn to the place behind her desk where the easel had been.

'Did you complete it?' he asked hopefully.

She thought about lying, but if she told him she had finished it then he'd want to see it, so instead she said, 'No, I didn't finish the painting.' And she felt like apologising though she was unsure why. 'There seemed little point.' Her words sounded cruel and that was not her intent. His skin became more pale, his features seemed to cave to the centre of his face, he looked as though he were about to cry. 'Anyway, how are you, Alfred?' she said quickly, breezily.

'I am . . .' he stopped to scratch vigorously at the whiskers at his throat '. . . much as you left me.' He looked around the wilderness – frightened, clearly – and then back to her. 'You seem to have fared well. I remember this desk.' He nodded, smiled lopsidedly, his expression unsteady, as though he were about to start laughing or screaming or both. 'I did always like your office,' he said, then added, 'lots of light,' with a tremor in his voice.

'I tend to think of it as inconveniently spacious,' Magdelena said, 'and I didn't leave you.'

Alfred ran his fingers through his hair and decided to put on his hat, carefully tipping the brim to shield his eyes. 'Why am I here, Magdelena?'

Okay, down to business then, if that's truly what you want. She pushed one of the folders to the edge of her desk. 'I take it you've heard about Leonard?'

Alfred shrugged his shoulders. 'He does this every few centuries or so; you know this. Gets tired of being Satan and wanders off to find himself, or some such mid-life crisis nonsense.'

'You are to retrieve him.'

'What was it last time? Ah yes, he wanted to open a barber shop.'

'Times are different now.'

'And before that, he wished to become a Druid.'

'The humans are much more volatile. He cannot be allowed to disrupt the natural order of things.'

'Two weeks,' Alfred said, growing in confidence before her eyes. 'Two weeks and he'll be back in Hell with his tail between his legs.'

Magdelena rose from her seat, taking the folder and walking over to stand in front of him. 'You're going to Earth, Alfred. You're going to bring him back before he ruins everything.'

And just as suddenly, his self-assuredness crumbled away. 'No.' He shook his head. 'I cannot go back there.'

'I'm sorry.' She held out the folder. 'I am so very sorry.'

'Are you?' he said, pushing it away. 'This couldn't have worked out better for you, could it?'

'What are you talking about?'

He stood sharply, and Magdelena clawed her toes inside her shoes, determined not to take a step back.

'I am talking about how you could not have arranged this better, Magdelena. If I am gone, then the shame and embarrassment of being associated with me is gone too.'

'Alfred, how could you even—'

'And then the great and illustrious career of Magdelena Cane is free to thunder on, unabated.'

'Now, you just listen to me, you ungrateful shit, ' she thrust a finger at the space between his eyes, 'I have done my best for you for the past hundred years. I have protected you, I have tried to make you well again. I have let you cower in the basements of Purgatory, wallowing in self-pity over one mistake. One mis—'

'One mistake,' he cried. 'One mistake! I lost souls, Magdelena! I lost the noble souls of fighting men! I did not account for them and they were lost, consigned to limbo!' He dropped back on to his rock with his head in his hands. 'And because of this Mr Gee is right: I deserve to be sacrificed.'

Magdelena wiped her eyes with her sleeve. 'No one is talking about being sacrificed,' she lied.

'You have seen the outcome when we interfere with the affairs of men. One of us pays. One of us always pays.' He snatched the folder from her. 'And this?'

'Mr Gee wishes you to take others with you.' Her voice sounded hoarse. Though she was swallowing down her own tears, her throat remained barren. 'He says you will need them when you find Leonard.'

'I know these men,' Alfred said. He flipped to the last page, read the name and smiled at her. '*He* will never come. Mr Gee must know that.'

'I imagine he knows you would say that.'

'Of course he does.'

'And he knows that you will try, all the same.'

Alfred stood and tucked the folder underneath his arm. 'Then let's get this over with.' He pulled his blazer straight and fastened the button before extending his hand. 'Goodbye, Magdelena.'

'Don't be like this.'

'Goodbye,' he said again.

She turned and walked back to her desk, saying, 'I will see you when you return.'

Without another word, Alfred straightened his hat and set off in the direction of the sun. She watched him as he ambled away, shrinking away from her until he was swallowed by the waves of heat rising from the parched soil.

He's just one man, she reminded herself. *One small and frightened man. If that is what you want then creation is full of them.* And saying the same words out loud did not bring them an echo of truth.

† † †

Over the course of a hundred years, Alfred Warr had learned to be wary of many things: the staccato crack of gunfire, the screams of the dying, the sight and smell of human blood, wide open spaces – very much like the one he was walking through now – and to a lesser extent, Magdelena Cane. It wasn't the woman herself, though he, above all others save Mr Gee, knew how formidable she could be. No, the most troubling thing about Magdelena Cane was what she could make men do. He had known, he had always known, that one day she would be his ruin. He was not worthy of her and he'd tried to hate her for it, but still his desire for her coursed through him as wild and unfettered as the Euphrates, as agonising as the shame that had torn at him for almost a century.

And now, after so long, Mr Gee had decided he would be punished for his failure. He would be sacrificed on this quest; it was the way of things. Alfred walked until he found himself approaching the basin which marked the boundary of Magdelena's office. The high canyon walls reduced the sky to a blue sliver. He felt oddly at ease as he travelled the narrow path; the shadows enfolding him provided something akin to comfort, and before long he realised he was dragging his feet. He didn't want to go outside, to Earth. He didn't want to be humanity's scapegoat.

The wraith was waiting for him when he stepped from the canyon into the glass lobby. Alfred smiled pleasantly, embarrassed that he'd forgotten her name. She may have smiled back; it was hard to tell. She glided along the glass corridor at such a speed that Alfred needed to run to stay with her.

'Have you got everything you need?' she asked as she reached the elevator.

Alfred said that he had.

Then she took a key from around her neck and inserted it into the elevator's control panel. 'He should be easy enough to find,' she said as the doors slide aside. 'Just follow the chaos.'

Alfred took a deep breath and stepped into the elevator.

The wraith said, 'Bon Voyage,' and the lift doors closed. Alfred shut his eyes; this was the part he hated the most. A bell rang softly and then he heard the sounds of gears and chains slowly turning, as though he were on a roller coaster car being drawn slowly uphill. The bell chimed softly again and Alfred's stomach hit the wall, the rest of him following a moment later. Time and space roared like a gale in his ears and stripped the moisture from his open mouth. The elevator gained speed, travelling horizontally, on course for the mortal plane, outside the human psyche. The elevator's interior was little more than a blur of dark wood and velvet green. Alfred began to howl; his ribcage creaked and his tendons stretched and flattened against his bones and just as he thought he could stand no more, the lift stopped sharply. He was thrown to the floor, landing awkwardly on his side. He lay there for a minute, fighting for breath, then used the safety rail to haul himself to his feet. He straightened his tie and smoothed down his hair, tucking it beneath his hat. He gathered the papers and did his best to sort them into the folder.

The elevator doors opened and he stepped out into a white, dimly lit room. No, it was very much less than a room; his single step covered its entire width and ended with his thighs pressed against a miniature washbasin.

Clearly, this wasn't right. He opened the folder and checked the first page. His instructions were quite explicit: he was to find Pietro Lantosca before attempting to secure Leonard Bliss, and Lantosca was not here. He looked around, though there was very little to see. Above the basin was a mirror set too low to have served anyone taller than a child, and to his right, a lavatory, obviously designed with the same child in mind. The cubicle trembled slightly and a low droning sound emanated from beyond its thin walls.

Yes, there has been some mistake, he thought. He'd been dispatched to the wrong location and he'd probably have to endure another hideous journey to correct it. A few choice words to Magdelena's wraith when he got back – whatever her name was. He turned around, a feat worthy of a contortionist in such a small space, and found himself facing a blank wall where the elevator should have been. He swore under his breath, and turned again to find his nose pressed against a thin folding door. Alfred pushed it to one side and was hit by the overpowering stench of livestock in transit. He staggered back into the cubicle, choking on his own bile. The droning sound filled his head, pressing his consciousness to the back of his skull.

'Are you alright, sir?' A female voice belonging to a daughter of Gaul; Alfred recognised the poetic resonance in her speech, though he had not heard the language spoken since the Somme. He felt a small and firm hand on his shoulder which he gently pushed away.

'I'm fine,' he gasped, swallowing the saliva foaming into his mouth. 'I just need a moment.'

'Do you need medical assistance, sir?'

'No, just a moment, as I said.' He fell to his knees and emptied his stomach into the lavatory. 'And perhaps some privacy.'

'I wish I could sir, but the pilot has requested that all passengers return to their seats.'

'The pilot?' He wiped his mouth with his handkerchief.

'Yes, sir. Didn't you feel the turbulence?'

'Turbulence?'

'Yes, turbulence,' she said impatiently. 'A few moments ago. You must've felt it.'

Alfred rose unsteadily to his feet and tried his best to make himself presentable. As he turned to face her, the stewardess looked oddly startled, as though he'd just unvanished in front of her. She was slim and extraordinarily pretty and Alfred thought if she were more so then she would look very much like Magdelena. The stewardess poked an expensively manicured little finger into her ear. 'Sir,' she said, her voice was as unsteady as he felt, 'you must return to your seat.' She also looked very frightened beneath her thin veil of make-up. At first, he thought it was the natural first reaction on encountering a Horseman of the Apocalypse; such an appearance would not bode well for any plane in flight. But the device attached to her psyche should have shrouded her perception of him, replacing him with something comfortingly logical. But he could hear the machine inside her head, spinning uselessly, as though its drive chain had broken loose.

'I must insist,' she said firmly, finally.

Alfred cursed Leonard under his breath and stepped out of the cubicle with the stewardess rustling behind him. He made a left turn and looked for an empty seat. The reason for the stewardess's distress became apparent: oxygen masks swung from overhead while the cabin crew squeezed past one another, moving from seat to seat trying to calm the passengers who seemed to be in the grip of an aircraft-wide hysteria. Some were praying, many were crying. A young mother was holding her child so tightly that two stewardesses were desperately trying to separate them so that the little girl could breathe.

Well, Alfred thought, that certainly explains the smell.

The plane was almost full, so he was near the end of the cabin before he found an empty seat, next to an old woman, much older than he was perceived to be, with thin white hair and wearing a hideous flower-print dress. She fanned herself furiously with the emergency procedures.

'That was something, wasn't it?' she said, as he slid into the seat and removed his hat. 'I mean, Jesus. I thought, that's it; we're screwed.'

The stewardess placed a comforting hand on his shoulder, did her best to conjure a reassuring smile for them both, then moved on.

'I mean, what the fuck *was* that?' the old lady said. Her fanning became more frantic. 'I thought it was a bomb. Did you think it was bomb?'

A man with a round pink face popped up above the headrests in front. 'That's what I thought,' he said. 'I thought, *Mikey, that was a fucking bomb. We are all screwed.*'

'Seriously screwed,' the old lady agreed. She turned to Alfred. 'What did you think? Did you think we were seriously screwed or what?'

'Or a missile,' the pink man continued. 'It could have been a missile.'

'Sonny, if it was a missile then we wouldn't have had time to even think about how totally screwed we are.' She turned again to Alfred for support, who nodded and smiled, more apologetically than he had intended.

'So what was it? It felt like something had hit the plane.'

Alfred felt himself swallow. He suddenly felt very hot.

'Came from up front somewhere. The washroom, maybe.' Another head appeared, less pink and much more angular. He looked at Alfred through bottle-glass spectacles and said, 'Didn't you come out of the washroom?'

Alfred pressed his hands against his thighs to stop them shaking. 'I think you're mistaken, young man,' he said, none too convincingly. 'I have been sitting next to this good lady since—'

'Since about two minutes ago.' She stared at him, a look of firm disownment tightening her face. The machinery – bolted to the underside of her psyche, between her childhood dreams and the pit where she'd buried her most shameful desires – hissed and sighed and spun down to a halt. A small wisp of smoke, that none but the Horseman could see, escaped her right ear. Alfred's hands began to shake.

'You okay, sonny?' the old lady asked, her tone one of suspicion with all traces of concern painstakingly hollowed out.

'Now I think about it,' said the angular man, 'I don't remember you going *in* the washroom.'

'Well, unless your job is to observe the lavatorial habits of every man, woman and child on this flight then I cannot say I'm surprised.' Alfred's voice was shaking, and it occurred to him that the machinery was driven by faith, and without Leonard, the nature of faith was as unpredictable as the flights of destiny.

The angular man smiled, flipped open a small, thin wallet and draped it over the back of the headrest so Alfred could read his ID card. Yes, of course, Alfred thought gloomily; observing passengers' comings and goings between the seats and the lavatories was indeed his job. 'Thaddius Stone,' he read. 'Air Marshal.'

The round-faced traveller whispered, 'Oh, crap,' and slowly sank down into his seat, even as the other passengers around them began to take a keen interest; Alfred found himself looking over a sea of expectant, suspicious faces while the machinery remained worryingly silent.

The ID card vanished as fast as it had appeared. 'Now, we all know who I am, sir. Perhaps you'd like to share a little something about yourself. We can start with your boarding pass, if you don't mind.'

Alfred opened the folder and fumbled through the pages under the stern yet passive eye of the air marshal. A thorough search through the loose leaves of paper failed to produce anything resembling a ticket or boarding pass.

'Okay,' Stone said calmly, 'how about a passport?'

Alfred loosened his tie. It didn't help. 'I think I may have lost it,' he said, 'or it was stolen, perhaps.' This wasn't working; he was making things worse.

'Y'see, now I really think about it,' said the air marshal, 'I can't recall you getting on this plane.' Alfred reached for his pocket, and the air marshal reached for his own. 'Steady there.'

Slowly, Alfred pulled his handkerchief free and mopped his face. He hated this place, this planet. He should have refused to come, taken his chances with the wrath of Mr Gee. But no, he had to come here to shine in her eyes, as he had all those years ago when she had suggested that he was merely Thomas Mort's bookkeeper, an accountant of human souls. 'I wonder if you could tell me,' he said, suddenly finding it a strain to draw breath, 'where this plane is heading?'

The air marshal smiled, nodded and a gun appeared from between the headrests. The old lady shrieked, and Alfred realised, even while sinking into the depths of a dark and fathomless panic, that he'd made the Celestial Field Operative's most basic mistake: he'd become terribly conspicuous.

The Book Of Leonard

Leonard: V

On the night that a charmingly modest man took one small step that bridged a divided world – and a million children looked to the moon and vowed that they would, one day, stand in his footprints – Daphne Unger and Alfred Warr dined unseen on the east wall of Vatican City and, like the mortals below them, gazed at the heavens. Alfred sat cross-legged, perched on the stones. Daphne sat too, in an old wicker bath chair that flexed and creaked beneath her enormous frame. Even the slightest movement caused her to wheeze and groan, and the chair to teeter precariously back and forth upon the wall.

'They've done it,' Alfred said. 'They've actually done it.'

Daphne took a pomegranate from the hand of her pet demon and swallowed it whole. 'To be honest, I did not think they would survive.'

'The astronauts?'

'The human race.' She snapped her fingers and the demon obediently handed her a napkin. 'Two world wars, Alfred. Two! What in His name were they thinking?' And she did turn a sour eye upon her wretched creature, who now seemed familiar to Alfred. The demon, he observed, was in the midst of the change: a transformation from human to sprite. Its fingers and toes had grown together to form hands and feet with just two large extremities. Its naked form was beginning to sprout the dark, oily fur that would, after one hundred years, cover its entire body. The creature's spine was curved and the vestige of a tail had begun to grow from its hindquarters. And yet there is something about him, Alfred Warr thought; he looked more closely. The creature's face was still human, a round countenance that was both unassuming and terribly sad. Its lips, along with its left eye, had been sewn shut with thin strands of barbed wire. This was Leonard's doing, Alfred knew; it meant that during its human existence, the creature did speak words that had doomed millions and had then turned a blind eye to their suffering.

Alfred looked intently at the unfortunate. Dear Lord, he thought. It *is* you.

'You *do* know him!' a delighted Daphne Unger exclaimed.

Alfred drew back from the demon. 'Not personally,' he said, 'but I am very familiar with his work.' At the merest thought of the war, Alfred felt a maddening itch at his throat and began to scratch most vigorously. Daphne leaned over and slapped his hand. Her chair creaked and tipped forward. She will not fall, Alfred reminded himself. Our kind rarely does.

'You'll bring it out in welts,' she scolded him and then sat back in her chair. The demon reached into a hamper and produced a leg of pork, which Daphne snatched from him and began to gnaw ravenously, tearing off strips of cooked flesh with her small pointed teeth.

'Are you are certain you do not wish to eat?' she said, waving the pork joint at the hamper. 'There is always plenty.'

Alfred said he was not hungry and then gazed out across the rooftops of Rome, stealing occasional glances at Daphne as she turned the pork leg to naked bone in moments. Two hundred years ago, Daphne Unger had been one of the most ravishing women to ever walk the Afterlife, rivalling his own sweet Magdelena in aloofness, poise and beauty. And now, as he regarded that same comeliness submerged in four hundred pounds of sebaceous flesh, it occurred to him that, even for an immortal, two hundred years was a very long time.

'Why are we here?' he asked.

Daphne shrugged, wiped the grease from her chins and accepted a glass of champagne from her changeling. 'Therapy, I think.'

Alfred sighed. *Therapy. Yes, of course.* 'And him?' he said.

'Heinrich?' Daphne smiled then reached out and squeezed the creature's genitalia as though testing a melon. The creature shuddered. 'Heinrich is a gift.'

'A gift?'

'From Leonard. He and I were quite a pair, once upon a time, back in the day.' She looked ruefully upon herself.

And by 'the day', Alfred assumed she meant the days of the black plague, when she and the devil had waltzed across the putrefying corpses of millions.

'Heinrich is on temporary release from damnation,' Daphne continued.

Alfred was not sure that he was.

'He will serve me for a thousand years: he will wash me, clothe me, cook for me, feed me.' She dragged the demon down by his penis then gripped his face in her portly hand. 'For the next thousand years, he will clean me after I've made my toilet,' she said, squeezing the creature's jaw, 'won't you, Heinrich?'

The demon did not make a sound, though a single tear escaped its sealed eye.

'And how is this therapy to work?' Alfred asked, fearing the demon's jaw would be crushed.

Daphne pushed the creature away and drained her champagne glass. 'How should I know? I'm only here because she thinks it'll help you.'

Magdelena, Alfred thought. Still trying, after all these years.

'I imagine she believes spending time with someone as equally broken will cure you. Foolish woman.' She took an apple from the demon and bit into it. 'And before demanding this favour, she had not seen fit to call upon me in fifty years! We used to be such good friends, you know: dancing at the Waldorf, cream teas atop the pyramids . . .'

'She is very busy these days,' Alfred said. 'She has not even found the time to paint, and you know how she loves to paint. And of course, she has had little time for me, but I understand that. Her work with Purgatory is important. vital.'

'Quite,' Daphne said, and smiled with sympathy before throwing the remains of the apple over her shoulder. 'And I wouldn't be surprised if the Department of Inhuman Resources has something to do with this; this has Gabriel Archer's effeminate stench all over it.'

In the distance, twenty or more rooftops away, two small boys ran and skipped across the tiles. They jumped the gaps between churches and scaled the spires to point at the stars. Alfred wondered what it would have been like to be young, instead of being imagined as a middle-aged man for all eternity.

'Ah, there they are,' Daphne said. She peered at the two boys through a pair of gilded opera glasses. 'The subjects of tonight's entertainment.'

Alfred asked her what she meant.

'Tell me, Alfred, do you *ever* read the memos?'

'Of late, I've found them difficult to lift,' he said.

At this, she did smile, again with the look of sympathy that Alfred had quickly come to loath. 'You sound almost human.'

'My time on Earth during the second great war has left me less than I once was.'

'Yes, I heard. You spent your years there weeping over dead Norwegians, by all accounts.'

'They were brave souls; they deserved no less.'

'At such a cost to yourself, Alfred. Twenty years later and you still appear old and weak. It is small wonder Magdelena has little time for you.'

At this moment, Alfred realised his time spent with Daphne Unger was not particularly therapeutic. 'Then what reason does she have, do you think, for rejecting you?'

Daphne turned pink – a deeper pink, and Alfred, feeling less guilty than he expected, returned his attention to the two boys scaling the walls of Castel Sant'Angelo. 'Why are we watching them?'

'They are important,' Daphne said, 'and tonight, their lives will change forever.'

'Surely such an observation does not require the time of two Horsemen—'

She raised a finger.

'—two Horsepersons of the Apocalypse. There is no war here, no famine.'

'Oh, I don't know,' Daphne said. She peered through her opera glasses. 'The round one looks ravenous to me.'

† † †

And so it was.

On this most historic of nights, young Pietro Lantosca stood on the parapet of Castel Sant'Angelo with his arms outstretched and his eyes fixed on the moon. He stood up on his toes and let the west winds cradle him. On a night such as this, Pietro thought, a moment is indelible: it will last for all time.

Pietro knew nothing of the wall upon which he stood and to which he trusted his life. It was as high and as grey as a mountain and Pietro fancied that it was made from stone as old as the Vatican itself. He came here, at night, whenever the opportunity for escape presented itself, when some emergency came to light that demanded the monks full and undivided attention: a fire in the dormitories, a flood in the orphanage kitchen; anything he and Salvatore could engineer with a pocket knife, matches, a ball of string and chewing gum. A distraction, so they could slip away to stand here and watch the sun sink beyond the walls of Vatican City. It was the most beautiful thing young Pietro had ever seen.

'Can we go now?' Salvatore said. 'It is cold and I am bored.' He screwed a finger into his nostril, to the point where it became a conjuring trick. 'And I am hungry.'

'Stand up here with me,' Pietro said. 'Then you will not be bored.'

Salvatore peered over the wall, at the people scurrying home in the twilight. He blanched and shook his head. 'If I stood there with you, Pietro,' he said, 'then I would be as mad as you.'

Pietro laughed and almost lost his footing. 'I will not let you fall.'

'I am fat and you are light, Pietro.' Salvatore examined the end of his finger before sucking the excavated morsel from it. 'How will you stop me?'

Pietro sighed and stepped down. 'Then tell me what you want to do.'

And Salvatore did twist coyly from side to side.

'Oh, not again.'

'I can smell them from here,' Salvatore pointed north-east, towards the lattice of streets beyond the Piazza Adriana. 'Fresh from the oven.' He inhaled deeply and Pietro wondered if he could truly smell fresh pizza from a league's distance.

'Do you not tire of eating?'

Salvatore smiled and shook his belly. 'Do you not tire of standing on this stupid wall?'

'How can you stand there, unmoved by our beautiful city?' Pietro exclaimed. He cast his arms open towards the sunset.

Salvatore scratched his head and shrugged his shoulders. 'How can you not like anchovies?'

Defeated, Pietro sighed. 'Come then, let us 'steal' you your precious pizza.'

Aside from their being charges of Father Manfredi, the boys shared little in common. Salvatore was the solid one: tall and overweight. His eyes were small and set deeply within pink folds of flesh. Pietro was small and slight for his eight years, swarthy and dark in complexion and temperament. His eyes were the colour of coals, as was his hair, save for the tiny circle of white on the right side of his scalp. Father Manfredi said the curious mark was the result of an angel breathing upon him while he slept. He said that it meant Pietro was one of God's protected ones, and as long as he did not stray from the path of righteousness then he would have nothing to fear.

But Pietro knew differently. He remembered his hair had been black two years ago, the night before he came to the orphanage. He remembered it had been black when he'd heard the explosion as he lay in his bed, listening to his mother and father fighting in the next room. And he remembered pushing open the door and seeing his mother dying in a pool of her own blood. He remembered his father placing the gun between his teeth and the crimson fountain that sprang from the crown of his head. Pietro remembered that before coming to the orphanage, his hair had not a trace of white.

The boys skinned their knees descending the Castel Sant'Angelo, then ran the city's dusk gauntlet of mopeds and motor cars, across the Piazza Adriana and then east along Via Cassiadoro, Salvatore driven by his hunger, and Pietro chased by his memories.

At the corner of Via Cicerone, Pietro hid behind a telephone kiosk. Salvatore arrived moments later, making harsh rasping sounds from the pit of his lungs. He doubled over then dropped down next to Pietro and said, 'How can you run so fast on an empty stomach?'

Pietro scratched the white on the side of his head. 'How can you run at all when you are always so full?'

Salvatore leaned out from behind the kiosk and looked across the street to where Signor Ocello was opening his Pizzeria for evening custom. 'It is almost time,' Salvatore said.

'Would it not be easier just to ask him if he has any pizza to spare?' Pietro smiled weakly at the passers-by who looked at the boys with amused suspicion.

Salvatore turned to look at him as if he'd gone mad. 'No,' he said. 'He is a foul and evil man who hates orphans as much as you and I hate the devil himself.'

Pietro sighed and nodded to a passing policeman, who smiled back and shook his head before going on his way.

'Have you forgotten how he beat me when I borrowed—'

'Stole.'

'—borrowed spare notes from the cash register his wife had carelessly left open?'

'You stole it,' Pietro said. 'And he did not beat you. He laughed at you and called Father Manfredi, and it was he who beat you, and then me for not stopping you.'

Salvatore sniffed. 'I remember it differently.'

'Besides, it was a year ago. I am sure that if we just cross the street and—'

'He almost saw us!' Salvatore pushed his friend back against the wall. Then he peered out from behind the kiosk. 'He has returned inside. Now, give me all the coins you have.'

'I will not!'

'It is part of the plan. You will call the pizzeria from this kiosk, and while he is distracted, I will take the pizza.'

Pietro rolled his eyes and handed over the contents of his pocket, less the safety pin, damp handkerchief and the meticulously polished mouse skull he carried for luck. Salvatore counted the coins then looked to the sky while making some vague calculation. 'You only have enough for about a minute,' he said. 'Do not dial until I have started speaking to them.'

And so while Pietro fed his hard-earned spending money into the telephone, Salvatore, demonstrating surprising agility and fleetness of foot for one of his girth, deftly skirted cars and motorcycles to cross the Via Cicerone and enter the esteemed premises of Miguele Ocello, self-proclaimed as the finest purveyor of speciality pizzas in all of Rome, and as he stepped across the threshold, Salvatore was inclined to agree. His nose twitched and saliva did flow in torrents about his back teeth.

At the far end of the shop, past the rows of white tables and chairs, Miguele Ocello hunched over the ovens, removing a palette from the middle shelf. He turned when he heard the bell above the door.

'Well, bless my boots. Young Signor Vecchi,' he said and smiled.

Signor Ocello was a surprisingly narrow man, Salvatore thought, for someone who had dedicated his life to the preparation of the most succulent concoction of tastes in the history of mankind. But Salvatore did also admire him for the effort he made in playing his role: from his chequered, tomato-stained apron to his rose-tinted complexion and that ridiculous grey 'W' of a moustache, thick enough to tickle the end of his bulbous red nose; to his dark hair, slick with cooking fat and parted neatly down the centre. It was only his lack of appropriate weight that did tarnish the illusion.

'And what brings you to my establishment on this fine evening?' Signor Ocello asked, and looked pointedly towards the cash tills.

'Should you not be with your fellow scallywags, watching the moon landing?'

Salvatore faltered, realising that he had forgotten to formulate a reason for entering the pizzeria. For the briefest of moments he actually considered saying *I wish to buy a pizza*, but immediately dismissed the notion as laughable and sure to arouse the demonic old man's suspicion. He looked across the street to the telephone kiosk, where Pietro was waving the receiver and pointing at it.

Salvatore shook his head: it was not time.

'Well?'

The boy, startled, quickly said, 'I have come to apologise.'

'If I remember, young Salvatore, the last time you came to apologise for stealing my wares, you took the opportunity to steal some more.' Signor Ocello stroked his moustache. His lips curled and Salvatore felt his flesh begin to heat, a situation made worse by the appearance of Signora Ocello, equally thin and twice as fearsome.

'And what do we have here?' Signora Ocello cast an unforgiving eye over the round young man shaking before her. 'You are the thief from the orphanage, are you not?'

'He has come to apologise,' Signor Ocello said, before Salvatore even thought about opening his mouth, 'for stealing.'

'Apologise, you say?' Signora Ocello looked to the cash tills. 'And is this an apology for stealing, or an apology for stealing when he last came to apologise for stealing?'

'I was about to ask him the same question.' Signor Ocello fixed Salvatore with a look that could sour milk. 'Well?'

The pair stared down at him, like ogres. Salvatore believed his legs were about to give way. He turned to the window and saw that Pietro had borne witness to his terrifying predicament and so had dialled the number. He swallowed and turned to face his tormentors, in time to see the wicked smiles drop from their faces. They meant to finish me off, Salvatore thought. Perhaps the oven, perhaps the refrigerator, or perhaps cut into tiny pieces and served on Signor Ocello's Six Meat Special, fabled throughout Rome.

'Yes,' Salvatore said weakly. 'I have learned my lesson; stealing is wrong and I shall never—'

Mercifully, the telephone rang. Signor and Signora Ocello looked at each other, grinned, then turned their most serious faces back to Salvatore.

'We will go to answer the telephone, young man,' Signora Ocello said. Her mouth did twitch as she spoke. 'You will wait here until we return, then we will hear your full and frank apology.'

'Indeed good wife, that is what we shall do.'

They turned a frightful glare upon him before shuffling to the small storeroom that served as their office. On his way, Signor Ocello was careful to leave an oven glove on the counter, and Signora Ocello moved a bowl of anchovies next to the stove.

'Hurry,' Signor Ocello said to his fussing wife. 'We shall miss this very important telephone call at this rate.'

When they had disappeared into the back room, Salvatore, scarcely able to believe his good fortune, struck. He took the largest pizza from the rack, folded it in half and tucked it under his arm before grabbing a handful of anchovies and running from the shop as fast as he could.

As soon as the shop bell rung, Signor Ocello stepped out of the store room and made a quick survey of what had been taken. He laughed loudly and his wife appeared, carrying cloths and a bottle of disinfectant. 'You indulge them,' she said. 'It is a poor example that will not help them later in life.'

'*We* indulge them,' he said, and kissed her lips. She blushed, and this did please him.

'Call Father Manfredi and tell him he owes us for the poor control he exercises over those in his charge.'

'Yes, dearest,' he said cheerfully. *And we would be just as lenient, had the good Lord seen fit to bless us with children of our own.* Signor Ocello heard a sniff and turned to see his wife wiping tears from her eyes. He took his her hands and pressed them to his chest. He nodded kindly and she smiled, just as sweetly, then pushed him away. 'We will have real customers at any moment. We must prepare.' She pointed at the bowl of anchovies. 'And throw those away,' she said. 'The boy picks his nose.'

† † †

'Do you not think,' Pietro said, approaching the subject furtively from Salvatore's blind side, 'that perhaps they are just . . . letting us walk away with the pizza?'

Salvatore belched spectacularly before answering. 'Why do you find it so hard to believe that we are cleverer than they are?' he said. 'He is an evil old man with an ugly wife. We are the good guys. That is why we always win.'

Yes, Pietro thought, I had forgotten that you live in a cartoon.

They sat on the orphanage wall, shadowed beneath the Basilica of Saint Peter, knocking their heels together and shaking the dust from their shoes. After they finished the last of the pizza they held an impromptu belching contest, which Salvatore won easily due to his uncanny ability to generate huge quantities of gas, seemingly on demand. Pietro often wondered if his friend possessed a second stomach.

'I wish to ask you something, Pietro.'

'Then ask.'

'Do you believe?'

'Do I believe what?'

'You know what,' Salvatore said patiently. 'What else is there to believe?'

Pietro scratched the side of his head and jumped down. 'Yes,' he said. 'I believe.'

Salvatore held on to the wall and lowered himself carefully to the ground. 'I cannot see how you can.'

'Because of my parents, you mean?'

'Yes, because of your parents.' He hurried alongside Pietro. 'Do you not question how God could make your father do such a thing?'

'I question Him, yes.' Pietro said, and scratched furiously at his patch of white. 'But I must believe. I must believe that somewhere my mother is happy and my father is at peace. I believe because I would surely go mad if I did not.'

Salvatore nodded and picked his nose. 'I do not believe,' he said and looked to the sky, waiting for a hand to descend from the clouds and crush him as though he was but an insect. 'If there was a God then he wouldn't have led my mother and father to abandon me on the steps of this place.'

Pietro said nothing, but looked ahead to a shape in black, barring their entry to the boys' dormitory.

'Preserve us,' Salvatore said. 'Father Manfredi.'

Manfredi was an imposing old man. At least one hundred years old, according to Salvatore's somewhat imaginative estimate. He stood a shade below six feet, with a sharp nose, folds of loose skin about his neck and small dark eyes. This, and his smooth scalp, earned him the nickname *L'avvoltoio*, for indeed he greatly resembled a great, brooding vulture in a cassock.

But this night, Pietro could see as they slowly approached him, the Vulture did not appear to be himself: his skin was a sickly white and his eyes were cast to the ground as though he were pressed upon by a great and terrible shame.

'Something is not right,' Salvatore whispered. 'He should be shouting by now.'

Father Manfredi clasped his hands together in front of his mouth and closed his eyes at the precise moment another man stepped from the shadows. He was a head taller than Manfredi and also appeared to be a priest – of sorts. His cassock was as white as new snow, and his collar, as black as the night. And around his waist hung a chain of metal rosary beads the like of which Pietro had never seen. Some of the charms appeared to be miniature knives.

Not so much rosary beads, he thought. Perhaps more like a garrotte. He felt himself swallow though he was unsure why.

Father Manfredi opened his mouth to speak. Instinctively, both boys squeezed their legs together should their bladders take fright.

'Children,' Father Manfredi began. The timbre of his voice was that of a child. Pietro was astonished. He looked to an equally bewildered Salvatore who simply shrugged his shoulders and relaxed his thighs.

'Children, this is Bishop Andrew.'

The white bishop stepped forward and Pietro could see that he would have been more at home in a boxing ring than a church. The muscles in his upper arms flexed under his cassock as he stretched out a massive hand towards them.

'Salvatore, Pietro,' he said, 'I am most pleased to meet you both.'

His skin was dry and rough with large calluses where his fingers joined his palms, and as they shook hands, Pietro felt the bones of his own fingers grind together. He grimaced, though he did not to cry out.

The bishop showed the beginnings of a smile and said, 'Good, very good. You're a strong one for your size, young man.'

But when he shook Salvatore's hand, the boy cried out as though bitten by a serpent.

'Well, perhaps with training . . .' The bishop rubbed his chin and then, puzzled, sniffed at his hand before turning to Manfredi.

'Anchovies, most probably,' the old priest said.

The bishop chuckled, a sound starved of all humour. 'And you say they have no living relatives?'

Manfredi looked to the ground and slowly shook his head.

'Good. Excellent.'

'This is the second time you have come in five years,' Manfredi said. 'Why do you take so much from me? Why not the other orphanages? It is unfair.'

The boys looked to each other and took a step away.

The bishop's false smile stayed fixed in place. He reached out and placed a hand on Manfredi's shoulder. 'You disappoint me, Manfredi. The other orphanages understand the honour the Church bestows in granting children such as these entry to the seminary.' He made the slightest of movements with his thumb and Manfredi sank to his knees.

Salvatore turned to run, but Pietro held his arm. 'It will do you no good,' he whispered.

'The orphanages belong to us,' the bishop said. 'And so do the children. You would do well to remember this.' He turned his smile on the boys and asked, 'Would you like to learn how to do that?'

Pietro said no, though he meant yes, and Salvatore nodded through fear more than any desire to incapacitate elderly members of the clergy.

'I will tell them,' Manfredi said.

'As you wish.' Bishop Andrew clasped his hands behind his back and walked towards the orphanage gardens. Father Manfredi watched him, waiting until he was sure the bishop could no longer hear them. Then he embraced the two boys. He held them until Salvatore began to cry and Pietro began to hate the strange old bishop who had come to lay waste to their perfect world.

'We are leaving, aren't we?' he said.

Manfredi closed his eyes. 'I am sorry, boys. Truly I am.'

'I do not want to go,' Salvatore wailed. 'Please, Father Manfredi. If we promise not to run away, or steal, or pee in the chapel font or—'

Father Manfredi raised his eyebrows and rolled his tongue around his mouth.

'You idiot!' Pietro said and punched Salvatore on the arm.

'Ah,' said Father Manfredi, smiling. 'So that *was* you. I did think as much. It no longer matters. Word of your adventures around Rome have reached the ears of the good bishop, and he believes your energies would be better spent in the service of the Church.'

'We do not want to go,' Pietro said flatly.

'And I do not wish you to leave, but our orphanage, like many in Rome, survives by the grace of the Holy Church. On rare occasions, they ask of us in return.'

'We do not want to go,' Pietro said, again.

'Do not make this harder, child.' And Manfredi embraced them again.

'Are we to be priests?' asked a tearful Salvatore.

Manfredi looked nervously over his shoulder. 'After a fashion.'

The bishop was pretending to read an inscription on the statue of the Blessed Mother. Surely, Pietro thought, he cannot hear us from there.

But Manfredi did appear to think so.

'Now, both of you,' he whispered, 'go to the dormitory and pack your things; you leave tonight.'

'But we have not said goodbye to—'

'I know, I know. There is no time. Now please, you must go. Do not keep the bishop waiting.'

Pietro squeezed his eyes shut to hold back the flood. He patted the old priest on the back and told him that he should not cry.

'Yes, you are right,' the priest said. 'God will protect you.'

'There is no God, Father Manfredi,' Pietro said. 'I shall protect us both.' And as he spoke, Pietro heard the strangest sound: an engine, old and poorly maintained, choking and grinding to a halt. Stranger still, the sound seemed to becoming from inside his own head, and only when the machine had stopped did he realise he had been listening to it for most of the night.

Perhaps most of his life.

'You must not say such things, Pietro,' Manfredi said, shaking him. 'Never say that, ever!'

'If there was a God, then he would not take us from our family – again!' There was movement behind him and to his right, but when he turned there was nothing there, save the old apple tree that he'd climbed on his second day at St Celia's, and then fallen from, breaking his wrist.

'You will see, Pietro,' Manfredi said. 'God loves you. He loves us all.' He pinched Salvatore's cheek and told him to hush; he had to be strong; he was to be a man from this day forward.

Pietro looked again at the tree, this time, from the corner of his eye. He could see them now, shimmering at the edge of a waking dream: an old man in a fedora hat and a white linen suit; and a woman so fat that huge folds of her spilled from the bath chair that curved inward under her enormous bulk; and the third: something less than human, yet more than animal, a creature that carried the sorrows of creation in its face.

'God in Heaven,' Pietro whispered, not daring to turn his head so he could see them clearly.

'Pietro?' Father Manfredi peered into his eyes then looked in the direction they were facing. 'Pietro, what is it?'

Pietro swallowed; he heard the man in the hat say, *I think he can see us.* The obese woman belched, hiccoughed and replied: *Impossible.*

'Father Manfredi,' Pietro said, hearing the sound of an old and poorly maintained motor hacking its way back to life. 'I think I am unwell.'

'You will feel better when you reach the seminary. Now, you must both go and pack your things.'

Pietro blinked slowly and turned to face the garden where the apple tree stood, quite alone.

'I thought I saw something, Father,' he said. 'Something most strange. I saw angels. Old and fat angels.'

Father Manfredi rose to his feet. 'An overactive imagination, Pietro.' He stroked the boy's hair and smiled. 'Or perhaps a sign that God is with you.'

~~'Or a sign,' said Salvatore, 'that you should perhaps stay away from anchovies.'~~

Sir, if I may, I don't think that any text of religious or spiritual significance should end with the word 'anchovies'.

M.C.

SEVEN

No sooner had Magdelena finished etching her critique than the telephone – the red one on her desk, the one she had come to hate with a passion that could ignite stars – rang. She stared at it, hoping it would stop, hoping it would melt, then snatched the handset from the cradle and spoke grimly into the mouthpiece: 'Mr Gee.'

'Good day, Magdelena,' he said, with the warmth of a gloryful dawn. 'And how are—?'

'I will not help you,' she said and threw the stone tablet down on the ground where it joined the thousands of others that littered the landscape. 'I refuse to take any further part in this meaningless indulgence.' She held her breath and waited for all that she was to come to an abrupt and symbolic end.

'I see.'

The universe, such as it was, continued, and so did Magdelena: 'Alfred Warr did not arrive in Rome.'

'I am aware of this,' Mr Gee said.

'We believe that his plane was diverted and he was removed from the flight.'

'That would be a fair assessment,' Mr Gee said.

'We cannot contact him and he has failed to contact us.'

'I am aware of this too,' Mr Gee said.

'He is missing. He is lost and alone and you expect me to waste time reading your stories of Rome's orphans and their involvement in the theft of pizza, time that would be better served trying to find him!'

'As I have often said, Magdelena, Alfred Warr is capable of so much more than you believe him to be.'

'You have abandoned him!' Magdelena said, her blood coursing through her veins with the force and viscidity of molten lava. 'You have abandoned him as you abandoned your own son!'

And then there was silence; a silence in which a thousand stars folded in on themselves and left Magdelena's world in darkness. She stood alone in the void, with nothing but the sound of her own lungs expanding and shrinking around her. She had gone too far, she knew, but swore that for Alfred Warr she would stand firm against anything that would befall her. 'You speak of fishes,' she whispered in the nothingness. 'You speak of tiny fishes while Alfred is lost to us. Punish me if you must, but I will not help you, not until you return Alfred Warr to the Afterlife. Not until you return him to me.'

And the nothingness sighed.

'I will forgive you, Magdelena,' Mr Gee said. 'I will forgive you because I love you as I love all things. But you must understand this – and I will never say this to you again – my will is final and it is absolute.'

'Return him to me.'

'Alfred's fate is woven into the very fabric of creation; I will not save him.'

'You are above all things,' Magdelena said. 'Return him to me.'

'As I did not save the children of Israel from the holocausts.'

'Return him!'

'As I did not save my only son.'

And again, there was silence. A moment from where Magdelena could see her anguish amplified and reflected in the one above all. His own son, she thought bitterly. *Then nothing I say will ever sway him.*

Magdelena's sight was restored along with her desert and her sun. But her heart remained cold, a fist of iron pounding inside her chest.

'I wish you to do something for me, Magdelena.'

'I am yours to command,' she said.

'I wish you to find a title for me.'

'A title?'

'For the newer testament. Something a little more in keeping with the times. Something a little less . . .'

'Biblical?'

'Mmmm. Perhaps. I've tried a number of variations on the classics, but nothing seems right. Anyway, see what you can come up with.'

'I'll do my best, sir.' Magdelena realised her nostrils were flaring; when she looked down she could see them.

'And one other thing.'

'Yes?'

'Perhaps, you could give Daphne Unger a call. She misses you, you know.'

'So I read.'

'Take her for lunch, perhaps.'

'Lunch?' Magdelena snorted.

'Something light, obviously.'

'I don't really think I have the time to—'

'This is not a request, Magdelena.'

'Sir, I must insist that I be allowed—'

'And as a reward for your good deed, I will tell you that Alfred will arrive, safely, in Rome.'

Magdelena's hand flew to her mouth.

'He will arrive safely, and will continue his mission.'

'Then please tell me what I must do to help him.'

'Speak to Pope Gregory XVII,' Mr Gee said. 'He will be able to tell you things which I may not.'

She wondered if Mr Gee would see inside her and behold the joy that shone like a new star. 'And what should I ask him, sir?'

'Well,' said Mr Gee. 'I would start with his murder.'

The star flared and burnt itself out. 'Excuse me?'

'His assassination.'

'You have sent Alfred to the Vatican, with his immortality faltering and an assassin at large?'

'So I would hurry, if I were you.'

'How can I—?'

The line disconnected and Magdelena realised she'd been handed a rose by the thorns: You giveth, she thought, and you rippeth away. She wondered again if Mr Gee would see inside her, and know how hard it was not to despise him.

EIGHT

FROM HIS APARTMENT WINDOW overlooking the Square of St Peter, Bishop Elias Bjørstad gazed out across the masses gathered before the resting place of the first disciple. The clergy gently pressed the crowds into lines that trod sombrely into the Sistine Chapel where Gregory XVII lay in state, while an army of priests moved among them, offering prayers and comfort to those in need.

And there were many.

Thousands, Elias thought, soon to be hundreds of thousands. He wondered if such as he deserved to hold sway over their values, their emotions, their very lives.

Did any man?

Night was falling and the lights of Rome shone from their mantles of concrete. He was tired; the dreams that had plagued him for as long as he could remember had become more frequent, more intense, of late. Dreams that spoke of him living the life of another man; a violent and hateful man who treated all around him with an arrogance and contempt that made Elias wonder why any god would put such a creature amongst the innocent and the weak.

Below, the crowds began to sing to warm their spirits, and Elias could look at them no longer. He walked slowly back to the living area, an ornate room of dark wood and crimson velvets. A set of oak doors separated the room from his sleeping chamber which contained a large writing desk, a small altar and a queen-sized, four-posted bed that, as far as he could tell, had its sheets changed thrice daily, whether he'd chosen to rest in the interim or not. Beyond that, there was a private bathroom which in itself was larger than any hotel room he had ever stayed in. Replicas of Michelango's finest works hung on every wall and every polished, gleaming surface carried a statue in fine marble.

And then there was the television, the like of which he had never seen. It was a 'flatscreen' according to the nun who was assigned to his laundry needs. Truly a wondrous device, no thicker than a paving stone. The nun had said that cathode ray tubes would soon be a thing of the past, and Elias realised how detached from the world he had become.

He sat in the armchair, sinking down until his knees were almost level with his stomach. The television obediently switched itself on and tuned into the Vatican's television station. Elias thumbed the remote, though it made little difference; every channel the world over carried the news of Pope Gregory's death. There were succinct words of remembrance from the leaders of nations; recollections of his good works, his leadership, his inspiration to his millions of followers; eulogies told of his generosity and his determination to see the Roman Catholic Church restored to its rightful place as humanity's moral beacon.

Elias watched with a heart that grew slow and heavy with each fleeting image. How could he hope to fill the shoes of such a man?

Then came a thundering knock on the apartment doors; the kind of knock that rarely waits for permission to enter.

Before Elias had time to open his mouth, the doors opened and Monsignor Vecchi swept into the gallery with three distinguished cardinals at his heels.

'Bishop Bjørstad,' he said.

Not so much a monsignor greeting his superior, Elias thought, as an executioner ensuring he had the right man.

Vecchi and the cardinals gathered around him in a perfect semi-circle and looked down with their hands clasped tightly before them: the 'prayers at the ready' repose, as Elias had once, foolishly, called it. He glanced at each of them in turn, unsure if he was supposed to rise respectfully, or stay pinned to his chair. Carlos Giordano, the Cardinal Secretary of State, raised an eyebrow, and that was enough to bring Elias to his feet.

'Your Excellencies,' Elias said, and bowed.

'And how does the evening find you, Bishop Bjørstad?' asked Cardinal Rossi.

'It finds me well, Your Excellency.' Elias replied.

'Is the accommodation to your liking?' asked Cardinal Giordano.

'The apartment is magnificent,' Elias replied.

'And the food is to your taste, I trust,' said Monsignor Vecchi.

'I have no complaints whatsoever, monsignor.'

Vecchi nodded, more to himself than Elias, then he turned and gestured towards the television set. 'What do you think?'

'I have never seen the like,' Elias replied. 'How, in the name of God, did they make it so thin?'

Martinez, the Secretary for Relation of States, nodded grimly. 'In his wisdom, the Lord has blessed the children of the east with agile minds and small, dextrous fingers.'

Everyone in the chamber turned to look at him. Unabashed, he stared back. Monsignor Vecchi coughed into his fist and moved quickly to fill the silence: 'Indeed, such is my incredulity that I often find myself watching television from the side.' He looked to each cardinal in turn until the chamber was filled with peals of strained laughter.

'Is there some way I can be of service to you?' Elias asked. He was beginning to feel that an almost surreal aura had gently cast itself across his evening.

The cardinals looked to Vecchi who, again, coughed into his fist. 'We are here, Bishop Bjørstad.'

'I would feel much more comfortable if you would call me Elias.'

'We are here, Bishop Bjørstad' – and Elias wondered if he'd perhaps only spoken inside his own head – 'for your answer.'

'My answer?'

Vecchi sighed and impolitely rolled his eyes. 'Do you, or do you not, wish to be Pope?'

Elias swallowed. The aura of surreality began to smother him. 'I thought I had more time.' He looked to the window, for the black smoke rising from the Sistine Chapel. 'The conclave does not begin for ten days at least.'

'As I have explained,' Vecchi said with an air of disintegrating patience, 'the conclave is a formality. The Curia would prefer that a decision is reached before the fires are lit.'

The cardinals nodded, somewhat eagerly, and it was then that Elias noted that they had carried an air of desperation into his chambers.

'What of the other candidates?' he asked. 'Cardinal Alejandro and Cardinal Czwerwinski?'

'They have withdrawn,' Cardinal Giordano said.

'Withdrawn?'

'Yes, they no longer wish to be considered for the position.'

'Of Pope.'

'Yes.'

Elias looked into each of their faces and saw no further explanation would be forthcoming, not from the cardinals at least, so he turned to Vecchi, who clicked his tongue and ran his index finger delicately across his eyelid. He suddenly looked very tired. 'Cardinal Alejandro has left.'

The other cardinals shuffled their feet and inspected their fingernails.

'He has left the Vatican?'

'He has left the Roman Catholic Church.'

'Oh,' Elias said. 'That is . . . somewhat surprising. He has been in the service of our Lord for over five decades. Has he converted to another faith?'

'No,' said Giordano, helping himself to a glass of wine. 'He has decided to become a professional footballer.'

'I see.' Elias looked at each of them in turn and then said, 'I beg your pardon?'

'You heard correctly,' said Rossi. 'He has returned to his native Spain where he will train intensively before trying out for . . .' He stopped and clicked his fingers.

'Atlético Madrid,' Martinez said.

Elias wondered if perhaps the Curia was again putting him to the test. 'They are a fine team,' he said, warily.

'An excellent team,' Martinez said, 'though I think their defensive line has lacked commitment of late.'

They stood in silence until Elias decided, test or not, he could not bear to let another moment pass without bringing the painfully obvious out into the light: 'I am sorry,' he said, 'but if I am not mistaken, Cardinal Alejandro will soon celebrate his sixty-fourth birthday.'

'You are not mistaken,' said Vecchi. 'And within a few days, the press will hear of this and the Church will be a laughing stock.'

'And what of Cardinal Czwerwinski?' Elias asked, nervously.

'He too has decided that the life as cardinal was no longer for him.' Rossi said.

'And he is now . . . ?'

'A professional skydiver.'

'Of course.' Elias squeezed his eyes shut until his eyelids ached, then snapped them open, just to be sure he was awake.

'Have you kept abreast of world affairs, Bishop Bjørstad?' Vecchi asked.

'I am afraid that I—'

'No matter.' He picked up the television remote and quickly switched through the news channels. 'The world has become a very strange place these past days,' he said, stopping at the BBC World News service. 'Did you know that the Japanese government has dismantled its nation's whaling fleet?'

Elias said yes; he had heard.

'Then did you know that the British government has introduced the two-day working week?'

'No,' Elias said. 'I had not heard that.'

'During question time, the Prime Minister said that working five days a week was extremely dull.' Giordano poured himself a glass of wine.

'He said he simply wasn't going to do it anymore, and if he wasn't going to do it, then he saw no reason why anyone else should either. And this was on the very same day their British National Party announced it would divert its funds to provide English classes for asylum seekers.'

'In New York,' Rossi said, 'Mafia captains have stated that they will no longer run extortion rackets and prostitution rings. Having decided that this is a poor way to conduct themselves, they will divert their significant resources to AIDS research.'

'We are hearing similar reports from Columbia and the Baltic states,' Vecchi said. He increased the television's volume and they stood and watched a news report on one bank's decision to stop the practise of giving loans. The CEO said that the paperwork generated was tedious and, quite frankly, not good for the trees. He went on to say that the bank would simply give money away, for free.

Martinez sighed and shook his head. 'And then there are the problems being reported within our own ranks: priests and nuns, when they are not leaving in droves to follow some childhood flight of fancy, are confessing to crimes against God and nature that you could not even begin to imagine.'

Elias thought of Sister Constance and slowly sat down.

'It seems,' said Vecchi, 'that the world is experiencing some kind of epidemic.'

'A pandemic,' Giordano corrected him, 'of honesty, generosity and courage.' The cardinals nodded in agreement.

The news broadcast continued, telling the story of a Philadelphia street gang that was rebuilding the school it had all but destroyed during a battle over territory just a week before.

'It has been but a few days, yet many are calling this the dawn of a new golden age: a time of enlightenment and understanding.' Martinez sighed and ran his fingers through his hair. The cardinal appeared troubled, though Elias could not understand why. 'And the Buddhists are being unbelievably smug about it. There is nothing on God's Earth that is worse than a smug Buddhist.'

'But this is all so wonderful,' Elias said, and to his surprise found himself filled with hope for the first time in months. 'For whatever reason, we, as a species, are reaching out to one another, for the betterment of ourselves and our brothers. Surely, this is a time of great joy.'

Rossi looked to the ceiling and sighed loudly; Martinez pinched his nose between his index finger and thumb then shook his head; and Giordano looked up at Vecchi as though the monsignor had spoken some soul-defiling blasphemy.

Vecchi swallowed and shrugged his shoulders apologetically. 'His view of the Church is somewhat . . . provincial, I grant you, but with my guidance he will perform—'

'Ah, now he chooses to be provincial, does he?' said Giordano. 'It is a pity his thinking wasn't more "provincial" when he was handing out prophylactics to Africans.'

'If I have caused some offence,' Elias said, 'then I apologise. I am sure Monsignor Vecchi is not at fault.'

'Isn't he?' Giordano turned the same accusatory glare on him. 'It was his suggestion that a wayward bishop should be installed as the next supreme pontiff. A bishop who seems to know little of the Church's higher function.'

'What higher function can there be but to guide humanity on its journey towards betterment and understanding?'

'Precisely!' Giordano thrust a trembling finger beneath Elias's nose. 'The word that you have little or no understanding of, Bishop Bjørstad, is *guidance*. Since its inception, the Roman Catholic Church has been the conduit between man and God: we are the Almighty's ambassadors on Earth; we interpret his laws and state his intentions; we alone have the final say in what is the correct and proper way for the populace to conduct itself. We,' he said, sweeping his arm outward to the Vatican at large, '*are* the conscience of the human race.'

The other cardinals murmured their approval, but Elias, from beneath the threatening glare of Monsignor Vecchi, shook his head.

'The path is not important,' he said, 'only the destination.'

Martinez cursed loudly, in Latin, before storming towards the door; Rossi made a peculiar, angry screeching noise in his throat. Giordano cupped his hands over his nose and mouth, closed his eyes and sighed loudly. He drew his hands slowly downward until they were clasped tightly below his chin. 'Vecchi,' he said, 'we will take our leave to begin preparations for the conclave. In our absence, you will explain to the good bishop how his life will be from this day on.'

With that, Rossi and Giordano joined Martinez at the chamber door. As they left, Martinez turned and said, 'You are a fool, Elias; a damned and godless fool.'

The door closed and Elias and Vecchi waited until they could no longer hear the echo of footsteps. Elias cleared his throat and asked what Cardinal Giordano had meant by his parting words: 'My life, from this day on?'

Vecchi rocked back and forth on his heels. 'Tell me, Your Excellency, if our followers now believe that they can find betterment without the guiding beacon that is the Roman Catholic Church, then what is to become of us?'

'I imagine,' said Elias, stubbornly, 'that we shall step down from the pedestal we have made for ourselves and join the rest of humanity in its rejoicing.'

'Mm.' Vecchi walked to the window that looked out over the Square of St Peter. 'Do you know how many people are employed by the Church? Do you have any idea? No, I'm sure you don't, so permit me to enlighten you.' He gestured for Elias to join him.

'On the rare occasion that my duties permit me, I enjoy walking along the streets that surround our hallowed walls. There are stalls that sell cards, and souvenirs and trinkets; beggars who can sketch the most wondrous images of Jesus Christ in mere minutes and will happily sell them to you for a handful of *lira*.' He opened the window and leaned against the frame. 'When I was but a child, I used to steal from a restaurant, not so very far from here. The most succulent anchovies you could imagine. They were like little scaled sweets.'

Elias looked down into the square where children ran in amongst the pilgrims, selling bottled water and gift cards.

'You see, Bishop Bjørstad, it is not just about the hundreds of millions who rely on us for their spiritual wellbeing, or the millions employed directly or indirectly by the Church. We must also consider the millions whose very livelihoods rely on our continued existence: the shop-keepers; the trinket-makers; the printers; the fringe churches; even those who make their living endlessly criticising us. Where would they be, indeed where would the city of Rome be, if we, as a religion, became irrelevant?'

Vecchi's argument was strangely seductive, as were all arguments that pleaded for things to stay the same. The Japanese economy would survive the loss of its whaling fleet, Elias reasoned, but could the United Kingdom continue to thrive now that its working population had been blessed with a five-day sabbath? And with that same reasoning, how long could the Roman Catholic Church survive if its followers chose to seek God of their own accord? As he often had throughout his life, Elias found himself torn in two; he had sworn allegiance to God and the Church, and now wondered if they were indeed the same thing.

'The death of Pope Gregory could not have come at a worse time,' Vecchi said. 'The world is in turmoil and we are without a conduit to Christ. If the human race truly is on the road to enlightenment, then the Church must be seen to be leading the way.' Vecchi turned to face him. 'The Church needs a leader, Elias; a strong, vibrant leader. The Church needs you.' He dipped his eyebrows at the corners to lend sincerity to his words.

'And what if I refuse?'

The monsignor looked out through the window and sighed. 'The choice is no longer yours.'

'That cannot be true.'

'If you refuse then you will be excommunicated.'

Elias felt his throat tighten, as though the noose were already in place. 'And do you mean "excommunication" through the office of the Pope, or "excommunication" by one of the apostles of the Inquisition?'

Vecchi smiled. 'At this time, there is no office of the Pope.'

The two men stood in silence, looking down at the crowd which was multiplying in size with every minute that passed.

'We must all do our part. The conclave will convene for two full days, after which you will be sworn in as supreme pontiff.' The monsignor turned on his heels and walked briskly to the chamber door. 'And I hope that you will be prove to be more cooperative than your predecessor, loved and respected as he was.'

'Monsignor Vecchi,' Elias said without turning away from the window.

'Yes, Your Excellency?'

'Have you not wondered why you and I and the Curia seem unaffected by this pandemic?'

'It had crossed my mind,' Vecchi said. 'I believe it is purely a matter of strength of character, of will.'

'Or is it perhaps that God deems us unworthy of such a gift as enlightenment.'

'Or perhaps he sees us as sufficiently enlightened to begin with.'

Elias turned and gave him a sour look. 'Do you honestly believe that, Vecchi?'

'All that matters is the survival of the Church,' Vecchi replied. 'What you or I believe is of little consequence.'

NINE

ALL THINGS CONSIDERED, ALFRED'S first day outside had started quite badly. To begin with, the plane he'd inadvertently manifested upon had made an emergency landing in Geneva.

'We're taking you off the flight,' Air Marshal Stone had told him.

Alfred said, somewhat desperately, that there was no need to go to any trouble on his account.

'I think you may be a terrorist,' Stone had said, flipping through the pages of Alfred's folder. 'You have a dossier containing nothing but blank pages. Is this some kind of invisible ink?'

Alfred explained that the documents had been prepared using a specialist typesetter, which meant their contents could only be seen by denizens of the Afterlife.

A muscle in Stone's left cheek had twitched erratically. He'd asked if the Denizens of the Afterlife was a middle-eastern terrorist group. Alfred, wisely, decided it was best if he stayed silent for the time being.

And so he was removed from the plane in handcuffs and chains. An armoured transport whisked him under police escort to the offices of the US Consulate, where he was treated very well, all things considered. He was kept in a small room with grey walls and a single table, three chairs and a water dispenser in the corner furthest from the door. He wasn't sure how long he was kept there; he'd forgotten his watch, the one synchronised with the heartbeat of the universe and which kept fastidiously good time. It could not have been more than a few hours, time enough for him to imagine the thousand unspeakable horrors that awaited him. He knew how brutal humans could be, and how they appeared to expend very little effort while being so.

Air Marshal Stone came to see him, and when the door opened, Alfred saw a sliver of daylight through the window at the far end of the corridor. The door closed; Stone sat down and asked him more questions about religion and fundamentalism. He asked Alfred if he had intended to blow up the plane.

Alfred asked, 'With what?'

Stone smiled without really meaning it. 'Wait here,' he said before leaving the cell.

Alfred wondered what else he could do but wait. He was left alone, without food or warmth, for another few hours. He began to feel a sense of cold panic rising from the pit of his empty stomach. He was hungry; that was a bad sign: a few more hours and he would be as vulnerable as a human. He tried the deep-breathing exercises that Magdelena had taught him, and reminded himself that he was still being treated remarkably well – all things considered.

The door opened and three suited figures stepped inside. The two men were in their late fifties and unusually tall, or so Alfred thought, with close-cropped hair and skin that looked as though it could be several inches thick. The woman was much smaller: barely five feet, if that. She wore a pair of large black spectacles that matched the colour of her hair, which was scraped back and tied in a long ponytail. She carried a large metal case that she placed on the table in front of Alfred and then took a step back so he could take a good look at it. One of the two men, who Alfred did not believe he would be able to distinguish between on a night with no moon, stepped forward, opened the case then took position by the door. The woman peered inside, tapping her lip and humming to herself as though picking from a confectionery box. She took out a large syringe and asked Alfred how much he weighed, roughly.

'I'm not sure,' he said calmly, though he felt like weeping. 'Is it important?'

'Kinda,' she said. 'This stuff's pretty experimental and I wouldn't want to kill ya.'

Alfred swallowed and resumed his breathing exercises; they did not appear to be working.

† † †

He woke with his face resting lightly against the stone floor, his head throbbing and the taste of rust in his mouth. He could hear the sound of a pen being tapped on the small desk a few feet above him. Below the desk, a pair of slender legs, crossed neatly at the ankles. He tried to sit up, but could not; he felt dizzy and he had the strangest notion that his brain had shrunk.

'I wouldn't try to sit up just yet,' said a voice from above the desk.

Alfred didn't feel at all well. 'I wonder if I may trouble someone for a glass of water.'

He heard the small woman whisper something. The door opened and a large pair of polished shoes left the cell.

'Well, I don't know quite what to make of you, Alfred – if that is indeed your real name.'

'It is my real name, and has been since the dawn of—'

'Yes, thank you. I get it.' The tapping became impatient. 'The truth drug did quite a number on you, Alfie. You've been talking all kinds of crap: some of it weird, some of it scary, some of it really, really funny. Poor Denny here damn near peed himself laughing, didn't you Denny?'

'Thought I was going have to relieve myself all over you, son.' The voice came from behind him, and Alfred realised his head was resting against someone's shoe.

'According to your statement, Alfie, you're not human, but a figment of my imagination.'

Denny sniggered.

'You're a – what was that word?'

'Manifestation,' Denny supplied helpfully.

'Yeah, a religious manifestation. You're a Horseman of the Apocalypse, right?'

'That was the scary part,' said Denny.

'And you've been sent by God, no less . . .'

'Without your horse,' said Denny.

'. . . to retrieve Lucifer, who is AWOL after a bust-up in Purgatory.'

The ankles uncrossed and then crossed the other way. Slender, Alfred thought, like the ankles of dear Magdelena.

'According to you, Alfie, if the devil doesn't get back to work, the progress of human civilisation will come to a crashing halt.'

Alfred tried to nod, hitting the back of his head against Denny's shoe. 'Without Leonard—'

'Leonard . . .' the woman said. Alfred heard papers shuffling on the desk.

'That's Lucifer's party name,' Denny said; Alfred decided that he didn't particularly like Denny.

'Got it, got it.' The pen tapping resumed. 'So answer me this: if Beelzebub is on vacation, then why is that a bad thing?'

'Leonard is the embodiment of the evil inherent in human nature, and without evil you cannot know the virtue of benevolence. Evil,' Alfred said, 'cannot simply cease; it must be eradicated, willingly, by the human race as a whole. Only then will you evolve to your true potential.'

'So you're saying there must be evil for good to flourish?'

'In a manner of speaking.'

Denny may have laughed but Alfred couldn't be sure. He thought, I should be more afraid, and wondered if perhaps the serum he'd been injected with had removed his fear of all things when it had removed his fear of telling the truth.

'You have very slender ankles,' he said suddenly, without inhibition or regret.

The woman drew her legs further beneath the desk and moved them slightly to the side. 'Why, thank you, Alfie,' she said, but he could tell she didn't really mean it.

'It is important that I resume my assignment.'

'The one given to you by Mr Gee.'

'Yes.'

The tapping stopped. 'What the hell am I going to do with you?' She sighed, and the cell door opened. The other pair of shoes stepped back inside, bringing three more pairs with it. Alfred swallowed and felt a line of sweat breaking against his hairline. No one had brought him any water.

'Here's my problem: I like you, really I do. But I don't know if you're a terrorist with a high drug tolerance and a whacked-out sense of humour, or if you're just plain fucking nuts.'

Two pairs of large hands took hold of his arms and hauled him back into his chair.

She nodded at the two men and smiled warmly, placing her spectacles on the desk. 'So here's what I'm gonna do for you, Alfie; I'm going to tell these gentlemen to take you for a little drive, put you on a jet and fly you to a little place we have out in Cuba.' She leaned forward and placed her palms flat against the desk. 'How does that sound?' she said. Her smile widened, revealing a mouthful of glowing white teeth. Lovely, Alfred thought, very much like the teeth of my own sweet Magdelena. Then he sighed and wondered if, for all time, everything everywhere would remind him of her.

† † †

And so now, all things considered, Alfred wondered if he was being treated well after all. Two of the larger men in suits half-carried, half-dragged him from his cell, then from the building and then out into a gravelled courtyard that encircled a large marble fountain. A large BMW four-by-four waited near the wrought-iron gates with its engine running. The woman, who Alfred had noticed had taken great pains to avoid telling him her name, walked ahead, barking orders and making calls on her cellphone. The suit to his right opened the BMW's rear passenger door and pressed down firmly on Alfred's head, forcing him inside. The woman climbed into the passenger seat up front; the other suit, Denny, jumped into the driver's seat, put the car in gear and pulled away.

'This place I am going to . . .'

'Cuba,' the woman said. 'Ever been before?'

Alfred said that he had. 'I arrived with the Spanish, as a matter of fact, in 1493.'

Denny shook his head and laughed. 'I am so going to miss talking with you, Alfred.'

Alfred couldn't remember Denny as having done very much talking. 'Where in Cuba?'

'Little facility we're putting together,' the woman answered. 'Guantanamo Bay. Heard of it?'

'No,' Alfred said. 'It does sound very exotic. One of those beach resorts, I take it.'

Denny and the woman looked at each other and chose not to reply, which in itself, Alfred thought, is very suspicious. He decided that if this 'Guantanamo Bay' was indeed a resort then it was probably one of a particularly poor standard.

The car lurched then gathered speed, leaving the gravel driveway and turning left on to the open track. Alfred didn't recognise any of the snow-dusted roads they drove through. The buildings, spaciously set from one another, were an odd mix of wooden chalets and old stone town houses. Traffic was light and extremely polite, so he guessed they were still in Geneva, heading north. The buildings grew further apart and the cars all but vanished; they travelled through open countrysides with the French Alps ahead of them. Denny and the woman chatted amiably to one another and didn't, thankfully, spare a second thought for their passenger. He guessed that they had known each other a long time; from the cuts of conversation, he gathered that Denny was married to one of the woman's close relatives, which hadn't stopped the two agents from sleeping together at every given opportunity. They spoke quite openly in front of him, and Alfred realised they could do so only because he was being taken to a dark and fetid hole from which he would never emerge.

'You okay back there, Alfie?' the woman asked.

Alfred chose not to reply as it didn't really matter.

The car made a sudden right turn into a meadow and carried on for another mile, stopping near a makeshift airfield beneath the shadow of the Alps. A plane stood waiting at the far end of the runway.

'Is this all really necessary?' Alfred asked.

'Well, that's what we're going to find out, Alfie, when we reach Cuba.'

They left the car in the charge of four more of the solidly upright, cheaply-tailored men and boarded the plane. Inside it was compact, though reasonably comfortable. There were only twenty seats, all in the same tan leather as the interior of the cabin. Denny pushed Alfred into a window seat near the front of the plane and sat next to him. The woman smiled and sat opposite them. She reached into her handbag and took out a fresh deck of cards and a packet of mints.

'Hope you play cards, Alfie,' she said. 'Denny here is hopeless.'

'I am not!'

'Not much of a poker face,' she continued. 'Not like you.'

Alfred looked passively at her.

'Yeah, that's what I'm talking about.'

The plane vibrated as something heavy landed against the fuselage. Denny looked calmly to the aircraft door and reached inside his jacket. The woman did the same without saying a word.

'Watch yourself!' shouted a voice from outside. 'Coming through.'

There was another impact against the outside of aircraft and someone cried out in pain.

'Hold him, for fuck's sake!'

Alfred felt a pull on his spirit: the draw of the Afterlife; a warning that he had just crossed history. He turned slowly and followed their eyes to the door.

'Denny, go see what the fuck's going on,' the woman said. She looked at Alfred as though he had something to do with it.

Denny was back a few seconds later, breathless. 'We got another passenger.'

'Fuck. Who?'

'That John Doe from the church fire in the Alps.'

'Here?'

'Yup.'

'I thought he was just nuts.' The woman turned and smiled apologetically at Alfred. 'No offence.'

'They think he murdered some priest,' said Denny, 'blew up a church and then dropped a hand grenade into a car, killing the driver.'

'Jeez, any little thing and they label you a terrorist.'

'Look, he's kicking up one hell of a fight out there. I'm going to help get him locked down.'

The woman nodded. 'Fine. The sooner we get him stowed, the sooner we can take off. Just watch yourself, okay?'

Denny grinned, produced a telescopic truncheon from his sleeve and hurried out through the door.

'He seems like a nice enough young man,' Alfred ventured.

'Yeah, one in a million,' the woman replied and picked a magazine from the rack beside her.

Denny was back a few seconds later, still breathless, and helping six agents carry a man strapped into a straitjacket. He turned and spun like a cracking whip, making it almost impossible to hold onto him; and he howled, screaming nonsense about demons and filing cabinets. His dark hair was wild and dishevelled and his eyes wide and spilling over with a strange, vacant terror. And he smelled, at least he did to Alfred. He carried the unmistakable stench of death and lies.

The seven men were jostled and bounced around the cabin as they fought to control the madman and carry him to rear of the plane.

'Careful!' the woman said.

'S'okay, we got it!' Denny brought the truncheon down across the man's stomach.

As he was manhandled past Alfred, their eyes met and history quietly sighed with relief. The lunatic ceased his thrashing, becoming limp and compliant. His eyes closed and he whispered, 'It has stopped. Thank the Lord in all his grace; finally, it has stopped.' He opened his eyes and fixed them on Alfred. And they were eyes the Horseman knew well. They were the eyes of a small, frightened child stolen from an orphanage in the black of night, and they were the terrified eyes of thousands of young men on thousands of battlefields. They were the eyes of a killer at war with his conscience.

'Friend of yours?' the woman asked suspiciously, holstering her side arm.

'Damnedest thing,' Denny said, taking his seat and wiping his face with a napkin. 'Takes one look at our man here, and he's as docile as a kitten. Weird, huh?'

'Yes, weird,' the woman said without taking her eyes from Alfred. 'Care to explain that, Alfie?'

Alfred said he wouldn't, if it was all the same to her. 'It seems every time I speak, things become decidedly worse for me.'

She laughed, a hollow shriek that gave Denny a start, even though, Alfred assumed, he must have heard it before. 'Trust me, Alfie,' she said, 'you don't know what "worse" is, not yet anyway.'

The plane departed without further incident, ascending in a rapid climb that left Alfred feeling rather sick. None of the other passengers seemed concerned, and the woman broke out the deck of cards as soon as the jet levelled out.

'Poker?'

Alfred politely refused and said he was going to try to get some sleep. As soon as he said this, he felt his eyelids begin to slide shut, almost of their own accord.

'Suit yourself.' The woman's voice began to fade, blending with the steady thrum of the plane's engines. 'How 'bout you?'

'Fine, but not for money this time.'

'Pussy.'

'For Christ's sake, Louisa, some of us got mortgages. And that cousin of yours ain't shy with the credit cards, if you know what I mean.'

'Okay, okay. Jesus.'

Louisa, Alfred thought. Your name is Louisa. And for a moment, he felt the shallow thrill that comes with a meaningless victory.

† † †

It may have been the turbulence that roused Alfred from his slumber, or the half-remembered dream of a localised war breaking out aboard the aircraft; he now possessed an indistinct memory of shouting and gunfire. The more he thought about it, the more real it became. In any case, when he opened his eyes he saw that he was quite alone and his wrists were no longer cuffed.

He thought he should call for someone, Louisa perhaps, then changed his mind. Instead, rising slowly from his seat, he took a cautious look around the cabin.

And as it happened, he was not alone. The agents who had accompanied him were at the rear of the aircraft, handcuffed, gagged and tied securely to their seats. Many were bruised and unconscious. Those that were bruised and lucid fought in vain against their bonds. The woman, Louisa, saw him and stopped pulling against the handcuffs that secured her arms above her head. She stared at him, as though this was, again, somehow his fault, and made muffled screams through the packing tape drawn across her mouth. Denny stirred at the sound, but did not wake. The blood had dried around his right temple so he did not appear to be in immediate danger; Alfred was thankful for that.

Louisa rattled her chains and gave Alfred an imploring look. He sank down in his seat and tapped at his bottom lip. He needed time to think. A course of action was required: a plan of some sort. He licked his lips and stretched himself to look again over the back of his seat. No, it was not a dream; and if he wasn't very much mistaken, two of the men, bound and gagged with strips torn from the seat cushions, were the pilots. Alfred felt himself swallow and he slowly turned his head to look through the window. The plane appeared to be climbing, though still flying dangerously low over the Alps. He rose reluctantly from his seat and walked forward, leaning into the ascent, though there was really no need. When he was standing before the door of the cockpit he took a deep breath and then knocked firmly.

'Come in,' a voice said. 'It is unlocked.'

Alfred opened the door and peered inside. He was relieved to see that someone was indeed flying the plane but, moving cautiously to the front of the cockpit, he was considerably less pleased to see who that someone was.

'Please, sit,' Pietro said.

Alfred settled warily into the co-pilot's seat and tried, unsuccessfully, not to stare at the dishevelled individual now in control of the flight. He was still wearing the straitjacket, its straps hanging freely from the arms and torso. At some point, Alfred noticed, the man had made an effort to smarten himself up, and when he saw the Horseman staring at him, he self-consciously smoothed down his hair.

'I apologise for my appearance,' he said.

Alfred said there was no need for apologies, then added that he could do with a little freshening up himself.

'This surprises me,' the man said, not daring to meet his eyes. 'You being what you are.' He seemed nervous, perhaps in awe. Alfred wasn't used to people being in awe of him. On the rare occasions when humans uncovered his true nature, that he was a representative of the Afterlife, he was usually faced with disappointment.

Pietro's hands were unsteady on the yoke, but it wasn't through unfamiliarity with the flight controls, or at least that is what Alfred hoped. The madman nodded without taking his eyes from the mountain ahead. 'I should have made more of an effort,' he said. 'It is not every day that one meets an angel.'

Alfred blinked. 'You remember me.'

'I remember you, I remember the fat woman in the wheelchair and the demon who, if my seminary history classes serve me well, was Heinrich Himmler.' He pushed on the throttle, increasing their rate of climb. 'The day I was removed from the orphanage, you were there, invisible to all, save me.'

'You were but a child then, Pietro Lantosca.'

The assassin smiled, in the same way a sleeping child smiles when caressed by its mother. 'It is so very long since I have heard that name.'

'And what name do you go by these days, Pietro?'

'I am known as Father Luke. I am—'

'I know what you are.'

The apostle looked down at his hand; he clenched and unclenched his fist and looked at it as though he could see blood running freely between his fingers. 'And my shame knows no end.'

'A priest, a penitent assassin – and a madman' Alfred said. 'A most unusual combination to find in one so young.'

'I am not insane,' Pietro said. 'I was tormented by my own conscience. It mocked me, tortured me, it . . .' he stopped and shivered '. . . it did filing.'

'Filing?'

'Inside my head! Taking my memories and cataloguing them. Moving papers, dropping folders, slamming drawers. It threatened to put the memories of my mother to the fire if I did not confess my sins. Can you imagine such a thing?'

Alfred said he could not.

'The sound was unbearable, unceasing,' Pietro said. 'And then, when they brought me on the plane, I saw you, and it stopped. That is when I knew that I had been right all those years ago: you are an angel.'

'I am not an angel,' Alfred said.

'I think you are.'

'I am no angel,' he said again, more firmly this time. 'I am a Horseman of the Apocalypse. I am a herald of misery. I am a portent of death.'

Pietro nodded slowly, without really understanding, then sniffed and asked the same tedious question Alfred had been subjected to since the dawn of man:

'If you are a Horseman of the Apocalypse . . .'

Alfred ground his teeth.

'. . . then why do you not have a horse?'

'It has and always will be,' Alfred replied, somewhat testily, 'a metaphor.'

Pietro shrugged and eased back the yoke still further, clearing a mountain peak by less than one hundred feet. 'You do not seem so terrible.'

The Horseman sighed and decided not to point out that he was no longer required to be terrible; officially, he was on sick leave. 'What do you intend to do with the people on the flight?'

'Have no fear, angel. I have had my fill of death for this lifetime.'

Alfred turned and looked down the gangway to where the agents, now all awake, were writhing and thrashing in a poorly organised attempt to free themselves.

'You yourself were secure and raving,' Alfred said doubtfully. 'Are you are saying that while I slept, you freed yourself from your straitjacket and handcuffs, subdued highly-trained military personnel and commandeered the flight?'

'It is what I am trained to do.'

'That is impressive.'

'No less impressive than an angel sleeping through a hijacking.'

It did explain the dream, Alfred thought. And the sound of gunfire. He wondered what had happened to the bullets. 'You could have been killed.'

'Yes, I had imagined that no one would dare fire on me in a pressured cabin. I was wrong. It is fortunate that the bullet struck your headrest rather than a window.'

Alfred swallowed and looked again to the agents. 'Still, to subdue men such as these in such a confined space . . . a most impressive feat.'

Pietro explained that every apostle received rigorous training in close-quarters hand-to-hand combat. A vital skill, he said, when called upon to kill someone inside a confessional booth. 'You would be astonished how often this is required of us.'

Alfred nodded and looked out ahead. It occurred to him that, even as a figment of human imagination, his existence had taken a decidedly surreal bent of late. 'Do you actually have a plan, Pietro?' he asked. 'Or do you merely intend to fly until our fuel runs out?'

Pietro looked at him, stunned. 'You do not have a plan?'

'Me?'

'Yes. You are from the Afterlife, after all. You are privy to all things. Why would you not have a plan?'

Alfred hadn't really given it much thought.

'Were you simply going to let them inter you in a Cuban prison camp?'

'They were taking me to a prison camp?'

Pietro shook his head. 'Archangel, why are you here, now?'

'Well, I was arrested on a flight bound for—'

'I mean here, on Earth.'

'Yes, of course you did. I am on a mission of great importance. I am here to find—'

'Leonard Bliss.'

Alfred's mouth fell open.

'My conscience explained it to me, while dusting the shelves in my head. You must escort him back to the Afterlife, yes?'

'I must.'

'Then I will help you.'

'And why would you do such a thing, assassin?'

Pietro leaned forward and tapped the fuel dial. 'If we are separated then I fear the voices will claim me. I do not wish this to happen. I will travel with you.' He turned to face Alfred. 'So where are we to go, Archangel?'

Alfred sighed and said, 'Rome. There is someone there I must speak with.'

TEN

'MURDERED, YOU SAY.' POPE Gregory XVII swallowed a mouthful of lightly whisked heaven then placed his cup on the table. He sniffed, scratched his nose and stared intently into the cup. 'Are you quite sure about this?'

'I'm afraid so,' Magdelena said with what she hoped was a sympathetic smile. 'My source is somewhat all-knowing.'

'Yes, of course he is. Forgive me.'

She had been unsure as to whether she should lead with the good news: that the enquiry had decided to permit him entry to the Kingdom of Heaven, in spite of the unprovoked assault; or the bad: that his premature arrival in the Afterlife was due to having been coaxed gently on his way. Either way, she had decided to tell him in the comfortable, non-threatening surroundings of the Purge Health Club, which the recently deceased pontiff had made regular use of while awaiting the outcome of the investigation. The club – all two thousand transparent floors of it – was particularly crowded this day, so Magdelena believed he'd be unlikely to create a scene by throwing furniture or weeping or something equally unseemly. She filtered his expression and body language through a lifetime's worth of emotional intelligence courses and saw that the news, good or bad, made little difference to him anymore. He sat across from her, wearing a sweat-soaked white T-shirt with his equally-white, stick-thin legs sprouting from inside a pair of large tennis shorts. The ensemble was finished with a pair of grey socks, brown leather sandals and a papal mitre that had seen better days.

'Murdered,' he said again, tipping the mitre to one side so he could smooth down his hair. He gazed over her shoulder, trying to focus on some point beyond the miles of swimming pools and running tracks, then he sighed and rolled his eyes upward as though trying to recall the contents of a shopping list. 'Well, goodness me,' he said finally.

'I'm sure this has come as something of a shock to you,' Magdelena said, thinking it would be nice if he demonstrated *some* indication he was at least slightly put out by it.

He noticed her looking at the mitre, so he smiled and removed it, placing it delicately on the coffee table. 'Yes, I know,' he said without waiting for her to speak. 'I am finding the adjustment difficult.'

'It'll be easier when you reach Heaven.'

'I do hope so,' he said. 'The disconcerting thing is that it feels the same when everything I've been taught says that it should not. I have so many questions and nowhere to begin. Am I really dead? I do not feel dead.'

'No one truly dies,' Magdelena said. 'When you cross over you live on in those that remember you.'

'So the Afterlife is a memory?'

'It is a memory and so much more: an idea, an emotion, a hope shared by billions throughout the ages.'

'A notion of faith so strong that it has manifested in the collective psyche of humanity.' Gregory shook his head. 'It does not seem possible.'

'And yet here we are.'

He leaned back in his chair and crossed his hands over his paunch, his expression contorting as if someone were trying to force the sum total of human experience into his ear. It was almost too much to comprehend, Magdelena knew. But he would try; they always did.

'I wonder if I might ask you something?' she said. 'Concerning your murder.'

His features relaxed and settled back into their proper place. 'Yes.' He sounded exhausted. 'But may I ask, is it common practice to tell your new arrivals that they were unlawfully killed?'

'No,' said Magdelena. 'But you are . . . were the Pope.'

'And I daresay you've had quite a few murdered pontiffs through your hallowed doors. Are they all afforded the same truth?'

Magdelena shook her head and thought, *He's astute. Annoyingly astute.* 'One of our field operatives, a good friend of mine, was recently dispatched to Rome to engage your successor in a mission of great importance. The operative – Alfred – is missing.' Magdelena leaned forward. 'I would very much like to know who killed you,' she said. 'If there is an assassin at work in the resting place of St Peter, then I need to know who he is.'

The former pontiff rubbed his chin and smiled. 'So that you may protect Alfred?'

'Yes.'

'And he is not immortal?'

'In some ways,' Magdelena said. 'We become increasingly vulnerable the longer we are outside. And Alfred's empathy with mankind makes him more vulnerable than most.'

The pontiff thought about this for a moment, and then the beginnings of an idea began to form, lending light to his countenance. He raised a finger in triumph; Magdelena was rolling her eyes before he spoke.

'The solution is simple,' he exclaimed. 'Have Alfred killed!' He sat back, grinning broadly, basking in the afterglow of his brilliance. 'If he is killed, then he will simply return –' he tapped the table to add weight to his point '– here!'

'If only that were true, Your Holiness.'

'Oh.'

'We are all part of this existence now. If we are killed, it is the same as if we are forgotten; we will cease to be. I cannot allow this to happen to Alfred. You must tell me of the dangers that lie in his path so that I may safeguard him.'

'You care for him a great deal, don't you?'

'I am concerned for a colleague,' she said quickly, and zipped her tracksuit to cover the flush she felt rising to her neck.

'I see.'

'We shared much a century ago, but that is behind us now. There is nothing untoward or improper about my—'

Gregory raised his hand. 'I was merely inquiring. Again, forgive me.'

Magdelena felt her face getting hot. 'Will you help me?'

'Miss Cane, a pontiff makes as many enemies as he does friends. If you're asking who would wish me dead then I will say, "Take your pick." Can your employer not help you?'

'He chooses not to. I think it is all to do with moving in mysterious ways.'

'Of course, of course.' Gregory nodded, though he still looked confused. 'Another question then.'

She wanted to say no.

'If I could tell you who killed me, what would you do with this knowledge?'

She set her jaw and said, 'Whatever it takes to save him.'

Gregory picked up his milkshake and sucked at the straw. 'Even if it means incurring the wrath of your employer?'

Magdelena felt the hairs on her neck tingle: a rare pulse of excitement that came when a new corporate game was afoot.

'If I may be so bold, Your Holiness,' she said icily, 'I find the extent of your knowledge somewhat surprising; who have you been talking to?'

A voice from somewhere near the bar called out to Gregory, and the throng of angels, wraiths and demons parted to allow Gabriel Archer through. He was dressed in a bright purple squash outfit, complete with matching shoes and racquet, a spectacle in puce; though she noted with some satisfaction he still had the black eye.

'Gregs, old man,' he said cheerfully, and snatched the chair that a demon laden with a tray of drinks was dragging to a nearby table with its foot. The creature stared sourly at the back of the archangel's head with all six of its eyes.

'You promised me another match,' Gabriel said, swinging his racquet, giving need for a number of wraiths to lean out of his way. 'At least give me the chance to win back a sliver of self-respect.' The archangel sat down and turned to the Head of Purgatory. He dropped the smile to greet her: 'Magdelena.'

'Gabriel.'

Pope Gregory apologised and explained that he'd run into her after their match and that she'd asked to speak with him.

'Yes, about Alfred Warr, no doubt,' Gabriel said, with a thin smile that was as annoying as it was false.

Magdelena fumed, tapping furiously on the leg of her chair.

'Actually,' said Gregory seeing she was about to boil over, 'it concerned my entry to Heaven; oh, and my death; I was murdered, you know.'

'No!'

'Yes!'

'But who would do such a thing? You're the Pope for His sake.'

'Well, as I was explaining to this dear, dear lady, the office of the supreme pontiff brings many—'

'Gabriel, what have you been telling people about Alfred and me?'

Gregory switched his attention between the two immortals, who were now locked in a silent battle involving only the eyes. He scratched his nose and rose to his feet. 'Think I'll head to the bar,' he said. 'That milkshake was heavenly, Magdelena. What was it?'

'Ambrosia,' she said, without taking her attention away from Gabriel, 'with whipped cream.' And she placed emphasis on the word *whipped* for the simple pleasure of seeing Gabriel flinch.

'Excellent. And can I get you both something to perhaps calm your nerves?'

'A flagon of Nectar,' Gabriel said, while trying to bore a hole in Magdelena's forehead through sheer force of will, 'topped with a Marrakech sunset and dusted lightly with a sprinkling of hope.'

'Splendid, and Magdelena?'

Magdelena asked, somewhat frostily, for a light beer.

Gregory said, 'I think the pair of you have much to talk about, and perhaps apologise for.' And with that, he hurried off towards the bar, which was several layers deep with toned demons and angels sporting salon tans.

Gabriel plucked at the string of his racquet, humming absently to himself. Magdelena rolled her tongue around her mouth and decided that one of them was going to have to be the bigger man.

'I'm sorry for punching you,' she said before she could think of a million reasons to stop herself, 'and for calling you a stupid little fop.'

'An *annoying* and stupid little fop,' Gabriel corrected her. 'And I apologise for calling you a whore.' He was about to add something, then thought better of it.

'We have an eternity together; we should really try to get on.'

Gabriel nodded while looking more than a little sad. He threw his head back, blew the air from his cheeks and stared into the sky; the sky that, as far as anyone knew, reached forever and an inch beyond. 'Do you know why I do this?' he said.

'Do what?'

'The clothes.'

'Sorry?'

He placed his racquet on the table. 'The pinks, the lime-greens. Surely you've noticed!'

'Well, yes, I'd noticed, obviously.'

'And you know why I dress like this?'

Magdelena thought that it was perhaps best she stayed silent for the time being. He leaned across and beckoned for her to come closer.

'To break free,' he whispered in her ear, then leaned back, smiling as if he'd won a game of chess, blindfolded. 'You, me, all of this: we are all defined by what humans perceive us to be. We are figments of their collectively tiny imaginations.' He stabbed his finger against the side of his head while reaching for his pocket with his other hand. He wrestled a packet of cigarettes free and flipped open the lid. 'But I've beaten them,' he said, catching a cigarette between his lips. 'How many of them,' he said, 'how many of them imagine the Archangel Gabriel as the kind of man who walks around wearing lilac sports gear?'

He began to look ever so slightly insane.

'None! That's how many!' He patted himself down for his lighter. 'You see! This is me! Me! Not an icon born of doctrine, but me! Doing something that none of them could possibly imagine I would do.' He looked at her, grinning wildly, waiting for her to say something. Congratulate him, perhaps. Tell him how grateful she was that he'd shown them the way to free themselves from the mediocrity of mankind's imagination.

'Is that really the best you could come up with?'

The archangel's smile dropped so quickly, Magdelena almost heard it land at her feet. 'Well, it's a token gesture, yes, but I am the Head of Inhuman Resources; I can't go off the rails completely.'

'Off the rails? Gabriel, you've hardly left the station. If you had really broken free, then don't you think you would have done something a little more . . . monumental?'

He sat forward in his chair, smouldering: a volcano in mauve. 'So what are you saying? Are you saying that humans imagine me to dress like this?'

Magdelena bit her lip and looked to the glass floor. There were some conversations that were never meant to happen.

'Oh, I see. You do think that. Okay, Miss I'm-So-Fucking-clever, please tell me why, in the name of Him, humanity would dress me in pastels.'

'Not all of humanity,' she said, apologising on mankind's behalf. 'Just a fair number of them. And I think it's a subconscious thing; just a feeling they get when they see all those pictures of you looking smooth and' – she could see this not going well – 'oiled.'

'They're oil paintings,' he said flatly. 'Oil paintings created by some of the greatest artisans in history. Of course I look "oiled".'

'That isn't really what I meant,' she said, praying for a fire drill. She could just stop, change the subject. There were so many more urgent things for them to talk about, and yet, at the same time, she was gripped with an almost destructive desire to see how this turned out. It was like watching a candle until you could no longer resist the compulsion to put your hand to the flame.

'Then what did you mean by "smooth and oiled". Artists like to paint me undressed, can't say I blame them; I'm in damn fine shape if I do say so myself.'

Magdelena stirred her water with her little finger.

'And it isn't easy staying this toned, you know. Personal trainers are fiends, Magdelena, sadistic, heartless fiends!' He held out his arm and flexed his forearm back towards his shoulder, his whole body shaking with the effort. 'Feel that,' he croaked. 'Go on.'

'If it's all the same to you, I'd rather not.'

'Go on!'

Magdelena swallowed. She reached out and gave his bicep a half-hearted tweak.

'For Christ's sake, Mags, put some effort into it.'

She rolled her eyes and squeezed harder. 'That's very . . . nice, Gabriel. Very impressive.'

He nodded with a grunt of self-congratulation. 'Nothing wrong with caring about your appearance, Magdelena. It's not as difficult as you might think.'

Magdelena pressed her lips together to keep her tongue firmly behind her teeth. She could feel her nostrils flaring.

'A bit of effort a few hundred years ago and Da Vinci might have painted you,' Gabriel said, and then as an afterthought that wasn't really needed, added, 'maybe.' He noticed that she was unwilling to look him in the eyes. 'What?' he said. 'What is it?'

'Nothing.'

'Come on, you're bursting to say something.'

'Really, I'm not.'

'Come on, let's have it. Is it the oil, the tan, the waxed chest, the clothes, the personal trainer? What is it? What is it about me that—Oh, my . . . Oh my God.' The cigarette fell from his lips. 'You think I'm gay, don't you?'

Magdelena put up her hands and realised she was trying not to laugh. 'Not me. Humanity.' This was not strictly true; she had herself painted Gabriel on many occasions, and his insistence on always reclining in a bed of laurel leaves had often made her wonder.

'Why?' he cried. 'Because I take care of myself and dress flamboyantly? My God, Magdelena, that is such a cliché!'

'I never said they were the most imaginative of creatures, Gabriel.' She placed her hands on the table and spread her fingers. It was meant to be a gesture of conciliation, something she'd heard on a resource management course.

Gabriel looked at her hands then glared at her. 'I was on the same fucking course, Magdelena.'

'It's the pictures, nothing more,' she said quickly. 'I'm sure it's nothing but a fleeting thought that passes through their heads when they're standing in an art gallery or—'

'A fleeting thought in the minds of millions that's kept me in pink sportswear for the past hundred years!' he wailed. 'It's true! They think I'm a homosexual!'

Magdelena looked around and smiled apologetically at the other customers then leaned forward to hiss at him: 'What the hell does it matter anyway? We're not in the Dark Ages anymore, you know.'

'Don't give me that political-correctness bullshit! I'm the Head of Inhuman Resources; I wrote the book on it. Is that why you hate me so much, Magdelena? I thought it was just professional jealousy.'

'So you're gay *and* delusional.'

'Ha! You see! You see!' He pointed a trembling finger at her and looked around amongst the demons and angels who were trying their very best to see nothing. 'Are we to add homophobia to your litany of crimes?'

'You are being ridiculous,' Magdelena protested, and while her sense of decency screamed, *No, you must not!* she spoke one of the Nine Universal Untruths: 'And I'll have you know that some of my very best friends are homosexuals!'

Gabriel curled his lip and thrust the cigarette in his mouth.

'You know you can't smoke inside,' she reminded him.

'This is the Afterlife,' he shouted, spitting the cigarette across the table. 'There is no "inside"!'

Pope Gregory XVII, with impeccable timing, returned with a tray of drinks. 'I can hear you from the bar,' he said, setting the tray down on the table. 'I had no idea the Afterlife could be such a stressful place.'

'Not for you,' Gabriel said, building himself up to a sulk of celestial proportions. 'It'll be an eternal fucking picnic for you.'

'We're having problems with personnel,' Magdelena said. 'It's putting us under a great deal of strain.' She looked pointedly at the Archangel Gabriel, who pointedly lit his cigarette.

'Ah, the redoubtable Leonard Bliss,' Gregory said. 'I take it he is the mission of great importance.'

Magdelena nodded. 'Sadly, yes.'

He took his seat and for a few moments he stared at his mitre with a squint, trying to see it from several miles away. He scratched his chin and opened his mouth, then closed it. Magdelena sipped at her glass; there was no need to hurry him, she thought. He is a good man; he will help me if he can.

'Now I think on it,' Gregory said, his voice thick with shame and disappointment, 'the Curia and I failed to see eye to eye on a great many things. We both desired a return to the Church's core values, but they wanted a more secretive approach, while I advocated a more open, accountable Church. Our discourses were often . . .' he stopped to rub ineffectually at a stain near the mitre's peak. Magdelena looked to Gabriel, who spiralled a finger near his left temple. '. . . heated,' the dead Pope said finally. He turned to the archangel and raised an eyebrow.

Gabriel quickly made a performance of scratching his sideburn. 'And that is enough to kill you?'

'This is religion,' said Gregory, eyeing him suspiciously. 'It shames me to admit it, but it takes very little.'

'So you think it was someone within the Curia?'

'Dear boy, I believe it was the entire Curia.'

'Then Alfred is walking into a viper's nest.' Magdelena sighed. She imagined the Afterlife without him, and found the mere thought of it almost too painful to bear.

And then Creation seemed to shrink away from her, as though it has looked around and was startled to see her there.

Pope Gregory asked her if she was all right; she said that she was, her voice echoing back from the furthest reaches of infinity. She looked at her hands and saw the cosmos reflected in her manicure.

Omniscience, she thought.

Creation, clearing its throat and regaining its composure, agreed.

It passed just as quickly, leaving her with the feeling that her brain had been vigorously scrubbed and polished. Her head hurt, and there was something new, alongside the ever-present thoughts of Alfred; an awareness and clarity she had not felt before.

She whispered her employer's name then opened her eyes to see Gregory and Gabriel looking anxiously at her.

'I think I may have been mistaken.' Magdelena got to her feet and began gathering her things. 'Mr Gee may be trying to help after all.'

'Hang on, where are you going?' Gabriel said, pushing back his chair.

'My office,' Magdelena replied, 'and you're both coming with me.'

The two men followed her out of the bar at a brisk walk: the pope holding his mitre firmly to his head, and the archangel leering threateningly at any demon who got in their way.

'You're overcompensating,' Magdelena told him.

'I know, I know,' Gabriel said. 'I can't help it.'

'I thought we might travel by tram.' The Pope said hopefully. 'I have yet to see many of the spectacular landmarks you have in Purgatory.'

'It is much quicker if we run,' Gabriel said.

Gregory XVII seemed to fold in on himself. He licked his lips and said, 'If it's all the same to you, I'd rather not. I'm a little too old to be tearing around the Afterlife at such a speed.'

Gabriel grinned and clapped him on the back. 'Nothing to worry about, Your Holiness,' he said. 'This,' he said, hugging the pontiff by the shoulders and shaking him affectionately, 'is simply how mankind chooses to remember you, the dull and unimaginative plebs that they are.'

'What Gabriel is trying to say,' Magdelena threw him a look with spurs attached, 'is that you can run as fast as you like now. All you need do is try.'

'Nevertheless,' Gregory said, 'I would rather take the tram.'

He is not ready, she thought. *He has yet to accept this, accept us.*

'Nonsense!' Gabriel scooped the startled Pope into his arms. 'Running is much quicker, good for the heart, not that it matters, and kinder to the environment. If we are to save our idiot Horseman then time is of the essence.' He turned to Magdelena and said, 'I will see you back at your office.'

As though his arriving first is written in the stars. 'No, Gabriel,' Magdelena said, with the barest hint of a smile. '*I* will see *you* back at my office.'

Gabriel raised an eyebrow. 'A race, then.'

'If you desire it.'

He smiled, showing a wide mouth filled with more than its fair share of perfect teeth. 'Dear lady, at this moment there is nothing I desire more.'

'Then as long as losing won't dent your sense of manli—'

And he was gone, leaving only the sound of a howling pontiff in his wake. Magdelena gave chase, knowing she would never forgive herself if, in any contest, she was defeated by an angel wearing lavender.

ELEVEN

MONSIGNOR SALVATORE VECCHI, PRIVATE secretary to the Vicar of Christ, laboured in his study, surrounded by maps and charts and printouts, and reminded himself that one day, one bright and glorious day, this would all be worthwhile. Despite the abundance of artificial light, his eyes hurt with the effort of keeping them open, lulled as he was by the sound of hymns and chants from St Peter's Square below.

Thousands had gathered in prayer with candles held high and hopeful, expectant faces turned towards the Basilica. They prayed for comfort and guidance. They prayed that before long the conclave would choose a man, blessed with the wisdom of the ages, to be the voice of God on Earth. They prayed that such a man would show them, morally and spiritually, how they should live their lives in the glory of the Lord's everlasting light.

Vecchi rose from his chair, stormed to the windows and slammed the shutters. Declaring one's love for God was all very well, but he'd never really understood why this could not be done quietly and in the privacy of one's own home. Where was it written that thou shalt annoy others with your self-serving mumblings and out-of-key singing? He'd had cause to attend mass on a number of occasions and he held a grudging respect for those who had the decency to mime.

He took his pen, a silver and gold affair carrying the papal seal of Gregory XVII, and tapped it against the map spread across his desk. The pen rested against a small patch of land to the west of Tel Aviv, and pinned to this patch of land was a cutting from an Israeli newspaper. The cutting told of the joyous return of an Israeli special forces unit, believed lost on a mission behind enemy lines. The unit brought with it a letter from the leaders of Palestine: a blueprint for everlasting peace between their two nations. The Israelis had welcomed the proposal without suspicion or condition, declaring the Palestinians their brothers, now and for all time.

This, Vecchi thought, will never do. He snatched the cutting from the map and moved it back and forth in front of his nose until the tiny letters came into focus. They had interviewed the returning soldiers, who'd babbled endlessly about spending their lives doing good deeds for others, rather than killing in the name of patriotism. One soldier told of their exploits in Rafah: how they'd spilled the blood of innocents, had been trapped like animals and then walked free with the blessing of those they'd been sent to kill. He'd told how they'd lived with Palestinian families who fed them and dressed their wounds and ensured their dead comrade was returned to them for their journey home. And all of this, under the sour and blackened eye of an angry shambling man who had appeared before them from nowhere.

Vecchi brought the sheet closer so he could study the name carefully; Leonard, it said. No surname or description. His name was Leonard and he was the most miserable man the soldier had ever met.

The name rolled and thrashed inside the monsignor's head, too wild and tenuous for him to grasp on to. He looked again at the map. This . . . contagion, this outbreak of virtue, had begun in the Middle East and spread like a plague, exploding outward across the oceans, carried to Europe, Asia, the Americas . . .

'A disease,' Vecchi murmured. An illness that affected the mind, perhaps, inhibiting all that was evil in the human spirit. The name 'Leonard' scratched at the inside of his skull and, without being fully aware of it, the monsignor reached across to a report marked for his eyes only. He walked to the centre of his office and stood beneath the chandelier, pouring through the detailed account of Father Matthew of the Inquisition. Vecchi had dispatched him days ago to excommunicate one of his brethren: Father Luke who had apparently gone mad during a failed operation in Montpelier. The excommunication had not taken place, however; Matthew had failed to reach the stricken apostle before he'd been handed over to the CIA. The monsignor cursed the Americans and their pathological need to involve themselves in any explosion not of their making, no matter how small it was, or where it occurred. Since the fall of the Berlin Wall, the work of the apostles had often become entangled with the machinations of the United States' secret service. Such encounters tended not to end well.

He walked back to his desk and considered sending another apostle to dispose of the irksome Father Luke.

Another apostle.

The contagion, this so-called 'Rapture', had taken its toll on the men who served the seminary: some, for reasons that were still unclear, had taken their own lives; others had simply left the service of the church. Their numbers were thin and Vecchi was reluctant to sacrifice another without guarantee of success.

No, he would send no more apostles. He sighed and fell into his chair. The scratching inside his head grew more intense and Vecchi was sure it was the sound of his own conscience trying to claw free of its cage. He'd long since learned to control his compulsion to do good, if doing so contradicted the needs of the Church. If he was unable to keep his sense of right in a firm chokehold then how could he serve? How could he have killed a supreme pontiff who'd threatened the stability of the Holy See?

How could he send a man to kill his childhood friend?

Vecchi poured a small measure of wine and thought of his ancient and feared predecessors: the scores of sullen and ruthless individuals who had held this most revered post before him. There was one in particular: Monsignor Claudio Conzenzas, the private secretary to Pope Innocent IV. It was Conzenzas who created the apostles of the Inquisition and had had thousands across Europe slain by the seminary's unseen hand. It was a record of achievement that no other secretariat had equalled in almost eight hundred years.

But Vecchi was close, so very close, and the thought of it prevented him from sleeping soundly at night. 'I do what I must to serve the Church,' he reminded himself. The scratching in his head became more desperate. He snatched up the report and stared at it, reading each word with an intensity designed to smother doubt from his mind.

Yes, Father Matthew had returned to Vatican City, reporting that he had witnessed a rabid and straitjacketed Luke being manhandled into a car. The lunatic had struggled and screamed, saying that his conscience was ransacking his brain and that it was all Leonard's fault.

Vecchi stopped reading and sat upright.

Leonard.

Somewhere inside his head, someone was whistling a hymn, though Vecchi, not being particularly religious, could not be sure which hymn it was.

Leonard.

The monsignor returned to the Israeli news clipping and read through it a second time. A common name, perhaps. Again, he could not be sure. But a name, uttered twice, thousands of miles apart. He sat back, tapped thoughtfully on the desk and wondered what he was missing. 'Who are you, Leonard?'

There came a knock at his door, then a respectful moment before the oak-leather panel swung aside. Sister Bernice, the private secretary to the private secretary to the Vicar of Christ stepped inside the hall, bowed and waited patiently for Vecchi to put away his train of thought.

'What is it?'

'I have news,' she said and stepped forward, placing a folded letter on the desk. 'Bishop Bjørstad has accepted your offer; he has agreed to be the next pontiff. Praise be.'

'Praise be, indeed,' Vecchi agreed, though he had given Elias Bjørstad very little choice in the matter. He took the letter and read it through, then again to be sure. 'Yes, praise be.' He rose to his feet, rested his fists upon the oak desk and looked down at his reflection in the polished wood; its hue masked his eyes, creating an abyss either side of his nose.

If I were a praying man, he thought, then I would surely fall to my knees and give thanks. 'Inform the Curia.'

'Yes, monsignor.'

'And tell the conclave that our new Pope has been found.'

'Yes, monsignor.'

'But no white smoke. Not until first light.'

'Yes, monsignor.' She bit her lip and looked to her feet, and Vecchi knew he had been given the best news first.

'What is it, Sister Bernice?'

'I have received troubling word from the seminary of St Fiacre. It is Father Matthew, the priest recently returned from Montpelier.'

'I know who he is, Sister Bernice. What of him?'

The aged nun cleared her throat. 'He is dead, sir.'

The news was not totally unexpected. Still, Vecchi found himself again in need of his chair; he sat down, slowly and without taking his eyes from the nun.

'He was found in his meditation chamber by his acolyte. It is believed that he poisoned himself.'

Yes, of course he did. Vecchi sighed and wondered if . . . when he was Pope, there would still be an Inquisition for *his* private secretary to command. 'Make the necessary preparations, Sister Bernice,' he said with his fingertips pressed against his temples. 'The world awaits our new leader.'

The Book Of Leonard

The Leonard Ultimatum: 6

AND SO IT WAS.

Three days after the much-beloved Pope Gregory XVII turned in his sleep and tasted poison on his lips, and on the day a demon tattooist inked a pair of indelible wings upon the back of Gabriel Archer, a Rapture did spread outward from the lands of the Middle-East. It was carried in the souls of travellers who journeyed to Africa, Europe, the subcontinent and the Americas. It freed the conscience of dictators and fed the morals of warlords. Across the face of Mother Earth, soldiers danced with their enemies, and thieves fell weeping at the feet of their victims.

It told all whom it touched that they must follow their dreams; they must love one another; they must sacrifice themselves for their fellow man, and so enter the Kingdom of Heaven.

And so it was on this very day, in a small church at the edge of the French Quarter of New Orleans and less than a stone's throw from the Mississippi River, seventy-eight-year-old Father Nathaniel Bouvrier stood before his altar, listening fitfully to his childhood dreams. The dreams told him that before the Church and God, before his dwindling flock, before everything else, he was a musician. So with feverish hands, he assembled the mixing desks and amplifiers and spliced them to the church's ageing sound system. He donned a set of headphones and spun vinyl disks upon the six turntables he'd set before him. And then, with a glaze to his eyes and sweat pouring from his brow, Father Nathaniel Bouvrier, seventy-eight, rolled the switches and laid down a trance that the world's greatest exponents of dance music would one day describe as 'crack cocaine for the ears'. The sounds brought the young, the old, the rich, the poor, the sheltered and the homeless. They danced and they drank; they ingested hallucinogens of questionable legality, and when the party spilled from the church and out onto the sidewalks, they made love in the streets. Their numbers swelled and thus was born a celebration of life, love and death, destined to consume the world for forty days and forty nights.

TWELVE

'"Forty days and forty nights".' Gabriel turned the slab around as though doom could be averted by reading the same text upside down. 'Things never turn out well when that old chestnut pops up.'

Magdelena took the tablet from him and threw it back on to the pile; the pile that had, while she had been away from her desk, grown into a pyramid of Babylonian proportions: thousands upon thousands of conveniently-sized tablets which were still, inconveniently, made from polished stone.

As an amateur writer, she thought, Mr Gee is nothing if not prolific.

'It would help,' said Gabriel, looking sourly at another slab, 'if we knew what we were looking for.'

'Anything that can help us to help Alfred, Gabriel, that's all. We'll know it when we see it.' Magdelena wiped her brow and picked out another tablet, then changed her mind and took another one.

'If he really wanted to help us, then why not just bloody tell us!' Gabriel shouted, more to the sky than her.

'Because it is not his way. It never has been. The humans have to learn for themselves; so must we.'

She shielded her eyes and looked to the pyramid. Halfway to the summit, Pope Gregory XVII (deceased) was making laborious work of his section. Two days ago, he was fired with anticipation at the prospect of examining teachings direct from God. A day later, he was mired in despair as he realised the human race was going to pleasure itself into oblivion, and a day after that, he looked . . . Well, he looked as she felt: drawn, tired and without hope.

And we should not be tired, she thought. Not like this. We are immortals, untouched by the mechanics of time. She could taste the sweat and dirt on her upper lip and dreaded to think what she must look like.

'This is hopeless, just hopeless,' Gabriel said. He discarded another slab, this time without reading it, then sat down on the ground. 'We've been at this for days Magdelena, and we've still got thousands of these things to go.'

'Some of us have been at it for days, Gabriel,' she said, taking up the discarded tablet, 'while some of us skipped off to Hell yesterday. Some of us decided it was more important to get a tattoo than to help Alfred. And now some of us are walking around under the sorry misapprehension that this tattoo makes us more manly and ironic.'

Gabriel sniffed. 'Just call Mr Gee; ask him.'

'I did. He didn't pick up.'

'Then try again!'

'There is no point, Gabriel!' She dropped the tablet mere inches from his head. He shrieked, like a child, and scrambled back through the dust, like a large crab. 'Bloody hell, Magdelena! You could have—'

'Oh for God's sake Gabriel, stop being such a little girl!'

Gabriel's face froze, and in that regretful moment, all of time seemed to freeze with him. Magdelena wished, like Mr Gee, she had the power to roll back creation.

'So,' Gabriel said, with a worrying lack of emotion, 'I'm gay *and* effeminate.'

'Gabriel, I am so very sorry,' Magdelena began. 'That wasn't meant to belittle your . . .'

He raised an eyebrow and waited.

'. . . difficulties.' Bad word, she thought. Such an awfully bad word.

He snatched up the tablet and shook it at her. 'I'm trying to help you, you know! You and bloody Alfred! Sitting in the middle of a desert, reading useless shit about—' he glanced at the tablet '—pizzas and Saint Fiacre! Just so your paramour, who you haven't fucked in almost a hundred years—'

'Have a care, Gabriel,' Magdelena said quietly, clenching her fists and sizing up his good eye.

'—can spend eternity hiding under your desk while you stroke his head like he's some sort of pet. Is that what the attraction is, Magdelena? Is he some sort of security blanket that makes you feel better about yourself? Is that what—?'

And it was then that she hit him, for the second time in three days, the second time in two thousand years. He pirouetted, a tight and perfectly-formed half-circle, then sat down in the dirt with a bump.

Magdelena shook her hand and pressed it into her armpit, suspecting that she had hurt herself more than she'd hurt him. The archangel struggled quickly to his feet, took a moment to steady himself and began pulling at his shirt to free it from his waistband. 'That is it! That is it! I don't care if you are his most favoured and I don't care if you are – and I use the term in its broadest sense – a woman! I'm going to thump you, Magdelena Cane. I'm going to thump you hard and in the face.' He put up his fists and began to dance from one foot to the other, ducking and bobbing more or less on the spot.

Several decades worth of personnel management courses had not prepared Magdelena for this, and so she improvised; she cast off a Jimmy Choo and thrust her instep into his groin, the immediate effect of which was a sharp pain lancing its way through her shin. She stumbled back, wishing on everything below the sky that she'd kept the shoe on. And Gabriel, too, fell backwards, his eyes bulging from his skull like clementines.

With his chest rattling on the arid air, Gregory XVII arrived at the base of the pyramid. 'Excuse me, but did you mention . . .' He coughed, wheezed and tried again. 'Did you say something about Saint Fiacre?'

Magdelena hopped back to her desk and leaned against its edge.

'What of it?' Gabriel said through clenched teeth. He pressed one hand over the fresh swelling on the left side of his face, the other over his crotch.

'I think,' Magdelena said, lifting her foot and resting it against the front of her thigh, 'I think I've broken my big toe.'

Gregory picked up the tablet and began to read; as he did so he thumbed the desk intercom. 'Rachel?'

'Yes, Your Holiness?'

'I wonder if I may trouble you for—'

'Two ice packs. They'll be with you shortly, sir.'

He turned to Magdelena, who was massaging her foot and blinking rapidly to clear her streaming eyes. 'This tells of two orphans,' he said, 'taken into the care of the Vatican.' He scanned down the tablet. 'I know one of them.'

Magdelena sniffed, hopped closer and tried to read over him. 'Lantosca?'

'No, the other one. Vecchi. He is . . . was my private secretary. He spent his formative years at the seminary of Saint Fiacre, of all places. I had no idea.'

Gabriel began a slow and painful journey to the desk, each step producing a terse grunt and a new facial contortion. 'And what,' he gasped, 'is so special about this seminary?'

'I know very little of it,' Gregory said. 'It is located in the grounds of Vatican City, somewhere near the east wall, I think.'

To Magdelena it seemed strange that a serving pontiff would be unfamiliar with any part of the Holy City, and when she voiced the thought to Gregory, he became oddly defensive: 'Neither I nor any of my predecessors would have need to visit such a place,' he said, and pushed his mitre firmly down on his head, lest anyone forget who he was.

'Fiacre,' Gabriel said, massaging his groin. 'I know that name.'

Magdelena remembered him too, from an informal gathering of saints past that she and Gabriel had attended many centuries ago. 'Did we not call him "Fiacre the Unfortunate"?'

'Fiacre the Dull, as I remember it.' Gabriel stepped gingerly over to her laptop computer and began clattering at the keyboard. Magdelena turned to Gregory, who stood with his arms folded and his lips sealed.

'Why does this place, this seminary, frighten you?' she asked.

'It does not frighten me,' the deceased pontiff shot back. 'I took no interest in it, nor did any of the Curia.'

'You must know something of it.'

'All I can tell you is that for a small, specialist order, it absorbed an inordinate proportion of the annual contribution: something of the order of eight million euros per financial year.'

'And you did not seek to find out why?'

'No pontiff has interfered with the business of Saint Fiacre's since the fifteenth century.'

'And what "business" would that be?' she asked, patiently.

'Pest control, as far as I know.'

Magdelena furrowed her brow. 'Eight million euros a year to control vermin around the Holy City.'

'Vermin spread disease,' Gregory said, as though reciting from a script.

'I've found him.' Gabriel turned the laptop around slightly so they could all see the picture on the screen. 'Saint Fiacre.'

Pope Gregory crossed himself, almost violently.

Yes, Magdelena thought, I do remember him. The saint had had a little too much to drink at the gathering and became quite maudlin as the evening progressed. She'd had quite a lot to drink herself but still had a clear recollection of his unhappiness over his sainthood. *I travelled much during my life,* he'd said, then belched, in her face. *But am I honoured as the Patron Saint of Travellers? No. No, I am not. The title is bestowed upon that glory hound Christopher; Christopher becomes the Patron Saint of Travellers for carrying our employer's son over a puddle. And what do I get? I'll tell you what I get, dear lady . . .*

'I don't understand.' Gabriel scratched at what he thought to be three days' worth of manly stubble. 'Why would anyone name a seminary after the Patron Saint of Sexually-Transmitted Diseases?'

The deceased pontiff crossed himself again.

'Well, if nothing else,' said Magdelena, looking at Gregory, 'it would certainly keep people away.'

THIRTEEN

ON THE MORNING OF the Papal Coronation, the US government, much to the planet's surprise, made a drastic and sweeping change in foreign defence policy. A spokeswoman for the Pentagon – an immaculately turned out colonel in the United States Air Force, with blonde hair twisted into a dome and glistening, vacant eyes – announced that the Joint Chiefs had come to realise that spending billions upon hardware capable of destroying the world several times over – when whoever was doing bad and evil things would most probably stop after the world was destroyed once – was, quite frankly, silly and wasteful. In light of this, the Joint Chiefs had decided to divert military resources into a global knitting programme.

'Excuse me?' said the only reporter in the press room without his jaw swinging free.

'You heard, Will,' said the spokeswoman, reaching under the lectern for her bag.

'I'm sorry, Colonel,' said another journalist, 'but it sounded like you said a "knitting programme".'

The spokeswoman placed an enormous roll-up between her lips and tried to light it. 'That's exactly what I said.'

'A knitting programme.'

'A programme designed solely to facilitate the production of knitted goods, yes.' She rooted around in the bag for another lighter. 'We're going to make blankets, ladies and gentlemen.'

'Blankets?' said the first reporter.

'Blankets for the world's needy?' said another.

'That's right: blankets for the millions around the world who don't have a blanket. Any of you guys got a light?'

The journalists, about thirty of them in all, looked at each other until one brave soul cautiously approached the lectern and handed the spokeswoman a lighter at arm's length. She said, 'Thank you,' and lit the joint, inhaling deeply and blowing a plume of white smoke into the air.

The same question, from the back of the room this time: 'The US government is going to cut defence spending and make blankets for poor people?'

The spokeswoman tapped the roll-up against the side of the lectern and said, 'Am I not speaking English?'

'Blankets?'

'Yes.'

'For the poor?'

'Yes, Jesus Christ, that's what I said.'

'But . . .why?'

She swayed a little and drew on the joint, then leaned forward to rest her elbows on the lectern and her chin in her hands. Her eyelids drooped; she smiled indolently and said, 'Why the fuck not?'

And it was there that the broadcast ended, returning to the news studio where two anchormen sat staring, wide-eyed and speechless.

Sister Ruth, one of Elias's attendants, switched off the television and crossed herself. 'Did you see that, Your Holiness?'

'I am here next to you, Sister Ruth. It is unlikely I would have missed it.'

'Smoking that . . . that filth!' she continued as though he hadn't spoken. 'On television!' She leaned forward and finished applying his makeup, a carefully prepared smoothing agent of her own concoction that would fill in the tired crows feet around his eyes. 'The audacity!'

She dabbed and brushed with angry, emphatic strokes near the corner of his right eye. 'The woman clearly needs God in her life.'

'Well, she clearly needs something,' Elias pulled away, fearing for his sight. 'Perhaps we should stop for a moment.' The voices in his head chimed their agreement, adding that perhaps someone in this room had a roll-up *he* could smoke. God knew he needed it, and he was the Pope, after all. What was the point of being the pope if the occasional small vice could not be indulged? I am not the Pope, Elias reminded them and himself. Not yet.

'I'm afraid we don't have time to stop, Holy Father.' Sister Ruth picked up a small circular sponge and dabbed it into a paste of her own design that would bring colour to his sallow cheeks. 'You're on television' – she crossed herself again, as though flatscreens were the root of all sin – 'in less than fifteen minutes,' then pointed the sponge at the clock placed judiciously above a large golden crucifix. From where he sat, Elias could see eight other clocks dotted around the papal apartments, there to remind the scores of people who made preparations for the coronation that time was precious. Nuns and priests, whose function he could not even begin to guess at, filled almost every inch of the floor space. As some left, others arrived, giving Elias the disquieting feeling that the room was the heart of some vast circulatory system. A cache of priests adjusted the cameras and recording equipment, while a group of nuns checked the lighting rigs and then checked them again. There were four more priests out on the balcony, and when a fifth joined them, the crowds in St Peter's Square cheered by mistake then groaned in twelve different languages. Three members of the Curia stood close to the entrance of the apartment's chapel, embroiled in a heated discussion with Monsignor Vecchi. Cardinal Möller wheezed from behind his oxygen mask and waved a withered finger at Leoni Rossi, the Cardinal Camerlengo. Rossi replied, and by way of a response, Möller reversed his wheelchair and tried to run over his foot. Carlos Giordano looked up to the heavens and blew out his cheeks. Elias doubted he'd ever seen anyone so miserable. Even Vecchi himself was shouting and waving his clipboard, pointing at it as though it were the commandments themselves. Elias wondered what the world would be like today if Moses had come down from Mount Sinai with a clipboard and a carefully typed list: The Ten items On The Agenda. No, he decided, things were more official when they were set in stone. He looked up to see Vecchi watching him. The monsignor excused himself from the argument and strode to where Elias sat having some sort of grouting applied to his chin.

'Not long now, Your Holiness,' Vecchi said his hands closed in front of his chest. He beamed unconvincingly, reached into his pocket then handed Elias a small box bound in vermillion. Elias eyed him warily, then opened it.

'The episcopal ring,' he said.

Vecchi nodded, barely able to contain himself.

'I am not the pope. Not yet.'

'The next few days are but a formality, ' Vecchi said. 'You are the supreme pontiff now.' He dipped his head towards the ring, urging Elias to put it on. Instead, Elias removed the ring from the box and slipped it into his pocket. He handed the box to Vecchi.

'After the ceremony then,' Vecchi said tightly.

'I think perhaps that would be best.'

They stared at each other, waiting for the air to crack.

'So, then,' the monsignor began again, 'I trust you are bearing well?' He looked closely at his fingernails, then found his reflection in a nearby mirror. He turned slightly towards it, pulling his stomach in and up.

'I would be much better, monsignor' Elias said, 'if important decisions were not taken without my involvement.'

With a single glance, Vecchi instructed Sister Ruth to bow and take her leave. 'There is something that troubles you,' he said, glancing first at his watch and then at the clock placed above the crucifix.

'It all seems so rushed,' Elias said glumly. 'The announcement, the coronation . . . I do not understand why everything is in such haste. I was not even consulted about the papal name. If this is the name I am to carry until the day I die then I should have a say in its choosing.'

'You do not like the name?'

'Do you?'

'It was Cardinal Möller's suggestion. We thought it would bring a lighter aspect to your reign.'

Elias beckoned Vecchi to come closer. He looked about to make sure no one else could hear, before speaking, slowly and deliberately: 'The Curia expects me to lead the Catholic Church as Pope Hilarius II? Was there even a Hilarius I?'

'Four-sixty-one to four-sixty-eight,' Vecchi said without allowing a second to pass. He looked at Elias with ill-disguised disappointment.

Nevertheless, Elias spoke haughtily and, for his sins, sarcastically: 'I apologise for being unable to name all two-hundred-and-sixty-four of my predecessors. If time avails itself, monsignor, then I will certainly endeavour to commit them to memory.'

'Two-hundred-and-sixty-five, Your Holiness,' Vecchi said with a serene smile.

'Pardon me?'

'You have two-hundred-and-sixty-five predecessors. You, Hilarius II, are the two-hundred-and-sixty-sixth supreme pontiff.' And he bowed deeply and, Elias thought, mockingly. Elias looked to the Curia who were still in the midst of a heated exchange, and wondered if he should not be part of it. 'I do not like the name,' he said, thinking if he did not brand his authority on this one small thing, then he would somehow be indentured for the rest of his days. 'I would prefer to be known as Innocent XIV.'

Vecchi looked at him as though he had just pushed over a nun. For a moment, Elias thought he saw a tell-tale flicker of rage, a faint tick in the muscle of his right cheek. 'That will be most difficult at this late stage, Your Holiness.'

'Nevertheless,' said Elias, 'that is my wish.' He wondered why in the name of creation he had chosen 'Innocent' as a name. Innocent, as a lamb to the slaughter.

'Perhaps we could think about changing your name after the coronation,' the monsignor ventured.

'You know as well as I do that these things have a tendency to stay once they are in place.'

'We will have to change the coat of arms.'

'Then the sooner we begin—'

'The banners inside St Peter's . . .'

'Will all have to be altered, I know.'

Both men stood firm, both men thinking that perhaps, somewhere between Tibet and the Vatican, a terrible mistake had been made.

'I wonder,' said Vecchi, 'if you are perhaps not the man we thought you were.'

'Is that necessarily a bad thing?' Elias asked.

'I do not know,' Vecchi said, looking again at his watch. 'And it appears we no longer have the time to find out.' He gave Elias a strained smile. 'I will speak with the Curia and see what can be done.' He bowed stiffly and walked back to where the Curia were now watching Elias with apprehension. Elias waited – for Vecchi to speak with them and then for Rossi to throw his hands in the air; for Möller to begin wheezing and groping wildly for his oxygen mask; and for Cardinal Giordano to look towards him and snarl – then he rose to his feet. A storm of nuns and priests raced to Möller's aid, pushing past Elias as he made his way to his study. I am but a figurehead, he thought. Nothing more. He closed the door behind him and rested his head against the panel. *And even as a figurehead, a chess piece, I am not worthy of this.* The voices in his head agreed; their clamour almost smothered the sound of footsteps behind him.

'Who is there?' Elias said. 'Whoever you are, please leave. I wish to be alone.'

'I'm afraid that will not be possible, Your Holiness.'

Elias turned his head without lifting it away from the door. By rolling his eyes he could make out two figures pressed together in the chapel doorway. The man on the left, the tall man with milk-white skin and oiled, dark hair, was dressed in a familiar perversion of the priest's raiment.

'God save me,' Elias whispered. An apostle of the Inquisition. Perhaps, he thought, requesting a new name had been a step too far.

'I am not here to kill you, Your Holiness,' the apostle said. His tone was respectful, deferential even, and yet Elias did not believe him. He turned and pressed himself against the door, finally catching sight of the other man, much shorter, white-haired, and wearing a thin linen suite and a white fedora hat which he tipped politely in Elias's direction.

Inside his head, the past lives of Elias Bjørstad shrieked in terror. 'You,' Elias said, pointing a shaking, accusing finger at Alfred. 'I know your face! I know you!'

Alfred smiled and held his hat in front of his chest. 'Indeed, young Elias. It has been such a long time.'

'I see your face in my nightmares!' Elias turned to run, but within the space of a heartbeat the apostle was upon him, one arm around his throat. Elias felt a thumb pressed firmly at the nape of his neck and immediately lost the feeling in his arms. His legs followed, giving way as if cut from under him.

'You must listen to us, Your Holiness.' Pietro whispered into his ear while dragging him back to the centre of the room. 'You must listen, and then you must come with us.'

'I cannot!' Elias said, his speech slurred. 'I am to be made Pope. I shall not be going anywhere with you.'

'You will have time for that,' Alfred said, 'but for now, you must accompany us. We have need of you. The world has need of you.' He smiled and laid a hand gently upon Elias's shoulder.

'Who are you?' Elias demanded.

'The pertinent question is, who are you?'

And as the man in the fedora spoke, Elias found himself savaged by his inner voices: memories of cruel and heartless men; men so far removed from God their redemption seemed impossible; men who railed against every instinct to be true and just.

'You are a reclaimed soul, Elias: born, lived, deceased, cleansed and then reborn again; saved from damnation for this purpose, this day.'

'Dear God,' he cried, 'I have done such . . . evil.'

Theft.

Murder.

Rape.

Bigamy.

He saw battles fought from longships and castles, brawls with swords and mace, guns and fists; he saw his many faces, scarred through violence, twisted by lust and avarice. He saw his many deaths: his crucifixion as a thief on the Hills of Calvary; his hanging as a pirate on the sands of the Ivory Coast; his execution as an enemy of the Third Reich.

The pontiff-in-waiting wept. 'I cannot . . . It is too much.'

'You must calm him,' Pietro said.

Alfred nodded. He knelt next to Elias and took his hands in his. 'You know, when we first met, you were moments away from being born. Indeed, it was an anxious moment for us all. As I remember . . .' he chuckled and scratched the welted flesh at his throat '. . . you seemed to have a rather large head, which unfortunately became trapped—'

'We are wasting time,' said the apostle, clamping his hands over Elias's nose and mouth. 'And you have an appalling bedside manner, Horseman.'

Elias tried to lash out, even as the world seemed to fall from under him. He heard the soft click of the door and a voice, Vecchi's voice: 'Pietro.'

The apostle released his hold, allowing the air to flood back into Elias's lungs.

The monsignor closed the door and stepped into the centre of the room, meeting the gaze of the apostle who rose to his feet.

'Salvatore.'

'So, the prodigal apostle returns.'

They looked at each other, appraising one another as one would appraise a curious work of art, or an opponent on the field of battle.

'It has been a long time,' Vecchi said. He cast his eyes to each man in turn: Elias, Alfred, Pietro, and then to Alfred once more. 'I feel I should know you.'

'I can assure you, sir,' Alfred said meekly, 'we have never—'

'There is a familiarity about you.' Vecchi turned to Pietro. 'He puts me in mind of the angel you spoke of when we were children.'

The apostle smiled thinly and nodded. 'Yes, there is a resemblance, now that you mention it.'

Vecchi approached the Horseman, who pressed himself against the wall until the wooden panelling cracked.

'The suit, the hat, the white beard.' He reached forward and touched the Horseman's trembling jaw. 'He is your angel. The one you saw on the day we were taken from the orphanage.'

Again, Pietro nodded. 'Yes, it is he.'

'Vecchi, you fool!' Elias hissed through his teeth. 'Run! Get help!' The apostle clamped a hand firmly over his mouth, and to Elias's dismay, Vecchi did something that was not altogether unexpected: the monsignor stood motionless, pondering his best course of action.

'He is as you described him,' Vecchi said. 'Every whisker, every line. So it is true? Everything we believe is real?'

Alfred cleared his throat and squeaked, 'To be accurate, I am not an angel. I am a Horseman. A Horseman of the Apocalypse.'

Vecchi smiled and made a show of peering around the room. 'You appear to be missing your—'

'Metaphor,' Alfred said, drily. 'I am missing my metaphor.'

'Salvatore, we are on a mission of great importance,' Pietro said. 'If we fail then it could mean the end of everything we hold precious.'

The monsignor nodded sympathetically and asked what was the nature of this 'mission'.

'We seek the devil himself,' Pietro replied.

'The devil, you say.' Vecchi scratched the bridge of his nose and asked for the tale to continue, but when Pietro opened his mouth to speak, he raised his hand. 'Not you,' he said then pointed at Alfred. 'Him.'

Alfred swallowed and stepped away from the shallow impression he'd made in the wall. 'I am not much of a storyteller, I'm afraid.'

'But this is not a story,' Vecchi replied with a crooked smile. 'It is the truth, is it not?'

And so, Alfred Warr recounted the events that led to Leonard Bliss's flight, the toll his absence was taking on the realm of mortals and the order from the One Above All to return him to the Afterlife, no matter what the cost. And while Alfred stammered through the tale, Elias wrestled with the realisation that he was a two-thousand-year-old soul, cursed for all time. 'Dear Christ, yes,' Elias said, and slowly opened his eyes. 'I am cursed.'

'In a manner of speaking, I suppose,' Alfred replied.

'For all eternity.'

'That is perhaps going a little far.'

'It is of no consequence,' Vecchi said. He glanced to each man and immortal in turn, waiting for them to join his train of thought.

It was Elias who eventually spoke for them by simply shrugging his shoulders.

Vecchi rolled his eyes and raised his hands to the ceiling. 'Am I always to be surrounded by fools?'

'Have a care, Salvatore,' Pietro growled. 'You address the Holy Father.'

'He is not the Pope,' Vecchi said, 'not yet at least.'

'I will never be Pope,' Elias said. 'How could one such as I ever be the conscience of millions?'

'You should pay more attention to history, Your Eminence.' Vecchi reached into his robes and retrieved his mobile phone. 'We have elected far worse.'

'Then you believe us,' Pietro said, watching the monsignor's finger waver over the *zero* key.

If he summons the Swiss Guard, Elias thought, then all is lost.

Vecchi smiled again, little more than a slight tightening of the skin around his mouth. 'Your tale is far-fetched to the point of ridiculous. You are lying, clearly: that is what my head tells me. You are either attempting some deception, the reason for which I cannot fathom, or you are under the influence of a most potent hallucinogen. And yet there is something of your tale that I find . . . compelling.' He approached Alfred, standing so close that their noses almost touched.

Alfred drew in his breath and held it there.

'Then there is you,' the monsignor said, quietly, thoughtfully. 'The man of his dreams.' He turned to Pietro. 'You will both remain in custody, apostle, until I am satisfied you are not involved in some conspiracy against the Holy Church.'

'No,' Elias said. 'They must be allowed to continue their journey, and I must go with them.'

Vecchi looked at him, his eyebrows raised. 'Really?'

'If I am to redeem myself then I must accompany them, aid them in finding this . . . Leonard Bliss.'

Vecchi thought on this for a moment, then decided to laugh. 'You are to be Pope, Bishop Bjørstad! Pope! I'm afraid your days of stumbling around the world in search of "the truth" are at an end. Your truth is here, within these sacred walls.' He looked to his phone, and Pietro used the moment's distraction to mount his attack: a leap that swallowed the distance between the assassin and the monsignor in a storm of white robes. Elias did not believe he'd seen anyone move so fast in all his lifetimes, that is until he saw Vecchi's response. The monsignor reached out with his free hand and caught Pietro by the ankle, curtailing his momentum and sending the apostle spinning into the far wall. Vecchi snapped his phone shut, sniffed loudly and, to Elias's astonishment, launched himself into the air, spinning and turning as a dark cyclone to land before Pietro who was already on his feet. Alfred held onto his hat and threw himself under the desk as the two priests traded blows and kicks in a silent ballet of unarmed combat.

'You must stop this!' Elias cried, finding himself compelled to protect both men, though enamoured of neither. 'I am the Pope!' He looked desperately around the room for some artefact with which he could assert his authority: a mitre, or a sceptre. All he could find was a leather-bound Bible which he snatched from the table and shook at the priests who fought and deflected with diligence and concentration. 'I am the Pope!' he cried again. The two priests were lost to all but themselves: a blow struck, countered, then mirrored. But it was clear to Elias that Pietro was faltering, so he took the Bible firmly in both hands and landed it as hard as he could at the base of Vecchi's skull.

The monsignor swayed, rocking back and forth on his heels, then slowly turned to face him, massaging the back of his neck. 'Your Holiness,' he said. 'Why on Earth would you do that?'

Elias dropped the Bible to the floor as the voices from his past lives sneered and told him the blow was worthy of a child; a small child; a very small child; a very small child blighted by polio.

Vecchi reached for Elias's throat, and again Pietro used his distraction to mount his attack. He rolled to his feet, a single fluid motion which ended with his arms locked about the monsignor's head and throat. He dragged him down to the floor where they continued their struggle, though this time it was Pietro who held the advantage.

'Do not kill him!'

'I . . . was . . . not . . . planning to.' Pietro strengthened his hold, keeping his own head out of the way of Vecchi's flailing hands.

'You are throttling him!'

Pietro tensed himself still further, and with a final spasm, Vecchi's arms fell limply to his sides.

'He is merely unconscious.' Pietro pushed the monsignor away. He jumped to his feet, dusted down his cassock and straightened the prayer beads that hung about his waist. 'Had I wished to kill him then I would have simply broken his neck.'

'Or he would have broken yours.'

'I would have defeated him,' Pietro said firmly, 'eventually.' He tapped on the desk with his fingertips. 'The battle is over, Horseman. You can come out now.'

Elias ran his fingers across the monsignor's throat, searching for a pulse. When he was satisfied that Vecchi would indeed recover, he sat down next to him with his head in his hands. 'I have hurt . . . so many.'

'Then perhaps this quest *is* your chance to redeem yourself,' Pietro said, 'both of you.' He sighed. 'All of us.' He rapped his fist against the wood. 'Horseman, the Swiss Guard will be here at any moment. We must leave.'

'I am sorry,' Alfred said from beneath the table. 'I seem unable to move my legs.'

'Are you injured?' Pietro said impatiently.

'No, I am merely petrified.'

'I know now why I lost my faith,' Elias said. 'I am not worthy of it.' He looked to the apostle. 'Did you not hear me? I cannot be the . . . What are you doing, Pietro?'

The apostle had knelt beside Vecchi's form and was running his little finger across the monsignor's lips. 'It is a sleep agent, Your Holiness, nothing more. It will give us more time.' He looked to the table and bellowed, 'Horseman!'

'Do not shout at me! Shouting will not help!'

'Then tell me, Horseman; what will help?'

'That is enough, Pietro' Elias rose to his feet and took slow, measured steps to where Alfred hid, acutely aware of the evil that walked in his shadow.

Or perhaps it is I who walk in theirs, he thought. Perhaps I am the shadow, a mere essence of good indiscernible in a sea of malice and selfishness. And he was so overwhelmed by these thoughts that he was trembling when he knelt on the floor and looked beneath the table.

Alfred sat with his knees drawn beneath his chin, rocking himself gently.

'Alfred, listen to me.'

The Horseman hid his face and whimpered softly.

'We will take this journey, Alfred, and we will take it together. The three of us will find this Leonard Bliss and the three of us will find redemption. But we must go together and we must go now.'

'Hurry, Your Holiness,' said Pietro.

'If you will not do this for yourself, Alfred, then please do it for Pietro and me. This is our chance to make amends for sins our past.'

'The Swiss Guard, I hear them,' Pietro said. 'If he will not come then we must—'

'Do not deny me redemption, Alfred,' Elias roared. 'Take my hand, damn you!'

The Book Of Leonard

The Preacher
and the
Thief: 1:7

AND SO IT WAS.

On the day Pontius Pilate washed his hands of him, and his people turned their backs to him, the Romans and conspirators came as one for the self-proclaimed King of the Chosen.

He was stripped and beaten through the streets of Jerusalem.

He was adorned with a circle of thorns.

He was taken to the Hills of Calvary.

He was tied and nailed to a cross of pine and hoisted high in the company of thieves.

He was spat upon and tormented, and when the crowds and the soldiers grew weary of their sport, he was left to die.

Only the whore remained, weeping. And the thieves: one embittered, the other repentant.

With the setting of the sun, the repentant did confess his sins and begged the preacher for forgiveness; it was granted, freely, and so the thief passed from this world, cleansed.

But the second thief did spit upon the prophet. He scorned him, and named him a false god.

'Where are your disciples now, oh King of Kings?' he said. 'In your final moments you have none to attend you. None save the whore from Galilee.'

The prophet closed his eyes and asked why he had been forsaken so.

'You speak to the air,' the thief said. 'If you were truly the son of God, then why does He not save you? Why does He not smite your enemies, make whores of their wives and slaves of their children? Why do you not simply climb down from your cross and walk away?'

And the prophet replied, 'Because he loves you. He loves you and would sacrifice his only son so you may find the path to salvation.'

'I have no need of salvation, preacher. We are born to sin. We are made to prey upon the weak. You and I will both die here this night, and beyond that there is nothing. I have lived my life free. I have taken whatever I desired: sustenance, clothes, money, lives.' The thief smiled at the prophet. 'I have taken your whore, preacher. She who weeps at your feet. I have taken her, as has most of Jerusalem. So you see, none of us are worthy of your divine redemption, and I am glad of it.'

The preacher was silent though his tears fell upon the whore weeping below. And where his tears struck and ran the length of her hair, strands of darkness changed to the most glorious white.

'No man is above redemption,' the preacher cried. 'And on this day, I will prove this to you.'

The thief laughed. 'And how do you seek to perform such a miracle, preacher?'

'You will die here, thief.'

'I know this.'

'You will die here, but you will not enter the Kingdom of my Father. You will be reborn, again and again, until the vileness has been cleansed from your soul.'

The thief began to laugh.

'You will roam this Earth, cursed and tormented by your past lives until you are deemed worthy of our forgiveness.'

The thief began to choke.

'You will know no peace, until you bring light to the world you despise.'

The thief exhaled and passed into the darkness.

~~And the preacher did look down from his cross. 'Go, harlot,' he said, 'for I will have no more of you.'~~

Sir, what happened in the New Testament should stay in the New Testament. There's nothing to be gained by rehashing this.

Sincerely,

M.C.

FOURTEEN

'YOU WILL TAKE THEM,' Pietro said.

Alfred looked into Pietro's outstretched hand. 'I have no need of such things.'

'You will take them all the same.'

'I will not.'

'Do not make me hurt you, Horseman.'

'You think that such as you could hurt such as I?'

'Shall we find out?'

Alfred looked at him and smiled. 'It was but a few days ago that you held me in the highest regard, Pietro. You believed me to be an angel.'

Pietro snorted and turned away from him. He walked to a pile of sweaters, picked out the two darkest and pushed them into a bag. 'You should find a change of clothes, Horseman,' he said. 'Do not think Vecchi will stop looking for us simply because we have left the Holy City.'

'I have no need to steal,' Alfred said, admiring a coat in the finest white cashmere. 'I will only be perceived by those whom I wish to see me.'

'Hmph,' said Pietro. 'And yet I was able to perceive you when I was but a child. You are not as infallible as you perhaps think.' The assassin looked to the rear of the store, where Elias was trying a pair of ill-fitting jeans and a denim shirt. 'No, Your Holiness,' he called.

Elias sighed, nodded and took off the shirt.

'Your thinking only stretches as far as your next kill, Pietro,' Alfred said. 'You must try to expand it across decades. If you had not seen Daphne and I on that day then you would not have known to accompany me on *this* day.'

Again, the assassin snorted, which Alfred took as a sign of concession, though perhaps not quite. 'In my world, time is a series of short red bursts,' the assassin said. He glanced at his watch, then through the empty pane of the storefront window. 'I suppose being immortal means that time is nothing to you.'

'It does not work that way, I'm afraid,' Alfred said. 'And I am surprised you would still think such a thing, considering how far I have diminished in your eyes.'

Pietro dropped the bag at his feet. 'All my life, I believed that you were an angel,' he said, 'and then I see you hide beneath furniture like a frightened child. Yes, Horseman, you have fallen far short of my expectations and that concerns me.' He looked over to Elias, who was trying on a Vatican baseball cap. 'It concerns me because we are being hunted by Salvatore Vecchi, one of the most formidable assassins the House of St Fiacre has ever produced,' he paused, thought for a moment and then added, 'Next to myself.'

'And you think that the two of us may not be enough to thwart him.'

'Oh, I will be enough, but should I fall before the final outcome then I wonder if you are capable, or even willing, to protect the life of the Holy Father with your own.'

Alfred thrust out his chin. 'I will do what must be done to see this mission through.'

'And I should trust the words of a man who hides beneath tables?'

'You think that I hide because I fear for my own life?'

'If not, then why?'

'Because after thousands of years watching men like you slaughter one another, I have grown tired of the tang of your blood in my mouth, the stench of your discharging bowels. I am, quite simply, sick of wading through your mud-stained entrails.'

They stared at each, without blinking.

'Make no mistake, assassin,' Alfred said, 'I do not fear for myself.'

Slowly, Pietro began to nod. He smiled, then took Alfred's hand. 'Then you will take these.' He placed a small pistol, a throwing knife and a silver metal cylinder – the size of a penlight – in Alfred's palm. 'If I am lost, then the life of the supreme pontiff rests with you.'

Alfred held up the cylinder and asked Pietro why would he need it. 'I see perfectly well on the darkest of nights,' he said.

'It is not a penlight, Horseman,' Pietro replied. 'It is a concussion grenade.'

Alfred almost dropped it.

'It should be effective against six clustered targets.' Pietro began to walk away before Alfred could protest, then he stopped and added, 'You will need to throw it.'

'I have seen grenades used before,' Alfred said.

'Good, good.' Pietro nodded but did not seem convinced. 'Do not use it anywhere within range of his Holiness.'

'I will not.'

'Remember that if your targets are apostles then they will also be carrying similar grenades. The effect will be devastating.'

'I will remember that.'

'And when you throw it, make sure that you—'

'As I have said not a moment ago, I am familiar with every grenade you could possibly imagine and many you could not.'

'And yet,' Pietro said, 'you thought it was a penlight.'

Elias returned carrying a holdall and dressed in a pair of large, comfortable jeans, a white T-shirt and a brown leather jacket. On his feet he wore a pair of brown moccasin shoes. He'd also kept the Vatican baseball cap, which drew Pietro's attention almost immediately. 'You cannot wear that, Your Holiness.'

Elias pulled it low over his eyes and smiled. 'Call it hiding in plain sight,' he said.

Pietro rolled his eyes. 'We have tarried far too long. I must arrange transport to the airport—'

'You mean steal a car,' Elias said.

'And then arrange passage across the Atlantic.'

Alfred sighed. 'Another plane hijacking?'

'If you either of you can think of any other way to transport a wanted assassin, a suspected terrorist and a pope across the ocean without attracting the attention of the authorities,' Pietro said, 'then I will hear your suggestion.'

'We should leave something.' Elias patted down the jacket as though he had a wallet to search for. 'We cannot simply take clothes from a store and leave without some kind of recompense.'

'I fear we have little choice,' Alfred said.

'No, I have so much to answer for. I will not add another count of petty thievery to my list of crimes.'

'In the light of your other crimes, 'Alfred said helpfully, 'I believe petty thievery will make little difference.'

'Nevertheless, I must find a way to—'

Pietro stepped forward and dropped a pile of notes on the counter. 'I believe that should more than cover the cost of the broken window and the damaged alarm, with enough left for the clothes we have taken. Now, can we leave?'

Elias and Alfred looked at each other, then obediently followed. They stepped gingerly through the broken glass and made haste towards a nearby car park. Alfred quickened his pace to draw level with Pietro.

'Where did you get the money?' he hissed.

'I found it,' Pietro whispered back, 'in one of the cash boxes.'

Alfred said nothing, though he nodded with resentment and admiration.

FIFTEEN

AS HE OFTEN DID of late, Monsignor Vecchi awoke with a start. Almost immediately, he was aware of the pain that lanced his thorax whenever he took a breath, less so the thundering inside his skull, more so the circle of grey, dry faces staring at him from above.

'You're a fool, Vecchi,' Cardinal Rossi said, 'a damned fool.'

Vecchi thought it best to say nothing, confess nothing, until he had gathered himself. Greater and wiser men had fallen into the abyss through a poorly chosen word spoken at an unfortunate moment.

The room was small and dark with a high ceiling upon which were painted replicas of the Basilica frescos. At first, the smell of candles and incense told him he was lying on a bed inside one of the many small churches within the City walls. But there was something else: the smell of ether and, looking beyond the dark marble arches to the open corridor, an unusually dense population of nuns.

The Vatican Hospital. Vecchi pulled himself upright and looked to his wrist; his watch was missing, replaced by a white plastic wristband that carried his name and blood type.

'The supreme pontiff, Vecchi.' Giordano closed the door, framing the question in much the same way as he might inquire to the whereabouts of a missing sock: 'Where is he?'

'How long have I—'

'We found you in the private study of His Holiness, alone,' Martinez said. 'I have lost a great many things in my time, Monsignor Vecchi: gloves; important personal documents; my favourite cassock. On a number of occasions Monsignor, I have even lost my faith, but even at my most absent-minded I have never misplaced a supreme pontiff.'

As its cardinals came and died with clockwork regularity, so the personality of the Curia changed as often as the seasons. The incarnation standing over him was, Vecchi believed, the most sarcastic he'd ever known. He ran his tongue across his lips; they were dry, naturally, but also carried a faint metallic taste that made the end of his tongue burn. The taste was new to him, but he suspected it was serpentine, a rare snake venom laced with a natural masking agent. It was the seminary's finest poison and in the correct dose would have induced a fatal heart seizure.

All the apostles were serpentine adepts, so his continuing ability to draw breath was no oversight; Lantosca had spared him. Perhaps it is the influence of this . . . Alfred Warr, Vecchi thought. Perhaps he clings to the remains of his innocence as a child clings to its most prized marionette. The monsignor swore that when they met again, he would make no such a mistake. He threw back the covers, swung himself clear of the bed and onto his feet. His legs almost gave way beneath him while his nakedness drew a collective gasp of horror from the gathered cardinals.

Möller cried out: 'Vecchi, have you forgotten yourself, man?'

'You say I have been here for two days?' He tied a robe about himself, and wondered if it was the effects of the serpentine that made his head throb. It was not a symptom he remembered reading about.

'The Pope,' Rossi said. 'Where is he?'

'Where have you looked?'

The Curia looked at each other, unsure if his impertinence should be admonished or ignored, and in their indecision, Vecchi saw something quite rare: their grey faces, usually rendered immobile by age and excess, had contorted into masks of translucent anxiety. Möller himself looked as though he had finally had enough. His lungs produced a hollow whining sound with every breath, yet he seemed unwilling to make use of his oxygen. Perhaps they have succumbed, he thought, to the malady that has afflicted the rest of the planet. But as far as he knew, this . . . Disease . . . entwined itself, like bindweed, throughout the sufferer's conscience, and no one in this room possessed one. So the question remained: why were they all so afraid? He asked what had transpired while he slumbered.

'Take a look for yourself,' Möller wheezed. He nodded weakly towards the window on the other side of the room.

Vecchi drew in his robe and strode unevenly across the floor, finding its chequered pattern difficult to cope with. The thundering inside his head grew louder as the window approached, and it was only when he was standing in front of it that he realised the sound wasn't coming from within him; it came from outside: outside the room, outside the hospital.

'What in God's name . . . ?'

The Curia stood, as ever, behind him, looking over his shoulder.

'It started yesterday,' Giordano said. He peered through the window, shielding his eyes from the pulsing lights.

'There must be twenty thousand of them.'

'At least.'

Vecchi was certain that if the window was open he would suffer a nosebleed. The rhythm pounded against his eardrums with the force and rapidity of a machine gun. And the lights, thousands of them; strobes casting hypnotic bursts of motion across the seething crowds; search lights probing the skies above the Basilica; lights of all colour that rolled and spun in maddening patterns across the mass of humanity that heaved and swelled in the square below. *His square.* Vecchi set his teeth and forgot himself. 'What the hell is going on?'

'I believe,' said Rossi, and he appeared none too sure of himself, ' it is called "a rave".'

'A what?'

'A rave. It's very much like a party, but with more people, more dancing and a substantially larger quantity of drugs.' Rossi's eyes had glazed over.

'I believe the English invented it,' Möller said.

Vecchi snorted. He did not see it as 'invented' as much as 'spawned' and, at times such as this, he understood why no englishman had worn the papal crown since the twelfth century. 'Why would they conceive of such a thing?'

The cardinals shrugged. This was where their expertise in the matter ended.

'It is just a dance party,' said Rossi, his eyes pulsing, 'with music.' Vecchi could hear the cardinal's foot tapping.

'I'm told they're usually the best kind.' The monsignor looked at him closely; his expression had slipped from fear to beatific; the malady had found him.

'These are the same people who were standing in devotion, waiting for us to elect a new pontiff,' Martinez said. At least he still looked confused, fearful, which Vecchi found reassuring. 'And now look at them. Dancing and fornicating like pagans beneath the resting place of St Peter.'

The monsignor put his nose against the glass and peered down into the crowd. Yes, many did appear to be engaged in acts of disgraceful lewdness; it was impossible to see where one body ended and another began.

Atop the colonnades to the south, a makeshift soundstage had been erected. Along with the musical instruments and turntables, the stage was equipped with the largest public address speakers Vecchi had ever seen. Thousands danced, copulated, or worshipped at the feet of the robed figure operating the turntables. The old man pumped his fist in the air in sync with what Vecchi could barely describe as music, while his other hand stayed clasped firmly over his left earpiece.

Vecchi looked closely at the old man. The light was poor and the distance a challenge, but the monsignor was blessed with the acuity of a sniper. 'Isn't that Cardinal deFlores?'

Rossi approached the window and looked out towards the soundstage. 'Yes,' he said. 'Yes, I believe it is.'

'He is usually so meticulous when it comes to attending the morning choir service,' Giordano said. 'We wondered what had happened to him.' He sighed deeply and closed his eyes, and when he opened them again, Vecchi noticed that they no longer seemed to reflect the light. 'The media is calling it "The Age of Enlightenment",' he said, sadly. 'A new era of peace, tolerance and hedonism.'

No, thought Vecchi, hedonism will never do. Peace without the guiding hand of the Church was unthinkable. Without the Church, this new age of tolerance would not be . . . tolerated. 'Is it . . . everywhere?'

Möller nodded; he seemed unable to speak so Martinez spoke for him: 'It began in the Middle East, found its way to the European states before oozing its way across the ocean, to the Americas.'

'What? What "found its way"? What "oozed"?'

'The Rapture,' Rossi said, his thin, wrinkled neck pulling his head back and thrusting it forth, trying to keep time to the music. 'It is the Rapture, praise be.'

The other cardinals looked at him; Möller shook his head.

'The Church of England is closing its doors,' said Martinez. 'They no longer have enough staff to maintain operations.'

The news saddened Vecchi more than he would have expected. He'd held something akin to warmth for the Church of England: a muted love that one might feel for a mentally deficient cousin. 'People are finding God,' he murmured, 'within themselves.' He turned away from the glass and realised that the Curia had heard him.

'Yes, yes, they are,' Giordano said.

'Yes! Yes!' Rossi sang, then clamped both hands over his mouth, his eyes wide. 'I . . . beg your forgiveness. I keep doing this; I seem unable to help myself.'

Vecchi returned to his bed and sat down, gripping the pressed sheets in both hands. 'We are all but done.'

The music, if one could call it that, came to an abrupt end, punctuated with a round of fireworks that filled the ward with a bright green light. Vecchi realised he'd been listening to the same drum rhythm since his awakening twenty minutes ago. His brain was numbed; his ears were bored and offended.

'My learned colleagues,' Giordano announced. 'If I may beg your indulgence, I would speak to the monsignor alone.'

Möller, Rossi, and Martinez looked at Giordano with ill-disguised suspicion. Giordano himself stood with his chin held high, clearly not feeling the need to explain himself any further. He was the Cardinal Secretary of State, after all.

'Again, forgive me, Cardinal Giordano,' Rossi ventured reproachfully, 'but surely any business you have with the private secretary concerns all of us.'

'I will not ask again.' Giordano spoke calmly, quietly, without inflection or malice, and in response the other cardinals glanced at one another then decided, as one, to take their leave. They filed sombrely from the chamber, Cardinal Rossi pushing Möller's wheelchair.

The doors swung shut behind them and Vecchi found himself regarding Giordano in an entirely new light, marvelling at how a man so small could cast such a commanding shadow.

'We are losing Cardinal Rossi,' Giordano said.

'It would appear so.'

'The others will follow.'

'Soon, I think.'

'And I will follow them.'

Vecchi said nothing.

The cardinal took a deep breath and turned to him. The light had returned to his eyes, but Vecchi suspected it would not be there for much longer. He would lose himself, become a godless hedonist like the poor wretches in the square below.

'What we did, Vecchi . . .'

'We should not speak of it, Your Eminence.'

'But we shall speak of it, monsignor!' The cardinal spat his words through clenched teeth. 'Because if what we did has wrought the end of the Holy Church—'

'Keep your voice down,' Vecchi replied sharply. 'None of this has anything to do with Gregory's death.'

'How can you say that? So soon after we end his life, the world is taken by this madness. We are assailed by our own consciences, compelled to confess ourselves. Do you not feel it? Do you not feel the weight of the sins you have committed throughout your life, Vecchi?'

'I feel it.' He did not.

'What we did was wrong!'

'What we did, we did for the good of the Church. We loved him, as we loved his predecessor, as we will love his successor. But his doctrine would have led the Holy See into a state of bankruptcy! We had no choice, Your Eminence. You must see that.'

Giordano closed his eyes and gripped his hands as though in prayer. 'I cannot go on like this. Our actions have unleashed an unspeakable evil upon the world.'

'No, Cardinal Giordano. You are wrong. This is not the presence of evil; it is its absence.'

The cardinal's eyes snapped open. 'You speak in riddles,' he said, 'and I will have no more of it.' And then his eyes thinned to white-hot fissures. It was an expression Vecchi had seen so many times and in so many ancient, threadbare faces. So many battles, he thought. So many sacrifices. He sighed; he should have known it would eventually come to this: every clergy for himself.

'This is your doing,' Giordano said quietly and without conviction or certainty, as though the monsignor's part in this had only just come to light.

He's writing the story of his escape, Vecchi thought, realising he was a but a minor character, an expendable, minor character.

'Yes, yes,' Giordano nodded to himself. 'It was you, Vecchi. You talked me into this. You said he would be the ruin of us!'

Silently, meekly, Vecchi's stunted conscience pressed him to confess.

'You poisoned me, Vecchi, as surely as you poisoned Gregory himself!' The cardinal thrust a trembling finger below Vecchi's chin. 'This is on you, Vecchi. All of this is on you!'

And though his conscience screamed, *No!* or perhaps because it had, Vecchi clamped his palm over the cardinal's mouth and, with his free hand, snapped the offending finger at the second joint. Giordano's eyes bulged, his face reddened and his scream burst silently against the palm of Vecchi's hand. He sank to his knees, as the monsignor released the finger and locked his hand about his throat.

'Forgive me, Your Eminence, but you left me little choice.'

Giordano screamed again, with more meaning this time; the end result was little more than a muffled squealing.

'I am going to allow you to speak now,' Vecchi said. 'If you scream, I will kill you. Please indicate if you understand.'

The cardinal nodded, then again, more vigorously, in case Vecchi had missed it. Slowly, Vecchi moved his hand away, keeping a grip on his throat.

Giordano appeared more furious than in pain. 'You broke my . . . I will see you imprisoned for the rest of your miserable existence!'

'I need you to listen, Your Eminence, preferably without speaking.'

'I have listened to enough from you to last me a lifetime, you maniac!'

'I have a plan,' Vecchi said.

'Another one? Hah! And who shall we dispatch this time? The President of the United States, perhaps?'

'I know what is behind the Rapture.'

Hearing his words, Giordano seemed to calm down. 'I do not believe you,' he said, though Vecchi could see that he wanted to. His eyes, drained as they were, almost pleaded with him: *Convince me, and I will follow you. Anything is better than this.* But what could he say? That angels walked the Earth? That everything they'd read, everything they'd been taught, was actually true? That Satan was real and feeling a little hard done by?

Vecchi remembered he'd once shared an evening meal with Pope Gregory XVII, not so long ago, before his doctrine of piety had taken the Church to the brink of ruin. Vecchi had tried to explain to him why the world was no longer the place for total religious devotion. The Pope had smiled and asked him what would be, in his opinion, the worst crisis the Church could face.

'Bankruptcy,' Vecchi had replied without waiting a heartbeat.

'Try again,' the Pope had said, spooning a layer of caviar onto a small white wafer.

Vecchi thought, long and hard, and said, 'Irrefutable proof that God does not exist.' Then he'd sat back, satisfied at having achieved checkmate so early in the conversation.

The Pope had laughed and shook his head again. 'No, Vecchi,' he'd said. 'What would destroy us is irrefutable proof that he *does* exist.'

Yes, Your Holiness, he thought. *I see it now.* He released Giordano and sat on the floor in front of him, folding his legs inward as though preparing to meditate. 'You must trust me, just once more.'

Giordano looked at him wretchedly, and then towards the door at the far end of the room.

He is thinking of running, Vecchi thought, out into the Square of St Peters, to confess his sins to that heathen mass.

But instead, the Cardinal said, 'What is your plan, Vecchi?'

The monsignor was astonished. 'Then you are with me?'

'Of course not, but if I do as my conscience demands then I am ruined, and so is the Church.' He managed a weak, unconvincing smile. 'And I am not so far gone that I will bring about my own downfall.' He closed his eyes and ground his teeth, no doubt to see off an offensive from inside his own head. When he opened his eyes a moment later, he added, 'For now.'

Vecchi rose to his feet. 'Give me three days.'

'You have two,' the cardinal said. He struggled up from his knees, grimacing from the pain in his hand. He examined his crooked, discoloured finger then shot Vecchi a sour look. 'Do not fail,' he added and then stood to take his leave.

Vecchi waited until he was near the door before calling out: 'Do you not wish to know what I plan to do?'

'I may succumb to your Rapture at any moment,' the Cardinal replied. 'The less I know, the better. If you succeed, then all will be well. If you fail then I don't imagine there will be any of us here to ensure you pay for it.' He stopped for a moment and then turned to face him. 'Again, does your own conscience not trouble you, Vecchi?'

Thinking that there was nothing to be gained by lying, Vecchi said that it did not. 'I suspect my prior vocation provides me with the mental discipline to resist its influence.'

If Giordano was cut by his remark, he chose not to show it. 'Well, that is good for you,' he said, then opened the door. 'Perhaps then, one day, you will be supreme pontiff after all.'

'I do not seek high office,' Vecchi recited automatically, 'I merely seek to serve the Church to the best—'

'Oh, spare me, Vecchi,' the cardinal said. 'I suspect neither of us has the time.'

The door clicked shut, and Vecchi found himself alone, assaulted by the cacophony emanating from the square below. The plan that he spoke of with such bravado was, at best, half-formed: a whispering, taunting conception that grew thorns when touched. And still, in the space of his own mind, he toyed with it.

For here were gods. Gods who stood no taller than men. Gods who hid beneath tables when faced with the merest human altercation. Yes, he thought. Here were gods. Weak gods.

Vulnerable gods.

The idea hardened, became transparent, glazed within the fires of its own ambition. His conscience cried, *No!* and so Vecchi closed his eyes, reached into his mind and thrashed it into silence.

He opened his eyes, took a deep breath, then donned his clothes and hurried from his hospital ward, down the marble staircases and out into St Peter's Square. The Swiss Guard was already in the process of erecting barricades beneath each of the arches. It will do no good, Vecchi thought, now the madness has found its home within our sacred walls. The Guard, as disciplined as it was, would fall to this Rapture and all would be lost.

And the heathen would storm the Vatican.

He fought his way through the crowd towards the Basilica, feeling as though the world were a fist closing tightly around him. The mass of naked flesh pressed against him. The sight of thousands, dancing and . . . mating, filled him with revulsion as the stench of human uncleanliness filled his nostrils. A hand grasped his sash and a young woman with flaming red hair and wild dark eyes used him as an anchor to claw her way from the mass. Vecchi tensed his legs, rooting himself to the stones, and took hold of her arm.

'Bless me father,' she cried. A score of powerful arms reached out and scratched at her, tearing crimson lines into her flesh, fighting to possess her.

Vecchi held her arm tightly and tried to pull her free. 'Stay with me, child,' he cried. 'I have you!' Her skin was slick with oil and sweat. His feet began to move, sliding across the stones. Closer to her now, Vecchi could feel her breath upon his face, her hold upon his tarnished soul. She caressed his cheek, pulling him by his collar towards her until her lips pressed against his ear.

'Bless me, father,' she whispered, and then smiled softly. The smile was welcoming, seductive. 'Bless me, father,' she said again, 'for I have sinned.' Her smile changed; her lips pulled back from her teeth into a snarl that was feral in both aspect and nature. Her free hand stiffened to a claw and swept down towards his eyes. Vecchi recoiled, bringing the heel of his hand down on her wrist. He heard it break, he swore to the Almighty that he'd heard it break, yet she laughed and released his collar. She began to slide away from him, melting back into the body of tangled naked flesh that divided and joined before his eyes. Then she was gone, and for the first time since his childhood, Salvatore Vecchi was unsure of himself: unsure of his power, his hold on the world around him. He had shrunk to nothing. He turned and he ran, not looking back until he had reached the sanctuary of the St Peter's.

A single fearful guardsman allowed him into the Basilica without challenging him for identification. On any other day, Vecchi would have taken the time to admonish him, perhaps see him demoted or thrown out of the Swiss Guard altogether. On any other day, he would not come to this accursed place. He found himself alone inside the most holy of churches, his heart pounding, his footfalls sounding out from the walls and the dome a hundred feet above him. He walked quickly to the papal altar, taking a moment to stand beneath the baldacchino and make the sign of the cross before reaching beneath the cloth and turning a large golden cantilever. A section of the floor rumbled aside to reveal a stone staircase that descended into the darkness. Vecchi took a breath and held it before making his way down into the caverns. Holding his breath in the tunnels was an affectation he'd carried with him since childhood; and since those early days, Vecchi had told himself that he did so to increase his tolerance for working underwater, or where the air was tainted. The true reason was far simpler: he disliked breathing the same air as the dead.

Far below the resting places of the saints, he sought out the second mechanism, a handle of bronze which rolled the section of the floor back into place some fifty feet above. The tomb closed over him, depriving him of light. He made his way along the dark passageway, running his hands along the damp walls to guide him. It was said that many a young advocate had become lost in these tunnels, succumbing to exhaustion and despair.

He only allowed himself to breathe when he reached a small wooden door, barely taller than himself. The door was made from ancient cedar wood and was shielded by inch-long metal spikes set into its panelling. The uppermost panel had been replaced with a small metal grille through which Vecchi could see a flickering light. The monsignor knocked once and almost immediately, a drawn, ashen face appeared from behind the grille. A pair of dark, wet eyes peered at him, and the face split into a smile that put the monsignor very much in mind of a grinning skull.

'Brother Vecchi,' the skull said. 'What brings you to the House of St Fiacre?'

† † †

The tunnel widened as it deepened. The moss-laden walls were slick with moisture, and the air carried a cloying humidity that made it hard to breathe. Vecchi followed his guide at striking distance, a childhood habit fostered within these very walls.

'The concealment tunnels have fallen into disrepair,' his guide said by way of an apology. 'It is has been years since we have seen their use. Why did you not use the chapel's main entrance?'

'I did not wish to be seen,' Vecchi said, *as you damn well know.*

'Of course, of course,' the guide said. He stopped at a narrow fork in the tunnels and tapped his lower lip before proceeding to the left. 'It is an odd superstition amongst outsiders,' he said. 'It is as if you believe entering the house of St. Fiacre will bestow some great misfortune upon you.'

'It is matter of reputation,' Vecchi said 'If the Inquisition chooses to name its seminary after the Patron Saint of Sexually-Transmitted Diseases then it should not expect visitors.' He was sure the guide had steered the conversation thus in order to taunt him.

The guide turned and smiled at Vecchi, holding the burning torch closer to the monsignor so he could examine his face. 'Your skin is strange,' he said. 'I do not remember it as so.'

'I do not remember you at all.'

The smile dropped, replaced by a discourteous snort. He aimed the torch ahead and once again they were on their way, travelling ever deeper below the foundations of St Peter's.

The air turned grey and Vecchi could smell the tang of sweat in the tunnels, accompanied by the grunts and cries of close-quarter combat.

'He is training the new initiates,' the guide said as they approached a heavy steel door at the end of the tunnel. 'Since the loss of so many apostles we find ourselves in need of fresh blood that must be trained quickly, and with so few of us to train them . . .' He turned the wheel at the centre of the door and pulled on it with all his might. 'Perhaps if you would return to us more often, Brother Vecchi,' he said, his voice strained by his labour, 'it would go some way to relieve us of this burden.' He straightened and caught sight of Vecchi's soured expression. 'Or perhaps not.'

The monsignor stepped past him, sorely tempted to break his neck.

'You know where the amphitheatre is,' the guide said. He pushed the door back into place.

Vecchi continued to walk towards the sound of combat, his eyes slowly becoming accustomed to the poor light. The lack of illumination was not neglect; it was deliberate, designed to foster greater awareness of the dark, and it was in the darkness that the apostles most often found themselves applying their ministrations. It was fortuitous that the lack of natural light led to the ghostly appearance of the apostles, a shared disposition that had wrought many a myth across the centuries. Myths which had served them well.

However, the environment had triggered a rare ailment in a young Salvatore Vecchi, leaving his skin a patchwork of varying shades that made it impossible for him to answer his apostolic calling. An assassin with such an unusual skin condition would be easily identified on leaving a place of an excommunication.

Vecchi arrived at the entrance to the amphitheatre and found that it was perhaps smaller than he remembered; as a child he came to believe that the cold grey walls that swept upward and closed above him were perhaps a darker incarnation of the sky; the same sky he and Pietro dreamed beneath on those hot summer days at the orphanage. The theatre was vast enough to encircle forty young initiates, who trained viciously in armed and unarmed combat under the close tutelage of four apostles. The initiates moved with a flowing grace, broken by lightning strikes and feints using sword, staff and fists, all within a sawdust circle that had borne witness to gladiatorial tournaments predating the Holy Church. Bishop Andrew himself was surrounded by eight of the young priests, who stood with quarterstaffs pointing towards him.

Andrew caught Vecchi's eye and returned his solemn countenance with an impish grin. With three sweeping arcs of his quarterstaff he dispatched the initiates with a series of blows and strikes that, within the space of a second, left them bleeding silently in the sawdust. And a second later, the initiates, and not one of them was above thirteen years, had sprung to their feet, holding their fighting staffs at arms. The bishop, panting, nodded approvingly. He bowed, and they returned the gesture without taking their eyes from him. So young and so wise, Vecchi thought. During a similar training match many years ago, he'd looked to the ground as he bowed; the subsequent blow to his skull had rendered him senseless for the rest of the day.

Bishop Andrew walked from the training circle, taking a light cotton tunic from the weapons rack and sliding it over a muscular torso of chalk-white skin that was pocked with bullet holes and knife scars. He approached, and Vecchi felt his own muscles tense. Less than ten feet away, Andrew stopped and turned back to his trainees who had not moved. 'My back was turned,' the old man said. 'I am displeased that you did not take the opportunity to attack.'

The trainees looked blankly at each other, and Vecchi smiled to himself. They could, he thought. *They simply knew better.*

Andrew approached him, shaking his head. 'They lack spirit,' he said, before he was out of the trainees' earshot. 'You and Pietro would have mounted a joint attack.'

'And we would have been defeated,' Vecchi said. 'If they lack spirit then perhaps it has been merely replaced by greater wisdom.' He held out his hand, but the Bishop ignored it, choosing instead to embrace him warmly.

'It is good to see you, my son.'

'And you,' Vecchi replied crisply, trying to hide his discomfort.

'We shall retire to my office.' Andrew gestured for Vecchi to lead on, but the monsignor himself knew better; Bishop Andrew was known for his rather brutal sense of humour. The old man grinned. 'Then you shall follow me.'

His office, a short walk from the amphitheatre, was unsurprisingly modest, especially when Vecchi compared it to his own private study. He had often found himself here as a child, and now it seemed much more dank and claustrophobic. It was slightly better lit than the rest of the chapel, which allowed an old man with failing eyesight to continue dealing with the mountainous paperwork generated by an order of religious assassins.

The office, of course, had no windows, so Vecchi forced himself into a small seat closest to the door. Andrew sat behind a desk and proceeded to arrange papers into large leather folders with broken seals. Every so often, he stopped and smacked the side of his head with the heel of his hand. Vecchi watched and waited.

Once the old man had finished, he leaned forward and clasped his hands on the desk in front of him. 'Now,' he said, his left eye twitching uncontrollably. 'How can I be of assistance to the private secretary to the Vicar of Christ?'

Whenever Vecchi heard those words, he suspected he was being mocked. 'I have need of all the apostles you can spare for a mission of great importance.'

'More apostles?' Andrew said wearily. He smacked the side of his head. 'I cannot spare them.'

Vecchi watched him with a raised eyebrow. 'I understand that circumstances have left our numbers greatly reduced, but you must—'

The bishop slapped his own face and shouted, 'Shut up! Shut up, damn you!' He leaned back in his seat, lost for breath.

'Your conscience bothers you,' Vecchi observed.

'For the past six days, and more intensely, it seems, since I cast eyes on you. I suspect it knows you are going to ask something of me that I should, in good conscience . . .' he chuckled to himself '. . . refuse.'

'Then perhaps it speaks to my conscience.'

Andrew produced a bottle of Spanish brandy from beneath his desk, along with two small glasses. He poured a measure into each and took an exaggerated sip from both before passing one to Vecchi. It was another custom amongst the apostles that Vecchi had to think on to remember. He nodded and tasted from his glass, satisfied it was not poisoned.

'You are quite the poisoner yourself,' Andrew said.

'When there is a need.' Vecchi brushed a mote of imaginary dust from his thigh. 'And speaking of need . . . the apostles I spoke of.'

'I cannot,' Andrew said, shaking his head. 'Until this epidemic of virtue is brought to an end I cannot risk sending another apostle beyond the safety of these walls.'

'If you give me the apostles then I will bring this to an end.'

'You will stop this madness?' The bishop asked, doubtfully. 'How?'

'Is it important how it is done?'

'When you ask me to risk my few remaining apostles then, yes, it is very important. Our numbers are few, Salvatore. Many have committed suicide or, like your friend Pietro, have abandoned their calling.'

'He is not my friend,' Vecchi said. 'I have not seen him since I left the seminary.' He wondered why that was important; or why he did not want to say he'd crossed paths with the lost apostle not two days before;

or how Bishop Andrew had recovered so quickly from a moment's weakness and now had him pressed into a corner. Vecchi twisted in his seat and cleared his throat. A means to explain this without sounding insane? There was none.

'The devil walks amongst us,' he said. 'He has taken human form and his presence here has led to this outbreak of virtue across the world.'

Andrew massaged his temples, sniffed loudly and after an excruciatingly long pause, told him to carry on.

'There is nothing more to tell. There is Satan and there is the plan: you give me four apostles, we find him in his human form and we kill him.'

After another silent breath no less painful than the first, the bishop had not burst into fits of laughter or alerted the Vatican Sanatorium that they had another priest in need of respite. Vecchi was unsure if this was a good sign or not. 'I understand that this sounds like nonsense—'

'Indeed it does.'

'But if you had seen what I have seen, a few short days ago.' He leaned closer and dropped his voice to a whisper. 'Do you remember that night when you took us from the orphanage?'

'To serve the Church,' Andrew reminded him, reminded himself, reminded his conscience.

'And do you remember Pietro claiming he had seen angels watching us from the gardens?'

'Indeed I do. It is a claim he stated time and time again, even under correction. Such a wilful child, unlike yourself.'

'It was no mere claim,' Vecchi said, allowing the barb to pass through him.

'Oh?'

'I have seen this "angel".'

'Oh.'

'He is as real as you and I and is exactly how Pietro spoke of him. And unless I am very much mistaken, he has not aged a day since our childhood.' He sat back and waited for the bishop's response. None seemed forthcoming. 'Well?'

'Salvatore, what do you expect me to say? Immortals? Gods? Is this what we have come to now?' He sighed. 'Do you know why you were allowed to leave the seminary without being excommunicated?'

And in honesty, Salvatore Vecchi had not asked himself this question. If an initiate was found unsuitable for service as an apostle then his choices were few: serve an apostle as his acolyte – or death. He had not suffered the humiliation of one or the finality of the other and had never thought to ask why.

'There has always been a third choice, Salvatore,' the bishop said. 'In the past, two of our number have left the seminary and lived to serve as supreme pontiff.'

For a moment, Vecchi thought his heart had stopped.

'We had hoped, we still hope, that you would be the third.' Andrew rose to his feet and walked around the table to tower above him. 'Our *business* is faith, Salvatore. It is not our place to believe, it is our place to enforce. If you choose to believe in mythical deities then I must ask myself if you really are the man to head the Holy Church.'

'I am!' Vecchi exclaimed. He could taste salt water in his mouth. Dear God, he thought, *I had no idea I desired it so much.* 'I am.' He repeated himself, more evenly this time. 'But if I am to lead the Church, then there must be a Church for me to lead.' He wanted to scream, to shout his joy to the world; if the House of St Fiacre believed that he should one day serve as the Bishop of Rome then nothing could prevent it. 'We are a faith, Bishop Andrew. If the people no longer require faith because the existence of an afterlife is a certainty, then what will become of us?' He stood, meeting the bishop eye to eye. 'Why do you think the apostles end themselves? Why do you think people now throw away their lives with such abandon? It is because they know. They know that there is a hereafter. And they seek to touch it, and they do not need us to do it.'

The bishop swallowed and returned to his seat. 'So you do believe.'

'Do you have another explanation for the madness?'

'No,' Andrew replied. 'No, I do not. But the very idea . . . God? Satan?'

'Give me the apostles.'

'Even if you find your Lucifer—'

'Give them to me and I will prove it you.'

'Even if you find your Satan,' Andrew raised his hand to keep him silent, 'how do you expect to destroy him? Is his power not that of a god?'

'Not while he travels the mortal plane. I have met another, like him: Pietro's angel, and I found him to be weak, vulnerable.'

'Salvatore—'

'Imagine, Your Excellency,' Vecchi said. He placed his fists upon the desk and spoke in his most reflective, most persuasive tone. 'Imagine the power, the respect the Holy Church would wield, for now and evermore, if we were to excommunicate *Satan*.'

He straightened and took a short step back, watching his words seep insidiously into the core of the warrior bishop.

'Kill . . . Satan?'

'Yes, Your Excellency. The eradication of evil, thanks to us. Thanks to the Church. The people would turn to us, once again.'

'Mm.' Andrew tugged thoughtfully at a wisp of hair above his ear. He clicked his tongue against the roof of his mouth and hummed to himself. 'I can spare three apostles.'

'I will require four.'

'You can have two.'

Fortuitously, Vecchi took heed of the bishop's expression before speaking again. 'That is not how you bargain.'

'It is how *I* bargain,' Andrew replied. 'Would you like to try for a single trainee advocate?'

Vecchi, angrily, shook his head. 'Two apostles will suffice. And one of the apostolic flights: the Learjet.'

And to his surprise, Andrew said 'Done,' without further discourse.

'I trust you still hold a suitable pilot's licence?'

Behind his thin, pale lips, Vecchi quietly ground his teeth, for now he was truly insulted.

SIXTEEN

NOT SINCE THE DAYS of Gettysburg had Magdelena witnessed such an influx. The gondolas rolled through the glass harbour in a conveyor: docking, dispatching and then casting off to join the other vessels travelling the celestial waterways between Earth and the Afterlife.

The dead queued a hundred rows deep, reaching back to the horizon.

Magdelena chewed thoughtfully at the end of her pen, crossed her legs and leaned to her left so as to get a better view through the glass partitioning of her harbour office. Below her, a thousand wraiths moved throughout the bewildered crowds, scratching down names and times of death. It had always been a unique source of wonder to Magdelena as to how few people knew the exact time of their passing, easily the most important event in a human's life.

'Are you even listening to me?'

She switched her attention back to the red-faced woman sitting in front of her. 'I do apologise,' she said, taking the pen from her mouth and placing it on the glass desk. 'As you can see, we are rather busy today and I should be helping my staff.'

'What about Percival?' the woman said.

Magdelena pushed a jar of sherbet sweets towards her and beckoned for her to take one. Sherbet, it seemed, had an immediate calming effect on new arrivals who were sometimes less than pleased at the timing of their demise. A few years ago, an eminent surgeon had sat in that very chair, berating her over his sudden arrival, as though it was in her power to reverse it. She'd waited for him to finish his tirade and then offered him a sherbet coin. He'd calmed after that, his demeanour much more conciliatory. He'd drowned in his swimming pool, he'd said, on his daughter's eighteenth birthday. They'd had guests . . .

Sherbet was the great leveller as far as Magdelena was concerned.

The woman sitting at the other side of the desk sniffed and dabbed her eyes with a pink satin handkerchief. Her makeup was an exercise in precision which had gone far beyond mere *application* and strayed perilously close to *architecture*. She wore an immaculate white suit: a padded jacket that narrowed impossibly at the waist and a matching A-line skirt, separated by a wide silver belt with a diamond buckle. She sat with her legs neatly crossed, making stroking motions with her hand over her lap as though someone had removed her pet and neglected to tell her.

Which, of course, they had.

'No thank you,' the woman said. 'This figure won't keep itself,' and she gave Magdelena an accusatory look, as though the Head of Purgatory was part of some otherworldly plot to make her fat.

Magdelena smiled, 'It doesn't actually matter now, you know.' She wished that humanity had blessed her with calves to carry off that skirt. 'You're beyond that.'

'No,' the woman said firmly, 'I am not beyond anything. There's been a mistake; I'm not supposed to be here. I want to find Percival.' Hearing herself say his name, the woman looked sorrowfully at her stroking hand and then clenched her fists against the armrests. 'And then I want to go back to Monaco.'

The sherbet gambit had failed, clearly.

'I'm afraid there has been no mistake,' said Magdelena.

'But when I . . . Died . . .'

She's said the d-word, Magdelena thought. *So there is hope.*

'My death was so . . . stupid. I mean, a plane crash, fine, but . . . Oh, Christ.' The woman stopped and looked around with a hand pressed lightly over her mouth. 'I didn't think I could be so terrified. There is so much time to think, but you can't. All I had going around my head was how much will it hurt when we finally crash. I just thought about the impact and the fire.'

Magdelena leafed through the sheaves of paper in front of her. 'It seems the pilot crashed into a mountain.'

'Three hundred people . . .'

'Yes, a tragedy.' She glanced down to the harbour where the rest of the passengers of flight A6718 had only just reached the front of the queue.

The woman blew her nose then said: 'The pilot just came over the PA and announced that he'd been unfaithful to his wife. He said that technology was evil, a curse.' Magdelena noticed that the woman had begun to sweat profusely, and that the mad stroking motions had returned. 'He said that technology had given us the internal combustion engine which filled the air with smog; and the internet which filled the mind with filth. He said technology gave us the automatic pilot which enabled him to cheat on his wife while flying a plane. He said he was being unfaithful right now, but his conscience had made things clear: it was time to stop.'

'Which is when he turned off the autopilot and shut down the engines.'

The woman nodded, sadly. 'Three hundred people . . .'

All accounted for, Magdelena thought, and pushed away a stray notion of Alfred Warr.

'He killed himself, the passengers, the crew and . . .' she stopped and looked to Magdelena. 'The co-pilot didn't stop him.'

Magdelena closed the folder and slid it to one side. 'The co-pilot may not have been in a position to stop him.' She felt her face turn red.

'Oh?' the woman said with a snort and a raised eyebrow. 'And what position was she in?'

Magdelena could remember better conversations. She risked another glance down to the harbour where Gabriel Archer and Pope Gregory XVII were waving anxiously to attract her attention. 'So,' she said briskly, 'how can I help you, Miss . . .'

'My dog,' the woman snapped. 'Where is my dog? Percival was in the hold of the aircraft. He should be here with me. Where is my fucking dog?'

'I'm afraid' – and Magdelena knew the conversation would probably not end well – 'that there is a separate afterlife for dogs.'

The woman's face turned a peculiar shade of blank. 'A separate afterlife,' she intoned, 'for dogs.'

'And cats.'

'Cats?'

'Yes, in fact there is a separate afterlife for every species on Earth.' Magdelena had often wondered what it was like in the krill Afterlife; crowded, most probably.

The woman leaned back in her seat and folded her arms. 'That doesn't seem very efficient to me.'

'It's not really a question of efficiency,' Magdelena said, watching the harbour floor from the corner of her eye. Gabriel was becoming quite frantic, and Gregory was waving his stained, battered mitre in broken semaphore. 'Most animals are quite resentful of humans. More often than not, humans are responsible for their deaths. It would be quite unfair for them to have to share the same afterlife as you.'

'I don't believe you.'

'Then it is a pity you cannot visit the lobster afterlife. You could ask them.'

The woman pursed her lips into a small red bullet.

'Look, we do have animals here. They may not be real, but you would be hard pressed to tell the difference. I have a pride of lions living in my office and somedays I forget that—'

'So you're suggesting I get a fictitious dog,' the woman said. 'You're suggesting I should waste eternity lavishing affection on some abstract imaginary creature.' She showed Magdelena a smile that only spiked at the corners. 'Like yourself.'

Magdelena felt her cheek twitch. *Imaginary creature;* the words took on a life of their own, thrashing and clawing inside the hollow that should have contained her soul. She sat back and breathed deeply, bringing her fingertips together to rest against her chin. 'Like many of your kind,' she said, 'you have lived your life from one burst of cruelty to the next. It is small wonder that the animals choose to go elsewhere.'

Somewhat surprisingly, the woman's smile didn't fade; in fact, it became rigid, fixed. Magdelena could hear her grinding her back teeth.

'How dare you.'

Down on the harbour floor, Gabriel was holding up his mobile phone and pointing to it.

'I'm sorry, Miss . . .' Magdelena waited for her to supply a name. She did not. 'I'm sorry but there really is nothing I can do.'

'Of course there's something you can do! You run this piece-of-shit operation, don't you? Get one of your weird transparent freaks to search your fucking harbour and find my dog!' She slammed her palm down on the desk and when she lifted it, there was a small photograph left on the glass. Magdelena turned the picture around. It was, she assumed, Percival; and he was, she assumed, a dog. His fur was dyed lavender and he wore a rhinestone collar fashioned into a bow tie that was as hideous as the woman's belt buckle. He had a miniature top hat strapped to his head and a fake moustache painted onto his muzzle.

'That was taken at a fancy dress party,' the woman said without an inkling of shame. 'I was Ginger Rogers.'

Down below, Pope Gregory XVII was stabbing a finger at the mobile phone Gabriel held aloft.

Alfred. Magdelena stood so quickly that her chair cannoned back and slammed into the glass wall. 'I'm sorry, I have to leave.'

'I'm not done yet!'

'I think you are.' She stuffed the paper sheaves into her bag and quickly checked her reflection in the glass: makeup, adequate; hair would just have to do. It then occurred to her that Alfred was on the phone and so what she looked like probably didn't matter. Calm down, you silly girl, she told herself. It's just Alfred.

'I will be making a formal complaint to your superior.' The woman rose to her feet, and the Head of Purgatory found herself wishing she was a shade taller.

'You can try,' she said, searching the drawers for her phone, 'but most days he's eye-deep in complaints.'

'I imagine that a lot of people tell you that you're something of a bitch.'

'Not as often as you'd like to think.'

'Well, the ones brave enough to are damn right: you are a bitch.'

'Miss Whatever-your-name-is,' Magdelena said on her way to the office door, 'You painted your dog. Let him have his eternity; he's well shot of you.' She slammed it shut then made her way towards the flight of stairs that would take her down to the harbour. The first step reminded her of her injured toe; it felt as though it were being crushed as soon as she put weight on it. The thought of seeking medical attention crossed her mind for the briefest of moments, but instead she chose to endure because she was a step away from godhood and gods were supposed to endure; and because there were others in far greater need than herself; and because at the other end of the archangel's phone, Alfred Warr was waiting.

† † †

'What kept you?' Gabriel handed her the phone and moved away, heading towards one of the processing gates where a small fight had broken out between a group of new arrivals. On another day, she thought, he would have left it to the wraiths, rather than risk a smudge on his tennis shirt. But of late, the Archangel Gabriel felt he had much to prove.

'Don't make it worse!' Magdelena called after him. He waved vaguely at her without turning around. 'And if you are hurt then don't come crying to me for sympathy.'

He stopped, turned and glared at her. 'I will not come crying,' he said, 'and if I did, it would not be to you.'

And up until this moment, she thought, we were starting to get along. She put the telephone to her ear and took a deep breath. 'Alfred,' she said, hoping that she did not sound too desperate.

'Magdelena!' Alfred cried, caring little for how he sounded.

Her heart tried to pull itself free of her chest. 'How are you?' she asked, her voice unsteady.

'As . . . as well as can be expected,' he said, and she imagined – she hoped – he was smiling.

'We had not heard from you since your capture in France. I . . . We were becoming quite concerned.'

'I was rescued,' he said, 'after a fashion. But I am well. I have the assassin and the supreme pontiff with me, so I imagine I am quite safe, spiritually and physically.'

He stopped talking as someone whispered to him. Magdelena strained to hear what was being said. 'Tell me where you are.' she demanded, and was surprised by the forcefulness in her voice.

'We are approaching John F. Kennedy Airport,' Alfred replied warily; her outburst had surprised them both. 'We will secure the final member of our retrieval team and then seek out Leonard.' The crowd was beginning to close in on her as more gondolas dispatched the dispatched, before setting sail again. The situation was becoming more desperate by the minute, and this was something she found increasingly intolerable by the second. Purgatory belonged to her. She had taken a ramshackle department run half-heartedly by a handful of demotivated demons and turned it into the model of celestial efficiency. The pride of the Afterlife. And to see it, like this: in disarray, without peace or harmony or orderly queues . . .

'You must hurry, Alfred.' She began to push herself free of the suffocating crowds. 'Our time is so short,' she said, and her injured toe throbbed in agreement. 'I was hurt, recently. Well, I wasn't hurt, I hurt myself and—'

'You are not healing.' The alarm in his voice did nothing to her assuage her. 'And what of Gabriel?'

Magdelena looked over to where the archangel stood directing the wraiths to break up scuffles between the newly deceased who were bitterly disappointed in what they found beyond the grave. Indeed, she thought, Earth is a global street festival; I too would be disappointed to find myself here. Her flesh grew cold at the blasphemy in her thoughts, not that it mattered anymore. Gabriel caught her eye and shrugged his shoulders in an exaggerated show of defeat. His own eye, the one she'd bruised, had not even begun to heal. In fact, it seemed worse. The flesh around it had darkened to a deathly grey and his skin seemed to have taken on a more translucent quality, as though some condition was causing him to fade away. I will be first, she thought. *More believe in him than in me.*

'Gabriel fares no better,' she said quietly.

'Their faith has become certainty, Magdelena,' Alfred said. 'They can no longer sustain us.'

'That is not true,' she said, knowing all too well that It was. The pain in her toes crept the length of her foot to her heel.

'Magdelena?'

'I am here, Alfred.'

'I will not fail you. Not again.'

'You have never failed me,' she said. 'You will find Leonard and you will both return.'

'Oh, Magdelena. I am to be sacrificed, we both know this is the way of things.'

'You will not die, Alfred Warr.' Her throat dried, even as the tears came. 'You will succeed and you will return to the Afterlife,' she said. 'You will return to me.'

She spoke and lit a flame within the psyche of six billion beings; a warm, soft light, a defiant light that shone in the darkness of a dying faith.

'I will be strong for you, my love,' Alfred said, and Magdelena thought that in one hundred years she had never heard him speak with such longing. 'I will be strong, and for you and you alone I will succeed. But Magdelena my sweet, I shall not return.'

'Do not say such things.'

'We cannot change what is to come.'

'Nothing is written in stone, Alfred.'

'The pyramids in your sanctum say otherwise.'

'How did—?'

'Gabriel told me.'

'Of course he did.'

'He said you had stopped reading it.'

'There was too much, and I have little time. If Mr Gee wants a reading group then he should—'

'I would like you to finish it,' Alfred said, with a solemnity that was rare, even for him.

'Alfred . . .'

'Please read it. When we were together there was so much of ourselves we held back. You were afraid that others would see you as weak . . .'

'Alfred, do not say such things.'

'. . . and I was afraid that if you saw inside me then you'd know how little of me there was. It is too late for me to know you, Magdelena, but if you read the pyramids then there is much you may learn about me.'

It sounded so very final. She could not bear it. 'You give up far too easily, Alfred Warr.'

'And you will love again, Magdelena Cane.'

It was not the answer she expected or desired, and though it was spoken with honesty and a genuine concern that she would not spend eternity alone, she found herself enraged – a strange sensation for someone so unaccustomed to any sensation at all.

Alfred said, 'I must go'

'If you must,' she replied, hoping he would stay on the line for just a short while longer.

The phone clicked and there was silence.

'How is he?' Gabriel said. She shrieked and threw the phone in the air, which he caught effortlessly and slipped into his pocket.

'How long have you been standing there?' she said in a continuation of the shriek.

Gabriel made a dry sniffing sound and turned to look out across the sea. When he looked back, a moment later, he wore a tired, hopeful expression, perhaps thinking she'd forgotten the question.

'Well?'

'Long enough,' he mumbled after a compressed pause. He looked at her, expectantly, steeling himself for the lash of her tongue. It didn't come, but he remained tense, tentatively asking if Alfred was all right.

'About as well as can be expected,' she said and set off towards the elevator at a brisk stroll. Gabriel followed, seeking to continue the conversation from beyond striking range.

'He'll be fine, you know. If there's one thing eternity has taught us it's that the Horsemen are a hardy bunch.'

'Not Alfred.' She stopped to sign a requisition handed to her by the harbour master. 'He's not like the other Horseman. He's not like us.'

The harbour master thanked her, grimaced at Gabriel, then glided on his way. He was replaced, almost immediately, by Pope Gregory XVII and young Ronald Weakes. The Pope stood, almost to attention; Ronnie seemed deferent by contrast, holding his cap and looking to the ground.

'Gentlemen, I have neither the patience nor the time,' Magdelena snapped. 'What is it?'

Pope Gregory opened his mouth, but it was Corporal Ronald Weakes who spoke: 'I have come to ask a favour, Ma'am.'

Magdelena took stock of the chaos around the harbour and then said, 'Yes?'

'A boat, Ma'am,' Ronnie said without meeting her eyes. 'One of the gondolas.'

Gabriel and Magdelena looked at each other and both said, 'What for?'

The deceased pontiff stepped in. 'We want to take the boat into Limbo, and search for Ronald's friends.'

'The Fighting Somersets,' Ronnie reminded them, as though they could have possibly forgotten. 'I . . . We want to search for them.'

Magdelena realised her mouth was open but made no attempt to shut it.

'We are doing very little here,' Pope Gregory said. 'In fact, I think we're rather getting in the way.'

Gabriel said, 'Do you have any idea how *vast* Limbo is?'

The dead Pope and the deceased soldier glanced at each other and shook their heads.

Magdelena said: 'That's the point: no one does. Limbo is so vast that mankind has never bothered to imagine its boundaries. It's limitless, and dark. Navigation would be next to impossible. No one who has gone there has ever returned. I'm sorry, it's out of the question.' She turned to leave, but Ronnie took hold of her arm. She looked at him sternly; he quickly released his grip.

'I'm sorry,' he said. 'I didn't mean to do that.'

She tried to soften. 'Ronnie, you've been here for so long now. Honestly, it's time you made your final journey.'

'I can't,' Ronnie said. 'I've sat here for eighty years, Miss, and it's only when I spoke to Mr Gregory here that I realised I'd forgot something, something really important.'

Gabriel rolled his eyes.

'And what was that, Ronnie?' Magdelena said.

'That Mr Gee helps those who help themselves.'

She sighed. 'That is true. But Limbo, Ronnie? Have the pair of you thought this through?'

'I am not ready,' Pope Gregory said suddenly. 'I am not ready to rest. Not yet.'

Magdelena looked at Gabriel, who said, less than helpfully: 'Mags, I don't think you're going to be able to stop them.'

Ronnie and the Pope nodded slowly. 'I'd rather do this with your blessing Ma'am,' said Ronnie.

'Oh, you would, would you? And what if I said we could not spare the loss of another gondola? What if I said I would just have you both locked away until you see sense?'

'You won't do that, Ma'am.'

'Really? Why on Earth not?'

Ronald Weakes swallowed and fired his final shell: 'Because you're lovely, Ma'am. You're brave and you're fair and you're generous and you're the kindest woman I've ever met, though it's fair to admit I haven't met many.' He wrung his cap. 'And because you know what it's like to miss someone Ma'am; miss them so much that it feels like you're walking around with a hole in you.' He took a long deep breath. 'And I miss them, Ma'am. And if I can't find them, then I want to be lost with them.'

Magdelena, her heart in her throat, threw Gabriel a stern look before he could point out that he wouldn't actually be lost *with* them. Then she turned her gaze on Ronnie. 'Well met, young man.' He'd employed a strategy against which she had no defence: flattery and honesty. 'I will be returning to my office now,' she said, 'to investigate the loss of another gondola.' She did not wait for their sighs of relief or their thanks, turning on her heels and walking away. 'I expect to see you both back here, someday.'

'Thank you, Miss Cane,' Ronnie called after her.

She tripped on the steps to the elevator; her vision was blurred. Tears, she thought, such a nuisance. Gabriel caught her arm and steadied her. 'Not sure that was wise,' he said.

'Well no,' she said, 'of course it wasn't.' Then she looked back and caught the eye of the Pope, who smiled and waved goodbye, mouthing a 'thank you' of his own.

SEVENTEEN

IT WAS NOT ALFRED'S wish to end the call. Now that he'd found the beginnings of his courage, there was so much more he wished to say. He wanted to tell her that she was the most precious thing in all creation. He would have said that in his universe her beauty was without parallel and that if he was a better man he would have seen them married a hundred years ago. Because like all creatures approaching their time, Alfred found that many things mattered little to him: the Afterlife, the apocalypse that never came, Mr Gee, his place in the cosmic scheme; all these things faded to a cold monochrome, leaving only Magdelena, shining inside his head, in all the colours of creation. Alfred found himself strangely at peace and, as he placed the phone in his breast pocket, it occurred to him that he might actually have Buddhist leanings.

'Yes,' Elias said wearily when the Horseman of the Apocalypse put the question to him. 'I suppose anything is possible.'

The journey from JFK Airport had taken over three hours: a slow procession west along Route 27, hampered by torrential downpours and the thousands of jubilant New Yorkers who, in spite of the inclement weather, had taken to the streets in celebration. Elias and Alfred were pressed uncomfortably together in the rear seat of the Fiat Uno that Pietro had purloined from the airport car park, and which he now drove wordlessly through the streets of New York, doing his best to avoid revellers who spilled from the carnivals, or leapt from the stages of makeshift street theatres, or simply fell from skyscrapers and landed, broken and smiling, on the concrete.

'Hold tight, gentlemen.' He slammed the brake pedal against the footwell and brought the car to a sliding halt. Elias lurched forward, slamming his head into the driver's headrest, while Alfred, who was not subject to the laws of inertia, held onto his hat as a show of solidarity.

Something slim and gaudily dressed formed a curtain of coloured diamonds in front of the windscreen, before crushing through the hood of the car with enough force to raise the rear wheels from the road.

Elias cried out: 'Dear Christ! What was that?'

'A harlequin, if I am not mistaken,' said Alfred, then asked if the supreme pontiff was all right.

'I am fine,' Elias said, as his world swam out to sea and then back again. He took several rapid breaths and crossed himself and was unnerved to find the gesture brought him little comfort.

'You are not fine,' the Horseman said. 'You are bleeding.'

'It is nothing.' Elias's world did somersaults. He placed his hand against his hairline and rolled his palm across the warm slick matting his hair to his forehead. He looked at his hand. Yes, there was blood.

'Stay here,' Pietro said, and pushed against the car door. It was jammed shut, so he turned in his seat, brought his legs to his chest and lashed out with his heels. The door sprung open and hung pitifully from a single hinge.

Elias slid the seat forward and followed him out, where his headache took a turn for the worse.

Outside the wreckage of the Uno, New York sweltered in a summer downpour. Thousands were singing, dancing, drinking and engaging in very public acts of a very sexual nature. Elias squinted at the doorway of a supermarket where a score of naked bodies writhed in a mass he could not separate by gender. He realised that he was strangely fascinated, almost drawn to it, as were the handful of women who walked, as though hypnotised, towards it, shedding their clothes as they did so. And the mass pulled at him too, like a vortex, while his past lives scorned him, told him to be a man, take what was being freely given, as he had so often taken that which was not. He turned his eyes back to Pietro who was looking closely at the harlequin embedded in the Fiat's engine space. 'Is he dead?'

'I hope so.'

Alfred extracted himself from the car, smoothed down his jacket and raised his hat to the crowd gathered around them. Some of them touched him then pulled away as though contact had burned their skin. But the others . . . The others looked at the corpse, which had somehow managed to raise the most serene of expressions in its final moments, and began to applaud. They cheered; they whistled; some even wept with joy. Alfred placed his hand gently upon Pietro's arm when he saw the assassin was reaching inside his jacket. 'There is no need,' he said. 'They do not mean to hurt us.' He tried to smile reassuringly, and Pietro curled his upper lip; the assassin clearly knew uncertainty when he saw it.

A girl, with auburn hair and vacant blue eyes, stepped from the crowd. She wore a pair of denim shorts and a soaked halter-neck top. Her feet were bare. All their feet were bare. She walked up to Alfred and then stood with her toes touching his shoes. She looked at him, through him as though she could see through to the back of his skull, and breathed a hint of cinnamon into his nostrils. Alfred felt his nose twitch. Her skin glowed under the unending downpour and he felt his own skin becoming uncomfortably warm.

'You ain't wet,' she said. 'Heaven's open . . .' She giggled quietly with a curved index finger pressed against her lower lip. 'Heaven's open an' you're as dry as a bone.' It was a southern accent. Alfred thought, Georgia perhaps. He recognised the soft laconic drawl from the whispers of the dying he'd catalogued during the American Civil War. She threw back her head and let the rain wash over her, into her mouth, into her eyes. 'This is wonderful. It's all just so wonderful.' Her head snapped back, her eyes fixed on him. 'Polynesia,' she said.

He raised his hat and introduced himself.

'I fail to see what is so wonderful about any of this,' Pietro said. With Elias's help he'd managed to roll the corpse from the car and now he stood with his hand inside his jacket, keeping a close watch over her and the gathered crowd.

'You can't see what's so wonderful about going to Heaven?' Polynesia said.

The travellers shared a look of confusion then pointed it at her.

'What the hell. Don't your voices speak to you?'

Elias cleared his throat. 'Not as loudly as yours it would seem.'

'My God,' the girl said. 'You don't know, do you?'

Again, they looked at each other. The crowd began to press towards them, giving Alfred the unwelcome feeling that he was a player in some bohemian horror movie.

'We must leave,' Pietro said, and the Horseman was very much inclined to agree.

'Heaven,' she made a triangle with her hands which she held out to them, 'exists.' She waited for her words to awaken them, then looked somewhat crestfallen when the travellers appeared none wiser. 'It's real. It's all real and we're all gonna go there!' She looked to the dead harlequin lying in front of the Uno. 'My husband. He's there already. He's done his good deed, got his place and he is gone!' She pirouetted, much like a ballerina, and the crowd cheered their agreement, but when she stopped turning she was holding a pistol.

Pietro yelled something that Alfred could not quite make out. A knot of fear materialised halfway down his throat. Pietro was aiming his gun. Alfred blinked and felt the world slide beneath his feet. The blink ended and he saw the assassin standing in front of the Pope, and Alfred himself was standing in front of the girl.

The world hadn't moved. He had.

'What did you say to me, Horseman?' Pietro growled.

Alfred had no idea. He looked to the crowd for someone to remind him, but they just stared glumly back.

'You said, "Don't shoot, you fool".'

Alfred blinked again. That did not sound like him.

'And you would do well not to throw yourself into my line of fire.' Pietro holstered his side arm and reached towards the girl, clicking his fingers impatiently.

'It wasn't for any of you,' she said, gingerly handing over the gun. 'It was for me. All I need is one unselfish act, just one. Something really big, something huge, then I get my place.' She eyed the gun, hungrily. 'I get my place in Heaven.'

Again, the crowd nodded cheerfully. Alfred was beginning to see the changes beyond the Afterlife through her. Where once the world was fuelled by greed, now it seemed that suicidal hedonists had inherited the Earth.

Elias was almost in tears. 'Child,' he said, his hands clasped together so tightly that they trembled under the strain, 'you would throw away your life before you've truly lived it?'

'Why not? Who wouldn't? I mean, before, we didn't know, not for sure. But now we do! We know it's real, and it's waiting for us.' Her vacant eyes came halfway to life. 'Heaven is waiting for us.'

The crowd cheered.

'Will you all please stop doing that!' Elias cried.

'We must leave.' Pietro looked east. The throng of thousands narrowed to a point somewhere beyond the horizon. Even if the car would run, progress would be slower by road. 'And we will have to walk.'

'It isn't far,' Alfred said, having produced a map seemingly from nowhere. Looking north he could see the Washington Square monument less than a mile away, but between it and them there was the crowd.

'It'll take you a while to make it through,' Polynesia said.

'Then the sooner we begin, the sooner we arrive.'

She considered this for a moment, twisting damp curls around her fingers, before nodding. 'Yeah, that kinda makes sense.' And then, to Alfred: 'Say, do you wanna fuck me?'

The crowd cheered on cue, while Alfred turned a radioactive crimson. 'I . . .' was how he started before he realised that ten thousand years of self-awareness had left him ill-prepared for such a question. 'What I mean to say is—'

'I kinda look at you and I see a guy who's real tired and really, really lonely—'

'Well, now you mention it—'

'And I thought to myself, 'Now here's a guy who hasn't been laid for a really, really long time.' Am I right? I'm right, aren't I?'

From the corner of his eye, Alfred saw Elias open his mouth, and then close it, quickly.

'And I figure, doin' an old guy; that's got to be a good deed, don'tcha think?'

And for the briefest of moments, a small, westerly corner of New York City became decidedly chilly. 'You think offering yourself to me will earn you a place in Heaven?'

The girl nodded. 'Hey, charity's charity.' She cast her attention around the crowd who again, maddeningly, nodded their agreement. 'And if you were a charitable kind of a guy,' she brushed an imaginary strand of lint from Alfred's lapel, 'then you'd help me get there.'

'You cannot just . . . fornicate your way into the Afterlife!' Elias bellowed.

Oh, but she can, Alfred thought. With Leonard absent, they all can. He wondered how Magdelena was coping with the sudden influx. Suicides took the longest time to process and she was such a fanatic for procedure. He gently took Polynesia's brushing hand and placed it by her side. 'Elias is right: I would not be enough. Your voices should tell you that.'

She twisted coyly, a slight movement from side to side accompanied by an impish grin. 'Would've been fun trying,' she said, and stood on her toes to plant a kiss on Alfred's lips. His body went rigid, aside from his toes which curled upward inside his shoes. 'Hope you guys find what you're looking for,' she said. She caressed Alfred's face, and he felt his heart lurch inside his chest.

'Who is to say we are looking for anything?' Elias asked.

The girl shrugged. 'Well, I figure if you're not joining the party you gotta be looking for something.'

'We should go.' Pietro set off north without waiting for a reply. Elias followed him without saying a word, leaving only Alfred, the girl, and the crowd.

Alfred said to her: 'Please don't do anything you will regret.'

'That's the most wonderful thing about all this, Alfred; no one can regret anything, not anymore.' She stroked his face and kissed him again, on the cheek this time. 'Your friends are leaving without you.'

He sighed, raised his hat and turned on his heels, hurrying after his companions.

'How do you do that anyway?' she called after him.

'Do what?'

'The not-getting-wet thing. How can you walk around in this shit and not get soaked?'

'It's complicated,' he replied, when in fact it was very simple. She seemed so sure of herself, of what was to come, a peace and certainty that he was envious of the moment she'd stepped from the crowd.

She laughed and rejoined the celebration. She waved and blew him a kiss. Alfred watched until he'd lost sight of her, then he turned and followed his companions, taking care to step between the raindrops.

† † †

The three-storey brownstone was nestled in the centre of four similar houses less than a mile north of the Greenwich monument. Elias found himself surprised at how unassuming it was, and then he wondered what he had been expecting: a palace of gold, perhaps, with hot and cold running myrrh.

'What amuses you, Your Holiness?' Pietro asked, somewhat humbly. He held a stolen umbrella above Elias's head, much to the pontiff's annoyance and embarrassment.

Elias said nothing. The celebration of life stopped a few blocks away, flexing itself around this street before resuming two blocks north. He could hear them: drums, trumpets, shouting, singing. Yet here there was an oasis.

'Why does the crowd avoid this place?' Pietro was becoming increasingly tense which, Elias knew, decreased the likelihood of finding Leonard without shots being fired.

'Their inner voices will be silenced in his presence,' Alfred said, 'as yours are silenced in the presence of mine. For that reason, I imagine their consciences will guide them away from his home.'

Pietro nodded, but remained taut. Elias noted that the assassin was probably nowhere near as anxious as he himself felt. But was 'anxious' the right word? Of course, he was apprehensive, but there was something else, something familiar. Elias recalled it was the same feeling he'd experienced a few days before, when he'd entered the Vatican.

'Is that him?' Pietro asked, pointing to a lone figure sitting on the stone steps. Elias could see the glint of steel in the man's hand, reflected in the subdued sunlight.

'No,' Alfred replied.

'He appears to be armed,' Pietro said.

'He appears to be whittling.' Elias realised the feeling he was experiencing was unworthiness, and felt oddly satisfied that he'd found his answer.

'He is whittling with a knife,' Pietro unholstered the sidearm from his jacket, 'which makes him armed.'

They crossed the street and approached the house. Elias told the apostle to put his gun away, which Pietro did under protest.

The man did not look up as they stood in a tight circle in front of the steps. He was dressed as the other New Yorkers were dressed: for a celebration that would last a short lifetime. He wore brightly coloured Bermuda shorts and an old safari hat. Around his neck hung a silver cross that, to Elias, seemed to shine much too brightly considering there was so little sun. He was difficult to age, perhaps in his early twenties, perhaps older. His hair was a sun-bleached blond though showing signs of whitening at the temples. His hands were large, thick-skinned, covered in small scratches and cuts and moved at unimaginable speed, the knife cutting and carving at piece of wood the size of a house brick. Sawdust and wood chip jumped and shot from between his hands, causing the three men to take a cautious step backward.

'I seek Jason Christopher,' Alfred said. He didn't look at the woodcutter, but cast his eyes to the middle second-floor window of the house. He smiled, as though someone was waving to him, but when Elias looked up there was no one there.

'Really?' said the carver. 'You are the second who has come seeking Jason in as many days.'

Alfred appeared not the least part interested. 'May we see him?'

'A very short, bitter man with a black eye,' the cutter continued.

'I assume he is available,' Alfred went on.

'He didn't stay long,' the woodcutter said.

'Tell Jason that Alfred Warr is here to see him, with a message from his father.'

The woodcutter looked up, finally. He rose quickly to his feet and stepped to one side. 'You will find him on the second floor.'

'I know. Thank you.' Alfred walked the steps with Elias behind him and Pietro forming a one-man rear guard. They entered the building, finding it poorly lit. The hallway, a wide reception area with a polished stone floor, opened out into a large circle with a collection of twelve wooden carvings, each one two metres high. They depicted gods and heroes from a number of religions and each cast a light into the otherwise dark hallway.

'Who was that?' Pietro asked.

Alfred removed his hat and straightened his jacket. 'An apprentice, I would imagine,' he said.

The wooden statues glowed, which Elias thought was such a shame: to carve things so beautiful and then make them into ornamental lamps. But when he touched one, an effigy of the Blessed Mother, it felt cold, and when he rapped it with his knuckles he realised that it was solid throughout. The wood itself appeared to bear its own light. Still, the statue was indeed beautiful: every line and crease of her robe seemed like silk to his eyes, and her own eyes of cedar followed his as he looked to the left and right of her. He touched her hand then snatched away when Pietro called out: 'Your Holiness!'

Elias looked to see that Pietro and Alfred had already climbed the first flight of stairs, halfway to the upper floor.

'We must stay together,' Pietro said.

Elias hurried to the stairs and stopped again when his eyes fell to another statue, carved so beautifully, so precisely, that it may well have been alive. It was of Jesus Christ, nailed to a simple, unvarnished cross. Elias approached it, though he could hear Pietro sighing loudly from the staircase. He pressed his face to its chest and felt tears between his skin and the wood.

'I think . . . I think I can hear him breathing,' he whispered. He looked to the floor, where another statue wept at the foot of the cross. He could not see her face, but she possessed a single braid that fell to her waist, each hair carved so delicately that Elias believed that they would move under the slightest breeze.

'Who is she?' he asked, then again when he realised he was still whispering.

'It is Mary Magdelena,' Alfred said, sadly.

Elias drew himself away from her, while still finding himself drawn to her. 'The whore?'

'If you will,' Alfred replied, icily. 'Come, he waits for us.'

'Our Lord and the Lady Magdelena,' Elias said, joining them, finally, on the staircase. 'They seem lost without each other.'

'It is just a statue,' Alfred said, pushing his way past Pietro who reached out for Elias's hand. Elias told him that he was perfectly capable of walking a flight of stairs.

'Still,' the supreme pontiff continued, 'I think it is the most wondrous statue I have ever seen.'

'Really,' Alfred said, disappearing around the curve of the staircase. 'I think it is somewhat self-indulgent myself.'

Elias looked again, and felt sure that all the statues heads had turned just so slightly, to look back on him.

He joined his companions on the second floor, where an expansive landing joined several rooms from which the sounds of delicate labour drifted. Elias counted twelve rooms in all and so decided that there was one industrious apprentice in each. The door to the thirteenth room was open, and he felt his heart pounding and his legs weaken as the room drew nearer. He followed Alfred and Pietro inside and wondered whether he should simply bow or fall to his knees, prostrate himself before his . . . His what? His employer?

'I wouldn't if I were you,' the woodcarver called down, without looking away from the eye he was shaping with a sharp chisel. 'The floor is covered with splinters.' He stood on a scaffold at least five meters above the floor, working an enormous statue that Elias felt sure must be his finest work to date. It was the same woman who was weeping at his feet in the lobby, though taller, much taller; standing upright, her head craned to look to the stars and her hands held high and out as though welcoming those same stars to her embrace. She was breathtaking, and indeed Elias had forgotten to breathe.

'You do this deliberately,' Alfred was shouting, waving an indignant finger up towards the woodcarver. 'You do this to annoy me! Well, it won't work!' It clearly had.

Pietro seemed to be examining the room for the missing space. Indeed, Elias was beginning to feel as though his perception was broken; the house was not large enough to hold a room of this size.

'Alfred,' the carver squatted down and tossed a lump hammer into the air. 'My father and Magdelena may make it seem so, but the whole of creation does not revolve around you.' The hammer landed a few centimetres from Alfred's shoes, and when they looked up again, the carver was standing among them.

Jason Christopher could best be described as remarkably ungodlike. His skin carried a deep middle-eastern tone to it, though it lacked the rough quality that Elias assumed of skin darkened in the shadow of the desert. He also had blue eyes which Elias, shamefully, expected. His hair was a mass of brown matted curls caked in dust and flakes of wood, as was his beard, which appeared sparse as well as untidy. He wore a pink tie-dyed shirt that was ripped across the chest and covered in paint splashes, and around his waist was tied a green sarong lined with golden braid. 'Jason Christopher,' he said, and extended a large gnarled hand towards Elias. Elias shook it, and felt his eyes bulge from his head as his fingers slipped across the hollow in Jason Christopher's palm. Bile rose into his throat and the room began to spin.

'I . . . I am—'

'I know who you are, Elias. It is so very good to see you again.'

'I beg your forgiveness,' Elias said weakly, 'but have we met?'

'Once,' Jason Christopher said, 'briefly.'

'Perhaps you should sit down, Your Holiness.' Pietro took his arm.

'I am fine, Pietro, please.' Elias straightened himself and cleared his throat. 'How may I serve you?'

This seemed to amuse Jason Christopher. His face broke into a broad grin, revealing two orderly rows of nicotine-stained teeth. 'And Leonard said that you didn't believe.'

'Who? Who said this?' Pietro said, ready to slaughter any man or deity who would spread such an untruth concerning the supreme pontiff.

'Pietro, do you have any idea who this is?'

Pietro said, 'With all due respect, Your Holiness, I know who he *believes* himself to be.'

'When did you start carving her?' Alfred demanded, thrusting a trembling finger beneath Jason Christopher's nose.

'Why, Alfred,' the woodcarver replied with a serene smile, 'is that a euphemism?'

Alfred exploded. 'Do not toy with me, Jason! You carved her at Bethsaida, after your little conjuring trick with the loaves and fish. You carved her again after your pilgrimage,' he made enraged quotes in the air, 'to Galilee. And again! Before your last supper!'

Elias wondered what Jason Christopher had really been doing if, as Alfred was implying, he wasn't on a pilgrimage in Galilee. The Horseman was still ranting and Jason Christopher stood shaking with his arms folded tightly across his chest and his hand pressed over his mouth to stifle his laughter.

Elias touched Alfred's arm and told him that that was quite enough.

'No, let him carry on,' Jason Christopher said. 'I haven't had this much fun in decades.'

'We have come on a mission of great importance.' Elias had no idea how one should address the Holy Son. The correct etiquette had never been covered during all his years of religious study because, of course, no one in the Catholic Church had seriously expected to meet him.

'Jason'll do just fine.' He walked over to a workbench and picked up a chisel, seemingly identical to the one he'd left on the scaffold. He examined it, selected another one, exactly the same, then crouched down and began etching at the toenails of Mary Magdelena. He stopped to caress her foot, then flashed Alfred a smile.

Alfred fumed.

'Perhaps, I should call you Mr Christopher,' Elias said, scowling at the Horseman. He is a Rider of the Apocalypse, he thought. *It is time he behaved like one.* 'You know why we are here?'

'Of course.' Jason Christopher chiselled delicately at a cuticle, with his tongue poking from the corner of his mouth. 'My father sent you on a quest to find Leonard Bliss, and he would very much like me to go with you. The answer is no.'

'I beg your—'

'You heard me, Elias. I'm not going with you.'

'You do not have a choice, Jason,' Alfred said. 'None of us have.'

The woodcarver sat down and crossed his legs, partly so he could delicately sand Magdelena's toes, but mostly to demonstrate his intransigence. 'I have done my part,' he said. 'I will do no more.'

'You make it sound as if there is some divine limit to the sacrifices that are asked of us,' Alfred said.

It didn't appear to be going well. Elias glanced at Pietro who was looking at the King of Kings as one might examine a game pheasant. The assassin cocked his head to one side, thoughtfully tapping at his throat. Pietro was a priest trained for direct intervention; he was no doubt thinking of the best way to stun Jason Christopher and then organise transport for the four of them.

'You speak of sacrifice,' Jason Christopher was saying. 'You, of all of us, have sacrificed almost nothing.' Alfred started to protest, but Jason was having none of it. 'You, who has hidden beneath Magdelena's skirts for more than half a century . . . You, least of all, can speak of sacrifice to me!'

'You know nothing of my suffering!' Alfred cried, his face darkened to a blood red. 'You know nothing of what I have seen. I have borne witness to men slaughtered like cattle, women defiled in ways you cannot imagine.'

In a single, fluid motion, Jason Christopher rose gracefully to his feet; feet that, Elias saw to his horror, ran with blood from puncture wounds driven through to the sole. He strode across the room towards Alfred, who straightened his back and thrust out his chin.

Elias looked desperately to Pietro, imploring him to intervene. The assassin simply shrugged his shoulders and glanced at his wristwatch.

Jason Christopher stopped a few inches short in front of Alfred Warr, thrust the chisel beneath the Horseman's nose and from there cast what he thought to be his winning lot: 'In your long and pointless existence, Alfred, have you ever known the pain of crucifixion?'

'Oh, this again . . .'

'Yes, Alfred! This again! Until you have been tied and nailed to a cross, hoisted and humiliated in front of thousands and suffocated slowly under the Calvary sun, then you cannot tell me that you have suffered! I will not hear it!'

'This martyr's fixation of yours grows tiresome, Jason. Tiresome and dull.'

And so it went on.

Pietro slid his feet through the sawdust without leaving a mark. He stood next to Elias and said, 'You do *know* what this is about?'

Elias looked to the statue of Mary Magdelena. 'I am not blind, Pietro.'

'Forgive me, Your Eminence.' Pietro joined him in admiring the towering statue. 'To cause such bickering amongst demigods . . .' he said. 'She must be quite extraordinary.'

Elias sighed. 'One day, you will see for yourself.'

'My kind,' Pietro said, shaking his head, 'do not enter Purgatory. We will be delivered straight to the underworld.'

'Is that what your conscience tells you?'

'Yes, even now. Unless I find a way to redeem myself.'

'Then you are fortunate,' Elias said. 'My own conscience cannot bring itself to acknowledge me.' He thought that the next life, if his soul was recycled again, would be a very lonely place for him, trapped inside his future self along with the savages of his past.

Alfred and Jason were leaning towards one another, their foreheads almost touching, gesticulating wildly as they traded accusations and insults.

'You are worshipped,' Alfred was yelling, 'worshipped by millions, and still you complain. Still, you waste your existence cutting wood and selling trinkets at craft fairs.'

'And what of you? War: the Horseman of the Apocalypse, who loses control of his bodily functions at the sound of a gunshot.'

Alfred slapped the chisel across the room and pointed a finger at Jason's left eye. 'You call me a coward? How dare you! You, who crafted the instrument of his own demise.'

'I had no choice!'

'You even polished it!'

At this, Jason Christopher seemed to calm down. He took a deep breath and a step back. 'I am a craftsman.' He sniffed and turned away. 'It is my nature.' He walked over to the chisel, past a hanging rack of ten identical chisels, and picked it up, checking the handle for damage.

'Yes,' said Alfred finally. 'And revulsion of war is mine.'

They looked at each other, and under the stoic gaze of Mary Magdelena, a silent accord was reached. Elias's pulse had quickened during the exchange. He took a handkerchief from his pocket and wiped the perspiration from his neck.

Pietro seemed motionless, standing with his eyes closed in silent meditation. Elias wondered if this was the resting state for apostles when they found themselves with no one to kill.

'Your feet,' Alfred said.

Jason shrugged. 'It comes and goes. Worse since Leonard arrived on Earth.'

'I feel myself growing weaker each day,' Alfred said. 'They no longer believe in us.'

'Oh, they believe in us,' Jason said, stepping over Magdelena's feet and making his way to a window, leaving a thin trail of blood in his wake. 'But that belief is driven by certainty, and we are creatures of faith.' He moved the cloth curtain aside and looked down into the empty street. 'We are fuelled by their desire for our existence, in the face of incontrovertible evidence.'

Elias understood; the Roman Catholic Church was driven in much the same way.

'Then you see why you must come with us,' Alfred implored. 'Leonard Bliss must be found. He must return to the Afterlife and resume his function.'

Jason nodded. 'To keep their consciences silent.'

'You have seen what is happening. Now that they know there is a Heaven, they are ending their lives to reach it. This cannot be allowed to continue, Jason. You must help us.'

'You are right,' Jason said. 'It cannot continue. But I will not go with you.'

Pietro sighed his exasperation. 'We waste our time here!'

Elias told him to be silent.

'Alfred, it is not that I do not wish to help you. It was just never meant to be.'

'How can you say such a thing?'

'Because it is true. I know these things.' Jason gently tapped his left temple. 'Much as Thomas Mort does.'

'Ah, your fabled omniscience.' Alfred folded his arms. 'How blessed you are.'

'If you can call knowing the time and place of your own painful death such, then yes, I am blessed.'

'He is not going to come with us,' Pietro said, 'so we should not stay here any longer.'

Jason said, 'You are the assassin.'

'I am the apostle, yes.'

'And you would leave without knowing where you are to find Leonard Bliss?'

'You know where he is?' Pietro stood upright with his hands at his side, his trigger fingers twitching.

'He came here two days ago and he too wished for me to join him.'

'Join him? Join him where?'

'You can still come with us,' Elias interrupted.

'I cannot, Your Holiness' – and Elias felt his heart soar to hear one such as he refer to him so – 'for it is not inscribed in destiny. This is my father's doing, you see. We have been estranged since the crucifixion, and he merely seeks a means to bring us closer.'

'And you would deny him?'

Jason shrugged and said, 'Fathers and sons.'

Fathers and sons, Elias thought. *We made our gods in our own image. Why should we be surprised that they are imperfect.*

'You will find him in New Orleans,' Jason said. 'He's decided to settle there.'

'New Orleans?' Pietro said. 'Why?'

Jason said he did not know. 'My omniscience does not reach as far. He said in a few years the town would be lost and abandoned. He said it would suit his situation very well.' His smile grew distant. 'As it would mine.'

Pietro nodded. 'New Orleans then.'

Elias and Alfred agreed.

'Then give my regards to my father the next time you see him,' Jason sank to the floor, crossing his legs as he did, then hunched his back and began chipping away at the small exposed section of Mary Magdelena's calf. Alfred watched him with a fierce grimace, and Elias found himself wondering how many in the Afterlife were obsessed with this woman. His past voices, depraved as they were, longed to meet her.

'Your work is a marvel,' Alfred said without meaning it and wishing the others to know he didn't mean it.

Jason snorted and put down his chisel. 'And it doesn't bother you,' he said. 'It doesn't matter to you that each time we intervene in the affairs of man, one of us is sacrificed.'

Alfred's voice wavered. 'It is the way of things.'

'It is the way of things.' Jason echoed and shook his head. 'And you do not care who is next?'

As he often did, Alfred looked to his shoes for the answer. 'I care very much. I imagine that your much-vaunted omniscience has given you a glimpse of what is in store for me.'

'For you?'

'Yes, for me. I am here, ready to face what is to come, while you, the supposed messiah, hides among humanity. And yet you still have the audacity to belittle my existence.'

Elias shivered; the air had turned decidedly cold once again

'Oh, Alfred,' Jason picked up his chisel, 'look at you: the martyr, forever denied his place in the limelight.'

Elias felt the temperature in the room drop still further. At first he thought it was merely his imagination, a reaction to the lack of warmth between the gods prattling in front of him. That was his first thought, until he noticed his breath: the clouds of condensation billowing from his mouth when he exhaled. He looked to Pietro who was flexing his fingers to stave off the sudden onset of frostbite. It was much as it was on K2, when one of Pietro's brethren had snatched him from death. His jaw began to tremble, rattling his teeth He tried to imagine what would happen if the two came to blows. Would every window in the room spontaneously shatter? Would Greenwich Village crumble into dust? Or perhaps the entire eastern seaboard would simply fall into the ocean.

To his credit, Jason Christopher chose not to escalate the war of taunts any further. 'As I said, Alfred, not everything revolves around you.' He wiped his nose and coughed, initiating a fit of sneezing that cleared both his sinuses and the atmosphere in the room. When he finally stopped, he scratched at his stubble and tapped the chisel lightly against Mary Magdelena's ankle. 'She did love you, you know.'

Alfred stood up straight and pulled his jacket taut. 'I needed people to tell me that a hundred years ago, not a few hours before I cease to exist.'

'You're as old as creation, Alfred. You shouldn't need anyone to tell you anything.' Jason Christopher smirked in a most un-messianic way and shook his head. He went to work on the ankle, shaping and moulding it as though it were as malleable as water. 'You will forgive me if I don't see you out,' he said, which Pietro took as their cue to withdraw; he was at the door in four strides.

'We're leaving,' he said, should no one have noticed.

Elias followed him, more than disappointed that he'd met the Messiah whilst in the company of an assassin and a petulant demigod. He hoped it wouldn't count against him. The voices of his lives past berated him, told him not to be such a wet fish.

They left the way they had come: past the row of twelve closed doors from behind which came the sounds of ferocious industry.

'Always twelve,' grumbled Alfred. 'He is so predictable.'

'Can we continue without him, Your Eminence?' Pietro asked.

Elias said that he didn't know. 'But I see we have little choice but to try.'

'New Orleans then.'

'Yes, New Orleans.'

Outside the three-storey brownstone, the Rapture had begun to encroach on the previously untouched corner of the Village. The sounds of drums and singing, trumpets and joy seeped through Elias's skin. He turned back and looked to the building they'd just left. He pulled his coat tight against the downpour and looked to Alfred, whom the afternoon rain steadfastly avoided. 'Will you know what to do when we find him?'

'No,' he replied. 'Contrary to popular belief, I am not blessed with the wisdom of ages.'

'I have yet to hear anyone say that you are.' Elias looked around to see where Pietro had gone. The assassin was a few metres away, outside a delicatessen, already hard at work on stealing another car. The pontiff was relieved to see that it was a Chrysler, much bigger than the Fiat Uno they'd been forced to abandon. We will be comfortable at least, he thought. His past voices cheered him, saying that at last he was starting to think as one of them.

EIGHTEEN

IT WAS A SIGHT that Magdelena never imagined she would see; for the first time in human history, night had fallen across the drylands of Purgatory.

The sounds of the desert winds were trapped and broken by the thousands of tents that stretched to the horizon, and there was not a lion or zebra or gazelle to be seen.

Magdelena decided that she did not care for the night.

'This cannot go on,' Gabriel Archer said. He was dressed in a smart double-breasted business suit of the finest wool. Another first; Magdelena couldn't recall ever seeing him wearing a suit before.

He was also ever so slightly drunk.

'We are at breaking point.' Gabriel reached for the wine bottle for the fifth time in twenty minutes.

Magdelena leaned forward and gently placed a hand over his, holding the bottle firmly to the table. The archangel glared at her. 'It is for the pain,' he said. His eye, far from healing, looked worse: an enraged crimson, like a birth mark, swollen and closed with ripe pustules covering the lid.

'Still,' she said, holding down the bottle. Gabriel softened his hand.

'Clear heads,' Daphne Unger said, gnawing on the remains of a guinea fowl. She reached for the bottle, her eighth glass in fifteen minutes, and no one did anything to stop her; Daphne Unger's constitution did not require it. 'Always good in a time of crisis. Cheers.' She downed the glass in one swallow, placed a pudgy bejewelled hand across her chest and released a quietly demure belch. Her pet demon, who had been squatting quietly beside her bathchair, leapt into life, scrambling over her enormous frame to dab at the corners of her mouth with a silk handkerchief. Magdelena understood the creature had once been a high-ranking official in the Nazi party whom Leonard had appointed to the unenviable position of Daphne's carer, a position that required it to perform tasks too terrible to contemplate. And now of course, Magdelena found herself contemplating them. The creature selected the morsels it fed to her very carefully. Clearly, it had developed an almost preternatural affinity with Daphne Unger's bowel movements and did all it could to keep them manageable, for her sake as well as its own.

'Is something wrong, Magdelena?' Daphne said.

Magdelena looked her directly in the eye and thought, Yes, as a matter of fact, you nauseate me. It was not Daphne's immensity that disgusted her, but her lack of self-control. It was a trait Magdelena abhorred in anyone. It was a trait she'd seen in herself of late.

'Is there something about me you find displeasing?'

'Why would you say that?' Magdelena said without a moment's self-reproach.

'We used to be such good friends, you and I. And yet when we meet for the first time in fifty years, you have so little to say to me.'

'I do not feel we have the time for this,' said Thomas Mort, who was tired and so spoke with little emphasis or conviction. Magdelena had never seen him so withdrawn. For one such as he, a Horseman of the Apocalypse who truly revelled in his work, to be brought so low was a sorry sight indeed.

'Well, perhaps we should make time, as she does not return my letters or phone calls.'

Magdelena glanced at the phone perched at the far end of her desk, one hundred metres away. The red phone. The phone she had come to hate. The phone that had steadfastly refused to ring as the Afterlife slowly collapsed under the weight of the dead. Mr Gee, she thought, have you abandoned us, as you abandoned Jason Christopher? As you abandoned Alfred Warr? She looked at the empty chair between Thomas and Gabriel and felt her heart drop to the pit of her stomach. 'Daphne, now is not the time. We have far more pressing matters to discuss.' She rose to her feet, feeling her injured toe bite at her for doing so. Inside her shoe, it had turned black and the nail bed had grown raw and infected. She winced and then coughed to disguise the pain. 'I have heard from Alfred. He has spoken to Jason Christopher who believes that Leonard was en route to New Orleans.'

Gabriel groaned and leaned back in his seat, pressing his palm against his forehead. 'Not that stupid bar idea again . . .'

Magdelena shot him a look that could have pierced steel. 'What bar? You know about this?'

'He may have mentioned something about it, over drinks.' Gabriel twisted nervously in his seat.

'And you didn't think this was worth mentioning to me?'

'It didn't seem important,' Gabriel said desperately. He turned to Wolfgang Pochs, who was attempting to slide under the table. 'Isn't that right, Wolfgang?'

Magdelena rounded on him. 'You knew about this too?'

Wolfgang Pochs, the Horseman whose remit mainly covered pestilence, coughed, as usual, sneezed, as he was always doing, and then swore, as he often did. 'You're a fucking coward, Gabriel,' he said and undulated his thin hips to work his way back from under the woodwork. 'He did say something about it, a couple of times. But he was just shooting his mouth off. You know what Leonard's like.'

'No one thought he would actually do it,' Gabriel mumbled, like a child who'd just narrowly escaped a spanking.

Magdelena cast her eyes around the table, past Daphne, Gabriel and Wolfgang, settling on Thomas Mort, who was doing his very best to look elsewhere.

'And you knew.'

Thomas made a low, rumbling sound in his throat that may have been a *yes*, a *no*, or *this really has nothing to do with me*. In the scheme of things, it didn't matter.

'So everyone knew about this, except me.' Magdelena dropped into her chair and rested her face in her hands. Her back creaked and her toe screamed. 'If I had known this . . .'

'What?' Gabriel said. 'What could you have done? This is preordained, Magdelena . . .' he heaved a massive stone tablet onto the desk '. . . if you'd bothered to read about it. They will journey to New York, retrieve the Messiah, steal a car and head to New Orleans.'

Magdelena stared at the stone tablet as though it had bitten her. 'Then it is not "preordained",' she said. 'Jason Christopher is not with them. He stayed in Greenwich Village.'

The Horsemen and the archangel exchanged glances.

'Are you sure?' said Thomas, glancing at his wristwatch. 'Mr Gee is rarely wrong about these things.'

'He is this time,' Magdelena said and felt oddly uplifted.

Rachel, accompanied by three other wraiths who looked startlingly similar, floated from behind the first row of tents, carrying trays of refreshments. The line of wraith security guards let them through, and they proceeded to set out a light lunch of ambrosia.

'This does not make any sense,' Thomas politely refused a plate. Daphne asked if she could take his.

'Nothing has made sense since Leonard left,' Magdelena said. 'So, Gabriel, you called this meeting with a proposal.'

Gabriel quickly swallowed a mouthful and stood up. He bowed stiffly to the others around the table and then cleared his throat. 'Friends,' he began, 'the Afterlife is facing its most significant crisis since the Flood. With Leonard out of action, the human conscience has been given free rein. This, as many predicted in the past, has proven disastrous.'

Wolfgang stifled a yawn.

'The humans now know that there is an Afterlife and, after spending a few days indulging themselves as a kind of "goodbye cruel world", they kill themselves and are now clamouring at our gates, demanding entry.'

'You said you had a solution, Gabriel,' Magdelena said impatiently, but Gabriel was waltzing with his own ego and refused to be distracted.

'Quite simply, we cannot cope.'

'We have room,' Thomas said weakly, 'for the time being.'

'Exactly,' Gabriel flashed him a smile as though he'd spoken on cue. 'For the time being. But as more of them commit suicide, the human consciousness contracts.' He brought his hands together in a slow clasp, in case someone at the table did not know the meaning of the word *contracts*. 'And as their group consciousness contracts, so does the faith that fuels the Afterlife – fuels us.' He looked around the table to make sure he'd driven the point home. 'Heaven,' he said with theatrical gravity, 'will shrink. And we will cease to be.'

'Gabriel, the solution,' Daphne said, while her pet demon fed her a portion of suet, which would help bind her digestion.

'We grow weaker by the hour.' Gabriel walked behind Thomas and placed his hands on the Horseman's extraordinarily broad shoulders. 'When even stalwarts such as Mr Mort here' – he squeezed the horseman's collarbones and ignored the hostile rumble that came back – 'look as though they're at – if you'll pardon the expression – death's door; no offence.'

'None taken.'

'Then we know it's time for drastic action. It's time for thinking outside the box. We need to step outside our comfort zone. We need to look beyond the trapezium of our own expectations. We need to—'

'Gabriel!' Magdelena shouted.

'—close the gates,' he finished, somewhat meekly.

There had been something of a silence around the table as he'd spoken, only marred by the sounds of civil disorder from the tented camp a few hundred yards away. The silence remained, though it seemed strangely more pronounced.

'What do you mean,' Daphne Unger said, her mouth full of fondant icing and her voice thick with disbelief, '"close the gates"?'

'Exactly what it sounds like.' The archangel sounded less sure of himself. 'We must close Purgatory Harbour. No one in or out until the crisis is resolved.'

Magdelena wondered who, aside from Leonard, ever went out.

'Impossible,' Wolfgang said.

'There is still enough room,' Thomas Mort growled.

Gabriel made a sweeping gesture across the vast expanse of refugee tents. 'Yes, but for how long?'

The thought of closing the gates had not occurred to Magdelena for the simple reason that it was unthinkable. 'If we close the harbour then the souls of the deceased will be lost.' She thought of young Ronnie Weakes. 'I'm sorry Gabriel, it is out of the question.'

'I am not talking about permanent exclusion. Just until we can get Leonard back to work and clear the backlog.'

'I am perfectly capable of clearing any backlog without closing the harbour,' said Thomas. 'Did we close Purgatory for Pompeii? Did we close it for Hiroshima? Nagasaki? Did we close it during the great wars? We will cope. We always do.'

'This is different,' Gabriel said.

'And what about the Flood?' Daphne chipped in.

'There weren't as many of them to die during the Flood, and with our power fading with the losses of the faithful—'

'And with such a small pool of faith, we were far less powerful then.' Magdelena closed her laptop. 'But we shall cope. We will not close the gates to them. That would be . . . inhuman.'

'You're making a mistake, Magdelena.'

'Gabriel, do you remember what happened the last time souls were lost before they reached us?'

Gabriel said nothing.

'Let me remind you: we were left with a broken man, no – a child, who has taken a pope and vowed to search Limbo until his friends are found; and a Horseman of the Apocalypse driven insane with guilt. I will not allow it, Gabriel. The gates will remain open.' She stood and the others joined her.

Gabriel looked to each of them in turn. 'Then I will go over your heads. I will go over all of your heads. I will petition Mr Gee directly. You forget that I have his ear.'

'He has no favourites amongst us, Gabriel,' Magdelena said as the others filed away from her desk, 'and if he favoured one above the rest then it would be Jason Christopher.'

Gabriel curled his lip, showing a corner of his perfectly straight teeth. He waited until he was sure the others had moved beyond earshot then leaned forward to whisper into Magdelena's ear: 'You are weak,' he said. 'You are all weak.'

Magdelena turned away; his breath reeked of death. 'This malice,' she said, her own breath unable to escape from her throat, 'this is not like you Gabriel.'

'You think that because mankind casts me as an angel, I will not consign them to oblivion?' The scar on his face glowed, changing from decaying flesh to something akin to molten rock. 'I will do this, Magdelena, if it will save us. I will do this and more!'

'I think this is not about the humans. I think this is about something else.' She placed a hand upon his arm and pressed her fingers gently, which served only to anger him further.

'If you think this is about my homosexuality, Magdelena, then you do not know me.' He took her hand, holding her fingers inside his fist. 'You do not know me at all.'

'Then tell me, Archangel,' with a minor contortion of the wrist her hand was free, 'tell me so that I may know you.' She gestured at the chair vacated by Thomas Mort, and Gabriel obediently sat. He tried to put his head in his hands, but the scar seared the flesh on his palms, causing him to cry out.

Magdelena quickly poured water from the jug on to a napkin. She knelt in front of him and pressed the napkin between his hands. He snarled at her and struggled, but she held his hands together, firmly between her own. 'The cold will soothe you.'

He fought on, and she responded in kind, increasing her mass to match his strength. 'Gabriel, please!' The earth began to crack beneath them, and Magdelena could see by the insanity in his eyes that he wasn't fighting her; he was fighting the Afterlife, his very existence. But the scar had weakened him, more than Magdelena's own injury had her; within a few moments he was spent. He slumped forward in his seat, his chest heaving.

'I tire of this,' he said. 'I tire of being nothing more than a dream, a figment of their banal imaginations.'

'It is the same for all of us,' Magdelena said. She soaked another napkin. She tried to clean his palms, but Gabriel was having no more of her. He rose to his feet and reached for the wine bottle.

'And I do not know how you stand it. This eternal treadmill, being everything they expect us to be until they decide they no longer need us.' He waved the bottle at her. 'I do not care whether I am gay or not,' he proclaimed, then drank.

'Really?'

'Of course I don't. In fact, many of my closest friends are . . .' he stopped and looked up, narrowing his good eye. 'That is not true. I do not have any homosexual friends to speak of.'

'Acquaintances, then.'

'Yes, acquaintances,' he agreed. 'My point is that while I care little concerning my sexual orientation, I despise having it decided for me. If I am gay then so be it, but to have something so personal dictated, arbitrarily, by a species I neither like nor trust . . .' He took another mouthful and set the bottle down on the desk. 'I cannot think of anything more unfair.'

Magdelena bit her tongue.

'We are soulless things, Magdelena. Hollow creatures made in their image because they lack the courage to face their own mortality.'

'Then this plan of yours,' Magdelena said, 'to close the gates. It is not about saving us; it is about punishing them.'

Gabriel's nostrils flared, but he did not deny it.

'We cannot survive without them. We exist because they exist. To contemplate such a thing while they throw themselves at our gates . . . That is blasphemous, Gabriel, and if you were in your right mind you would know this.'

'They deserve nothing more,' he said. His face remained grey and unmoved, save for the raging red scar about his eye. 'And if we fall with them then perhaps that would be better than . . . all this.' He rose to his feet, rocked back on forth on his heels. Satisfied that he had the measure of himself, he turned and walked away, cutting an uneven path towards the tented camp, where the wraiths were doing their utmost to keep the surging crowds at bay. A number of banners had appeared amongst the crowd. *Heaven Can't Wait,* they read.

From the edge of the camp, Gabriel called out to her: 'Think on this, Magdelena; if we are nothing but lies, then what is your love for Alfred Warr?'

Magdelena's breath caught in her throat; tears burst silently behind her eyelids. She took a moment to breathe again and thought, This? This is what pierces you? Mere words, spoken by a drunken archangel?

'Love cannot be imagined Gabriel! Not by us, not by them.' He *could* hear her, she was sure of it. 'Somewhere inside us, their imagination ends and we begin.' Yes, he could hear her. He was simply being childish. 'And I begin with my love for Alfred! Do you hear me?' She wiped her eyes with her sleeve, yelled 'I know you can hear me, you little shit!' then sat down heavily in her chair. She took three cleansing breaths and held her hand out.

Shaking.

Three more breaths and the rest of the wine and her hands were still trembling. She tried to stand and found she could not; it was the pain from her injured foot. Her ankle was beginning to look discoloured and, unless she was very much mistaken, there was a faintly unpleasant odour coming from inside her shoe. Without allowing herself time to think, Magdelena slipped off the shoe and near-wretched at the sight.

Her large toe was shrivelled and black; the nail, lifted from its bed, was embedded in a film of viscous pus; her instep had turned purple-black, along with her second and third toes.

Her two smaller toes were missing.

Magdelena swallowed. So this is to be our end, she thought. *Gabriel will turn to ash and I will simply rot away.* She tried to take comfort in the knowledge that Alfred would be faring better, being closer to the source of faith than they themselves were in the Afterlife. He would falter eventually though, as would they all.

He will falter and he will stop.

She closed her eyes and thought of oblivion. The ceasing. Everything you are, everything you ever knew suddenly vanishing into nothingness, lost forever. When Magdelena opened her eyes she realised her heart was beating rapidly. What gods will they choose after us, she wondered. Would they need gods at all?

She picked up the stone tablet Gabriel had left. It was like the thousands of others: smooth, white, inscribed in gold and extraordinarily heavy. Alfred said the tablets were the key to knowing him, and at the time she'd been hurt, insulted even; the idea that she, above all others, didn't know all there was to know about Alfred Warr ... She, who had coaxed him back from the brink of madness.

And yet, he was outside, on Earth, fighting for humanity and the Afterlife. Fifty years ago she would not have believed it of him.

The Book Of Leonard

Leonard: VIII

AND SO IT WAS . . .

That the summer of seventy-two was a time of flight.

It was the summer of seventy-two when the students of Columbia University fled from tear gas and batons.

It was the summer of seventy-two when the villagers of Trang Bang fled from allied napalm.

And it was on one humid, mosquito-laden night in the summer of seventy-two that Alfred Warr fled through the jungles of South Vietnam, carrying a dying soldier in his arms.

'Hanoi,' he gasped. 'Hanoi cannot be far.'

The soldier reeked of ill-hope and a surfeit of diseases the scent of which Alfred could not begin to identify. Alfred knew not where he was running to. And in truth, he did not care. All that mattered was that he could bear the sight of human suffering no longer. He could no longer stand by and observe in silence, tallying the fallen before their journey to Purgatory.

The foliage grew more dense; vines thickened to twisted branches as wide as he was tall; flowers lanced into thorns that tore at his arms and his face. His linen suit was stained with moss and his own blood. A few short years past, the very notion of physical injury would have been unthinkable, but Alfred had lived with this war since 1969 and in that time he'd forgotten how to be immortal, how to walk amongst men, unseen. And so when he had travelled to the camp with Wolfgang Pochs and Daphne Unger, his heart had touched the soldiers imprisoned there. They were dying. But the manner in which they were dying took hold of Alfred Warr and broke his spirit cleanly in two. They had no food, no medicine; they lay in their fever and their filth, near naked in a night so dark it taxed even the eyes of the immortals who watched over them. The prisoners were ravaged by starvation and disease and had barely the strength to raise their heads.

But one did find such strength, and he reached out to the Horseman of War.

'Alfred,' Daphne Unger said. 'Alfred, he sees you!' She carried with her a fathomless hamper, a gift from Leonard Bliss, from which she brought forth joints of meat and bottles of wine.

The Horseman had stepped from the shadows to place a gentle hand upon the soldier's brow. The soldier did not appear very old, twenty-one at best, and by the tattered, filth-encrusted remains of his uniform, Alfred surmised that he was a centurion of the United States Marine Corps. He'd reminded Alfred very much of Ronald Weakes, the young soldier whose comrades he'd misplaced during the first great war.

The marine had asked of him: 'Are you an angel?'

Alfred had said, no, he was not an angel.

'What are you doing?' Daphne had looked nervously about her. 'Alfred, whatever you are thinking—'

'I can save him,' he'd said. 'He is not too far gone. I can save him.'

'Don't be ridiculous! Look at him!'

'If I can get him to a hospital . . .'

'We are miles deep inside the most inhospitable jungle on Earth. There are land mines everywhere, Alfred.' Daphne had waved her arms, trying to draw the attention of Wolfgang Pochs, who was taking down the particulars of two soldiers expiring in the same cot.

'I will save him,' Alfred had said.

'You will do no such thing,' Daphne had replied. Pochs waved back then carried on making notes. 'Oh for goodness' sake!'

She had once been a beautiful and treasured friend of his own Magdelena, which held no surprise for Alfred; he believed that beautiful women gravitated towards each other, as though the effects of pulchritude could be amplified by standing close to others who bore it. But Alfred knew if she did not bring her consumption under control, then Magdelena would have nothing more to do with her. Her weight did point to a weakness of spirit, and Magdelena, Alfred knew, spared little time for the weak.

'Wait here,' Daphne had said to him. 'Do not move. I will get Wolfgang to talk some sense into you.' She'd hurried away, clutching the fathomless hamper to her chest.

'You are lost, are you not?' The soldier spoke, his voice could barely be heard, yet in the stillness of the trees it was as though he were screaming.

'I am not lost,' Alfred panted, wondering if he was indeed heading south as he'd hoped.

'Put me down,' the soldier whispered. 'I need to rest.'

'We are almost there,' Alfred lied, then tried to remember when this had become second nature to him. 'You will be fine.'

'I appreciate what you're trying to do, but I think we both know that is not true.'

Alfred battled on through the undergrowth that seemed to grow more dense with every step. His pace slowed, his limbs dragged down by the weight of the jungle. He longed for the moonlight which concealed itself above the trees.

He heard a bark followed closely by a rush of air that rustled the leaves, not more than a few hundred yards behind them: the sneeze of Wolfgang Pochs, the Horseman of Pestilence. Alfred tried to run, but his act of defiance had left him all too human; his limbs had nothing more to give.

The stakes of bamboo ahead curved towards him; he slowed and changed direction, heading east. The shafts moved again, cutting off his escape. There was another choice: west, but Alfred, in his panic, turned and tried to run back the way he'd come. The bamboo trees snapped shut. The twisting of nature was not a natural skill of a Horseman; Mr Gee himself had intervened.

Wolfgang Pochs stepped from the undergrowth, a thin spindle of a man, spilling over with nervous energy that manifested as a near infinite number of physical ticks. His blond hair was thinning into a horseshoe about his cranium; and his nose, a straight slope that started in the centre of a very prominent forehead. Wolfgang looked upon Alfred with unbridled rage. He said, 'What the fuck do you think you're doing?'

Alfred felt his knees begin to give way.

'No, come on, tell me. What the fuck do you think you're playing at?'

Daphne Unger thrashed and beat her way through the undergrowth and stood panting with her hands pressed against her knees. 'Why do they not fight their wars near a health spa?' she said miserably. 'You caught him, then.'

'With Mr Gee's help,' Wolfgang said. 'Alfred was about to tell me what he planned to do with the marine, here.'

The marine raised his head and peered through Daphne and Wolfgang, his eyes stopping short of the bamboo forest behind them. 'Why have we stopped?'

Alfred said, 'We have company,' and laid him gently against a tree.

'I see no one else.'

'Truth be told, you should not be seeing me.'

'Why do you keep doing this?' Wolfgang demanded of him. 'You would think that after one screw-up you would just do as you're told for the rest of eternity, but no, not you. What is it, Alfred? Does destiny not agree with you?'

Alfred removed his hat and pressed at his brow with a silk handkerchief. 'I sometimes do wonder myself.'

'We have to take him back, Alfred,' Daphne said.

Alfred's legs finally buckled and he sank to his knees. 'If you wish to take him, then you will have to kill me first.'

The soldier opened his mouth to speak, but Alfred raised a single finger to his lips.

'You are being ridiculous,' Daphne said. 'We do not fight amongst ourselves.'

'No, I am not being ridiculous; I am being tired. Tired of this endless cycle of death and paperwork. And I know that you tire of it too, Daphne.'

'He is lying,' Daphne said quickly. 'He knows nothing of me. I fear the strain of this war has proven too much for him. Again.'

But Alfred remained stoic in his determination. Throughout the twentieth century he had been unsure of a great many things, but not this: the soldier would live. Not because he meant something to Alfred, or because he deserved to survive this terrible war above all others. No, he would live because something of the Afterlife needed to change. The human race had evolved, was still evolving. They should evolve too.

'We both rage against destiny,' he said to Daphne, 'even as we are caged by it.'

'I see,' Wolfgang said, folding his arms. 'So you voice your concerns through acts of insubordination.'

Alfred chose to say nothing in reply.

'And yet I do not see Daphne wilfully circumventing a process that has been in existence since the dawn of reason.'

'She chooses to express her sadness in other ways,' Alfred said, looking to the fathomless hamper. Such a strange gift, he thought. It was one of Leonard's odd predilections, to guide others to their own damnation, even those he professed to love. Perhaps that is why, the Horseman thought, he excels so at a task he claims to despise; malevolence is his nature.

'That was hurtful, Alfred. Very hurtful,' Daphne said to him. She threw the hamper into the undergrowth, then looked back to be sure of where it landed.

'And for that, I am sorry,' Alfred said. He stooped down to retrieve the fallen soldier. 'But unless either of you is entertaining the notion of physically restraining me, then I shall be on my way.'

'No,' the young soldier said, with such strength and fortitude that Alfred knew immediately that someone else was speaking through him.

'Put him down, Alfred. Now.' The soldier looked sternly upon him, and Alfred reverently complied, laying the stricken man gently down near a cluster of bamboo roots. He took three paces back to stand between Wolfgang and Daphne and removed his hat, holding it respectfully at his chest with his head bowed. 'Sir, I—'

'Do you think I am a cruel God, Alfred?'

'No, sir, I do not, but I wished—'

'What you wish for is immaterial. There is only my will and the destiny of all things, preordained since the beginning of time.'

From somewhere above the trees, they could hear the drone of low-flying aircraft. Alfred looked to Wolfgang in horror, and Wolfgang turned the same expression on Daphne.

'I will return him to the POW camp, sir,' Alfred said.

'It is too late,' the soldier said. 'Your action has brought more Vietcong soldiers looking for the escaped POW. The movement of such a large number of troops has alerted the Americans, who have, in turn, alerted their allies to the south. The planes you hear will lay waste to this entire region.'

'No, no. I am sorry, I will return him to the camp.'

'Every village from here to Da Nang will be little more than a charred memory. Thousands will die, Alfred. Because of you.'

'You can stop this! Why will you not stop this?'

'Because I cannot. When will you realise that destiny, simply, is? You cannot change it; you cannot shape it to your will. This soldier will die. His brothers, his sisters, his mother, his friends; they will not let his passing be forgotten. They will not accept him as Missing in Action. Their grief and rage will galvanise millions. Their loss will be instrumental in bringing this war to an end. That is destiny, Alfred, and no matter how many must suffer, destiny must stay its course.' The soldier rose to his feet. He placed a hand upon Alfred's shoulder. 'If I could, do you not think I would change this? Do you not think I would have altered the way of things to save my own son?'

Alfred's tears fell on the undergrowth, and the poison of self-loathing they contained caused the jungle floor to sprout thorns of the smoothest, sharpest bamboo. 'I am sorry,' he said. 'I am so sorry.' He felt a hand, a large and powerful hand, upon his shoulder. Wolfgang and Daphne were gone; starvation and disease would no longer lay waste here. Once the planes dropped their payload there would only be death, sudden and unjust; the department of Thomas Mort.

'Leave me,' he said. 'I will stay here with him.'

'Were you not listening?' Thomas said. 'This is not your choice to make.' As ever, he had thrown himself into the part; he was dressed in the plain black combat fatigues of a VietCong sniper. On his head he wore a *nón lá,* a conical hat he'd woven himself from palm leaves. On his feet he'd strapped a pair of sandals he'd made from the tyres of an abandoned American jeep. Of all the Horsemen, Thomas Mort was the one who enjoyed his work the most. And even on this day, the day of his downfall, Alfred Warr saw this as an irredeemable character flaw.

The soldier slipped gracefully to the jungle floor and lay still.

'The planes are almost upon us,' the Horseman of Death said.

Alfred began to weep, and Thomas Mort shook his head. 'Oh, Alfred,' he said. 'You really have done it this time.'

NINETEEN

MAGDELENA SNAPPED THE TABLET in two with her bare hands, just as the phone – the red one, the one she didn't care for one way or the other – rang.

'Mr Gee,' she said without emotion.

'Magdelena,' he said, and as she'd expected he was somewhat less than his shining self. 'I haven't heard from you in such a long time. I thought perhaps you'd given up on me.' He sounded genuinely concerned that she'd stopped reading the Newer Testament, and she had. But he knew all things past and all things to come, so his concern, Magdelena decided, was disingenuous.

She pursed her lips and drummed her fingers lightly against her desk. 'Is that what you thought?'

He paused for no other reason, she believed, than he thought now would be an appropriate place to pause. To be so powerful and yet so disconnected. She had never envied him, but it was only now she understood why. Did he really feel anything for the souls clamouring to be allowed through Purgatory and into Heaven? Did he care for the hundreds of thousands of refugees held crying and shouting, restrained by wraiths just a few hundred yards from her desk? Her office was overrun and she was not sure she cared herself.

'What else was I to think?' he said plainly and then ploughed on without waiting for a reply. 'But what did you think?'

'What do I think?'

'Of the chapter. It's the one about Vietnam if I'm not mistaken.'

Of course you're not, and you know you're not. 'Yes, sir. The one about Vietnam.' She perched on the edge of her desk and smiled at the two halves of the tablet lying at her feet. The gold lettering no longer shone and the marble had already faded to a dull grey. She hadn't thought that the writing might be alive.

'Well?'

'Well what?'

'What did you think?' He was beginning to sound impatient.

'Well . . .' She took a deep breath, 'I thought it was self-indulgent, among other things.'

And in the silence that followed, someplace else, a civilisation of billions looked to the skies and saw a meteor scorch the heavens; and as one, the billions breathed their last . . .

'Self-indulgent,' Mr Gee said. 'How do you mean, self-indulgent?'

'It reads like an omniscient ego trip, sir. Like a god watching his underlings stumbling and searching for their place in his tableau of creation.' Her heart beat faster; defiance was exciting. She could see why Alfred revelled in it. 'And I believe your characters lacked any real sense of being, if you understand my meaning.'

'No, I can't say that I do.'

'Well, let's try to ignore the fact that you *do* know what I mean because you are God and so you know absolutely everything—'

'Magdelena—'

'I find myself stunned, truly *stunned*, that you know so little about us: those who have served you since the beginning. You paint Alfred as some kind of disobedient buffoon who steps from the path of destiny whenever the desire takes him. That is unfair and untrue. Alfred is a good man, a man who cares deeply for his duties and the people whom they affect. Everything he has done, every misstep, every mistake, is because he cares. That is more than can be said of any of us.' She took another breath and closed her eyes. 'It is more than can be said of you.'

She was as stunned a few moments later when she opened her eyes and found her world had not come to an end. She could hear Mr Gee on the end of the line, breathing heavily; and when she listened more closely, Magdelena thought she could hear ten thousand angels at his shoulder, tutting their disapproval.

'On the subject of insubordination,' he said, 'perhaps Alfred isn't the one I should be concerned with.'

'Perhaps not, sir.'

'So, what else?'

'I'm sorry?'

'What else did you not like about the writing?'

Magdelena was caught off guard, not expecting her existence to have continued long enough for her to furnish him with further criticism. 'I suppose there is your portrayal of me.'

'Oh?'

I am being tested, she thought, or perhaps I am being judged. 'You seem to think that I do not care for Alfred Warr. You seem to think that I would put my career, and how people see me, over his welfare.'

'And you think this is wrong?'

'I know it is wrong.'

She heard him scratching at his chin. 'And yet you have hidden him away for almost a century,' he said, 'as though you were embarrassed by him.'

'That is untrue,' she shouted, in spite of herself. A number of wraiths, among those she'd charged with holding thousands of desperate souls away from her desk, turned to look at her.

'Or perhaps you were embarrassed by your relationship with him.'

If this is some sort of test, Magdelena thought, then it is an unjust one.'You are mistaken. I have hidden him away to protect him, to allow time for his mind to heal.' And without a moment's thought she added, 'I care for him, sir; more than I care for anything or anyone. And because I care for him I will do anything to see him safe.'

The thinking came afterward: memories of the few, fleeting, wonderful times they'd spent together; and the rest, when they'd circled each other, snatching fragments of love and then retreating to the safety of solitude. After the memories came the tears. She'd cried far too much of late; it was beginning to annoy her.

'I see,' Mr Gee said.

Magdelena wiped her eyes with the heel of her hand. 'Of course you do.'

'If you love each other then you both have an odd way of showing it.'

'Thank you, sir.' If she was to be plagued by these irrational bursts of emotion then she would have to arrange for Rachel to keep her supplied with boxes of handkerchiefs. 'For my part, I can say that to run Purgatory I have to appear more resilient than my male counterparts, of which there are a great many.'

Mr Gee chuckled. 'Are you saying the Afterlife is a hard place for a career woman?'

'Are you saying it is not?'

Mr Gee was silent for a moment, and in that silence, Magdelena thought she heard ten thousand angels gasp.

'You know, I honestly didn't know you were going to say that.'

'Then today has been one of surprises for us both, sir.'

'So it would seem.'

'This book of yours,' she began, 'would I be right in assuming that you have no intention of writing a new Bible? And that this book was for my benefit alone?'

At the other end of the phone, ten thousand angels sighed as if to say, 'At last!'

'Did you honestly think I have the time to write a whole new path for humanity? It is why we have a marketing department.'

'Of course.'

'Did you learn anything from the little you've read?'

Magdelena thumbed her intercom to summon Rachel. 'Yes, I'm afraid I did.'

'Good, yes. That is very good.' He sounded distant, apologetic even. 'Do you know that Gabriel came to see me?'

'He threatened to, yes.'

'Some nonsense about closing the gates of Purgatory until the crisis is over. I don't know what gets into him sometimes.'

'Actually, you do,' she said, and again, for just a moment, Mr Gee fell silent. Magdelena looked out to the horizon where the displaced souls had swelled to an unimaginable number. She'd already cancelled all leave for the ferrymen, put the wraith patrols on triple shifts. There was more she could do, if only she could clear her mind to think of it. But closing the gates . . . No, closing Purgatory had never been an option.

'We exist for them,' Mr Gee said, as though this alone was enough to excuse what was to come. 'They brought us into being and when they have no further need of us then that is when we shall cease. It has always been the way of things, Magdelena.'

She inhaled sharply. The air felt hot, used, already breathed and exhaled by millions. 'If . . . When Alfred dies down there, it will not be the same as Jason Christopher, will it? Enough of them believed in Jason to bring him back. But no one knows Alfred. No one believes in him. He will just disappear, won't he?'

'Yes,' said Mr Gee quietly.

And the only emotion she felt was surprise, and even then the only surprise was how little she felt. After all, at its most primeval, she thought, that is what love is: sacrifice. Jason Christopher sacrificed himself for his love of humanity, and Alfred had been doing the same, for ten thousand years, for the very same reason. This is how immortals ceased to be: they loved. Alfred loved mankind, and she loved Alfred so very much.

She thought she heard Mr Gee sniff; she definitely heard him clear his throat.

'May I ask you something?' she said.

'Anything.'

'It concerns your son.'

He hesitated, and the ten thousand angels at his shoulder began to whisper among themselves. But Mr Gee had made a promise and if nothing else he was a deity of his word. 'Go on,' he said cautiously.

'You must have known Jason would not go with Alfred to New Orleans.'

He said yes, he did know. He, unfortunately, knew everything.

'Then why did you send Alfred for him at all, if you knew he would fail?'

He replied without hesitation: 'Because I care little for the intransigence of fate when it comes to my son. That is most strange, do you not think?'

'I think it's called "faith".'

'Is it indeed? Can't say I care for it.'

'No, sir . . . Sir?'

'Yes?'

'Alfred . . . Will he suffer?'

He said nothing, and in doing so answered her.

'Oh.'

'I am sorry, Magdelena,' he said, and that was his farewell.

Magdelena put down the phone and her heart broke. Everything Alfred Warr ever was, everything he could be, it would all be lost to oblivion, dissolved to nothing. A few would mourn his passing, and then the cycle of creation would carry on. The few mortals that knew of him would die and he would be forgotten; and since her own memories, in part, were the memories of mankind, Magdelena knew she would forget him too. Perhaps ten years from now, perhaps ten thousand years; as ever, the time was unimportant, only the inevitability of what was to come.

I will not allow it!

'Ma'am?'

Magdelena raised her head. 'Rachel,' she said. 'How long have you been there?'

'Long enough.' The wraith looked shyly to the earth. 'I am sorry. I should not have been listening. It won't happen—' She raised her hand to her mouth. 'Oh, ma'am,' she cried, 'surely there must be someone else!'

'Rachel?'

'I have never cared much for him, but to see you so unhappy. Surely Mr Gee can send someone else. Why him? Why not Gabriel?'

'Rachel, stop this.'

But Rachel did not: 'None of the wraiths like him, you know. He's arrogant, and he's rude. He thinks he's Mr Gee's gift to women—'

'Rachel . . .' Magdelena reached for her, taking both her hands in her own and squeezing them tightly. The wraith's blood coursed in torrents through her veins. Gabriel said he mistrusted the wraiths; their transparent skin made them difficult to read. It was only now that Magdelena could see how untrue his words were. Rachel's emotions, her anguish, her fear for her, were here, on show for creation to see: her heart thundered like a steam hammer, her lungs expanded and contracted like bellows, and there were tears, something Magdelena had never seen from a wraith before, flowing in diamonds of salt.

'And he looks through us,' she said, almost screaming with the injustice of it. 'He looks through as though we don't exist. You must call Mr Gee, Magdelena.'

And it was the first time in a thousand years that Magdelena had heard Rachel speak her name.

'You must call him and tell him that Gabriel Archer is more than suitable for—'

Magdelena let go of Rachel's hands and took her into her arms. Her flesh was soft and almost unbearably hot, not cold and hard as many imagined wraithkind to be. Rachel placed her head beneath Magdelena's chin and cried in a way that was almost like music, her tears warming the flesh of Magdelena's throat.

'What is wrong with you, Rachel? Why are you being like this?'

'Because I know you,' the wraith said. 'I know you will try to save him with no regard of the risk to yourself.'

'He would do no less.'

'And you are sure of this?'

'Everything Alfred has done is to prove himself worthy of me.'

'No one is worthy of you,' the wraith said. She turned away, and Magdelena found the effect sad and strangely unnerving. She reached out and placed her hand gently on Rachel's shoulder.

'I can still see your eyes, you know.'

Rachel made a sound from somewhere in her throat, like small glass ornaments being shattered over and over again. She was laughing, or so

Magdelena thought. She turned around and pulled herself upright, floating exactly four inches above the ground so that her eyes were in line with those of her employer. 'I will fetch your finest coat,' she said. 'I understand the weather is somewhat inclement in New Orleans.'

'Yes, so I'm told.' Magdelena nodded gratefully.

' And I will see that it is cleaned,' Rachel said, 'when you return.'

TWENTY

'Is there anywhere in this country where it is not raining?' Elias pulled his coat tighter and then yanked his baseball cap low over his eyes. To his left, Pietro Lantosca was eyeing a gun shop across the street from where they had abandoned the car. To his right, Alfred Warr, doomed Horseman of the Apocalypse, looked to the heavens.

'What plagues you, Horseman?' Pietro said without looking at him. 'Do you miss home?'

Alfred removed his hat and scratched his head. Elias fancied that he looked less well than he did six hours ago. There were spots of rain settling on his jacket. It occurred to Elias that Alfred no longer stood apart from this world; he was bleeding into it, becoming one with it, something less than a god.

Alfred wiped his face with his handkerchief and looked forlornly at it when he realised it was damp. Up until now, his relationship with the handkerchief had been little more than a comforting affection.

'You are unwell,' Elias said.

The Horseman turned to him and smiled. He pointed at one of the many roads that criss-crossed the main thoroughfare, filled with revellers who danced in and among the gaudily coloured buildings, intent on celebrating themselves into the grave. They moved in a vague, fluid synchronicity with a pounding dance rhythm that blasted from every public address loudspeaker mounted on every streetlamp. Their eyes were glazed and their bodies, lacking food and water, were far beyond the point of exhaustion. Elias could see the dead, left on the streets, in dumpsters and doorways. And next to them, people made love: two, three, four at a time.

Heaven awaits, but for now, lose yourself, Elias thought.

'This way,' Alfred commanded and began walking south, towards the Mississippi.

'And you know this, how?' Pietro said, still looking longingly towards the gun shop.

'I just know.'

New York had left them unprepared for the abandon that had taken New Orleans. The atmosphere was much more intense, the people pressed more densely onto narrow streets. The music was louder, the lust more desperate, more depraved.

'When we find him,' Elias asked, 'how will you convince him to return with you?'

Alfred tripped over a couple who were fornicating next to a fire hydrant. He apologised and raised his hat. They didn't seem to care. 'I will offer him what he wants,' he answered.

'Which is?'

'His freedom.'

Pietro shrugged. 'He seems quite free now.'

'No, he is not.' Alfred stopped and put his fingers to his lips. 'He is still tethered to the Afterlife and he will not relinquish that. To do so would make him mortal. No, he will return. The question is how much damage will be done in his absence.'

The world's financial system had collapsed, food production had fallen to nothing, people were starving, the sick lay dying in hospitals and were quietly glad to do so: Elias wondered what more damage was left to be done. 'So what is it that you offer?'

Alfred took a deep breath and shivered. 'I will take his place. I will shoulder his burden as the CEO of Hell.'

'That is what this is about?' Pietro said. 'He wishes to change the terms of his employment?'

'I believe it is. Leonard has been the director of Hell since the beginnings of man. It was his punishment for interference.' Alfred started walking again, heading towards a wide alleyway, away from the mass of the crowd. 'It is a thankless task. Necessary, but thankless. You spend your days listening to the worst of humanity telling you that "there must have been some mistake. I'm not supposed to be here. I demand a right of appeal".' His voice took on a more sarcastic, mocking aspect. '"Whatever I've done, I didn't do it; it was my brother/sister/cousin/mother/dog/pet shark."' He stopped. The other two were staring at him. 'As I said, it is a thankless job, and I think that perhaps he has had enough.'

'Then why would you do it?' Elias asked.

'Because I deserve no more,' Alfred said, and appeared to shrink.

'I feel I ought to point out,' Pietro said, 'that self-pity is a most ungracious trait in a god.'

'How many times, Pietro? I am not a god.'

'You claim to be immortal, so how can you disclaim godhood?'

'Have you not listened to anything I have said over the past three days?'

'I have listened, yes. And I think you are a fraud.'

'So you do not believe in God?'

'I believe in God, Horseman. I just do not believe in you.'

Alfred smiled. 'Then why did you come?'

'I follow the supreme pontiff. It is as simple as that.'

As much as the exchange amused him, Elias felt compelled to intervene: 'His presence calms the voices in your head, Pietro. Surely that must prove something.'

'And only mine, Your Holiness,' Pietro replied. 'He has not waved his hand and set everything right. He has not clicked his fingers and sent Leonard Bliss back to Hell. In fact, his contribution to this venture has shown him to be nothing but human, and not a particularly useful one at that.'

Alfred clenched and unclenched his fist. 'You have a very outmoded view of godhood, he said, 'which matters not; as I've said, I am not He.'

They walked on in sullen silence, past a row of apartments and small houses, churches, bars and delicatessens. Alfred's pace began to slow, though the look of determination spoke of someone who believed they were running as hard as they could. As they entered another street that gave passage between eight churches, Pietro raised his hand and brought them to a halt.

'What? What is it?' Alfred followed the line of his gaze, looking up at the rooftops. 'I see nothing.'

But Elias could see them, moving in the shadows. He was about to shout out a warning, but heard the crack of a pistol as he opened his mouth. A figure toppled from the roof and landed broken at their feet.

'We must find cover!' Pietro trained the pistol across the roofline, firing two more shots, while Alfred bundled Elias into a doorway.

'Dear Lord,' Elias said, pointing to the body on the ground. 'I know this man. He is the apostle who took me from K2.'

He lay with his eyes open and blood leaking from his left ear. Elias thought that even in death he looked no less menacing. 'Pietro, you have killed an apostle!'

'Forgive me, Your Holiness, but I do not believe he was here to aid us.' Destiny agreed with him: a shot rang out and the window next to Elias dissolved, showering both he and Alfred with glass. Three more gunshots, followed by a burst of automatic fire that forced Pietro back into the doorway of a small church. He looked across the street and licked his lips, preparing to launch himself from a standing start.

'There is no room,' Alfred shouted.

'And you would never make it.' It occurred to Elias that the plan was to separate them from their apostle, which meant, perhaps, that they didn't mean to kill them. Still, it was a simple and clever tactic: divide and conquer. 'How did he find us?' he whispered.

'Who? Do you know who is doing this?' Alfred pressed himself further into the doorway as another bullet sung past his nose. He reached an answer before the pontiff had time to speak. 'Your manservant,' he said, shaking his head.

'We prefer the term "private secretary",' Elias said and couldn't imagine for the life of him why it was particularly important.

Across the street, Pietro fired another round towards the rooftops.

Alfred shouted, 'Do not waste your ammunition.'

'I have done this before, Horseman.' Pietro fired again and pushed himself back against the doorway. 'We are hemmed in. You must take the supreme pontiff and leave.'

'That is out of the question!' Elias shouted. He tried to step from their hiding place but Alfred pulled him back. 'We go together, Pietro, or not at all.'

A third voice spoke with a calmness and familiarity that on another day Elias would have welcomed. 'That is very noble of you, Your Holiness.'

'Vecchi.' Elias shook his head. He shouted to the rooftops, demanding to know what, in God's name, the monsignor thought he was doing.

'I am here to aid you in your quest, Your Holiness. I am here to help you to find the devil who walks among us.'

Alfred raised an eyebrow and showed it to Elias.

'You come to my aid by opening fire upon me? Your supreme pontiff?'

'A case of over-zealousness on the part of my companions. A misunderstanding. We should lay down our weapons and discuss how we are to deal with Leonard Bliss.'

Deal with him? Elias looked to Alfred who shook his head. The Horseman appeared much calmer than he'd expected. A few days ago he would have been searching for a table to hide beneath. His short time on Earth had hardened him, clearly.

'He seeks to separate us from our apostle,' the Horseman said grimly. 'I have seen this tactic many times on the battlefield: drive a line of between the strongest and—'

'Us?'

Alfred grinned. 'We have very little combat experience. That is the truth of it, I'm afraid.'

This was not what Elias needed to hear. 'You are the Horseman of War! How can you have "little combat experience"?'

'It is more of a clerical role,' Alfred replied. His smile broadened to the point of inane. 'More of a book-keeping position, truth be told.'

'Why are you smiling like that?'

'Honestly?'

'Is now a good time to lie?'

Vecchi called out to them: 'I await your answer, Your Holiness.'

Elias risked leaning out from the doorway so he could better see the rooftops. 'Can you at least tell me how many you think we are dealing with?' he hissed.

'I suspect two.' Alfred squinted, trying to see through the rain. His suit clung to him and the storm had wilted his hat. None of this, Elias thought, bodes well. 'And I think he plans to kill Leonard,' the Horseman continued, 'whether we surrender or not.'

'I think you are right.'

'That cannot be allowed to happen.'

Elias muttered, 'Really?' under his breath.

Alfred stared at him in disbelief. 'Hell will not run itself, Your Holiness.'

'I thought *you* were going to run it.'

Alfred licked his lips. 'I am unsure if destiny has that in mind for me.' He pushed Elias back against the wall and looked out. 'I think that perhaps my journey ends here.'

'Gentlemen,' Vecchi said, and punctuated his words with a burst of gunfire. 'Just tell me where I may find the Trickster and I will be on my way.'

'Tell him nothing, Your Holiness,' Pietro shouted.

'Pietro.' Vecchi sounded genuinely pleased that the apostle was still alive.

'You are endangering the life of the Holy Father, Salvatore. Where is your sense of honour, your sense of duty?'

'What I do, I do for the Church, and if you did not still think as a child you would understand that.'

'What I understand is that you have changed little from the pizza-thieving little *monello* I dragged through the seminary's training.'

Vecchi came back, his voice sitting tightly at the top of this throat. 'You dare to—I do what I do for the good of the us all, you fool! We stand at a turning point in history! We can kill the devil, and you would stand in my way.'

'This is not about the Church, Salvatore.'

'That is *Monsignor Vecchi* to you, Priest.'

'This is about your ambition.'

'He is distracting him,' Alfred whispered to Elias. 'We should be ready to make our escape.'

'Do not be ridiculous. They will cut us in two the moment we step from this doorway.'

'We have little choice. We cannot stay here.'

'And what of Pietro?'

Alfred looked across to where Pietro stood, counting out his remaining rounds while throwing insults to the rooftops. Their eyes met and Pietro gave the Horseman a single grim nod. Alfred acknowledged it with a barely perceptible nod of his own, leaving Elias with the unwelcome feeling that an entire conversation had just passed him by.

'We are leaving, Your Holiness.'

'How? We are pinned down!'

'Pietro will cover us.'

'And who will cover Pietro?'

Alfred did not reply. Instead, he pushed Elias out of the doorway and shouted for him to run. And so Elias ran. He heard the crack of gunfire and an automatic rifle burst in reply. He heard a cry and another body hitting the ground. He turned his head and he saw Pietro, his face calm, his eyes clear and the hint of a smile on his face, before he folded inward under a hail of bullets.

Glass shattered either side of them and he felt Alfred pushing him forward, clear of the street and into the crowd. They fought their way through a sea of people, and headed towards a row of apartment buildings that had been painted with murals of Heaven. Exhausted, deafened by the cacophony and yet somehow exhilarated, Elias took a flight of stairs four at a time and ran the length of a fire escape, the sound of Alfred's feet only a few yards behind.

Please God, he thought. Let that be Alfred. He wanted to run forever, but his body said otherwise: the onset of exhaustion was as sudden as it was final. 'I cannot go on,' he gasped. 'I must rest.'

Alfred slowed to a halt and leaned against a window frame, making a loud wheezing sound from inside his chest. 'We cannot remain here.'

'You are right,' Elias said, standing straight and looking back the way they'd come. 'We must go back for Pietro.'

'There is nothing we can do for him, Your Holiness.' Alfred took hold of his arm, and it was then that Elias saw that the Horseman's formerly pristine jacket was stained with blood, a crimson circle just below his left breast.

'Alfred . . .'

The Horseman blinked rapidly and tried to raise a smile. 'Well,' he said, 'I must say this has been an experience.' Then he slid down the wall until he was sitting on his heels. 'You know, I didn't even feel it.'

'I will seek help.'Elias removed his coat, rolled it and pressed it beneath Alfred's jacket.

'Ever since I came back, Your Holiness, I have felt things that I had forgotten for so long. My heart is beating so fast. And my mouth . . . my mouth is so dry. And so are my eyes. You know, I do not believe I blinked while we were running.' He coughed and added, 'I do not think I have ever felt so alive.'

'We must get you on your feet,' Elias said, but Alfred was now a dead weight, bound to the fire escape. 'I do not understand. How did he find us?'

'It can only be you. Some device you have carried with you from the Holy City.'

'Dear God.' Elias rummaged frantically through his pockets. 'It is the episcopal ring.'

'Give it to me,' Alfred said.

'This is my fault. I have brought this upon us.'

'Your Holiness, give me the ring.'

'I didn't want to leave it. This is all my doing.'

'He will be upon us within minutes.' Alfred reached up and took the ring from him. 'Now you must go.'

'And what will you do?' Elias pressed harder; the bundled jacket was already stained through. It seeped through his fingers.

'I will delay him as long as I can.'

'Alfred, you can do nothing. I will explain to him—'

'Try to understand, Elias, I have known this man since he was a child. I have watched him grow from a greedy little boy into the ambitious priest who murdered your predecessor.'

'You are mistaken,' Elias said, though every strand of his being told him that Alfred spoke the truth.

'I know you believe me.'

Elias wondered if these agents of the Afterlife were able to see into each other as easily as they could see into mortals. He tried to look in every direction at once, expecting to see apostles swarming about them like carrion crows.

'You must leave, find Leonard. Follow the path to the river.'

'But how will I know him?' Elias asked, feeling the Horseman's heart fading beneath his touch. 'I have never seen him before.'

'You will know him,' replied Alfred. 'Everyone knows him, especially men of faith. Now go.'

Elias nodded and gently rested Alfred's head against the wall. 'You will not die,' he said. 'You're a god. You will not die.'

'If enough believe in me, then I will live on.'

'I believe in you, Horseman.'

Alfred smiled. 'Then let us hope that you are enough.'

They embraced, briefly, for Alfred was in far too much pain, then Elias rose to his feet. The demons of his past lives were oddly silent, yet still his sorrow and his shame knew no end. He turned his back on the fallen Horseman and made his way unsteadily along the fire escape. He did not look back, knowing he would return to him, he would call for help, and they would both die there, waiting for aid that would never come.

'If I could perhaps encourage you to hurry, Your Holiness,' Alfred called out.

'Yes, yes.' Elias' response was more irritable than he'd intended. He was about to turn around to apologise, but instead he bit on his lower lip and ran down the staircase to the street. Again, fighting every instinct to look back, Elias plunged into the crowd and was swept away towards the river.

The Book Of Leonard

Chapter IX

AND SO IT WAS . . .

On the day that money ceased to be legal tender, because none was earned; and the day crime was legalised because no one cared; it was on this very day that Alfred Warr, for want of a more fitting expression, breathed his last.

Alfred lay alone on a metal walkway, not one league from the Mississippi River, his life pouring slowly from a small hole between his fourth and fifth ribs. In his final moments, the Horseman chose to focus his fading consciousness upon Magdelena Cane. He counted every strand of her hair, first black and then white. He followed the line of her braid to the small of her back. He gazed into her eyes and remembered the flecks of darkness he saw there; the darkness that came with reluctant longevity. He wished he had longer to truly savour the memory of her calves, but the sound of footsteps forced him to look outside himself. He hoped against all hope that it was her, and his heart sank further when Salvatore Vecchi stepped from the shadows.

The warrior priest approached and crouched down. He gently brushed Alfred's collars and marvelled at how his fingers passed through him.

'So this is how a god dies,' Vecchi said.

'I am no god,' Alfred replied.

Vecchi stirred his fingers, making ripples through Alfred's core.

'I would very much appreciate it,' Alfred gasped, 'if you would not do that.'

The monsignor's smile of compliance stayed for but a moment. He tore his hand from him and Alfred did cry out; the frigidity of the man's touch was unto death itself.

'You have cost the lives of many, for one so young,' Alfred said.

'I have done what needed to be done for the good of the Church.'

'I see,' Alfred said. 'For the good of all.'

'Indeed.' The monsignor looked about him and scratched at his nose. 'But tell me,' he said, 'how does a god end his days in Louisiana?'

And all Alfred could offer was: 'Fate.'

Vecchi nodded and sat back on his heels. 'You took the ring from him.'

'The tracking device? Yes.'

'Then I have underestimated you.'

'You are not the first.'

'If there was something I could do for you . . .' Vecchi began.

'I understand,' Alfred said.

'Your wound appears to be very serious.'

'Yes, I know this.'

'Fatal, in fact.'

'Yes.'

'I know of such things.'

'I do not doubt your expertise.'

'Of course, of course.' He held out his hand. 'The ring then.'

'You will never find him,' Alfred said, 'not in New Orleans.'

'Oh, I shall find him,' Vecchi said. 'I am extremely adept in such matters.'

'And then?'

'Leonard, I will kill. Elias . . . ?' He shrugged his shoulders. 'I do not know.'

'What is one more dead pontiff to you?'

Vecchi's nostrils flared, his eyes burned, and Alfred thought the monsignor would end him there and then. 'The ring,' Vecchi said and snapped his fingers.

Alfred reached slowly into his pocket and dropped a small metal circle into Vecchi's outstretched palm. Then he closed his eyes and filled his mind with thoughts of Magdelena.

'What is this?' Vecchi said. He held the ring by its tiny metal rod and peered at it.

'It is a firing pin,' Alfred said, Magdelena's smile playing in sepia behind his eyelids, 'from a concussion grenade.'

TWENTY-ONE

ALTHOUGH THE PUBLIC CONVENIENCE, situated at the intersection of Treme Street and Espianiade Avenue, less than an angel's leap from the French Quarter, was considered by many to be the last word in hygiene, privacy and convenience, Magdelena Cane could not help but wonder if the celestial elevator could have found her a more disquieting place to land.

She opened the door and stepped out into a street party that refused to be washed away by the Atlantic storm lashing the city. For the first time in fifty years, Magdelena felt mortal rain against her skin. It was different to the rains of the Afterlife; it had a much more solid feel to it, more like gel than water. She marvelled at how much she savoured it; she could easily have stood there for the next fifty years, letting the rainwater course channels over her flesh. She pulled her raincoat tightly about herself and took stock of her surroundings. The city was more alive than she'd ever remembered, in the throes of a Mardi Gras that would last for all time. She took a single step towards the surging crowds, and her foot reminded her that haste, while possible, would be very painful. She reached down and pressed against her gangrenous toe, forcing a putrid black liquid to ooze from the seams of her shoe. It hurt, it looked awful and it smelled worse, but she reminded herself that it was her own fault and the wound she'd inflicted upon Gabriel

Archer was worse by the mere fact it was so visible. She took a deep breath and limped determinedly towards the crowd.

Magdelena did have a plan, of sorts: she would find Leonard and hope that nearby she would find Alfred. She politely tapped the shoulder of a young man who danced frantically, completely out of step with the music thundering around him. Clearly he was in a world of his very own. Perhaps, she thought, it is why I am drawn to him.

He turned, his wild eyes roaming the length of her slender frame, then he stopped dancing. She was out of place: with this party, this town, this world. He could tell. She could tell he could tell.

'Why ain't you dancing?' he asked hoarsely, his throat stripped raw by days of endless celebration. He took her by her hand and her waist and spiralled in a lopsided waltz through several pools of rainwater. He stopped and planted a kiss on her lips that caused a stutter in the movement of her lungs. The crowd cheered them both, and in spite of everything, Magdelena felt somewhat flattered. Nevertheless, she pushed him gently away and told him that she could not dance, not on an injured foot.

'But perhaps you can help me,' she said, startled that after so many centuries her head could still be turned by the attention of men. It was as if she'd learned nothing in Galilee. 'I am looking for Leonard.'

The man ran his fingers through his dark hair and smiled, somewhat condescendingly. 'Honey, I know a lot of Leonards, you're gonna have to be a little more specific.' He spoke as a Gaul might; Magdelena knew then that she was close to the French Quarter. 'What is he? Black, white, tall, short?' He looked thoughtfully, upward and to his left, then ventured, 'Single, married?'

'Yes,' Magdelena replied.

The reveller looked at her as though her brain was seeping from her ear. 'What, he is black *and* white, tall *and* short?'

'He is all of those things and more,' she answered impatiently, touching his arm. 'Have you seen him?'

'Lady, I cannot help you if you don't—'

'Think harder,' she said.

The man seemed to deflate. He rolled his eyes and then, suddenly, became rigid. A tremble coursed through him and he shivered as though noticing the rain for the very first time. 'I . . . I have seen him,' he said. 'A short, heavy-set kinda guy, going bald, wearin' really thick red spectacles, real nasty black eye. Not my type at all.'

Clearly he was.

'Could you tell me which direction he was heading?' She was jostled by a woman and man, whose naked, enmeshed bodies undulated into her. Magdelena gave them a look that had once sundered civilisations.

'Towards the river, I think,' her thrall said. 'Try along Bourbon Street. Guy looked like he needed a drink.'

She thanked him, waved to the crowd, who cheered back, and set off in the direction he'd indicated.

'Hey,' he called after her. 'How come your coat ain't wet?'

She turned around and said, 'It's a Versace. Why in Heaven's name would I allow it to get wet?'

He tapped at his chin and opened his mouth to ask a series of questions, but stopped as the ground beneath their feet rippled. Then came an explosion and, less than a hundred yards away, two buildings collapsed into an alley.

TWENTY-TWO

ELIAS HEARD THE EXPLOSION too. He heard himself whisper Alfred's name
and felt a tear run between his lips. It was the first of many; a few
moments on and he stood shaking and weeping as never before. He
covered his face with his hands and sank slowly to his knees. I cannot
go on, he thought. I am so close and yet I cannot go on.

The Atlantic storms pounded the streets and the sound of music and
joy filled his ears. Who was he to think he could – should – bring all
this to an end?

'Man, are you okay?'

Elias raised his head.

The woman smiled down at him and hoisted the child higher so he
sat in the cradle of her hip. She was young, perhaps on the wiser side of
her twenties, with a cascade of strawberry blond hair and freckles so
dense they stood out, even in the rain. The rest of her skin possessed
the whiteness of lilies, which gave her the aspect of tainted porcelain.
Elias chided himself for the thought, while his past lives jeered. The
woman and child were both drenched from the ceaseless downpour, as
was he. 'Don't I know you?' she asked. She wore rosary beads about her
neck, fastened with a gold clasp that also held a large crucifix made
from dark wood. A Catholic, Elias thought, a practising Catholic.

'I'm sorry,' she said. 'Aren't you the Pope?'

And a devout one at that. As far as Elias knew, his name had never been made public. He struggled to his feet.

'Oh my God; it is you! What are you doing here? Have you come for the Rapture? Oh my, I'm forgetting myself.' She dropped to one knee – a struggle while holding a child – and kissed his hand. 'Where is your ring?'

Elias opened and closed his mouth and eventually managed to say, 'I lost it.'

She looked up in horror. 'The episcopal ring?'

'I will have another one made,' he said, unconvincingly, then took the child while she struggled to her feet. After she'd dusted down her knees she stood staring at him. To his dismay, she made no move to take the child back.

'I am Sister Catherine,' she said and shook his hand.

'You're a nun.'

She nodded and beamed. 'For my sins. I saw you speak at an all-faiths symposium four years ago.' She looked coyly to her shoes and added, 'I've been a something of a fan of yours since then.'

'Really?' Elias couldn't see it.

'Why, yes. You spoke with such conviction, such fire. I was inspired, truly inspired.' She reached out and stroked his arm. 'You are a wonderful man, Bishop Bjørstad. I am so glad that you will be our conduit to God.' Then she put her hand to her mouth and chuckled softly. 'Not that it matters now, of course.'

'What do you mean?' The crowd had grown louder; thousands of people packed into one street. Elias took her hand and led her to the sidewalk, just as crowded but somewhat quieter. 'What do you mean by that?' The child started to squirm, so Elias put him down but held tightly on to his hand. The thought struck him that if she were a nun . . . 'Whose child is this?'

She shrugged while twirling a lock of hair around her index finger. 'Dunno,' she said. 'I found him near the park. Thought I'd take him with me.'

'With you? Where?'

She appeared to be trying to pout, though the overall effect was of someone sucking an oversized cough sweet. 'To Heaven, silly.'

Elias felt the blood in his heart cool. One of the voices from his past lives cried out: *She wants you! Accost! Accost!*

'You mean to kill yourself,' Elias said quietly.

'Of course! I figured you're here to do the same.'

'And the boy?'

'He's coming with me.'

The child looked up to him and nodded, and Elias found his resolve suddenly restored. He took her hand and placed it around the boy's. 'Sister Catherine,' he said, 'I need to ask you something, and it may seem an odd question but I must insist you answer honestly.'

'Of course, Holy Father.'

'I need you to tell me the last time you saw Leonard.'

'Leonard?' She looked puzzled. 'I don't think I know anyone called —'

'Please,' Elias said desperately. From somewhere behind him he heard the sound of glass and metal being smashed and crushed. A cheer went up from the crowd and when he looked round, he saw a man lying on top of a crushed police car.

'Y'see,' Sister Catherine cried, 'we can all go to Heaven, right now. Isn't it wonderful?'

'Leonard.' He tried again. 'It is very important that you remember him.'

She took a cautious step away, taking the child with her. 'I told you, Your Holiness, I don't know anyone called Leonard.'

'Close your eyes,' Elias said, 'and try to remember.'

'Holy Father, I—'

'I order you!'

She closed her eyes. 'I'm sorry. I'm trying, I really am. I just have no idea who you are—' She stopped and her brow furrowed. 'Wait, I think I feel something.'

Elias clasped his hands together and prayed.

'No,' she said, opening her eyes. 'I'm sorry; it's gone.'

And at that moment, Elias knew the true meaning of despair. 'It's fine,' he said, as one of his past lives suggested he beat it out of her. 'I'm sure you did your best.'

'Say, did you say you were looking for Leonard?'

Without hope, Elias looked to the elderly couple fornicating at his feet. 'We seen him,' gasped the old lady. 'Tall guy, rake thin, masses of long grey hair and a big pirate's earring, black eye.'

'You did say Leonard Bliss?' the old man said, slotting his words between effort-worthy grunts.

'Yes!' Elias cried, 'Yes! Which way did he go?'

'Headed for Moonwalk Quay, by the looks of it,' the woman said. She pushed down on her husband's buttocks. 'C'mon Mike, put your damn back into it!'

Elias thanked them, though they'd already lost interest in him, and turned back to Sister Catherine who was watching the couple with eager fascination. 'Sister Catherine, I want you to promise me something.'

'Anything, Holy Father.'

'Take care of this boy and do not harm him or yourself until I return. Do you understand me?'

'Yes, Holy Father,' she said excitedly. 'You wish for the three of us to depart together.'

'No . . . ! Yes! Yes, that is what I wish.' Elias took both her hands and squeezed them. 'I will return soon, and we shall leave for Heaven together.'

Another body landed on top of another car.

'Hurry back,' she said.

Elias promised he would return and then ran as fast as he could in the direction of Moonwalk Quay.

TWENTY-THREE

HAD THIS BEEN A normal day then the police force would have cleared the streets. Had this been a normal day then a cordon several blocks wide would have been cast around the site of the explosion. Had this been a normal day, house-to-house searches would have revealed whether or not a second bomber was lying in wait.

But this was not a normal day, and so Magdelena Cane was able to stumble over the rubble that had once been two apartment blocks and feel the essence of that which had once been Alfred Warr.

The crowds of singers and dancers and love-makers did nothing to stop her, and Magdelena was grateful for that. I must remember to thank my lord and master, she thought bitterly, caring little whether he could hear her or not.

'Alfred.' She stood atop the ruins in the pouring rain and softly spoke his name. There was so little left of him now, barely a memory, and that too would fade from human consciousness. Alfred was not like Mr Gee or Leonard Bliss or Gabriel Archer: stories of him were not told in script or rhyme; he was not feared or worshipped. He was a less-than-significant immortal who held a minor administrative function; the celestial equivalent of a middle manager.

And yet Magdelena loved him, faults and all, like no other in the cosmos. She plunged her hands into the debris and searched for his spirit. But there was nothing. He was gone and he would not return.

'I am sorry, my love,' she whispered, 'but I am not enough.' She lacked faith, she lacked hope, but what she lacked most of all was mortality: the invisible 'use by' date etched into each and every one of them; the one true certainty that kept them striving, kept them fighting, kept them hoping for something better after they were given over to the soil.

She needed *them* to believe in Alfred Warr, and she would offer everything she was in return. She closed her eyes and spoke to the One Above All.

'Release me.'

There was no reply, and she thought, This must be what it is like to be human: to pray and hear nothing. But they prayed anyway, because they had faith – while she had His phone number. Magdelena flipped open her mobile, dialled *1* and put the phone to her ear. It rang four times then made an oddly organic clicking sound.

'Hello?'

'Release me,' she demanded.

'Magdelena—'

'I demand you release me.'

'Magdelena, please—'

'You have kept me immortal for two thousand years, so I know it is in your power to make me human again.'

'You are human,' he said reproachfully.

'No sir, I am not. I am a figment of human imagination, and so are you.'

And in the silence that followed there was time enough for a star to collapse and incinerate the thousand worlds in its shadow.

'I have served you,' Magdelena said, 'in all things without question.'

'Hmph.'

'Nearly . . . without question, as I served your son. I have asked for nothing—'

'Ahem.'

'—almost nothing in return.' She dabbed her eyes with her sleeve. 'I have to save him, sir. And I can only save him if I can believe in him with my whole heart, without sight or reason.'

'You seek faith.'

She nodded because she knew he could see her. 'Ronald Weakes told me that we ourselves have no faith. I think he is right, and it is why we cannot save ourselves. We know too much, sir, and without the unknown to believe in, we are incomplete.'

Mr Gee sighed, and the ten thousand angels at his back sighed with him. 'You will be reborn in human form,' he said, 'and you will not know of your past lives. You will know nothing of the Afterlife. You will know nothing of him. How can you hope to believe in him when you will not know of his existence?'

'I love him more than life itself. I believe that will be enough.'

'And you will love him, though you can never be with him again?'

'Love is perhaps strange like that.'

And again, Mr Gee was silent. Perhaps he deliberates, she thought. He might agree; he could refuse; and Magdelena wasn't sure which frightened her more. It suddenly occurred to her that she had not said goodbye to Gabriel.

'You must have known,' she said. 'You must have known all along that I was the one to be sacrificed.'

'Magdelena . . .'

'This is why you wrote the book for me. You wanted to show me that Alfred was worth giving my life for.'

Again, Mr Gee was silent.

'There was no need, sir. I already knew.'

He took a breath that could have altered tides. 'You will never know the sorrow I will feel for you.'

'No, I expect I will not, so do not make this harder for both of us.'

'There is no return from this; you do understand that.'

'Yes sir,' she said, and wished he'd hurry before she changed her mind.

'I will miss you terribly, Magdelena Cane.'

'I will miss you too, sir.'

'That is the truly awful thing,' he said. 'You will not.'

She heard him moving stone across stone, and someone whispering in his ear. Finally, the scrape of a steel across the monoliths she assumed were her release forms.

'Magdelena Cane.'

Magdelena closed her eyes.

'I release you.'

And without sound or flash of light, Magdelena Cane was no more.

TWENTY-FOUR

ELIAS WONDERED IF HE was the only man left on the planet who could genuinely say he was unhappy. The rain was as relentless as the celebrations, and without Alfred's influence close to hand, the voices of his past lives raged and thrashed inside his skull. The ceaseless beat of the drums called for him to abandon his quest and lose himself to the Rapture, and the voices inside his head agreed.

I have work to do, Elias told them. Important work, and then as an aftershot he added, And it is you who are weak. The voices fell silent then burst into laughter. 'I shall show you,' Elias shouted. 'I shall show all of you!'

Seeking Leonard Bliss proved to be as simple as inquiring to his whereabouts: 'Yeah, I seen him,' replied a man eating fire next to a hot-dog stand. 'Kinda tall, real thin, long black hair, bruised eye, and oily white skin. Looked liked one of them goth kids.'

'Yeah, we saw him, just a couple of minutes ago,' said the two men kissing outside a ransacked church. 'Real big guy. His muscles had muscles. Black eye, waxed chest, neat moustache, leather chaps. Real tight butt.'

His companion slapped him on the arm. 'I'm standing right here, you know!'

'Yes, that sounds like him,' Elias said wearily. He wondered if they perceived Leonard as they themselves wished to be perceived. He'd once heard a cardinal say that true evil is never further than the closest mirror. Though that was Cardinal Moynahan, he reminded himself, and Cardinal Moynahan was quite mad.

So Elias walked on, feeling he was closer and yet moving still further away. The rain seemed to beat down on him alone; the thousands around him simply revelled in it. But it wasn't just the rain; the population dropped from above like stricken birds, smashing into cars, sidewalks, other revellers. Each landing brought a cheer from onlookers, and Elias tried to imagine the countless souls clamouring at the gates of Heaven.

The people fell thick and fast around Jackson Square, so much so that Elias was forced to seek refuge inside a tavern, pressed between a police station and a fire house. It was deserted save the bartender who sat on stool watching a television programme: a documentary telling of the Yakuza's famine relief work in the Sudan.

'Ain't all this something,' he said without turning around.

Elias took a seat and said that it was. They both watched the documentary roll into a news report telling of the UK government's imposition of the one-day working week.

'One day's plenty,' the bartender said. He turned and blinked, as though he'd just realised Elias was there. He seemed unsure as to what he should do next.

'Perhaps you could serve me a drink,' Elias said helpfully.

'Yeah, yeah sure.' He looked around under the counter, for what, Elias had no idea.

'A Scotch,' Elias said, and then, at the insistence of the voices from his past lives, added, 'A double.'

The bartender was back on familiar ground. He measured out a small glass and placed it in front of Elias with a napkin. Elias fumbled in his pockets, realising he had no money.

The bartender smirked and raised his hand. 'Relax. It doesn't matter.'

'I am so very sorry,' Elias said, raising his voice above the jeering in his head. 'I will arrange for payment as soon as—'

'Look around you, friend.' The barman pointed at the TV screen. 'Who gives a fuck about any of that shit anymore?'

Elias declined to agree but asked, 'Why are you not out there with them?'

'Ah, now there's a tale.' He began wiping down the woodwork with a fresh cloth. 'This whole *do a good deed then kill yourself* thing just doesn't sit well with me.' He tapped the side of his head. 'No conscience you see. Nothing to tell me what a bad boy I've been.'

'Oh.' Elias suddenly wished Pietro was with him.

'I'm a . . . Damn, what did the shrink say?'

'A sociopath,' Elias supplied, and slid slowly from his barstool.

The barkeep clicked his fingers. 'Yeah, that's it! That's what he said! An evil murdering sociopath.' He laughed and shook his head then froze. 'You know, he really shouldn't have said that. It was kinda rude.'

'Yes,' Elias agreed, glancing at the door. 'Very rude.'

'You know what I did?' said the barkeep, who Elias now suspected wasn't a barkeep at all.

'I'm rather hopeful that it was some sort of traffic offence.'

'Killed a buncha people, six in fact, in this very bar.'

On the screen, the Chinese government was announcing free elections along with a euthanasia programme that would deliver one billion people to the gates of St Peter within a year.

Elias breathed, 'God help us.'

'Looks to me like he's helping himself.' The bartender-that-wasn't refilled his glass. 'You're looking for Leonard.'

Elias looked at him, forgetting for the moment that he could be murdered on a whim. 'How did you know?'

'Because I told him you would come.'

The voice came from the corner, from a table tucked invisibly behind the jukebox. There seemed to be nothing unusual about the voice, except that on hearing it, Elias found the incessant cursing of his past lives stopped. He rose to his feet, picked up his glass and made his way slowly to the corner, painfully aware of how the temperature seemed to rise with every step. Standing by the table was like standing at the mouth of a furnace. The sullen individual sitting there wore a pair of paisley swimming trunks; a T-shirt that proclaimed in fiery lettering, 'Better the Devil You Know'; and a red baseball cap with two cloth horns sewn into its sides. His hair burst from beneath the cap in untidy spikes of grey. He didn't look from his glass as Elias nervously took the chair opposite. Instead, he kept his head down, tracing his finger across the table, scorching his name into the wood.

'So, Elias Bjørstad,' the devil said. He spoke quietly, and yet with each syllable Elias thought he could hear the agonised screams of millions. 'You have escaped me more times than I care to remember.' He looked up to reveal a face very much like Elias's own, perhaps older and with a black eye that looked on the verge of necrosis. And as well as the heat, there was a smell, not sulphur as he'd expected, but something else, something vaguely familiar.

Elias's past lives remained silent, hoping, he presumed, that they would not be noticed.

'I am here to ask that you return to the Afterlife,' Elias said. He wished he'd cleared his throat first as his voice came as a strained whisper.

'And they send you? No one else?' He looked past Elias's shoulder, squinting as though someone invisible may be standing behind him. 'Hmph. They really did send just you.'

'There were others,' Elias said, suddenly remembering what the smell was: embalming fluid. He swallowed so he wouldn't wretch. 'They did not make it.'

'I see.'

'I am sorry.'

'Oh, no need to apologise. I'm sure it isn't your fault.' The devil sat back in his chair and crossed one leg on top of the other. He was wearing plastic sandals and odd socks. 'So, I will hear your petition.'

'I beg your pardon?'

Leonard sighed impatiently and rolled his eyes to the ceiling, and kept them rolling until the whites showed. 'You are here to convince me to return to the Afterlife, are you not?'

'Well, yes, but—'

'Then get on with it.'

Elias had no place to start. He was used to offering his counsel to those in distress, those who had reached a crossroads in their lives and did not know which way to turn. But those people were human. Leonard Bliss was decidedly not, outward appearances notwithstanding. He cleared his throat and decided to lead with a question: 'Perhaps if you tell me what troubles you.' He had to stop himself from adding the traditional 'my son'.

'What troubles me?' The devil rocked his chair forward on to four legs and slammed his arms down on the table.'Can you not see what troubles me?' He jerked an angry thumb to his right eye. 'He punched me!' he cried petulantly. 'He punched me, in the face.'

Elias noticed that tiny flames danced on the surface of his tongue. 'So, you are looking for . . . an apology?'

'An apology?' Leonard looked at him in disbelief. 'You think this can be fixed with an apology?'

The barman placed a tall glass of water on the table and left without a word.

'I thought it might be a start.'

The devil leaned back and fumed. For a moment, Elias believed the audience was over, but then he spoke again, his tone now soft, but still laced with the suffering of many. 'You have no idea what it is like,' he said. 'Everyone and everything hates me. They scream and spit at me from their cages, and I tell them: "It's not my fault! You condemned yourselves!"'

It occurred to Elias why Alfred Warr had been sent to retrieve him: they were very much alike.

'And they write things about me,' Leonard said. 'In pamphlets and cartoons.' He leaned closer, beckoning for Elias to do the same, which he did, reluctantly. 'You would not believe the things they scratch on the walls of the lavatory cubicles. Slander! Things about me, and latex, and goats. Can you imagine such a thing?'

Elias said he could not. A vague notion began to form in his strangely silent mind that perhaps Leonard just needed someone to hear him out.

'I have *never* behaved inappropriately towards a goat. And then there are things they say about me and Magdelena Cane. Untrue! That bloody woman would break me in two.

'I try my best for them: the contemporary music appreciation society; the life-drawing workshop; the Chinese for Beginners class. I paid – out of my own pocket – for a day trip to the Lake of Eternal Suffering. They said they had a wonderful time, and yet still they mount legal challenges, trying to bargain their way out of Hell. And I ask myself: "Why do I bother? Why in the name of Mr Gee do I waste my time with these whining and unappreciative—"'

'Leonard,' Elias said, so sharply he surprised himself, 'perhaps there is something that you want. Something that – and believe me, no one is belittling your own suffering – something that would ease your mind and make you consider returning to work.' It seemed harsh, perhaps a little unfeeling, but Elias was aware that while Leonard spun his tale of woe, outside they were still hurling themselves from rooftops.

Leonard sniffed and set his jaw. 'I am sorry if I'm boring you.'

'You are not boring me, ' the pontiff lied, 'but as long as you remain . . . indisposed, then more people will kill themselves to reach Heaven. We thrive on uncertainty, Leonard. We live to discover: new things throughout the cosmos, new things in ourselves. As much as we need to be generous to each other, to love one another, we need to know evil, we need to face temptation so that we can make the choice to strive for something better.'

Leonard regarded him as a scientist might regard the contents of a petri dish. 'You speak eloquently, Bjørstad. I remember a past life of yours when you could barely grunt.'

'I was a different man back then. Now, I believe I have bettered myself. This was the decision I made when faced with the evil I was.'

'It took you long enough.'

'Yes,' Elias said, sadly, 'by all accounts, it did.'

Leonard placed his finger on the table and left it there until he'd burnt a fingerprint. 'And would it not be simpler just to prevent people from being evil? You live your lives being lovely to one another and then just go to Heaven after a lifetime of harmless breeding?'

'That is existing,' Elias said. 'It is not the same as living.'

'No,' the devil said thoughtfully. 'I don't suppose it is.'

'We need to grow, Leonard. That is our purpose.'

'Until you no longer need us?'

'Perhaps,' Elias said, 'perhaps not. I do not know.'

'You make the possibility of oblivion sound like an adventure.'

'And yet it is a possibility that we mortals must face eventually, and we must face it without the certainty of something beyond. That is the essence of the faith upon which you thrive.'

Leonard looked at him, a question on his lips that Elias generously saved him the embarrassment of asking. 'Why else do you think your eye hasn't healed?'

And slowly, almost imperceptibly, the devil nodded. He took off his cap and scratched at his scalp, sending flakes of dry skin into Elias's water. 'There will be conditions.'

Elias moved the glass to one side. 'I do not have the authority to grant conditions.'

'You are Mr Gee's representative on Earth,' Leonard said. 'You have the authority.'

This did make a surreal sort of sense. 'Go on,' Elias said doubtfully.

'I will need holidays.'

'You have just had one.'

'Regular holidays. One day for Jason Christopher's birthday is somewhat insulting.'

Elias took a deep breath and spread his fingers across the table. It was unpleasantly warm to the touch. 'What did you have in mind?'

'I would like four weeks, paid, during the year.'

It sounded very reasonable and very human, though Elias remained doubtful. After what he had witnessed over the past few days, he was uncertain that humanity could cope with the eradication of evil for one month out of every twelve. 'Do you not have some kind of personnel section to negotiate for this kind of thing?'

'We do,' Leonard said. 'But it is run by a preening idiot.'

Four weeks sounded like a very long time. 'Four weeks every century,' Elias heard himself say.

Leonard looked annoyed, judging by the way smoke billowed from his nostrils without a cigarette in sight. 'That is unacceptable.'

'I do not believe so,' Elias said nervously, without taking his eyes from Leonard's festering facial scar. 'You are growing weaker. The more people die then the less are here to believe in you. You will cease to exist. Eventually, you all will.' He tried to add a note of finality to his words, but his voice, his courage, failed him. And now Leonard Bliss was looking at him, deciding whether to speak further or simply wipe him from existence.

'You know, I could kill you with a thought.'

'I imagine you could, and that would be one less believer to sustain you.'

Leonard scratched at his cheek, making the scar weep.

'So,' Elias said cautiously, 'would four weeks every century be acceptable?' Leonard may have nodded, but he wasn't sure. 'Was that a "yes"?'

'Yes!' The force of Leonard's reply shook the bar's foundations. Plaster fell from the ceiling, and the glasses hanging in racks closest to them shattered into fine powder.

'Good,' Elias croaked. 'Now, is there anything else?'

And there was. Leonard reeled off a list of demands, to which Elias agreed, negotiated down or ruled out altogether. He negotiated the request for early retirement down to an increased pension because he could not imagine a situation where an immortal could ever claim it; he agreed to a council of demons where the hellspawn could air their grievances to Mr Gee; he agreed to a review of Leonard's employment terms, but refused any scheme that involved a job share between demons, angels and wraiths. He refused the indoor swimming pool because in his limited experience, no one who was simply *given* a swimming pool ever actually used it.

They spoke for over four hours. They spoke of humanity's past and its myriad futures. They spoke of the struggle of good against evil, of respect and hate. The homicidal barkeep served them spirits and snacks, while outside the people and the rain stopped falling.

Leonard was smiling, and that made Elias nervous. 'Finally, after so many centuries,' the devil said, sipping his sixteenth vodka of the day, 'a pontiff I can actually work with.'

The Book Of Magdelena

Chapter I

AND SO IT WAS ...

On the day Israel and Palestine declared an end to their ceasefire; and the day that Meir Bashevis of Rosh Pina passionately kissed his best friend Zivah Mahel, the woman who, through six decades of unspoken longing, had nursed him through alcoholism, depression, the divorce from his first wife and the death of his second; on the day Leonard Bliss walked back to the Afterlife and faced the wrath of Mr Gee . . . On that very same day, the conscience of mankind shrank from a roar until it was once more a quiet rumbling that occasionally caught humanity unawares.

And so millions stepped away from the ledge, rose from the rail tracks, released themselves from the noose, took the pistols from their mouths, their heads from the ovens, and decided that perhaps it was better to be called upon than arrive unannounced.

The world had swayed, and now it righted itself. The poor returned to work and the rich watched them leave. Greed once more became a commodity, and faith, a curiosity. The days of Rapture became a byword for conspiracy: a mass hallucination, a contaminated water supply, something seeded in the clouds, something that poisoned the food chain. Nations regarded one another with suspicion. There was talk of invasion; there were plans to make war.

Mr Gee watched and smiled. He repaired the machine; the one bolted to the underside of the human psyche, protecting it from madness should it ever encounter byproducts of its religious beliefs. The machine groaned and whirred, clanked and stirred.

And one year on, all that was, was once again: talk of war was forgotten; and for all things wrong with the world, everyone blamed the Americans.

But something had awakened in the mind of humankind: a desire to walk a different path; a road to enlightenment.

TWENTY-FIVE

WHEN ALFRED WARR CAME back into existence his ears popped so violently he thought his end had come no sooner than he'd begun. He dropped to his knees, clutching his head as all the sounds of creation burst against his eardrums. A hurricane of air froze his nostrils, the summer breeze flayed his skin and the naked sun blistered his scalp. But it was good. All of it was good; it meant he was alive. He coughed; he wretched; he lay in the dirt, gasping. He clenched his fists, taking handfuls of dust and forcing it between his fingers.

Alive.

He had been returned. He took short rapid breaths, waited for his senses to calm. Slowly, the world eased around him: the breeze simply cooled; the sun gently warmed. And in the air he felt the gentlest change, like someone drawing ripples through a stream.

'I thought I would find you here.'

The voice was familiar and carried an air of contempt, though he couldn't quite place it.

'And where is "here" exactly?' he asked.

The voice paused before answering, and Alfred thought it curious that he could not see her feet. 'Roquebrun,' the voice said crisply. 'The South of France.' A transparent hand reached down to help him stand. He took it; it felt like soft glass.

'You are Rachel,' he said. 'I remember you.'

The wraith gave no indication that she was listening. She cast a sour transparent eye over him and shook her head.

Alfred swallowed and fastened his jacket. 'How have I returned?' he asked.

The wraith did not reply; she turned slowly and then drifted towards a winding path that led to the base of the mountains and the village beyond.

Alfred followed, and it was a pattern of behaviour that felt horribly familiar. 'Where is Magdelena?'

'Come,' Rachel said. 'There is much you must learn.'

They passed unseen through the townsfolk who walked the same path. The path widened as they came in sight of the bridge joining the two halves of Roquebrun across the river.

'I came here once before,' he said, hoping to light the spark of conversation, 'with Magdelena. It was a long time ago. Between the wars, I think.' It occurred to him that he wasn't sure exactly how long ago that was. 'How long have I been gone?'

The wraith said, 'Eleven years,' without slowing or turning around.

Yes, Alfred thought. There is contempt there. 'That is a long time.'

The wraith did not reply.

'Jason Christopher came back in three days.'

She spun and drifted to him, stopping when their noses almost touched. 'Many more of them believe in Jason Christopher than believe in you.' And then she turned and drifted away again. Alfred followed, listening to the run of the waters and the sound of bicycle wheels on cobblestones. It was very much a time between wars, he observed, which meant, most likely, that at least one was due.

Eleven years. The Afterlife was timeless, but he'd spent his existence walking the path of history alongside mankind, and so Alfred was sure he felt it: the passage of time was as real to him as it was to the human race.

When they reached the village square he was thinking that perhaps he could settle here. Not forever of course; perhaps for twenty or thirty years. He thought that after so long apart, Magdelena could take respite and join him. 'I do not understand; why is she not here to greet me?'

Rachel stopped again, but did not turn around. Alfred's first thought was that she could no longer bear to look at him, such was her repugnance. But as he watched her, he saw that she seemed unsteady, gently swaying as though borne on a crosswind. 'She is no longer of the Afterlife,' she said.

Alfred blinked. The air around him seemed to grow as thick as oil. 'That is impossible.'

'She wanted to save you,' said Rachel, 'and she was willing to surrender her immortality to do so.'

'No, that is not right. Who is running Purgatory? I need to speak to the Head of Pu—'

'You will speak to me.' She turned and Alfred could see liquid crystals streaming for her eyes. 'I have been running Purgatory for the eleven years since she left us.'

Much had changed, and Rachel explained it all to him with a solemnity that made Alfred feel that much of it was his fault. Pope Gregory XVII and Private Weakes had sailed into Limbo with Magdelena's blessing, and returned five years later with the lost souls of the Fighting Somersets. Following a week-long celebration, Gregory took his new position as the Head of Inhuman Resources, and Gabriel Archer, still very much in the closet, had moved across to run the new legal research division, which he perceived as a more dynamic career route for one so obviously masculine.

And young Ronnie Weakes, who had waited so diligently since the end of World War I, joined his comrades in their ascension to Heaven.

Rachel stowed the past decade into a few short sentences, and Alfred heard very little of it.

'And what of Monsignor Vecchi?'

'It was most strange,' Rachel said. 'On the day of his judgement, his conscience showed itself to be something akin to an abused spouse: quiet, meek and fearful. It refused to speak out against him.'

Alfred sighed. 'Then he ascended.'

'Without the testimony of his conscience,' she said bitterly, 'I could do nothing.'

Alfred felt only the mildest sting of disappointment. The system of judgement was not perfect; Magdelena had always said so, though it hardly seemed to matter now.

But Rachel continued, explaining that Heaven did not sit well with Salvatore Vecchi: 'He became . . . difficult, melancholy. He believed that destiny had cheated him from his eventual place on the papal throne.' She smiled, perhaps. 'Destiny and you.'

'Then I am glad that I am useful for something.'

'And then of course there was Pope Gregory XVII. Facing the man he had sworn to protect, the man he'd murdered, each day, until the end of days . . . The prospect was too much for him to bear, and then the sense of deprivation, of loss . . .'

Alfred stopped walking. 'What are you saying?'

'His rosary beads and his shoes were found in the Celestial Gardens, beneath a noose tied to the apple tree.'

'He chose non-existence over Heaven,' Alfred said. 'Then perhaps he possessed something of a conscience after all.'

They travelled on, Rachel stealing glances at him for every other step that he took.

'I should have done more,' she said. 'Vecchi should not have ascended. If I were—'

'Magdelena?'

Rachel bowed her head.

'She was much loved,' Alfred said.

'Yes. Yes she was.'

'The sacrifice,' he said. 'It was to be me.'

'Yes,' she said, 'yes it was.'

'We will speak with Mr Gee. We will see to it that she is restored.'

'Do you not think that I have tried?' she said, showing her deepest revulsion, even through transparent eyes.

Hate me if you must, Alfred thought, it is insignificant when compared to the the hatred I feel for myself. 'Did you offer yourself in her place?' he asked though he knew it was not her sacrifice to make.

'I did. As did Pope Gregory XVII and Private Weakes and half of Purgatory.'

The streets of Roquebrun grew narrow, and low buildings of polished stone rose either side of them. Despite its small size, the village seemed to carry an international air. Alfred recognised the denizens of at least two dozen countries, and they all appeared to be walking in the same direction. Unseen, they joined the flow of human traffic on its journey to the village square. The passage through became choked with cars and vans parked either side.

Illegally, Alfred suspected, and was sad to see that he still concerned himself with things that did not really matter. The vans carried the insignia of various news media organisations from around the globe: the BBC was here, as was CNN, Sky, Fox News and Al-Jazeera; their respective crews hurriedly unloaded equipment and pushed their way through the crowds.

'Why are they here?' Alfred asked.

'You will see,' Rachel replied.

'Why did I come back to this place?'

'I imagine you were drawn here,' Rachel said. She made a sharp left turn and floated in front of a gift shop. In its window it carried models of the Eiffel Tower, the Arc de Triomphe. 'Like everyone you see here, you were drawn to her.' She beckoned for him to come closer.

Alfred complied, following her crystal gaze into the shop window. He spied a pretty little thimble that he thought would have made a lovely gift for Magdelena, and for a moment, his sense of loss threatened to overwhelm him. He folded his lower lip between his teeth and squeezed his eyes shut.

She is . . . gone. She is gone. Forever.

But that was the strangeness of immortals: those afflicted with unceasing longevity could not truly grasp the concept of eternity. And so an eternity without Magdelena simply felt like a dull ache around the outside of his heart, when he knew it should be so much more. So he pressed his head against the glass and tried to shrink forever to its lowest terms. Look at it, he told himself. Look at a time far from now, when the human race is no more, and their sun has burned itself out, and their galaxy has collapsed, and the universe itself is nought but a speck in the nothingness; imagine the day after that and see that you will have reached it without ever again feeling Magdelena's breath upon your cheek.

'Why do you weep, Horseman?' Rachel asked.

'Because,' Alfred said finally, 'because I have seen the true meaning of despair and found I care little for it.'

Rachel may have nodded, Alfred wasn't sure. He wasn't sure he cared. She pointed at the glass, at a picture sitting between the French national flag and a large jar of confectionery. He wiped his eyes on his sleeve and peered through the window, and then he looked more closely. The brushwork was almost alive; every line, every flourish spoke of the almost inhuman talent possessed by the artist. It depicted a battle, fought in the mud of the Somme, where soldiers died needlessly beneath the sombre grey of a winter sky; thousands of them, torn and scattered all the way to the horizon. Their anguish clawed at him, taking the breath from his body, and when he thought he could lose no more to the painting, he saw himself, dyed into the carnage as if to be invisible. He looked almost comical in his linen white suit and fedora hat. It was only the greyness of his skin and the sadness in his eyes that joined him to the rest of the painting. He wondered if others could see it, or was his image for those of the Afterlife and the few humans sensitive to them.

'It is me.' His words left his mouth, as soft as air.

There was another painting further back. Another war, the jungles of the South Pacific, and again, the senseless waste. And he was there, standing sadly among the dead and the dying.

And there were more: Korea, Viet Nam, and places Alfred recognised though the wars were unknown to him. But in each painting, there was always the thin grey ghost in the linen suit and the fedora hat.

The people inside the little shop were as mesmerised as he was. Some wept as they purchased the paintings, others could not bear to look at them, running from shop in floods of tears.

'The artist,' Alfred said. 'How does he do this? These pieces are extraordinary.' And then Alfred knew, and the knowing tore even more from his being. 'It is her,' he said to Rachel.

Rachel inclined her head slightly – what passed among wraithkind as an approving nod. 'It is how you were brought back. Her love and sorrow for you is in the paintings, and the paintings touch them.'

'I must see her.'

'She will not know you. It is not her; it is but a whisper of her.'

'She will know me.'

'She cannot even see you.'

'She has told of me in her paintings,' Alfred said angrily. 'She will know me. She will remember me. Take me to her!'

His ferocity pressed Rachel back. She seemed surprised, though not unpleasantly so. 'It is a pity,' she said. 'If you had shown half this arrogance a hundred years ago then you would have been a better Horseman.' She drifted away from the window and rejoined the river of tourists and reporters flowing towards the village square. Alfred hurried to catch her.

'You are in my service now, Alfred Warr.'

'I am aware of that.'

'And you will find me less forgiving of your . . . lapses.'

Alfred said nothing.

'I have never thought much of you, if I am honest,' she said.

'If I am honest, I have never much noticed you.'

'But Magdelena saw something in you that was worthy of her time and her love. Whatever it is, I hope to discover it for myself.'

Alfred decided he cared little if she discovered it or not.

The road became a minor thoroughfare lined with cafés and pebbled houses. The buildings were taller here and bleached white, which offered something approaching shade from the ferocious sun. Rachel had not finished speaking, though Alfred had quite finished listening.

'I think that perhaps it was the love you have for the humans that she found so endearing. I think it is why you suffer so when they harm one another. Perhaps you need to cultivate a level of detachment.'

'If my love for mankind is the reason Magdelena loved me,' Alfred said, 'then do not expect me to forsake it.'

They completed their journey without another word. Alfred's pain screamed silently inside him. He began to wonder if he would still be in such agony the day mankind ended.

The village square was as quaintly beautiful as he'd expected; the cobbles formed a neat circle, six stones deep, around a small, well-tended ornamental fountain. Lilies and chrysanthemums were neatly arranged in abundance, encircling the fountain and the pyramid of pictures behind it. The crowds had stopped and obediently sat in a half circle that stretched to the edge of the square and spilled into the streets beyond. The journalists had set up their equipment a respectful distance away. Rachel and Alfred drifted through the crowd, stirring some of the more sensitives ones, who felt a ripple of cold as the field agents of the Afterlife passed through them.

'Here,' Rachel said, pointing at the artist, sitting with her legs folded on the edge of the fountain. The spray of water soaked her hair and the back of the pale yellow summer dress she wore.

Alfred gazed at her and understood. His heart sank and his universe, in its entirety, sank with it.

He looked at Rachel who may have been watching him; it was difficult to tell. 'How can one so young paint so beautifully?' he asked, though the answer did not matter to him. All that mattered was that he had truly lost her.

The child seemed oblivious to the crowd, engaged in painting another picture that depicted man's desire to destroy himself. Her hands flashed almost mechanically between pencils and brushes, adding marks and strokes without any apparent attention to where each would go.

'She cannot hear and does not speak,' Rachel said, and Alfred found his anguish could run still deeper. 'She was found as an infant eight years ago, here, next to the fountain. The villagers take care of her, and have resisted all attempts to make her a ward of the state.'

Another picture finished. She held it out and waited for someone to come from the crowd to take it. A young woman ventured forward and took the picture in both hands. She thanked her between sobs and returned to her place on the cobblestones. The girl picked out another canvas, replaced it, selected another, and began to sketch again, with sweeping, balletic strokes of her pen. Her face seemed serene, devoid of any feeling or passion, an expressionless contrast to the life she imbued in the canvas.

Alfred, captivated by her, asked why the authorities did not simply take her away.

Rachel smiled, making the extra effort to ensure it showed. 'She has a guardian, someone of considerable influence.'

There was a raised murmur from the crowds. The journalists looked bewildered for a moment, then began talking among themselves. One shouted 'He comes!' and pointed to a passageway leading away from the square. The cameras and microphones swung towards it as an old man dressed in jeans and a blue satin bomber jacket appeared at its mouth. He walked with a cane, the result of a pelvic misalignment, according to Rachel. Still, he looks buoyant, Alfred thought, for want of a better word, and more presidential than pontifical: upon his head he wore a vermillion baseball cap with the Vatican seal sewn on its front.

'Elias,' Alfred said, and found a small spark of joy kindled within him. 'He still lives.'

'And is still Pope,' Rachel added, somewhat proudly, as though she had something to do with it. 'He has reformed the Roman Catholic Church: the replacement of the Curia, the ordination of women, a more sympathetic view towards contraception, the founding of a holy order with the express remit to investigate the clergy accused of crimes against those in their care. He has dissolved the Inquisition.'

'A wise move,' said Alfred. 'At least no one will try to kill him for the changes he has wrought.'

'Unlikely. His popularity among his followers would make this a poor strategic move. Besides,' she nodded towards a tall figure stepping into Elias's wake, 'he has a rather formidable private secretary.'

Pietro Lantosca was older now, though the lines around his mouth said he'd learned to smile during the years of Alfred's non-existence. A livid scar ran from the grey of his left temple, below his eye and disappeared under his chin. Alfred guessed that the battle in New Orleans had gone better than expected, though not as well as it might.

Elias waved at the cheering crowds before taking his place next to the little girl, who didn't acknowledge him; she carried on with her painting while the supreme pontiff fielded questions from the crowd and the gathered journalists: Who is she? Why has the Roman Catholic Church taken such an interest in her? How can such a young child possess such a prodigious talent? Who is the ghost in her paintings? Now that he had recovered from his hip surgery, did he have any plans to take up parachuting again?

The questions came and Elias answered with grace, humour and great humility. The crowd did indeed love him, as Rachel said, and they sat in an obedient awe of both the supreme pontiff and the little girl.

'We must leave,' Rachel said. 'There is much to be done.'

'I would stay a while longer,' Alfred replied.

'To do so would serve no purpose. She cannot know you.'

'I understand, but still I would like to stay.'

She tried to look disapproving, for the good it would do. 'Then do not delay too long. The world stands again on the brink of war.' She looked to the child and smiled with an almost painful longing. Then her faced hardened and she turned to him. 'I will see you in Iraq, Horseman.'

Alfred watched her lessen to a mist and drift away on the winds. He sighed. The Middle East, he thought. Again.

Though this time it would be different; *he* would be different. He would honour her. This time he would be the Horseman he was reborn to be. He moved through the crowd and sat next to the little girl on the edge of the fountain. The picture was of a war fought in the sand. Men were dying, but he wasn't there. Not yet. It saddened him that Elias and Pietro could no longer see him, but it was a sign that their own demons were at rest, and for that Alfred was grateful. He looked to the child and her radiance struck him with hope.

'I will watch over you,' he said. 'Now and for always, in this life and your lives that follow, I will always watch over you.'

And though she did not take her eyes from her painting, the little girl smiled – a smile so very much like Magdelena's. He closed his eyes and saw a tiny cottage, someplace else, where they were not immortals but people; where they lived, and married, and raised children, and grew old together, touched by the passage of time and caring nothing for a life hereafter.

And when Alfred opened his eyes again, the little girl and the crowd had gone, and the day had become dusk. He rose slowly to his feet, buttoned his jacket and straightened his hat.

East then, he told himself and started walking with the sun at his back, along the cobbled road that would deliver him to the sea.

27230463R00189

Made in the USA
Charleston, SC
06 March 2014